THE NOTORIOUS DR. AUGUST

Also by Christopher Bram

Gossip
Father of Frankenstein
Almost History
In Memory of Angel Clare
Hold Tight
Surprising Myself

THE
NOTORIOUS
DR. AUGUST

HIS REAL LIFE
AND CRIMES

CHRISTOPHER
BRAM

WILLIAM MORROW
AN IMPRINT OF HARPERCOLLINS*PUBLISHERS*

HarperCollins books may be purchased for educational, business, or sales promotional use. For information please write: Special Markets Department, HarperCollins Publishers Inc., 10 East 53rd Street, New York, NY 10022.

FIRST EDITION

Designed by Bernard Klein

Printed on acid-free paper

Library of Congress Cataloging-in-Publication Data

Bram, Christopher.
    The notorious Dr. August : his real life and crimes / Christopher Bram. — 1st ed.
       p. cm.
    ISBN 0-688-17569-4
      1. Pianists—Fiction. 2. Clairvoyants—Fiction. I. Title: Notorious Doctor August. II. Title.
PS3552.R2817 N68 2000
813'.54—dc21
                                              99-055805

00 01 02 03 04 BP 10 9 8 7 6 5 4 3 2 1

In memory of J.M.B.

And no visit is complete without a performance in our own Pavilion of Harmonia, home to the Finest Musical Artists of the Continent and America. This season we are proud to announce the return of the celebrated Dr. August: The Metaphysical Pianist. This World-Renowned Clairvoyant of the Keyboard has baffled experts the world over, performed for The Crowned Heads of Europe, and thrilled music lovers and novices alike with his Supernatural Sonatas. He is the very man whose diabolical melodies once terrified an entire family to death! Are you brave enough to listen? (Four shows daily. Children must be accompanied by parents.)

—"Come to Dreamland," advertisement, *New York World,* 1909

THE NOTORIOUS DR. AUGUST

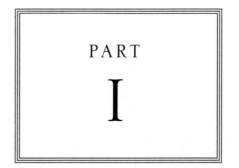

PART

I

1

LIFE is eternal, but lives are short. Immortality is my rock as well as my bread and butter. Yet I still love the mortal, the temporal, the physical—the luxuriant overcoat of the Oversoul. My own coat is in tatters, but I remain inordinately fond of it. As my sojourn here approaches its end, my Metaphysicals suggest that I record a few scenes from my time among naïfs and knaves, gods and ghosts. And with the friend whom I loved for sixty years. Loved yet never understood. Perhaps I can begin to understand him now that he is dead. A message from the other side assures us that he has departed the world, this time for good.

Very well, then. I was born. In 1850 in New York.

I end my days in the city where I began, a fine irony for someone who has been out in the world and beyond. But we're in another part of that city, and a whole new century. When I was a boy, this was a mere village north of town, a handful of steeples and rooftops visible across the meadows from the promenade atop the high walls of the old reservoir at Forty-second Street. Now Harlem is a city within the city, a realm of squealing children and fussing mothers by day, laughing men, braying autos, and raucous new music by night. I like this music, loose, humorous grab bags of mood and melody performed by self-made royalties: King Oliver, Duke Ellington, Prince Jazz. It pours from the clubs when you walk me through the raccoon-furred crowds of Lenox Avenue on snowy evenings, a bald white crow in dark glasses on your tolerant, guiding arm, or insinuates itself through the ether into a radio cabinet in our snug little rooms outside time.

It has been a marvelous age of invention: radio, aeroplane, electric light, the telephone, and fellatio. Oh, yes, the last was invented in 1862. By Giacomo Barry Fitzwilliam, my uncle.

Well, he was not really an uncle but a distant cousin. And I suspected early on that he did not invent that intimate act, or it would not bear a Latin name. Uncle Jack was neither a Roman nor a priest. He was a musician, a gloomy violinist with drooping whiskers and the lean build of a bat or badly furled umbrella. He toured the smaller cities of the East as "the American Paganini," believing he paid Paganini a great compliment. Everything unkind that gets said of musical artists—that we are vain, petty, self-centered, and mad—can be said with perfect justice of Uncle Jack. I was his accompanist for a time, on the piano in smoky theaters and drafty town halls, aboard trains and coaches where I tended our luggage, and in the sagging beds of cheap boardinghouses. I was also adept on the melodeon, pipe organ, and transverse flute.

Aunt Ada turned me over to this pompous scarecrow when I was fourteen. Her tiny rooms on East Thirteenth Street, behind the Academy of Music, were crowded by her two ambitious, pushing, opera-singing daughters. "Augustus, you are in my way." "Augustus, take this note to the theater." "Augustus, you are in my chair." Their enormous balloon skirts squashed through doorways and whistled against the wallpaper. Quarters became more crowded still with the return of their adored brother, wounded at Chancellorsville, and there was no longer room for me.

We were a musical household, in the pseudo-Italian manner of Irish Protestants. A piano was always present, and I can no more remember learning to play than I remember learning to speak. I must have taken in some of my beautiful mother's gifts with her milk before she passed away in my infancy. Accompanying my cousins when they rehearsed for auditions or lullabying my aunt when she was incapacitated by headache, I first enjoyed music for the pleasure that it gave to other people. Orphans are quick to mistake the satisfaction of others for love.

Life with Uncle Jack quickly disabused me of that notion. But I cannot claim that his bedtime attentions were torture. He loved fame more than he loved the flesh, his own as well as mine, and he was the flautist there, believing I offered him a magic elixir of youth. All I had to do was lie back and enjoy. His erratic needs gave me a useful trump card in our constant contest of master and servant. I spent my early years living by the seat of my pants, including those occasions when I didn't wear any.

Should I speak of such things? I compose this for my Metaphysicals, and my own amusement, yet wonder now if some publisher might not remember the notorious Dr. August and offer money for his story. The Eternal is very fine, but it doesn't buy dinner. Form may follow function, but function follows cash. Never mind, Tristan. Write it all down, my recording angel, every word. Later we can delete and shape and lie.

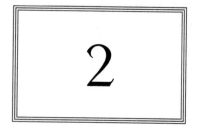

2

I have lived a picturesque life. I see my life in pictures, even now when I am blind. I still dream in pictures.

But music sustains and animates the images. Here at my piano I can finger the keys to unlock my thoughts and memories. The spirits sometimes offer tunes that help me with the words. A pity you cannot write music, or we could include this improvised accompaniment. Perhaps the music is the true story and my words merely a way of beating time. But you can deceive with music as well as words.

Do you recognize this one? No, not spirits, but Schumann. "Träumerei" from *Kinderszenen.* Have you forgotten all your German, my boy? "Dreaming." *Scenes of Childhood.*

Picture a river in summer, a wide estuary with a sandy bank framed by trees. Pillars of cypress stand out in the water on either hand, forming a little cove. Figures populate the scene. All are male, all but one are nude. Three sit up to their chests in the shallow green water. A fourth strides toward the shore, plowing the surface with his groin. A fifth lounges on the bank, sunning his mossy front. The sixth, a small boy with lank brown hair, paper-white skin, and elfin ears, sits cross-legged on the sand and serenades them with a flute. The scene has the arcadian quiet of a painting by Poussin or Puvis de Chavannes, names that meant nothing to me then.

But look closer. These Greek gods are marred by sunburn, bony joints, and shrunken bellies. The pastoral is spoiled by scabs of soap suds drifting on the water and, along the shore, homely pairs of broken boots. Wet wool uniforms and tattered cotton drawers cover the bushes, drying after a wash. These noble warriors have just finished doing their laundry. And there is a seventh figure, fully dressed, an augmented seventh who sits on a log in the foreground like a mortal visitor, head lowered over busy hands, a wide-brimmed hat like a straw halo squeezed over a loaf of nappy hair. He is a large African youth, broad-shouldered and muscular, yet he uses a needle on a pair of trousers with surprising delicacy.

I see the scene from far away, yet I was there. I am the boy with the flute, piping Schumann to a troop of Confederate cavalry in the last summer of the Civil War. I was their captive, their prisoner of war. More accurately, I was their pet while they decided what to do with me.

Very well, then. Enough medias res. The story of my capture.

In the summer of 1864, working the towns south of Philadelphia, Uncle Jack found the pickings lean, the wartime bookings sparse. He decided to try Virginia and the armies of the Union around Hampton Roads. We booked a passage to Point Comfort. And he was right. Soldiers were more appreciative of our music, and less discriminating, all except a regiment of German immigrants who recognized my uncle's flamboyance for the rank Irish ham it really was. Now and then we performed in a house with a piano, a badly tuned Chickering or other American-made crate, a good excuse for my own poor playing when I accompanied him on the "Kreutzer" or other difficult piece. I was no prodigy as a youth, not in that age when people who played the piano were as common as those who can now drive motor cars. More often than not, Uncle Jack performed alone, a grasshopper in a black frock coat, sawing and swaying under the night sky for officers who sat by their candlelit tents and smoked melancholy cigars. Crowds of soldiers stood in the shadows under the trees or perched in the branches overhead. And in the darker regions behind them, among the mules and cooking fires, crouched the camp laborers, former slaves whom some said this war was for, but were invisible here. I barely noticed them myself.

My uncle's program was always the same, a little Beethoven, a little Paganini, a medley of animal impersonations—rooster, cow, and cockatoo—and for the encore, our rendition of "Just Before the Battle, Mother," a duet for flute and violin. My uncle took on a look of high artistic solemnity while he milked his sobbing instrument and brought a mob of soldiers to tears.

We were fed and fêted and paid quite well, sometimes from regimental funds, often out of private pockets. Armies were more casual affairs in those days. We worked our way from camp to camp up the north side of the James River, then crossed to City Point behind the siege lines of Petersburg. Grant had just made his last great assault on the town, the Battle of the Crater, where the soldiers exploded a mine under the earthworks, then charged into the gap and were trapped and slaughtered. The army settled in for a long siege.

City Point was a boomtown, a vast slum of tents and warehouses under tumbling clouds of smoke from a hundred steamboats docked along the river. We gave an afternoon concert in a new hall roofed with canvas and floored with sticky raw pine. It was part of the hospital, so our audience was full of bandaged faces and missing limbs, men tapping feet that were not always there. Usually too full of my own concerns to notice other people's sorrow, I was terribly moved that day. I hated the Rebels who'd maimed these men, and was glad our music could offer them a few sweet spasms of sentiment.

"That was lovely," Uncle Jack sniffed afterward, wiping his own damp eyes and catfish whiskers. "If only tears were dollars."

But one man's were. A Maine colonel who'd lost an arm was so touched by our mother duet that he wanted to share it with his brother, who was on picket duty downriver. Uncle Jack bargained and wheedled until the colonel hired us for a visit, paying handsomely and loaning us two horses so we could ride down under the escort of his music-loving lieutenant. We were safely behind Union lines, so they said.

We left City Point in the cool of early morning, the camp already noisy with mule teams, clattering wagons, and blacksmith hammers. Uncle Jack and Lieutenant Gill trotted ahead of me while I played with the reins and stirrups of the new beast between my legs. I had no experience on horseback, but my animal seemed to know his business, so I let him take charge. I wore my short blue jacket with brass buttons and a little straw hat with a narrow brim and fluttering ribbon. I carried my flute in a satchel hung from my shoulder. We left our baggage in the colonel's tent.

"Boy! Don't loiter," Uncle Jack snapped. "My late cousin's child," he told the lieutenant. "I let him accompany me out of love for her memory. He's proved a disappointment musically."

Never cordial with me by daylight, Uncle Jack was quite nasty that morning. He had been in a frisky mood the night before, whereas I hadn't. But his insults didn't bother me. I knew he was a fool, and you cannot be too intimidated by a man whom you've seen bobbing for apples under your nightshirt.

The lieutenant asked about famous musicians and composers, and Uncle Jack happily held forth.

"Oh, Joachim is a genius. A great genius. He admires me enormously, you know. He attended my concert twice in Berlin."

Needless to say, Uncle Jack had never been near Berlin, or anywhere on the Continent for that matter, yet he chattered away. He looked quite ridiculous on horseback, tall and rickety, bouncing along with his high silk hat jammed over his eyebrows. He never noticed that a trouser strap had come loose and his pant leg jiggled up, exposing a frayed shank of dirty linen.

Very soon we were in open country. The traffic of wagons and couriers died away; the air was no longer white with dust. The sun climbed higher, and locusts roared in the trees. The countryside appeared to have been stripped by locusts. The split-rail fences had been burned up in campfires. Green cornfields were trampled flat. Houses had been picked clean for lumber or firewood, so all that remained were timber skeletons and chimneys. When I saw a house still in one piece, with even its windows intact, I knew that we were very far out.

The sun blazed all morning, leaving me stupefied, drowsy. My head emptied of thought, my jouncing hindquarters went numb. Toward noon, however, we entered a forest, a long, cool cathedral of towering pines. The road was infinitely straight, the wagon tracks covered with pine needles, as if it had been months since anyone passed this way. The carpet softened the tread of our horses so there was only a piney hush, a jingle of reins. It might have been beautiful if only Uncle Jack had stopped talking.

"And Liszt," he was saying. "The greatest genius of them all. Wrote a Transcendental Étude for me. Liked it so much he transcribed it to piano for himself."

By now even the lieutenant was growing dubious. He glanced back at me to see if my expression supported or mocked my uncle's claims. But he stared right past me, his eyes popped open, and his face turned white.

"Oh, murder!" he cried. He pulled hard on his reins, swung his horse behind mine, and shouted, "Ride like hell!" He slapped my horse, spurred his own, and took off. And my horse leaped after his, a jolting spring of muscle that flew out from under my legs and tumbled me backward into empty air.

The next thing I knew, I was flat on my back on hard clay, looking at treetops, every ounce of breath knocked out of my chest. I sat up in time to see three horses, one of them riderless, galloping off in the distance.

Before I could understand what had happened, my patch of road exploded in a thunderstorm of hooves. New horses pounded over and around me, tearing up earth and sprays of needles, beating the ground like a kettledrum. I clutched myself in my arms as they swept overhead, massive shapes spurred by a pack of wild devils. There was a loud "Yee-haw!" as they tore after my companions, and a gunshot. I slapped my hand over my heart as if shot.

But my heart was still beating—I was nothing *but* a beating heart. I remained sprawled on my fanny in a slow rain of dust and needles as the world rushed off without me. The rumps of riders and horses pumped madly down the road, the thud of hooves diminished to a patter like falling acorns, and I was forgotten, abandoned.

Then a shadow fell over me. I looked up. I saw a calm horse up above, a bronze statue of a horse gazing down with one round eye like a ball of brown glass. Beyond the eye was the squint and frown of a man, a soldier with a blond beard and gray campaign cap, a Rebel.

"Will you look at this, Isaac. We caught us a Yankee baby."

I thought he was talking to his horse, until I heard a second rider clomp up on the other side of me. It was a colored boy on a nag. He had a sack of cornmeal drapped over the withers and a saddlebag full of vegetables. A live chicken hung by its feet from the bag, studying me along its upside-down beak.

"Does your mama know you're playing soldier?" said the white man. He wore gray trousers, but his shirt was civilian homespun.

"I'm no soldier, sir."

"The hell you ain't. You a courier? What's that you're carrying? Hand it over."

I stumbled to my feet and surrendered the flute bag twisted around my shoulder. I dusted myself off and saw my dangerously blue jacket. I desperately looked around for the hat that had flown off my head, but the dapper crown with a velvet ribbon that would prove my civilian nature was nowhere in sight.

The Rebel extracted a shiny barrel with valves and silver wires from my bag. It took him a moment to understand what it was. "You're fife and drum," he said.

"No, sir. I'm an artist, sir. A musician."

He didn't know what to make of that. "Well, wash you in the blood of the lamb," he muttered.

Hearing a rising thud of horses, I looked up the road, hoping my uncle and the lieutenant were returning to tell this fellow my true identity. But it was only the pursuers, a half dozen breathless, red-faced Rebels. "They got away, Sergeant Tom. We was too loaded down with loot to catch them." Their saddlebags, too, were full of produce, ears of corn and green apples. One of the riders clutched his own chicken by the legs, all the life shaken out of it.

"I told you leave them be," said my captor. "We're supposed to be running from Yanks, not chasing them."

I stood half ignored in the road, surrounded by men on horseback like a frog being sniffed by a pack of dogs. These were the enemy, the Secessionist traitors, and traitors were monsters capable of anything. I felt that Uncle Jack had abandoned me to them as punishment for last night.

"What're we gonna do with this one, Tom?"

"You tell me. You were the ones hot to catch them."

The soldier with the dead chicken said, "Let's hang him. They'll be hanging us soon enough." He lifted his bird and shook it. "Let's string him up right here so the bastards'll see who they're dealing with."

My heart froze, my skin went cold. I pictured my lifeless little body dangling over the road.

But the others frowned at the angry man, embarrassed that he could propose such a thing.

"Let's take him prisoner," said a man in spectacles. "We've never had no prisoner before, Sergeant."

"We're supposed to be foraging for grub, not boys," the sergeant grumbled. "Still, don't seem right to leave him out here. What's your name, son?"

"Augustus Fitzwilliam Boyd, sir."

He made a face. "Lot of name for not much boy," he said. "All right. We'll take him back and see what the captain says. We either turn him over to the regiment as a prisoner when we rejoin them or we just let him go in a day or two. He rides with you, Isaac. Up you go, Billy."

The nag stumbled closer. The white palm of a brown hand was held out to me. I took it and climbed up, slipping and sliding over horsehair until I found myself pressed against a Negro back.

"Hold on to my waist," the Negro said gruffly.

I did, and was surprised, like when you handle your first snake and find that they're smooth and dry. It was like putting my arms around any man. The only Negroes I'd ever spoken to were minstrel players, white men in darkface. I half expected this one to rub off on my clothes.

I remained frightened, stunned. I kept looking back as we trotted up the road, wanting the Union army to come to my rescue, yet fearing it, too, because it would mean shooting, and I might be killed. I held on to the colored boy who seemed so much older than me. I couldn't see his face. I had noticed nothing except his color, but he sat so sternly in the saddle that I pictured him looking quite fierce.

We turned off the main road into the woods, down a narrow track, Rebel cavalry riding in front and behind me, a terrified white boy sharing a nag like an ambulating sofa. To this day I cannot stretch out on a horsehair couch without feeling its cushions heave and flex like muscles.

$$3$$

W E rode for an hour and came to a camp by the river, in a grassy clearing around a shacklike house with a porch. A dozen motley soldiers stood up around the fire or wandered over as we rode in, pleased to see food, startled to see me. There were leafy lean-tos all around and a buckboard wagon stranded by the house. After the orderly rows of tents in Union bivouacs, this camp looked no better than a hideout for bandits. The former owners of the property had supported themselves by fishing, and tarred nets hung in the trees like great rotting spiderwebs, but the only boat left behind was a flat-bottomed punt no bigger than a coffin sitting in the grass.

Sergeant Kemp—my fair-haired captor's name was Tom Kemp—took me to meet the captain. "Come along, Billy," he said, without grabbing or touching me, as if I were a stray cat he didn't want to spook. He went up on the porch and knocked on the door. I noticed a hole in the seat of his pants, a great rip with a polka-dot handkerchief stuffed inside. Anyone who cared for such niceties could never murder me, I hoped.

A hoarse voice called out, and Kemp opened the door. It looked like a garden shed inside, with tools in a corner and greased paper on the windows. A tallowy figure lay in a mass of bedding on the floor, an old man of thirty in an open shirt soaked with sweat. I thought he was drunk at first—I had seen my share of drunks—

but the room stank of night soil and sickness. He stared at me with yellow eyes while Kemp told him who I was.

"A Yankee puppy?" he said and laughed. "A calf? Fricasee him in butter. Stew him in his mother's milk. The flesh of a child. That'll fix me right up. The meat of the innocent. But then I'll burn in hell. Oh, no. Save me, Lord. I didn't mean to say that." And he pulled a blanket over his head. "Go away, Tom. I don't want you seeing me like this."

"Never fear, Captain," said Kemp. "I know it's just your fever talking."

He ushered me outside. "The captain came down with malarial fever two days ago," he explained. "We been holing up here until his fever breaks. He'll decide what to do with you once his head's right." Kemp spoke in a flat, laconic voice, a stoic soldier showing no fears over his commander's temporary madness.

It was Crawford, the fellow in spectacles, who proposed a wash. "We captured a bar of soap. Come along, Billy. You're ours now. We got to keep an eye on you. And you look like you could use a bath."

I followed them down to the river, a hundred yards away, and sat on a log while my captors shucked their boots and uniforms. They squatted naked in the shallows, grumbling and joking while they passed around a white brick of soap, rubbing and wringing their garments, picking out the lice. No, they were not devils, not even Wyatt, the man who'd wanted to hang me. He sat on his heels at the water's edge, all backbone and bony haunches, a skinny boy like a hairless dog.

None were much more than boys. Kemp, the oldest, was only nineteen, not so much their sergeant as an older brother whom the others obeyed according to their mood. His nudity was thicker and more adult than theirs. These were not battle-weary veterans but latecomers who'd joined up only this past year. They were part of the Confederate cavalry that roamed the countryside south of Petersburg, guarding Lee's last supply line to the west, playing havoc

with the Yankees to the east. They had come too far east and been
separated from their regiment. They expected to rejoin it as soon as
the captain was well enough to travel, either on horseback or in the
wagon they'd commandeered. They were a pack of boys under the
command of a grown-up now delirious with fever.

I was reluctant to undress in front of my country's enemy. But I
was hot, and the river looked cool, and they were not quite traitors
without guns or uniforms. I did not need to wash my clothes, so I
folded each item in a neat pile. I expected the Rebs to make fun
of my pale skin and scant hair as I tiptoed down to the water with
my hands cupped in front, but they only said, "Don't it feel good
to drown your fleas, Billy?" I was Billy Yank to them, a stand-in
for the whole Union army, a fantasy army of friendly fellows who'd
never hurt anyone. Crawford splashed and dunked me, but we were
all too tired for horseplay. We ended up sitting in the river with
our bare bottoms on velvet mud.

Kemp called Isaac down to mend his trousers while he soaked.
The colored boy sat on the log with a needle and thread to stitch a
red, heart-shaped patch into the seat of Kemp's pants.

"Play your fife, Billy," said Kemp. "Give us some music."

I waded ashore, took out my flute, and serenaded my captors with
a melody from Schumann. Even the birds stopped to listen. The
horses, too, who stood a few yards away in a shady grove around a
little stream, looking contentedly nude themselves without their sad-
dles. Out in the channel, a mile away, a string of Union steamboats
pushed upstream toward City Point, never suspecting that the enemy held a naked musicale on shore.

Those sunburned *ignudi* seem quite beautiful to me now, so
young and vulnerable. That afternoon, however, I was far more
conscious of the figure in clothes, the one they called Isaac or the
sergeant's Isaac or Kemp's Isaac. He was Sergeant Kemp's slave, of
course. It took time for me to understand that. He wore no chains.
He wasn't whipped or cursed. Kemp addressed him as if he were
family. The man mended his master's pants with rifles stacked a

few feet away. He could have grabbed one anytime, shot a few soldiers, and escaped. But then I could have, too, and I never even considered it.

I disliked sitting on the mud. I stood up, brushed myself off, and looked for a dry spot. There was only the log, but I sat there, although it felt strange to perch naked beside a slave.

"Don't you swim?" I asked.

He frowned, as if I mocked him, then understood that I didn't know the rules. "When I'm alone," he muttered.

I played another tune on my flute, Bellini's "Casta Diva," while the Negro continued to sew. His eyelids were heavy hoods, his cheeks scored and scarred by an old infection. He had a sharp, angular nose, like a white man's nose lightly pressed in his dark face. I mentally washed him white so that he might seem like any man, but his features remained odd and mysterious. His thick lips were pink-brown. His youthful beard looked both dry and delicate, like black lichen. Wanting to win his approval, I decided to play something he knew: I began to tootle "Dixie."

"Hey, hey, Billy!" Crawford cheered from the water. "We'll make a Rebel of you yet." And I realized that I was betraying my country with music, but played the song to its end.

Without a smile or a look, as if deaf to the tune, Isaac bit off the thread, got up, and draped Kemp's trousers over a bush with the other wet clothes. He trudged back up the hill to the fire where he was cooking dinner.

He intrigued me, enthralled and worried me, the very idea of Isaac. The difference of him, this man who was and wasn't like other men. I could find no language for what I wanted except a guilty desire to own him. Yes, here we were in a war to free these people, yet I wanted to own one.

The soldiers had eaten nothing but blackberries and river clams for three days, so they feasted that night like beggars at a banquet. The chickens were cooked up with onions in a stew called cush, and there was cornbread gritty with sand, roasted ears of green corn, and baked apples. A plate was carried to the captain in his shack. Everyone else gorged around the fire, all except Isaac, who took a portion of the food he'd cooked and ate it alone, sitting under the wagon as if eating were a private bodily function.

While they ate, they told stories about raids and close calls and ones-that-got-away, shared experiences they didn't need to tell each other, but I was a stranger, a new audience. They even spoke of their escapade that morning, Wyatt regretting that he hadn't potted the tall galoot in black. "Beg your pardon, Billy," he quickly added. "Forgot he's your friend." But I was sorry he hadn't shot the son of a bitch who'd abandoned me to the wolves, even now when the wolves turned out to be friendly.

When they argued over who would get me as a bedmate, I wondered if I'd been captured by a squad of Secessionist Uncle Jacks. But no, they only wanted to be good hosts and get a change from each other's snores and dirty feet.

"I'll settle it," said Kemp. "He bunks with me."

He spread out his blankets in the wagon beside the house, safely above the dirt and crawling insects. He took off only his boots, so I kept my trousers on. I'd slept in some strange beds that summer, but a wagon bed under the stars was the strangest yet. I lay back and saw the pink flicker of firelight on the fan of leaves overhead. I expected to fall asleep immediately, although the entire day had been like a sleep, a sleep full of dreams too unbelievable to frighten me anymore, a concussion of dreams. You might have thought that I'd landed on my head and not my butt when I fell from my horse.

Kemp remained sitting up, smoking a pipe before he turned in. "Where're your people from?" he asked, but only to prime the pump so that he could talk about his people, his and Isaac's.

He actually spoke of his family as *their* family, as if he and Isaac were blood. He missed them badly. Unbuttoning his mind for a boy, his soldierly stoicism gave way to homesick melancholy. Their farm was outside Norfolk, he said, a small farm, not a plantation. The town had been under Yankee occupation since the start of the war. Kemp had hated the bluecoats, insolent, trashy soldiers who were rude to ladies and mean to slaves. When Kemp beat up a soldier who spoke lewdly to a young girl—he refused to repeat what the soldier said—and the Yankee provosts were looking for him, his father finally gave in to his desire to join his schoolmates in the army. Better that his son risk his hide on a battlefield than rot in a Yankee jail. Kemp slipped across the river that very night. Isaac was sent along to look after him.

I asked how old Isaac was.

Fifteen, sixteen, or seventeen. Nobody knew for sure. Isaac's mother died a long time ago, and no one remembered exactly what year he was born. "But we grew up together. He was my little black shadow when I was a child. And my shadow grew. He's been like a brother to me. He's as brave as the rest of us here. And smart. You won't believe how smart that boy is. I love him like he was white." When the war was over, Kemp wanted to have their picture taken together, he and Isaac and Antigone, his horse.

Lately, however, he had begun to wonder what would remain when the war was over. "Death and destruction," he said. "War without mercy." He sucked on his pipe; the bowl lit up his grave face like a thought of hellfire. "There is no reasoning with a tyrant like Lincoln. Wyatt is a hothead, but he may be right. Not healthy to think on, but you're going to hang us if we lose," he said sadly. "Hang us all."

Before I could remind him that I was an artist and wouldn't hang anyone, his sorrow abruptly gave way to bitter anger.

"And now you're using our niggers against us. You know about that? Putting them in uniform and setting them loose on us like dogs. When Lee's men captured that nigger regiment at the Crater, when they surrounded them in that hole and they surrendered, they slit their throats, every last one. Nothing else you can do with mad dogs but kill them."

The sudden fury in his speech startled me, but our emotions were simpler back then, gentler when they were gentle, more violent when they became violent.

Kemp soon turned sad and sorrowful again, fretting over his parents and how they would manage without him and Isaac to help with the coming harvest. I fell asleep to his murmurs and a steady sigh of wind in the trees, like a troop of guardian angels shifting around us in the dark woods.

I dreamed of city streets and featherbeds that night, and woke up to find myself on the hard slats of a wagon, in a gray forest beside a snoring youth. Sergeant Kemp's beard looked softer, wispier than it had the day before. I saw through the sandy curls to a homesick son inside.

It was early yet, and the trees were colorless, like clouds of smoke from the campfire that had burned to ashes in the night. The camp was perfectly still. A single bird began to sing, just three notes, like this. A flat, A flat, D. I never learned the bird's name but can still remember the song I heard while I watched the smoke turn green and become trees again.

Needing to relieve myself, I pulled on my shoes and climbed down from the wagon. I saw Isaac inside the spokes of a wheel, wrapped in a blanket, fast asleep on the ground. I was startled to find him there. Had he heard his master's praise last night? It should seem no worse than a parent talking about a child in its presence, but I was oddly embarrassed for him.

I hurried into the trees beyond the fishing nets to what looked like a private spot and let fly with my watering can. Only then, while I splashed the leaves and my bladder ceased to press my brain, did I think of escaping. What might happen if I kept walking? Could I find the road and get back to City Point on foot? The trail to the main road was a few yards to my left. Back in the clearing a couple of men were already up, sleepily stirring the fire, but they couldn't see me out here.

I was tucking myself back in, weighing my chances, when I saw the sentry by the trail. He sat at the base of a tree, behind the trunk, but with his outstretched legs clearly visible.

"Excuse me," I said and quickly buttoned up. "Didn't mean to commit a rudeness in your presence." I should have known there'd be guards out here to keep me from fleeing.

But he didn't reply. I stepped toward him, wondering if he were asleep. I came around his tree and saw the front of his shirt, as red as paint, and a pair of spectacles askew on his lard-colored face. It was Crawford, and he looked dead. And all I could think was that he, too, had become homesick in the night and his heart had burst.

Just then there was a shout in the clearing, followed by a loud crack, like a dozen dry branches breaking. I looked back at the camp. Everyone was on his feet, jumping into boots, barking at each other. Then the branches across the clearing snapped again, and I understood: It was rifle fire. I could see nothing except foliage and silky smoke and sparklike flashes, so it was as if the trees had guns and were shooting at us.

I froze where I stood, twenty yards inside the woods on my side of the clearing, instinctively lifting my hands in the air.

I saw men roll on the ground, then jump up and run toward the river.

I saw Kemp and three others pressed against the house on the side away from the shooting trees, fumbling with their rifles.

Around the corner from them the captain stumbled out on the porch. He was barefoot but had thrown on coat and trousers. He held up his trousers with one hand, gripped a revolver in the other, and frantically looked for a foe, before he tripped and fell across the steps. He did not jump up again like the others.

"Run, boys! Get to your horses!" Kemp hollered and stepped out from behind the wall with his rifle and a revolver. He went down on one knee behind the porch and fired at the trees while the others ran for the river.

I heard a patter like rain in the foliage over my head. Only when leaves began to flutter down did I understand that bullets were snapping through the branches. With remarkable calm, as if in a trance, I took a single step to my left, so that another tree trunk stood between me and the shooting.

But it seemed less like a battle out there than a village street on the Fourth of July, all racket and confusion and nose-stinging drifts of burnt powder. The gunshots grew ragged, stopped, then started up again, like children were setting off a fresh string of firecrackers. There were voices, cries—"Good-bye, boys, I am dead"—and someone began laughing, hysterically, as if over the high jinks of a clown at the circus. A stranger suddenly appeared in the clearing, a bearded horseman in a blue coat who wheeled around on a muscular, prancing steed, looking for someone to cut down with the saber in his hand. But there was nobody left standing by the house. He shouted at the trees, "Call pursuit!"

A bugle blew strangled notes. Men shouted, and horses whinnied in the greenery. And a torrent of soldiery poured from the woods, blue-uniformed men on brown horses. My rescuers, I thought, and stepped forward with my hands still held high. The stream thundered past me and raced toward the river, grimacing, wild-eyed men who ignored the surrendering boy at their feet.

There was a whole company of Union cavalry hidden in the woods. The lieutenant and my uncle must have reported the ambush, and these men were sent out to hunt down the marauders. They'd found our camp last night, silently killed Crawford on sentry duty, and, under the cover of the wind in the trees, had taken up positions and waited for first light to attack.

The torrent dwindled to a trickle, the younger, less experienced riders struggling to catch up with the others. Finally one last horseman trotted out, at a leisurely pace, a handsome fellow with a square jaw and a dandy's black side-whiskers. He saw me, then the bundles of clothes scattered around the clearing. He reined in his horse and dismounted. "Don't move," he shouted, wagging a rifle at me. He hurried over to the bundle on the porch steps, the body of the captain. He emptied the dead man's pockets, taking his watch and leather purse, strewing letters on the ground, so the captain resembled a scarecrow who'd been stuffed with paper. The thief-dandy raced over to another body and began to do the same to him, then jumped back, startled. He approached the body again, put his rifle to its head, and fired. The corpse jolted and was still.

From underneath the wagon Isaac timidly stepped out, his hands raised as high as mine. The soldier saw him.

"Get out of here, nigger. You're free. You ain't a slave no more. We just liberated you."

He was approaching a third corpse when another horseman galloped back from the river.

"Cunningham!" he shouted. "Why you hanging back?"

"Taking a prisoner, Sergeant. We got a prisoner," he said in the most official tone imaginable.

I cried out, "I was *their* prisoner! They captured me yesterday when they ambushed me and my uncle on the road!"

The sergeant scowled. I was trivial, of no importance at all. "Cunningham, I won't have my men robbing the dead. Get back on your horse!"

The thief obeyed, smirking and shaking his head as if over a comic misunderstanding.

There was a fresh rattle of gunfire up the river. "Let's go, Cunningham. I'm not letting you out of my sight. You there!" the sergeant shouted at me. "Stay put till we come back! You're our prisoner until I'm told differently."

The sergeant and the thief galloped off. I didn't think to lower my hands until Isaac lowered his.

And there we were, no longer a slave and a prisoner of war, just two stunned boys in a clearing strewn with corpses.

Isaac walked over to the man whom the thief had shot. He rolled him over on his back, but I already knew who it was from the heart-shaped patch in the seat of his pants. The mouth in the soft blond beard hung wide open, permanently surprised by the gunshot to his head.

I expected Isaac to let out a cry or heartbroken groan, but he only stood up and frowned at Kemp's corpse.

"You stupid son of a fool," he hissed. "You great big fool of a hero. You love me like I was white, but you'd slit my throat if I raised a hand against you." And he spit at him. His mouth was dry, and the fleck of foam missed, so he spit again. "Your shadow, huh? Your little black shadow?" He had heard every word last night, Kemp's hatred of bad niggers as well as his praise of a good one. But his anger was terribly complicated.

"What're you staring at?" he snarled at me.

I was staring at his eyes, half closed around the water that spilled brightly down his cheeks. Isaac responded to his master's death with tears as well as spittle, yet tears did not soften his anger.

"Go find your friends!" he sneered. "You're free. You have no business here."

"They told me to wait," I insisted.

A rustle in the bushes caused us both to turn. A bronze mare trotted out, forlorn and riderless. It was Antigone, Kemp's horse, let loose when the other horses were mounted and ridden off. She came back to look for her master, circling the clearing, looking at Isaac, then me, never noticing the body at our feet, unable or unwilling to see humans once they were dead.

Suddenly, without knowing why, I began to weep. Like a baby. Not the sweet, shallow tears of music but deep, burning sobs. I buried my face in my hands but couldn't stop crying. Whether it was for Kemp and Crawford and the other dead or in sympathy for Isaac and Antigone, I cannot guess. Perhaps I cried only for myself, feeling no terror until now when I was safe and saw the bodies in the grass, any one of which could have been mine.

Oh, yes. It can still affect me. After all these years.

They say that we will soon understand time, that Albert Einstein and his theories will do away with it. But I love time. It keeps everything spread out, like music. A piano sonata without time would be just a loud, cataclysmic bang. And if time separates you from things you love, it also protects you from experiences that are too painful to hold close.

5

THE sun finally came up; the smoke-hazed clearing was flooded with light but no birdsong. All the birds had fled. I sat on the edge of the porch, folded in a heap, trembling and sobbing while I waited for my rescuers to return. When I eventually cried myself dry, I noticed that Isaac was dragging corpses over the ground. He didn't explain to me what he was doing, no more than he'd explain to Antigone. There were five corpses, counting Kemp's. Isaac laid them out in the bright green grass like freshly caught trout.

I sniffed up the last of my tears and said, "What're you going to do with them?"

"I don't know. Bury them, I guess. Except Master Thomas. Who I'm taking home."

"But he's dead," I said.

"God's truth." He went over to the abandoned punt and kicked at it. "A good enough coffin," he declared.

He took some tools from inside the house and began to pry up floorboards at the other end of the porch, where I remained seated, numb and staring. I couldn't stop looking at the bodies in front of me. Isaac had put Crawford's spectacles back on after hauling him from the woods, so he was more vivid than the others, flies swarming around the knife wound in his chest or walking on his bared white teeth.

"And you're going to bury the rest?" I said.

"That's right. Or you can start burying them."

It was too awful to leave them out where the flies could feast, and I couldn't just sit there while I waited for my cavalry to come back. I asked Isaac if there were a shovel, and he said to look in the house.

The shovel felt huge and heavy in my weak arms. The ground was soft and sandy, but my musical hands blistered easily. I don't know where I got the energy to dig, but I did, with a sudden anger as inexplicable as my tears. I dug with my back to the corpses, digging my first shallow trench at Crawford's feet. Isaac told me not to go too deep, so that the families could come back and dig up their sons without difficulty.

The Yankee sergeant never returned for me. None of the Union cavalry ever came back. They must have pursued Kemp's command down the river and into the countryside, forgetting the devastated camp they'd left behind. If Lieutenant Gill had reported that there might be a prisoner, the attackers must have forgotten in the fury of the chase.

While I clumsily dug, Isaac wrapped Kemp in a bedsheet from inside the house, carefully covering the bloody wound at the back of his head. He lifted him in both arms and laid his body in the boat. It was a tight fit at the shoulders, with a foot or two extra at the head and feet. He hammered the boards from the porch over the top, then trimmed the excess with a rusty saw. Kemp had been right. His shadow was smart, a wizard with his hands.

He had finished before I started digging the third grave, and he came over and worked with me. When we laid in the first man, Crawford, and began to cover him with dirt, it seemed no worse than putting him to bed. When Isaac got to his face, however, I had to cover it with a rag before he emptied the first shovel of earth on his glasses.

Isaac marked each grave with a board on which he carefully

scored a name with his bowie knife. He knew the full name of each man, and he could write, which surprised me.

It was noon when the last corpse was neatly tucked into its quilt of earth. Isaac said we should eat. He took out a handkerchief wrapped around a slab of cornbread, cold side meat, onions, and tomatoes. He waved his knife at the food, signaling me to share it. He ate as he had worked, grimly, silently. He treated the burial of these murdered men as if it was just another chore in a life of chores.

"Why're you doing this?" I said. "Why don't you just walk off now that you're free?"

He slowly chewed a mouthful and swallowed. "Because I don't feel free. Because I got to do this before I'm done with Master Tom and his family."

I couldn't understand. I did only what people told me to do. This was like a law in his heart, a rule that could not be removed until he performed one last duty.

When we finished eating, he said, "Looks like your friends ain't coming back. You want to ride with me? Until we run into them on the road."

"All right," I said. Even with the corpses safely tucked away, I could not stay in this glade of death.

We loaded the coffin boat into the wagon. Isaac coaxed Antigone into the traces and tied a makeshift harness, half rope, half leather, around her. We scavenged the camp for things he would need on the road—food and blankets, a water jug, a cooking pot, a sack of parched corn for Antigone, a weighty navy-issue revolver. And my flute, which I almost forgot. It was a three- or four-day wagon ride down to Norfolk, Isaac thought, depending on what he encountered and how cooperative Antigone might be.

She resented being reduced to a cart horse. Isaac had to lead her by her bridle up the narrow track toward the main road while she grew accustomed to her new role. I walked behind the wagon, watching the coffin wobble in the wagon bed that I'd shared with the man the night before.

When we reached the pine-needle highway, I climbed up on the seat. I was amazed by how exhausted I was, all life drained from my bones. Isaac sat beside me. He flicked the reins, and Antigone obeyed, but with her head lowered, as if ashamed. The wagon squeaked and rumbled behind her. The long pine cathedral rolled by us like unoiled stage scenery.

After a few miles Isaac said, "Take out your fancy whistle, Billy. Play us a tune."

"My name's not Billy," I said angrily.

"Whatever you're called. Give us some music, boy."

I was furious to have him address me in that insolent, bossy manner. "Go to hell," I told him.

We were coming out of the trancelike spell of the violent morning. The slave played at being a master; the little artist rebelled against taking orders from a Negro.

But then, as suddenly as it had come over me, my anger faded. "You can call me Boyd or Fitz or Augustus," I said wearily. "Just don't call me Billy."

"Fitz? Fitz. Yeah. Fitz." He liked the sound of that. "How about a song, Fitz?"

I took out my flute and placed the mouthpiece to my lips.

Let us end today with that picture: A pale boy and a dark boy sit side by side on a wagon pulled by a humiliated horse, bearing a makeshift coffin through a fairy-tale forest. And the pale boy plays a tune on a shiny flute, maybe "Träumerei" again. His mouth is dry, and he plays poorly, unable to keep the flute steady on the shaking wagon the melody sounding very thin and mournful over the low, drumroll rumble of wood.

6

WE ran into nobody that day, neither my indifferent rescuers nor our Rebel friends. We saw no civilians either. The forest road ran on forever, a long, lugubrious nave of evergreens broken only by an occasional patch of cleared ground that let in a slash of sunlight. We came out into the open around dusk and spent our first night under a chestnut tree off the road. Isaac slept under the wagon, but I took my blanket to the moss between the roots. I couldn't bring myself to sleep beneath a dead man.

The next morning we heated up the cush for breakfast, reharnessed Antigone, and resumed our journey. Antigone had completely resigned herself to being a cart horse; I began to resign myself to the possibility that I'd go all the way to Norfolk with Isaac. The Union army was there, and I should be able to find the means to get back to New York. I was finished with Uncle Jack, music, and war. I wanted only to go home.

The countryside was as flat and plain as a kitchen table, desolate and deserted. This was backcountry, with more scrub pine than fields, the fields fallow and choked with weeds. The few houses visible from the road were no more than cabins; all plantations and towns in the region were on the river, ten miles to the north. I covered my head against the sun with a slouch hat that had been tossed into the wagon with the other gear, an enormous floppy hat—

it must have been Crawford's—whose wide crown was held up only by my oversize ears. The brim drooped over the landscape like a tattered awning.

We were all new and strange to one another that day: me and Isaac and Antigone, and the body in the box.

In the early cool of the morning, I began to come out of my trance, the spell cast by yesterday's violence. I became more myself again, which meant I wanted to talk. Isaac wasn't much of a talker. When I tried to get him going with questions, he answered in miserly monosyllables. Yes, he and Master Tom grew up together. No, he didn't love Master Tom like a brother. No, the Kemps did not own scores of slaves, only him and his sister and her husband and the husband's mama. No, they were not one big happy family.

It took me a full hour to learn that much. I decided his race was as inarticulate as mules. He sat like a black rock beside me, elbows perched on his knees, his stoic face locked on the back of Antigone's bobbing head. His rough, scarred cheeks suggested the cheeks of an old statue corroded by its own tears, although his eyes were quite dry now.

"Why did you spit on Kemp when he was dead?" I asked him.

He grimaced and sighed and shook his head. Then he asked what life was like in New York City. I happily seized the new subject, rattling away about my aunt and bossy cousins, my hopes for fame and fortune, the music world with its feuds between the lovers of Italian dash and the new admirers of German seriousness. I enjoyed hearing my boyish magpie chatter again, as if the sound proved that I'd put the awful bloodshed safely behind me.

Isaac continued to face straight ahead, as if he weren't listening, as if I were speaking Greek. I knew he'd asked about New York simply to put an end to my pesky questions, but I didn't care. I wanted to talk.

Yet he paid more attention than I guessed. Isaac had spent his life pretending not to listen when white people spoke. He was a black sponge, only you could never tell which words soaked in and which ones rolled off. Between my speeches and anecdotes he slyly slipped me new questions: How much were men paid for their work up north? Could they move to any town they pleased? Where did city folk live? In short, he wanted to know what it was like to be free.

"You want to go to New York?" I said.

He grimaced again, annoyed his questions had given him away. Old habits of secrecy die hard. But he shook the reins, lifted his head, and boldly announced, "I don't know where I want to go. Or what I want to do. The best I could want before was to be hired out to someone in town, where I could be on my own. But all that's now changed. The whole world is before me."

Isaac had so many different voices that I cannot be sure which one he used during our first days together. He could talk like a mumbly darky when necessary, or in the high-flown tones of a slave preacher, or even the flat, laconic sentences of Master Tom himself. He seemed to prefer silence, so he wouldn't have to choose. Isaac had been a house slave in a small household, watchful and tight-lipped, yet well spoken when he spoke. He was a gifted mimic with a remarkable facility for language, one that served him well later in life.

I had a glimpse of his talent that very morning when we entered our first village. The place looked like a ghost town, its glaring white street empty except for a flock of scrawny chickens no bigger than pigeons. They were watched by a woman who stood on a ramshackle porch, her face hidden in an old-fashioned bonnet as deep as a cave. She cradled a heavy horse pistol, holding it in both hands like a rifle. She was expecting us. In that dead, silent country, one could hear the rumble and squeak of our wagon for miles.

"Just keep going," she told us. "No food for you here."

Isaac lifted his hat and spoke in a startlingly dim, slow, slurred voice. "No ma'am. Me and da young massa takin ma otha massa home. Put him in da cold, cold ground. We don't touch nothin, ma'am. Dis da road to Norfolk?"

"Norfolk?" she said. "Yes. But it's a long way." She respectfully bowed her bonnet, without lowering her pistol. "Sorry about your sorrow," she offered, addressing me although I hadn't said a word. "But no food for you here. God be with you."

"God be with you, ma'am," went Isaac, and he set his straw hat back on his head.

When we were out of earshot, I broke into a grin. "You should go on stage," I said. "So I'm your master now?"

"Only in name," he grumbled. "Only till we get to Norfolk."

An unattached slave looked dangerous, yet one with a white man, even a boy, seemed safely owned. But I had my wish. For a few days at least, in the eyes of strangers, I owned Isaac.

"How much are you worth?" I asked him. "If you were for sale." It was a rude question, but I was curious.

"Last heard, three thousand dollars," he said dryly. "In Yankee dollars."

Isaac's company made me wealthy beyond my dreams.

Then he asked me, "What's your price?"

"I'm not for sale," I said. "I'm white."

"No. You are not your own man," he said solemnly. "We have all been bought and paid for." It took me a moment to understand that he was quoting Scripture.

I quickly learned the game we had to play on the road. A few miles farther on, we came to a bridge over a creek guarded by two armed men on horseback, an old man and a boy. They wore no uniforms but looked official, either local militia or constabulary. I did all the talking. "Good day, sirs," I said, placing my enormous hat over my heart. "These are sad days. My man Isaac and I are bringing my poor brother home from the war."

They studied me and the coffin boat, giving no notice to Isaac. "Just so long as you're not deserters," they said. "Our own soldiers are deserting in droves. They can be as bad as the Yankees when their bellies need filling." They let us pass.

"You can call me Massa Fitz," I told Isaac on the other side of the bridge.

"I don't have to call you nothing," he grumbled.

We stopped at noon to fill our own bellies and water Antigone. There was a well under an enormous live-oak tree at a crossroads. The ground beneath the branches was beaten smooth. The pulley for the bucket hung on a limb. The water tasted brackish yet cool, our cold food sour yet tasty. After we ate, we sat against the base of the tree, Isaac napping with his straw hat over his face. I rested beside him, happy just to sit on solid earth that didn't squeal and rock from side to side.

The view outside the cool shade shimmered with heat and cicadas. The north-south road crossing our road was a narrow lane with a grassy strip down the center. I drowsily gazed up it, thinking of north and home, dreaming with my eyes open. Then a shimmer in the lane became a wrinkle, the wrinkle became a man, then three men, walking in single file toward us. Their beards were white with dust, their uniforms ragged and colorless. They were soldiers, yet with nothing military in their bearing. They lugged their rifles like hunters at the end of a bad hunt, one man using his as a walking stick, another carrying the stock as a yoke across his shoulders, arms hooked over the butt and barrel. He looked like a walking crucifixion. When the armed Christ saw our horse and wagon under the tree up ahead, he undid his arms from his cross and took the rifle in both hands.

I snapped out of my daze and frantically nudged Isaac. "Soldiers," I said.

He woke up just as the three deserters strolled into our shade. They promptly swarmed around the wagon.

"Lookee here, Jeb," one man said. "Mighty pretty mare."

"What they got in there?" said another, going to the wagon.

The third man, the armed Christ, stood before me and Isaac as we stumbled up from the tree. He held his rifle at the ready, grinning. His teeth were bad, his eyes red squints in a face like dirty dough. His feet were so caked with dirt and calluses that it took me a moment to recognize he was barefoot.

Neither Isaac nor I raised our hands in surrender, which would be an admission that we were being robbed.

"Smells like strong meat in that box," said the man searching the wagon. Being with Kemp all day, we hadn't noticed his changing aroma.

"Not meat," I declared. "It's my brother. Sergeant Thomas Kemp." If they knew his rank, they might show him more respect. "My man Isaac and I are taking my brother home."

The soldier stroking Antigone said, "Let the dead bury the damn dead, I say. Life and good horses are for the living."

I waited for Isaac to say or do something to protect our horse. But he just stood there, staring at the soldier's rifle, his shoulders falling into a deferential slouch even as his hands closed into fists. He was split between his hatred and his fear of these men, and silenced by his split.

So I jumped in. "You can't take our horse," I said. "How can I get my brother home without our horse?"

The armed Christ snarled, "Carry him on your back. Bury him right here. Why should we care? He's your kin, not ours."

"We take the wagon, too, Jeb?"

"Don't be a damn fool. That broke-down cart would only give us the slows." The man scowled at Isaac. "What you lookin' at, nigger? This stinking war is your fault. You and your master. Our family don't own no niggers."

"Hey, they got grub back here, Jeb," said the man going through the wagon. "And a gun. Will you look at this cannon?" He held up the navy-issue revolver that was supposed to protect us.

Their leader laughed. "Careless not to keep your sidearm by your side. All right, boys. Let's take the grub, unhitch the horse, and get out of here. We need to be out of this county by nightfall."

"What about his boots, Jeb? You could use some boots."

My barefoot captor looked down and saw my shoes, my preposterous high-buttoned boots. "Dainty little things," he said in surprise. "I couldn't fit my big toe in one."

"What about his nigger's shoes?" one of them suggested.

"I ain't gonna wear coon leather." But he continued to stare at my feet, pinching his eyebrows and frowning, seeing by my shoes that I was only a child. I saw my chance and grabbed it.

"Oh, please, mister," I cried in my most childish voice, a plea pitched close to tears. "I promised our mama. Our mama's waiting for me to bring poor Tom home. Our poor, heartbroken mama. If you were killed, wouldn't your mama be miserable if she didn't see you nicely buried?" Rebels had to love their mothers as blindly as Union soldiers loved theirs. All men loved their mothers back then, or pretended to. Not having one myself, I was scornful of all this mama-love, but not above using it.

A blush of sadness, a flush of shame came over out captor. "Shut up," he snapped at me. "Just shut your fool mouth." He turned away and looked at Antigone.

I was about to go to the wagon and take out the flute hidden under the seat for a few bars of "Just Before the Battle, Mother," when our captor suddenly growled at his comrades, "Damn the horse. Be nothing but trouble on the road. Leave the mare be. But take the gun and vittles."

"Such a pretty horse, Jeb. Our mama'd love this horse."

"Just shut your mouth, Zack, and fill our canteens. So we can get out of here."

"Whatever you say, Jeb. Big mistake, but whatever you say."

"Oh, thank you, sir," I said. "Thank you, thank you, thank you," as they took their turns at the well, then bundled up our food in one of our blankets and headed off.

I watched them tramp south, Zack still loudly coveting Antigone, Jeb still telling him to shut up, until they disappeared behind a tall stand of briars.

And Isaac found his voice again. "Hill country trash," he hissed.

"Nothing but low-class hill trash. They have no right to mention Master Tom with their foul, low-class breaths."

"Well, I saved our horse," I told him.

He shook his head and spat at the ground. "A small blessing," he said, offering no word of praise for what I'd done.

I'm not sure why I did it. The soldiers were right: The dead were dead, and we could've buried Kemp at the crossroads and been done with him. But I needed to prove to Isaac that I was good for something, and Isaac had knotted his mind on bringing Master Tom home. I went along with his knot, made no attempt to untie it.

We resumed our journey, and Isaac remained silent, a sullen, brooding silence. It's remarkable how many kinds of silence there are. This one was contagious, and I lost my desire to speak. And the deserters had taken our food, so we now had nothing to eat. The fields we passed remained barren, all weeds and thorn and withered tobacco brush. We tried eating Antigone's parched corn when we stopped that evening, but it was like chewing gravel, even when we boiled it in water.

7

THERE was rain the next day, not a downpour but a light cool drizzle. It settled the dust and slowed the ferment of poor Tom. I was now on familiar terms with Kemp, though I'd known him longer dead than alive.

We passed through a hamlet whose doors and windows remained closed against us. A dozen dogs of all breeds and sizes trotted after the wagon, begging for a taste of what smelled like bacon.

Isaac held his silence all morning. He sat hunched against the light rain, closed like a fist around something in his heart. My own heart was not nearly so keen as my stomach. Suddenly, out of nowhere, Isaac angrily asked, "Who am I? Who in God's name am I? I was a fool to want respect from that soldier trash. Not the respect owed the Kemps. I am not Kemp's Isaac anymore. That world is over. That world is finished. I am in God's hands now. The body of Thomas Kemp is in my hands, but I am in God's."

I thought it was his hunger talking, the inebriation of an empty belly. His mention of God didn't disturb me. People in that age were always dragging God into the conversation. I was from a family of freethinkers myself, and we weren't quite atheists but believed in a Supreme Being as vague, unworldly, and beautiful as . . . well, music.

"Providence," said Isaac. "It is all Providence"—and I only pictured a city in Rhode Island with a perennially disappointing box office. "The house of Kemp is of nothing now, and I am left to Providence. God will do with me as He will. If He wants me to be happy in Goshen, so be it. If He wants to drop me into the flames of perdition, that is His right."

Freedom was not very appealing if it left you a slave of God, I thought, but kept the thought to myself.

Words continued to tumble out of him, furious, hard-bitten accusations, directed not at me but like an argument with himself. The fires of hell led to home fires, fires of the hearth, and he spoke of the Kemps, his master and mistress, and his sister, Lucy. Stupid Lucy, ignorant Lucy, a foolish woman who thought that the Kemps were Providence itself, that the Kemps would provide. She once told him, "Don't go talking like that, Ike, or you makes our white people thinks you wants to be free"—he used his darky voice to imitate her. But the Kemps, too, were children of God, and God the Father saved only a handful of His children from the fires of hell. Isaac hoped Master Tom might be in heaven, but that was for God to decide, not the Kemps.

I didn't know what to make of this crazy, aimless hell talk. Isaac seemed so much older and wiser than me when he was silent. But underneath his manly mask was confusion, uncertainty, and fear. Religion provided words for his emotion. Strange to say, it never occurred to me that Isaac might have gone mad. Years of slavery followed by such sudden, violent freedom could unhinge any man's mind. But when you're young, the entire world seems half insane already.

I did not dare offer him solace, not even a pat on the shoulder. I didn't know what to say except "Food. We need to find food. You'll feel better when you get something to eat."

He raised his eyes to heaven and scornfully shook his head. But then, as if noticing his own hollow pit, he sighed and said, "Yes. You're right. Food for the body. *Then* food for the soul."

For all his religion, Isaac never opened his throat in song during our journey. We had no musty hymns or exotic Negro spirituals on our long ride east, neither "Asleep in Jesus" nor "Roll Over, Jordan." There was no music in Isaac, and what tunes we had were all provided by my pagan flute.

The sky began to clear toward sunset, and we saw a grand house in the sunshine up ahead. A stately brick box stood by the road, rain-washed and glittering, behind a miraculously intact white rail fence. It looked like a mirage at first, a pocket of plenty in that impoverished land. Yet there was no livestock in the yard, no human beings by the barn or slave shacks. The place appeared deserted. We rode through the gate, hoping there was a garden out back where we could scrounge forgotten vegetables.

I went up to the front porch and knocked on a heavy oak door. Nobody answered. I looked through a window, the glass so old that it swelled and crimped like running water. The low sun poured through elegant rooms inside.

An ancient colored woman hobbled across the yard, her head tied up in a rag turban.

"You there! Auntie!" Isaac shouted. She hurried off, afraid to even look at us, skating her rag-bound feet over the clay.

I tried the door. It was unlocked. I opened it slowly. "Hello?" I called in. There was silence inside. Even the clock in the front hall was still, the hands stopped at two forty-five, or maybe nine-ten: I remember only that the ornate clockface wore a sly, subtle smile.

"Don't go in," said Isaac. "You want your head blown off?"

But I'd already entered, and Isaac soon followed, stopping at the threshold to wipe his feet. "Rich folk," he whispered. "Old-time gentry."

Shafts of dusty amber light stretched through rooms full of fancy furniture from another era. There were no dustcovers on the chairs and sofas. Who lived here, and where had they gone? I couldn't guess. No portraits hung on the walls, only a single pale square over the fireplace that suggested they'd taken their image with them. But they'd left behind a piano. A great oblong box squatted in the back parlor, an old Broadwood imported from England. I went over and opened the keyboard. The keys were black and brown, like an ear of Indian corn. I tried a few notes. The treble end was hard and metallic, like broken chimes, but the lower octaves sounded fine.

While Isaac went into the other rooms, I sat on the stool and fingered the keys, hesitantly, as if it had been years since I'd seen a piano and couldn't remember how it worked. I was pleased to touch an old forgotten self again.

A tune came to me, one I didn't recognize. I let a pattern of notes trickle from my fingers. It began, in fact, as simply a set of finger movements, something physical rather than audible, a spider dance performed by my right hand. I played the phrase slowly, then again, more quickly. The phrase led to a new phrase, and another. I improvised an answer with my left hand. Something like this...

C-sharp minor, an agitated, unhappy key. That may have been only the out-of-tune piano, but it began to pour from my fingers, race out of my hands, a cascade of notes like the *presto agitato* of the "Moonlight" Sonata, which surprised me, since I'd been unable to master those pounding rapids on my own. Like this passage here. A similar steam engine of bass but with new phrases racing alongside, angry shouts and heartbroken laments. It grew under my hands like a fire, into a blaze of sound, a holocaust of chords and arpeggios, a furious, weirdly exuberant sorrow.

On that hollow, jangling carillon of a piano, I played better than I had ever played before. But the music did not originate in me. It came from somewhere else, leapfrogging my brain and going straight into my hands.

There it was, the first composition dictated to me by the spirit world, only I didn't know it at the time.

When it stopped coming to me, when I ran out of notes, I let it softly die. And I sat there, staring at the black-and-brown keyboard, gripping my suddenly ice-cold hands between my legs.

"Does it have a name?" said a voice.

I nearly jumped from my skin. But it was only Isaac—I'd forgotten I was not alone—drawn back to the parlor by the roaring piano. He looked impressed. It may have been gibberish to him, pure cacophony, but I'd been flying like a locomotive, which would have amazed anyone whose ideal of speed was a buggy ride.

"I don't know," I said. "I don't know what it's from. It just came to me."

I remained shaken, alarmed. I wondered if the piano were haunted and had somehow used me to play itself. Or had the music come from the corpse in the wagon outside? It had sounded demonic enough, though I doubted that the ghost of Thomas Kemp would speak in the style of Beethoven.

"Nobody here," said Isaac. "Everyone's run off. Except that old woman out back."

"There's no dead people upstairs?"

He treated the question as perfectly natural. "The rooms are all empty," he said. "But there's pickled tomatoes and preserved peaches in the pantry. And a feather bed upstairs. A master's feather bed," he announced and added, with a stern note of defiance, "I'm sleeping in a master's bed tonight."

We did not light a fire or candles that evening for fear of attracting a passing patrol or more deserters. We gorged ourselves on the tomatoes and sweet jarred fruit by moonlight. Food eased my anxious mind only so much. I remained nervous. There were no clues for where the owners had gone, why they had left their house in such apparent haste. I unhitched Antigone and brought her indoors, afraid she might run off or the old woman out back would steal her. The tall horse balked at the front steps and the door, but finally lowered her head and entered, stepping like a lady to the manner born. Putting her with the piano and sofas, an armful of hay on the carpet, was a nice sacrilege equal to a slave in a master's bed.

I did not want to sleep alone in that handsome haunted house. "Is there room for me?" I asked Isaac. The sharing of beds was commonplace in my century. "Or I'll sleep on the floor."

He shrugged. "Sleep where you like. It's a big bed."

I followed him upstairs to a moonlit room and a canopied bed like a mound of snow under a marquee. We undressed to our shirts and got in. Climbing clothed into that downy heap would have been as unthinkable as taking a bath in trousers. I was so tired, so empty that I didn't stop to think that I was sharing a bed with a Negro. Everything seemed to pour into me—linen, feathers, and Isaac. I sank into a deep sleep.

I dreamed that I stood in a forest, a burning forest with flames like music. Each fire had its own key, major or minor, a roar of sound like an idea of sound. Men screamed silently in the musical blaze. I caught glimpses of them in the flames, Kemp and Crawford and the sick captain. I was dreaming of Isaac's hell, only I stood unharmed in the midst of their punishment. The flames did not burn but merely warmed me.

I woke to find myself pressed against a man's warm back and backside, with my hand in a very intimate place. I knew it was Isaac but continued to hold him, the smooth, hard root of the man. It was good to touch something so familiar, like touching the piano downstairs. We ride our souls in sleep like horses, and sometimes the horse knows best where to go.

He softly moaned and stretched, and suddenly became still. He was awake; I was terrified that he'd be angry.

"This is magic," I claimed. "I know magic tricks and spells." My half-awake sleep self hoped that he'd be too innocent to know what I was doing. I lightly rubbed his lamp, as if to make a genie appear.

He let my hand continue a moment. "That ain't magic!" he snarled. And he swung around, grabbed my wrists and pinned me, so violently that I expected him to slap and punch my face. But he had my shirt up under my arms, his knees between my legs and his tongue in my mouth.

I had never been kissed. Uncle Jack didn't believe in kissing. It felt wondrous, like eating magnetic air.

My mind stood apart from my body, amazed by Isaac. The bite of his beard and press of bare hips were a revelation, a show of warmth and passion never hinted at by his stony daylight self. My body was delighted with the attention, my hands fascinated with his back, the skin like rough silk, the great weight of him. He wrapped his arms around me for the naked lightning of souls, first mine, then his, with a loud duet for flute and trumpet.

We lay there, heart to galloping heart, our breaths in each other's face, our hearts stripped of their foreskins. His open eyes were so close to mine that I seemed to look into the infinite spaces behind the stars. Then his head jerked back and he stared at me, sharply, as if seeing me for the first time, understanding that he had been intimate with a man—a white man.

He blinked, he frowned. "That's how *we* do it," he muttered. He rolled off, turned his back to me, drew himself into a ball, and promptly fell back asleep.

I remained awake, breathless, amazed. It had been nothing like my sessions with Uncle Jack, which were all in my privates. This time my entire body, head to toe, heart and soul, had become a private part. I cautiously scooted against Isaac's back, put my arms around him and fell asleep, too.

When I awoke the next morning, Isaac was already up and lacing his shoes. "We better get going," he said in his usual stony manner, as if nothing had happened in the night.

But I already knew. His silence was in yet another key, a different indifference. I was immediately ashamed of last night, frightened by what he must think of me. My shame contained not only fear but a strange new fondness for Isaac, a tenderness that made me crave his respect.

Downstairs in the parlor Antigone towered over the squat, dead piano. She looked more profoundly wrong by day than she had by moonlight. I led her back outside. Isaac and I breakfasted on jarred fruit, with as few words as possible, and loaded a box of jars into the wagon. He didn't mention last night, so I didn't dare mention it either. Soon we were on the road again, the sinister mansion rumbling behind us and disappearing in the misty trees.

The morning was cool and damp, uncomfortable for us but a kindness to the corpse. If only we could've preserved Tom like fruit in a jar.

Finally Isaac said, "I had a dream last night. A sinful, childish dream."

"I know," I confessed. "I had the same dream myself."

He refused to look at me. "It's bad enough to do it as a boy," he said angrily. "But now I am a man. A free man. I must put away childish things."

"Forgive me," I said. "It won't happen again."

"It better not," he declared. "Or I'll leave you on the road. Out here in the middle of nowhere." He blamed me, and like a criminal or a man in love, I took full responsibility.

"It will never happen again," I insisted. "I promise."

Because I knew he was right. It was a boy's vice, and we were no longer boys, not after all that we had been through.

"Fine," he said. "Good. We need never speak of it again."

And I was relieved, overjoyed that we put it behind us so quickly. I could not tell him about Uncle Jack, of course. And I couldn't ask about the black boys with whom he had done his childish thing. I gladly passed over the latter. Picturing pickaninnies in each other's arms would have been too humiliating, making me feel that I was no better than a slave myself, a shameless beast, and no longer white.

8

IT took us four days to reach Norfolk. It would have taken longer
if we had had to go the long way around, but the ferryman at
Gosport, a tobacco-chewing Charon, took pity on a dead Confederate
and carried us over the river for free.

The wide water was a forest of masts and rigging and smoke-
stacks, a floating metropolis that dwarfed the real city on shore. We
did not head into town from the landing but back out toward the
country, past trim little houses on a wide, sandy street. There were
people here, men on horseback, ladies in buggies, a squad of marching Union soldiers, all of whom frowned and shivered at the sight
of us. A sad air of mortality clung to the two boys and their mournful horse, not just an air but a smell. The coffin now stank like a
crate of rotting fish. Yet Isaac sat up very straight and tall, looking
quite proud as he traveled this road that he knew all too well, toward
home.

The houses gave way to fields, and then we came to a new batch
of houses and a church, a stark white Presbyterian thing. Next door
stood a pale rectory of whitewashed bricks behind a picket fence.
There was a sign on the gate: THE REVEREND JOSIAH KEMP. Neither
Kemp nor Isaac had mentioned that their people were church mice.
Was this the source of Isaac's God?

We creaked through the gate and up a rutted drive. The whitewash of the house was badly faded, the front lawn reduced to a ragged vegetable garden. A hayfield out back looked half chewed where someone had attempted to harvest it.

A door flew open in the kitchen wing of the house. Out ran a stout, gray-haired white woman in a great skirt of plain cloth. "It *is* Isaac! Our Isaac! Isaac has returned!"

She was followed by a wide-eyed young woman in similar dress and a solemn man in whiskers, shirtsleeves, and a black clerical shirtfront. He was the spitting image of Tom Kemp, only the spit had dried and turned gray.

"But where is Master Tom?" the mother cried. "Did our Tom send word when he will be——" Then she saw the lidded boat in the wagon and understood the rich smell in the air. She froze, she swayed. She sank in a heap of crinoline, her skirt billowing up as if the earth were water, swallowing her until all that remained were her open mouth and staring eyes.

"Dearest wife," her husband said and embraced the kneeling woman. "Be not afraid. Our boy is with the angels." And he broke into tears.

"My darling brother!" the girl cried and threw her arms around both parents.

Isaac and I stood by, respectful of their sorrow yet remaining apart from it, like undertakers.

After the first wave of sorrow passed and Reverend Kemp had helped his wife to her feet, he came over to me. His iron-gray muttonchops and mustache formed a solid frowning curve, so he looked quite stern even with tears streaming into his whiskers. He said through his tears, "You served with Tom? Thank you, sir, for bringing him home." And he embraced me, a complete stranger.

I had to explain that this was all Isaac's doing, and I'd only been along for the ride.

"You, Isaac?" said Reverend Kemp. "Yes. Of course. You always had a good soul, a great heart." And he embraced Isaac, sobbing on his shoulder as fearlessly as he would sob on a handkerchief. Isaac remained straight and composed, his hands at his sides.

"Take Tom into the parlor," commanded his mother. "Take him into his home where he belongs."

The father, Isaac, and I tugged the coffin from the wagon and carried it through the front door. The family was too full of grief to care that it was only a rotting punt and stank to high heaven. I felt the weight inside and pictured the corpse again: blackened, shriveled, oozing. We set the boat on two straight-back chairs, and Mrs. Kemp laid her face on the makeshift lid, sobbing on the splintered slats. I was afraid she'd want it opened so she could look upon her son. But her husband took her in his arms and said they should let Tom rest tonight, now that he was home.

"You must be hungry after your journey," he told us. "When did you last eat?" Food is the steadying ritual for mourners as well as comforters. "Come into the kitchen. We take all our meals in the kitchen. Since the servants ran off."

"What?" said Isaac. "Lucy and Samuel and Granny Jones? *They* ran off?" The news took him completely by surprise.

"Their names are no longer used in this house," Reverend Kemp flatly declared. "Come."

We followed the Kemps into the kitchen, where the day was fading in the window and firelight flickered on the bricks. I sat down at a large slab table. And Isaac, still blinking in amazement over the flight of the others, drew out a chair and sat beside me.

The Kemps stared at him, as they might stare at a dog who had just quoted Shakespeare. Their slave sat himself at their table? Then Mrs. Kemp, her eyes still flowing like a spring, said timidly, "Yes, Isaac. You should eat, too. You must be ravenous. You boys have come a long way with our Tom."

While mother and daughter stirred the fire, shifted a pot, and cut bread with new, awkward expertise, there were sharp whispers from the daughter and hushing sounds from the mother.

They didn't sit with us while we ate. Even Reverend Kemp, who had put on his coat, remained standing. It was my first hot meal in days, and I ate greedily while the reverend asked me questions, addressing me, not Isaac. You were with Tom at the end? He died in battle? Did he die bravely? Did he die quickly? I said he died bravely, which was true—although his bravery had looked like foolishness—and that he died instantly. They did not need to know that their son had lain there half dead until a scavenger put a bullet in his head.

Isaac showed no concern for what I told them but hungrily ate while he brooded on something else. "They even took the old woman?" he muttered to himself. "Did they leave no word for me?"

"Who? Oh. *Them,*" said Reverend Kemp scornfully. "They left without a word. They took off in the night like thieves. It is a vile thing to learn that for years you held scorpions to your bosom, Judas Iscariots."

"But you are home, Isaac," said Mrs. Kemp. "We knew you would not abandon us. You were always true and faithful."

And Isaac said, quietly, calmly, "I came back only to bring your son's body home. I am not staying." He continued to eat while he let his declaration of independence sink in, carefully mopping at the gravy with a piece of bread.

"What did I tell you!" the daughter shouted. "He's gone bad like the others! The insolent way he sat himself at our table."

"Hush, Jane, hush," said Mrs. Kemp. "He brought our Thomas home. He's still family. We can reason with him."

"They're all alike!" the daughter cried. "They take food from our mouths and run off the first chance they get!"

For a moment, I regret to say, I hesitated in my loyalties, feeling that Isaac was in the wrong. These people had lost a son. This was not the time for them to lose a servant. It was as though my pity, a plate of stew, and their white skin were enough to make me one of them.

Reverend Kemp approached the table. He gazed down at Isaac

from a high pulpit of silence. He laid a firm hand on Isaac's shoulder. "No," he declared. "You will not follow them. You are wiser than they, Isaac. You always were. Not just more clever but wiser, deeper, more pure. Your place is here, and you know it."

Isaac stiffened at Kemp's touch. He kept his head down. "No, sir. My place is in the world of free men. My soul is mine to do with as I please."

Kemp struggled to keep his temper. "We raised that soul up, Isaac. We clothed and fed and trained it. We gave you everything. We taught you to read and write."

Isaac shut his eyes and took a deep breath. "No, sir," he said. "It was Tom who taught me to read. Against your wishes."

"Tom?" said Kemp. He jerked his hand away as if Isaac were a hot skillet. "You call him *Tom* now?" The face in the righteous whiskers was turning red. "You think you are his equal because he is dead?"

Isaac took another bite of stew. He had to work hard at his show of indifference.

"Look at me when I speak to you!" Kemp commanded. "You insolent whelp! Look at me!" And he struck Isaac, hitting his face with the back of his hand, knocking the spoon to the floor.

The blow made me flinch, but Isaac promptly recovered. He sat very still, then resumed chewing what was in his mouth.

"No, Josiah!" cried his wife. "Reason with him."

"One cannot reason with a viper!" cried Kemp. "Look at me!" he shouted and raised his hand for another slap.

Only this time Isaac grabbed his wrist before the blow hit. He gripped the wrist and looked at Kemp: It was *not* the look that Kemp had wanted. Master and chattel glared at each other. The caught hand made a fist.

I broke my silence. "But he brought your son home!" I shouted. "He brought his body a hundred miles!"

"You take his side in this?" cried the daughter. "Who are you anyway? Where are you from?"

Before I could answer, before I could even tell the truth, I saw the change in Reverend Kemp's face as the fight went out of his fist. His eyes were wide open, as if seeing Isaac for the first time, and his righteous whiskers folded around his mouth. He did not appear frightened but baffled, confused. He could not have been more stunned if a chair had jumped aside, refusing to be sat in. He glanced at his wife and daughter to assure himself that he was still real.

Isaac slowly stood up and released Kemp's wrist. "I am going," he announced. "But remember this: Your property did not steal itself like a thief in the night but as a man. A free man. And I'm taking things Tom owes me. Things that are rightfully mine." He turned and strode out of the kitchen.

The father remained by the table, stunned. The Kemps all looked at each other in amazement. A piece of furniture had just given them a speech. When we heard Isaac on the stairs, the Kemps hurried out to the front hall, and I followed them. They climbed a narrow staircase to the room that had been their son's.

Isaac had opened a chest, a clothes press, and spread a blanket on the bed, where he was laying out a dark suit—the shadow of Tom Kemp. "I brought back the body his soul once wore," Isaac declared. "He can leave me his second-best suit. Like a brother would. He'll want his best suit for the grave."

"He's gone mad," said the daughter. "He's not our Isaac anymore. He's a thieving stranger who's broken into our home."

But nobody went for a gun. The Kemps watched dumbstruck from the doorway as Isaac set a shirt on the suit, and a change of linen, then rolled the clothes in the blanket and tied it into a bedroll. He laid the bedroll over his shoulder and faced them with icy dignity. "The Crawfords, Bulls, and Lassiters?" he said. "Tell them their sons are buried near Claremont. At Wigandt's Landing. And there's a Captain Pelham. I don't know who his people are, but he's buried there, too."

He came toward the door, and they fearfully stepped aside, afraid to be touched by this stranger.

He went down the stairs, then paused coolly at the foot. "Thank you for your hospitality," he called up. "The meal I just ate. My first meal as a free man. Much obliged," he said, and went out the door.

"Isaac!" I shouted. "Wait for me!"

The confusion of the Kemps instantly turned to anger with the forgotten guest. "This is *your* doing?" they charged. "*You* filled his head with ingratitude and treason!"

"Not me," I said and backed toward the stairs. "You cannot fill that man's head with anything. And it's not treason, it's freedom."

I hurried down the stairs and out the door and caught up with Isaac in the growing darkness. He had only stopped at the wagon to get a few things, and I wondered if he forgot that I was even here. He showed no surprise when I appeared, but grumbled, "You should have kept your mouth shut in there. You could've stayed and eaten and bathed and rested a few days before you went back north."

"I couldn't pretend I was on their side," I told him.

"No?" he said. "I guess I should thank you for your loyalty. I don't know what good it does me, but thank you."

I fetched my flute from under the seat. Antigone was still hitched up, and she swung her head around to look at me with a round, bottle-brown eye. For a moment I thought she wanted to go with us, but she turned away and tossed her head, as indifferent to our fate as God.

The Kemps watched us from a window, then came to the door. The father and daughter began to shout. "Scorpion! Judas! Get away from here. We don't want you! We're finished with you!"—pretending to be the agents of his departure. They remained by the door, afraid to come closer. And then Mrs. Kemp cried out, "You had no business taking Tom's clothes! You are not his brother!" she sobbed. "You're a nigger!" she cried. "Only a black-assed nigger!"

We walked toward the gate, Isaac maintaining an eerie, preternatural calm while his "family" shouted names at his back. One can only begin to imagine what he felt: indignation, fear, hope, confusion. A slave is a stranger to all, even to himself, so long as he remains a slave. Now that he was free, who was he?

We reached the road, and Isaac stepped more briskly. He held his head high, and his stride became exultant, even happy, angrily happy—one can be joyful in one's anger.

"I knew my act would go unrewarded," he said. "But that was for me, not for them. I should thank the Lord for hardening pharaoh's heart. Now I can walk away without regrets. I am truly free. Amen."

"Amen," I agreed, uncertainly.

Because it suddenly felt very queer to walk alone with Isaac on that dark, dust-soft road back toward town. I missed the rumble and squeak of our wagon, the comforting gait of our horse, even the presence of a corpse at our backs. It was just me and Isaac now, with nothing to explain why we were together.

"Where will you go?" I asked.

"I don't know. The world is open to me. I never been out in the world. Until I went to the war with Tom."

I said nothing. Then, "Do you want to come north with me?"

"No. I was considering it. But no. I need to find my sister. I need to find my feet in a place that I know. And it will be hard enough for one man to find a ride north, much less two."

He was right, of course. There was no practicality to my invitation, no rhyme or reason. I did not really expect him to go with me to New York. It was only my reluctance to say good-bye to Isaac after all that we had been through. But I could calmly accept that we would go our separate ways. After tonight, or the next night, depending on how long it took me to find a passage home, we would part forever.

There was no moon yet, only a scatter of stars to show where the earth ended and the sky began. We didn't speak. Our footsteps sounded as soft as heartbeats in the talcum dust. The usual dog barked somewhere in the night, and the road stretched ahead of us, pale and straight, with an inevitable fork somewhere up ahead in the dark.

PART

II

9

THERE was the thunder of drums, a joyful blare of brass, and cheering, endless cheering. Crowds stood five deep in the redbrick canyon of Broadway and roared at the long blue columns marching through. The ranks of soldiers rolled in the distance like blue wheat, under flocks of flags and a dense sway of bayonets like a sunlit haze of needles.

New York again, home. Nine months later, and the war was over. Oh, yes, this is the Radetzky March I am playing, a gaily martial quickstep of the Habsburgs, more evocative of plumed helmets and shakos than of drab blue American cloth. But the tune brings that day back to me in all its colors. There was no John Philip Sousa yet, and our music was still European, even when we celebrated something as American as the triumph of the Union.

It was spring, and shop windows that had been hooded with crêpe a month ago for Lincoln now bloomed with red-white-and-blue bunting. Handkerchiefs fluttered like butterflies as row upon row of sun-brown soldiers swung past. The gentlemen in tall hats and ladies in little bonnets along the curb shielded their own delicate white faces with black umbrellas and pastel parasols. They cheered each torn, bullet-riddled regimental color as if the flags were men. They cheered the generals, too, who lifted their hats and set their horses prancing to the tunes brayed and twittered by regimental bands.

I watched the parade while perched on the iron sill of a shop window, in order to see over the mushroom mob of umbrellas. Standing beside me, holding my arm for balance, was Fanny Gaskins, a pretty girl of my age with red hair, lace gloves, and freckles peeking through her rouge. We were both in our Sunday best: me in a fancy cravat, yellow waistcoat, and porkpie hat; Fanny with her flounces and ribbons stuffed into a short green hussar jacket. Two overdressed fifteen-year-old dolls on a storefront, we probably looked like a sentimental illustration of young love from *Harper's Weekly*. Yet we were not what we seemed.

"Hurrah!" Fanny called out, like a little girl pretending to be a lady. "Hurrah!"

I cheered, too, though not as often. After all, I'd "seen the elephant" myself, as people said of the war, and the passing ranks of soldiers did not make me think of heroic deeds but of youths bathing in a river, and pointless murder. I wondered how Fanny connected these men with her own wartime experience.

This was the first great parade of many. We spent the rest of the century in parades, celebrating our nation's survival of slaughter. The great public event of my age took place at the start of my life, so the world seemed like a solid, settled place in the years that followed, with no historical dramas as dangerous as those of my own making.

"What a day!" cried Fanny. "There is only one word for today. Splendifluous! What a splendifluous day to be an American!"

"There's no such word," I said.

"No, Professor? Well, there should be."

I studied the spectators at our feet, taking in the fine clothes, furtive glances, and moistened mustaches. "Tonight's going to be a long, splendifluous night," I muttered.

"Now, don't be vulgar," said Fanny. "I don't want to think on that. I thank you not to remind me."

But it was true. The city was full of gentlemen who'd come to town for the great victory to-do, and there was nothing like the sight of so many ladies out in public to awaken a healthy man's appetite.

Fanny and I worked together. Not in a fashion shop that our smart clothes suggested but in another trade. I had a new calling in life. To give our profession its proper name: I was a whorehouse musician, and Fanny was a whore. Yet "whorehouse" is not the right name either. Roebuck's was nothing like the public houses downtown—noisy, sordid places on crooked, saloon-lined streets, with *carte de visite* photographs of "soiled doves" pasted in the windows as if they were actresses. We were a private, respectable establishment, on a good street in the West Twenties, a five-dollar house with genteel ladies, good liquor, and fine music, the last item provided by me.

A wave of laughter rolled through the crowd as another regiment marched by. I soon saw why. At the rear, riding a threadbare mule, was an old Negro in a frayed suit and stovepipe hat. The mule was hung with banging pots and pans, a stumbling goat tethered to its tail. A sulking child-soldier gripped the mule's bridle, the regiment's drummer boy, who clearly resented being reduced today to an escort for the regimental mascot. The old man, however, showed no shame but sat up straight and proudly tipped his hat at the crowd, which only made people laugh harder, Fanny and I laughing with them. Yes, I laughed, too, thoughtlessly joining in, finding mirth in the low spectacle only because everyone else did.

Church bells began to toll in different parts of the city, the hour making itself heard over the din. Three o'clock: We were due back at the house. I hopped down from my perch like a boy, then offered Fanny my hand like a gent and helped her to the sidewalk. She held my arm as we walked behind the good citizens, looking like a perfectly respectable couple.

We were halfway down the block when a tall, dark, domed figure abruptly stepped into our path. His teeth were angrily bared, his sharp nose indignantly raised at us. Two rawboned wrists stuck from his coat sleeves.

Fanny let out a gasp, pressed a hand to her throat, then said, "Oh, it's you! I don't recognize you in that hat. You gave me such a fright, Isaac."

Yes, it was Isaac, in the second-best suit that he was outgrowing, and a new round-domed hat like a brown egg, a prehistoric bowler with almost no brim. Fanny should not have been surprised. Isaac had been with us at the start of the parade, but his new hat confused her.

"Did you see that uncle on a mule?" he petulantly snapped. "Out there like a fool for all the world to laugh at?"

"Yes, pitiful," I said, wondering why he took it so personally even as I regretted my own laughter. "Excuse us, Isaac. We're overdue at the house."

He fell into step alongside me, shaking his head in anger, so full of anger that he forgot we were not alone. "No Negro regiments in this parade. No black men at all. Just a fool riding on a mule. It's an insult. An insult. Don't they remember who this war was for?"

"You shouldn't take it to heart," I said. "People just want to forget the war and laugh again."

"Amnesia!" said Isaac. "Insult and amnesia!"

Fanny looked straight ahead, pretending not to know this well-dressed Negro chatting with her escort.

When we reached the corner, I said, "It's going to be a late night, Isaac. You don't have to wait up for me." I said it solely for Fanny's benefit. Isaac never waited up.

"Insult and amnesia," he repeated, tipped his hat at Fanny, and, still grumbling to himself, took his leave of us.

Fanny and I strolled up a cross street, away from the roar and throb of the parade. "I do declare," she finally said. "Your man Isaac gets crazier every day. I don't understand why you keep him on as your servant."

"He can be forward," I admitted. "But no more forward than you are with those whom you serve."

Fanny loudly sniffed at the comparison. "Well, intimacy leads to certain liberties," she said pompously. "But your man doesn't have that excuse."

"No. He certainly doesn't," I said, speaking the truth. "But we've been through too much together to stand on ceremony."

Oh, yes. Isaac had come north with me. Of course. He was my servant only in name, and in the eyes of others. Nevertheless, almost a year after we met, we were still together.

10

How did we make our way north? I did not mean to skip over that, Tristan, only it was a dreary business getting out of Norfolk. Stranded in the wilderness, I'd been homesick for cities, but a city is an even meaner wilderness when you have no money. Isaac and I were two masterless servants in a city of men without masters: sailors between ships, Yankee and Confederate deserters, freed or runaway slaves, and refugees of the war.

Isaac went around with me my first day in Norfolk, wanting to see how a free man did things. I made a very poor teacher. We went first to the army headquarters in City Hall, where I stood in a room like a train station packed with stranded women, children, and old men. I expected the government to help me, though they'd done such a poor job of it so far. But the army could not care less about a lost musician. The name Giacomo Fitzwilliam meant nothing to the corporal at the desk. When his questions began to indicate a suspicion that I was a deserter, and he went to speak to a superior, I quickly slipped out the door and rejoined Isaac on the steps. Next I tried the docks, thinking I might find a New York–bound boat where I could stow away, but most of the ships were moored out in the channel, and the few docked vessels were guarded by soldiers. I offered myself as a waiter or dishwasher on a passenger steamer, but the steward took one look at my dirty face and sneered, "Go back to the farm, pig boy."

Isaac did not scoff or laugh at my failures but coolly took them in, conning them like lessons in grammar.

We spent the night in the yard of an abandoned tobacco warehouse, a fenced-in lot full of huge empty casks. Set on its side, without a top or bottom, a tobacco hogshead makes a good shelter, despite the peppery smell of dried leaf. We weren't the only ones playing Diogenes in that yard of barrels. There were sullen, wary blacks in one end of the yard and loud, drunken, bottle-breaking whites in the other. Isaac and I had nothing to do with either group but kept to ourselves. We slept side by side that night, head to toe, two sardines in a cigar box.

The next day Isaac went off on his own to hunt for news of his sister. We agreed to meet back at our hogshead that evening. I couldn't tell him of my new plan, for fear of what he'd think of me: I had decided to backslide and be "a boy" again. The world was full of Uncle Jacks, the town full of Yankee businessmen. I thought I could attach myself to one long enough to get a ticket back home.

But I was not very appetizing, even after I washed off at a public pump. I still had my flute, which gave a look of purpose to my loitering. I did not prowl the streets like a common prostitute but stood in the mud outside saloons and hotels, playing for the occasional penny pitched into the floppy hat at my feet while I tried to catch an eye. I caught no one but did pick up enough pennies to purchase some bread and cheese, which I took home to our hogshead to share with Isaac. He, too, had had no luck. The town was full of strangers. All the slaves whom he had known were vanished, fled. No familiar soul remained who could tell him what had become of his sister.

The following day did not start much better. An old Southern gentleman with a long white beard spoke to me for quite some time, then invited me to join him for a brief visit to a nearby stable, which I politely declined. By nightfall I had parked myself outside a gaslit hotel on Granby Street, the brightest windows in town. Businessmen lounged in a bright lobby on the other side of the glass, sharing tips and rumors and chaws of tobacco. I was piping a melancholy tune when a fat man with a round, bland face came out of the hotel and hurried by, deep in thought. He suddenly stopped, turned around, and listened a moment. He stepped in closer. His face remained bland as he looked me up and down, but I thought I'd found my pigeon.

I quickly finished my tune. "Good evening, sir. You obviously have an ear for fine music."

"You a musician?" he said. "A trained musician? Yes? Come with me." He grabbed my elbow and hauled me off, so quickly that I hardly had time to snatch up my hat.

His name was Roebuck, he said, Asa Roebuck. He and Mrs. Roebuck and their three stepdaughters were in the entertainment line. They had just lost their piano player and badly needed music. When he heard that I played the piano as well, he was certain he'd found his man. They were crossing the bay to Point Comfort the next day, where they had a two-week engagement, then would work their way up the coast to New York. He offered me room, board, travel expenses, and three dollars a week.

Thrilled by my good fortune, my miraculous change of luck, I instantly wanted more. "I have a manservant," I said. "Will you take him on, too?"

Roebuck showed no surprise that a boy begging in the street might have a servant. "Hmmm," he said. "He a strong fellow? Strong back? We happen to be short a luggage man." They had lost their porter at the same time they lost the piano player, when the two men had had a disagreement over a fifth ace and the porter argued his point of view with a broken whiskey bottle. He had been sentenced to be hanged that very afternoon.

So I already had a pretty good idea that these people weren't the Hutchinson Family Singers. I didn't learn the exact nature of their entertaining, however—the steps the stepdaughters took to make a buck—until I arrived at their boardinghouse. It was early yet, and the sole guest in the parlor was a shy, beardless ensign. The Roebucks did not receive enlisted men. The trio of so-called daughters all dropped the officer for me.

"What a little doll!" they cried, pinching my cheeks and petting me, three overdressed, thickly painted girls who were not much older than I: Mary Anne, Mary Ellen, and Fanny, the youngest.

"A *dirty* little doll," said Mrs. Roebuck. The lamp revealed the state of my clothes, which had been hidden on the dark street. Luckily there was a piano in the parlor, and I immediately proved my worth with renditions of Bellini, Foster, and a few half-remembered hymns. So it was agreed: My servant and I would report the next morning and go with them to Point Comfort.

I hurried back to the hogshead and told Isaac my good news, hesitating before I added that he could share it, if he wanted. He listened, he thought, he frowned. There was much for him to frown at: leaving his hometown, working as a servant, the company of whores. I did not think he would accept. My proposal was chiefly a gesture of friendship, a way to thank him for getting me to Norfolk, and a display of my own cleverness.

But then, with a confused lift of his eyebrows and an abrupt, uncertain smile, Isaac made the most momentous decision of his life and mine. "I could, couldn't I?" he said. "There's nothing for me here. My sister and her husband are God knows where. And I want to see the world. I want to go north." And he must have wanted to remain with me, though he never said so. Who else did he know in this new world without masters? "Thank you, Fitz. Thank you." He gripped my hand in both of his and gave it a warm, manly shake. "This is a gift that I will never forget."

We spent two months in Point Comfort, not two weeks, in a drafty summer house down the beach from an army camp. The officers had plenty of ready cash, business boomed, and there were no problems with the authorities. The local commander, a New York politico-turned-colonel, adored Mrs. Roebuck, a handsome, buxom woman who worked alongside her daughters. The Roebucks' marriage was chiefly a business partnership, Mr. Roebuck a silent partner except in times of crisis. As servants to servants, Isaac and I blended into the household. I pottered away at the keyboard each night, learning to coax musical honey from a clanking cottage piano; Isaac ran errands and cut firewood and did whatever heavy work Mrs. Roebuck required. We were treated as equals, more or less. Again Isaac took in everything with a solemn, studious detachment, as if it were all a lesson. He kept his lessons and opinions to himself, however, even with me, keeping deeply inside himself, a turtle in its shell.

"I suppose it's meet and fitting," he admitted to me one night in the room we shared in the attic. "Very meet and fitting. That a preacher's slave start his free life in white man's Babylon. White people should hold no mystery for me now." He was dryly amused, like an old, sarcastic turtle.

The turtle did not come out of its shell until we stood side by side on the third-class deck of the steamer bound for New York. We went directly to New York from Point Comfort. The politico-colonel had a business associate back home who offered the Roebucks a whole house there, complete with furnishings, bed linen, and bribed magistrates. The coastal steamer slid past the headlands, and all around us was ocean, miles of ocean. A slave in a seaport, Isaac had never been to sea, of course, but he wasn't frightened. He gripped the rail and took in deep, heady breaths of open space. "It's like we're steaming through the sky," he said with an ecstatic grin. "Sailing up to heaven."

He stood there all night long, lost in a hypnotic reverie while the vessel plowed through the stars. I went to bed. I rejoined him the next day when we entered New York Harbor, wondering what he would see: heaven or Babylon?

He saw a bay crowded with sails and ribbons of smoke, immense and open—there was no Statue of Liberty yet—and an elongated island that bristled with shipping and wharves. Inside the masts and rigging were towering buildings of five and six stories, nearly as tall as the church steeples, street upon street of them, hard-paved streets loud with the clatter of wagons, horsecars, and omnibuses, and more people than Isaac knew existed in the world. He was overwhelmed. He tried to resume his turtle stoicism, but his eyes remained wide, his mouth half open. Then he began to scan the crowds frantically for something else: other black faces. He looked relieved when he saw some.

I was overwhelmed myself, but with my own questions. This was my home, the scene of my real life, only who was I now? That first night, while Isaac unloaded trunks and the girls explored the new brownstone house, I went downtown to see Aunt Ada.

Cousin Beatrice answered the door, took one look at me, and fainted. She collapsed at my feet, and I was touched; I'd never guessed I meant so much to her. But she thought I was a ghost. Uncle Jack had returned a month ago and reported that I'd been killed, shot dead in an ambush by Rebel monsters. They had mourned their poor little cousin, then digested my death. But here I was, miraculously resurrected. They were thrilled, for an hour or so. The dead can be tiresome when they stay past supper. Cousin Ted had recovered from his wounds to become the new head of the family. He was glad to hear I'd found employment and would not be dependent on them. They had packed my few belongings in a little trunk, which they'd intended to sell but now gave the trunk to me to take to my new home.

And so I stayed on at the Roebucks', where I still had Isaac. I was suddenly anxious about him, afraid he would bid farewell now that we were in Freedomland. But Isaac stayed on, too, while he learned the ropes of urban life. He went out alone in the evenings. He did not want me to show him my New York but insisted on discovering his own city, exploring it on foot, walking up and down it like a man pacing off a piece of property he might buy. He returned from his expeditions confused and alarmed. It was a world of strangers out there, and while white people did not treat him like somebody else's dog, the way they did in Norfolk, they pretended not to see him at all. He met other colored men and women, but they were all cold and aloof, he said, treating him like a hayseed, no better than a field nigger.

His one pure joy during those first months was his discovery of newspapers. Isaac became a great reader of papers. He was amazed by their ubiquity, left out on tables, stuffed in ash barrels, or blowing around in the street, and he could pick one up and start to read, even in public, without fear of anyone's ripping the sheet from his hand and demanding to know where he had learned to read. His first important purchase with free man's wages was a fresh *New York Tribune*, still damp from the press, for a penny. His second important purchase was a two-dollar Bible, despite my advice that he should save the money toward a winter coat.

Isaac and I again shared quarters in the attic, until the weather turned cold and I confronted Mrs. Roebuck, said I'd proved my worth and deserved an increase in salary so I could afford my own place. She reluctantly raised my pay to ten dollars a week. I invited Isaac to come with me. "It's not good for man to be alone," I said, secretly tickled by the flexible uses of Scripture. And Isaac accepted, treating the move as a moral practicality. He announced that he was finished with serving harlots and should end his employment here, especially with Mrs. Roebuck threatening to dress him up in livery.

I found a boardinghouse for us a few blocks away, on Twenty-fifth Street east of Madison Square, the new center of town. New York was slowly climbing north. It was a shabby-genteel neighborhood, on the edge of a warren of wooden slums and mud lanes. I told the German landlady that I had a servant, a colored servant. Isaac was accustomed to this fiction. Other boarders had servants, too, who all lived under the eaves, but I explained I was sickly and often needed help in the night. That was fine with Mrs. Kuntzler.

She disliked putting a colored man in with the white servants, and she had an available room with servant's quarters, a space no bigger than a cupboard. I offered to pay Isaac a small salary until he found a job, but he refused. He would be no more beholden to me than he already was.

He looked for work as a carpenter. The color line was temporarily blurred, smudged. It had not yet become an institution. After the Draft Riots a year ago, black people were treated more kindly. They could at least ride the horsecars. Yet the craft trades remained closed to men of color. Isaac ended each day of wandering from cabinet-makers to carriage shops to building sites wearier and more exasperated, yet he never raised the possibility of returning to Roebuck's, or back to Norfolk.

He now called himself Isaac Kemp, which surprised me. He took the name of the owners whom he had disowned. When I asked why, he said that he had spent his life as Kemp's Isaac, and those were his syllables. He thought he could make them his own by reversing their order.

We slept with the door between our rooms wide open, often chatting before we dozed off. Sometimes, especially on cold nights when he needed to talk something out, Isaac invited me to join him in his bed for conversation. When I invited him into mine, however, he always refused.

I remember one night when I lay propped on my elbow beside him, his bare feet like two cold stones under the blankets, while he addressed the ceiling in an urgent, worried whisper. He had seen a dog-and-rat show that afternoon. A grinning colored man had accosted Isaac in an alley and invited him, for a penny, to join the men and boys, black and white, going down into a cellar. A little bull terrier stood in a pit dug in the floor. When the crowd finished making their bets, the colored man emptied a box of hungry rats into the pit. They rushed the terrier, who seized rat after rat, biting their necks and shaking them to death, while men of both races cheered and laughed. But the rats kept coming, and the dog was finally overcome. Isaac was disgusted. "What is to become of America?" he sadly concluded. "What is to become of our country?"

Surprising words from a newly freed slave. The uppermost question on my mind was "What is to become of Augustus Fitzwilliam Boyd?"

So there we were. In the mix of chance and choice that make up any life, there was more chance than I care to admit in our remaining together. Isaac would have called it Providence, which is a Christian name for fate, which is a pompous word for luck.

Was I in love with him? Such a question, Tristan. What an odd thing to ask when we both know— But yes. Oh, yes. I loved him. From the bottom of my lonely orphan heart. Yet it was an unnamed love, an airy devotion, a white love, not in race but invisibility. It wrote white upon the page for weeks on end, flaring up as a mild fever only when Isaac was cross with me or turned cold and aloof. Love would squeeze my heart and flutter my gut for a day or two, until it subsided again in our routine of days. Because there was nothing I wanted from Isaac except his company, which he freely gave me. I had left the childish vices of my time with Uncle Jack safely in the past.

One might say that I loved Isaac like a brother, only in my experience most brothers love each other either indifferently or irritably. My love was friendlier, more tentative and respectful. Such love can be like a brook that seems as still as glass, until you impede it with your hand and it suddenly swells and sputters around your fingers. So long as my love had no impediments, it was invisible.

Did he love me? Ah, there's the rub. I think he did, in his terse, manly fashion. I cannot define the cut of his love at this time. He may have loved me merely as habit and haven. Who else did he know in the world? He *said* that he was living with me only until he found his feet as a free man and took his place in the world. I often suspected that this was a ruse, a masculine disguise of a deep, tender affection. At other times, however, I fully believed him.

11

But I had more pressing matters on my mind than love. With the war over, the world went back to its business, and I needed to get on with mine, my career in music. Childhood had ended, and I itched with ambition.

The music trade of that age was a loose, haphazard affair—instrumental music, I mean. You could not throw a rock without hitting an opera singer or choral group. For real music, however, there was only the Philharmonic Society, which gave a scant four concerts a year, its members supporting themselves in private lessons or playing at dances and balls. The only other orchestras were in the theaters, and I refused to give myself to the pit. I was quite the snob for a whorehouse piano player. My goal was to break into the concert cafés, musical saloons that paid a handsome wage to seasoned performers. I was still too green but could season my craft at Roebuck's. I invested my earnings in books of music: Liszt, Chopin, Spohr, and Schumann. I had turned my back on the Italians. The myth that I cannot read music was something we later fabricated for the paying public. I thought I could always compose if I failed as a concert virtuoso. My ambitions were naïve but not completely absurd. After all, Brahms in his youth is said to have banged the ivories in taverns and brothels.

It was nearly a year after my return before I saw Uncle Jack again. In the little music world of New York, I'd heard he was touring New England, then that he was back in town, performing in a concert café on the "good side" of the Bowery. I went down to see him one night, out of idle curiosity, nothing more. But I did not ask Isaac along or even tell him where I was going.

I found the old catfish-whiskered scarecrow in a bright café, piously sawing away among potted palms and brass spittoons. An insipid blond boy accompanied him on a piano. Uncle Jack had easily replaced me, of course. Ladies and gents sighed wistfully over their beers, pleased by his music, which sounded awful to my ear—wet, cheap, soppy stuff. The violin is such a mawkish instrument, with none of the quick, precise emotion of the piano. The solo violin gave Victorian music its bad name.

When I went up to him during the interval, he was not at all surprised to see me again. "Where did you run off?" he said, as if it had been my choice that I was left sprawled in a road in Virginia.

He introduced his new accompanist, a cheese-faced waif named Egmont Mumpitz—Uncle Jack had joined the shift to things German. The spotty boy studied me with the simpering look of a new mistress examining her predecessor.

"Egmont has the gift," said Uncle Jack. "He lives for music. That was your problem, Gussie. You lived for your life. One must surrender one's life to music, but you love your life too much."

I knew he was talking simply to hear his own chatter, and nastily told myself that Egmont's one gift was that he probably gave Uncle Jack no lip, only prick. Yet the charge stuck in my craw. I wanted to be a serious artist, and feared I wasn't. I did not mention Roebuck's, nor did Uncle Jack, although he must've heard what I did to make ends meet, how far I'd fallen.

But Roebuck's was not the lower depths for me. It provided a comfortable situation for a young man exploring his art. The piano was a good one, a new Steinway, American-made but superior to anything yet produced in this country. A tall box like an upright grand, it had a full keyboard, cast-iron frame, and rich, full tones, which were invaluable for playing Schumann. I was much taken with Schumann that year, not just the snappy, famous tunes but whole piano suites—*Papillons, Carnaval, Waldszenen,* sketchbooks of brief, lean, musical pictures, demanding to the fingers yet loose and free in the ear. The piano does not quite sing with Schumann; it speaks, like a man talking to himself in a hundred different voices, shifting from sorrow to wit to anger. Schumann gave me a brand-new vocabulary of quicksilver moods, quirky harmonies, and odd, almost jazzlike syncopations. And I learned that I performed better when I could ignore the score and improvise, stepping free of the cage of bars and staves on the printed page.

Now and then a gentleman might ask for a particular piece, Verdi or Stephen Foster or "Casta Diva"—even the hurdy-gurdies on the streets played "Casta Diva" back then—but generally they let me play what I wanted. Their minds were on other things. We received only men of means at Roebuck's: bankers, lawyers, judges, and college students, who were all sons of wealth in those days. We had our share of Champagne Charlies, but most of the guests remained on their best behavior downstairs, smiling to themselves while my music cast a veil of high-toned decorum over their lewd intentions. Dancing was not permitted, and the piano covered any unseemly noises from the stairwell. I quickly became inured to what these men did upstairs with my friends, blocking it out as a matter of no relevance to my life.

The ladies were as well behaved as their visitors. Mrs. Roebuck saw to that. She floated through the soft gaslight like a society hostess, making introductions, offering refreshments, delicately slipping greenbacks up her sleeve.

The first floor was a series of densely decorated parlors full of fringed curtains and floral wallpaper. The taste of the decade treated women and furniture as equals. With their own layers of fringe over florals over stripes, the dresses blended into the sofas and drapes, a clash of patterns tumbled together in a kaleidoscope. Women wore their hair center-parted and tightly cinched, so their heads looked glossily upholstered in silk. At least the balloon skirts had begun to shrink, which allowed for more room at any mixed gathering.

I was on friendly terms with all the gay ladies, who were so much nicer to me than my cousins ever were. A male without authority or lust, I was a refreshing change for them. There were more stepdaughters now, although the fiction of family had been dropped. Women came and went. A pretty actress named Euphemia stayed for six months before she returned to her life onstage. Mary Ellen left to become a banker's mistress. Mary Anne left under a cloud. She drank, discreetly at first, but her drinking deepened, grew worse, until one evening she stumbled and spun through the rooms with gin on her breath, falling into laps and collapsing on the floor. When Mrs. Roebuck disciplined her by demoting her to a maid, Mary Anne walked out in a huff. We were all sorry to hear that she landed in a common cathouse on the waterfront. The prostitute world was as finely layered as society.

But Fanny remained. Cheerful, spirited, red-haired Fanny, who was my age, roughly. She said she was fifteen but must have been older. Well, youth was a commodity in her trade. She had grown up in a Quaker orphanage, run away, and been discovered begging on a street corner by Mrs. Roebuck, who took her on as a wash girl. But Fanny was too pretty to be wasted on laundry. The gay life was a step up for her, and she enjoyed it. She was the house pet, the resident jester. Out on the street she played at being proper, but indoors she laughed and clowned and mocked people. She called the cocky, strutting college boys "rabbits," for their quick fuses, and a pince-nezed lawyer, one of her regulars, became "Nebuchadnezzar," after the king who went mad and ate grass on all fours. I was "Professor," for being so serious, or "Dr. Mouse," a reference to my ears. We fell into each other's company like the youngest brother and sister in any family. She often sat beside me on the piano bench to whisper her jokes and try to make me laugh and scramble my playing.

All right. Our life was not really as easy as I make it sound. Fanny was not always the thoughtless, carefree creature that I've painted. One afternoon I arrived early at the house to find her sitting alone in the back parlor, on a window seat behind a curtain, in tears. She'd encountered Mary Anne on the street that morning, plying her trade at ten o'clock. The cathouse at the docks had expelled her, and she was now a common streetwalker, her complexion ruined by drink, her once plump body rail thin.

"She had been so beautiful!" cried Fanny. "More beautiful than I. It broke my heart to see her. She asked for money, but I knew she'd spend it on gin. So I lied and said I had none. Was that awful of me?"

I assured her it wasn't, then sat beside her to offer my sympathy.

But Fanny needed no sympathy. She made a fist, struck her knee, and declared, "That will not happen to me. No. I will not stay in this life. I was made for better things. I will find a man with money. By hook or crook. He will set me up in a shop or even marry me. One way or another I will put this behind me, Professor. I will. You don't know how determined I am when I set my teeth in something."

I thought she was only whistling in the wind, yet we were in similar situations. The same abyss opened under both of us. I needed success not just for reasons of pride and self-esteem but because failure in this life was so deep and terrible.

That evening Fanny was her cheerful, mocking, bubbling self again, holding hands with men old enough to be her father.

Meanwhile Isaac was making his way in his own world with its own hours. Our schedules were askew, and we saw less of each other. He found work as the assistant to a carpenter, a German Jew fresh off the boat from Hamburg. New York was awash in all kinds of Germans. The man did odd jobs in the German neighborhood on the East Side known as Kleinedeutschland, sheds and roofs and privies. He spoke little English, but Isaac soon picked up a few foreign words and phrases. He had a remarkable ear for language, while my German remained restricted to the strudel lettering on sheet music.

I never met this Jakob Hirsch but always pictured him as a dry old man with a gray beard. He was amused when a darky began to speak his tongue, and decided to teach it to Isaac while they worked, so that they might have real conversations—about God and politics. Hirsch was an atheist and radical. Isaac would come home with wood shavings in his hair and odd new phrases in his mouth, such as "opiate of the people." Isaac held his own with the man and was quite disdainful of his beliefs, as amused by a godless Israelite as Hirsch was by a German-speaking *schwarzer.* But he seemed to like the fellow, which annoyed me.

When Mrs. Kuntzler asked me why my servant went out in the mornings dressed in work clothes, I told her only that I slept until noon, didn't need him, and didn't know what he did.

Isaac was not the only Negro at the boardinghouse. Despite her pretensions to gentility, Mrs. Kuntzler could not afford a white or even an Irish cook. Her cook was colored, a proud, stocky woman with a cinnamon complexion, meaty arms, and a young husband who worked as a barber: Lydia and Jackson Freeborn.

They lived downtown in Little Africa, but Jackson often came up for meals, and Isaac took his supper with them in the kitchen. I ate in the dining room with the other boarders. When Isaac began to talk more often about the Freeborns, I became curious, anxious. He spoke of them critically—as their name indicated, they'd been free for several generations and could be quite condescending toward a former slave—but less critically than he spoke of Hirsch. He was clearly taken with them.

One night after supper I heard their laughter downstairs. Instead of hurrying back to Roebuck's, I tiptoed down to the kitchen. I did not expect to find them singing and dancing but thought I might catch Isaac in a more unbuttoned, relaxed mode. I found him sitting quite properly at the oilcloth table with Jackson, while Lydia washed the dishes.

Isaac was startled to see me there. "Did you need me for something?" He did not call me "sir" or jump to his feet but frowned at my invasion.

"Uh, no, Isaac. I just wanted to, uh, ask Lydia for a cold glass of cider. My throat is awfully dry."

I wanted Isaac to invite me to join them at the table. He didn't. My presence made him uncomfortable, embarrassed.

Lydia dried off her hands and poured me a glass of cider. I stood in the corner and sipped it, quite slowly, waiting for the men to resume the conversation I had interrupted.

I was thrown to see Isaac with others of his race. He was usually so full of Isaac-ness that he seemed one of a kind. In the company of the Freeborns, however, he suddenly became black. I found myself sniffing the air, as if to smell their color. Despite what white people say, there is no Negro smell. Now that I am blind, I find that all people have their own specific aromas, different sonatas of the nose. I can't claim that blindness makes me color-blind. I can still catch race, not in voices but in expectations, the different mix of hope and fear. And in touch, of course. One of the glories of blindness is the liberties one can take with strangers.

I drank my cider, and Jackson resumed talking, refusing to be silenced by my presence.

"Politics ain't for the likes of us," he continued. "Getting on in the world is what we're about. Heh-heh. And that means lying low, staying invisible. Since when we're visible we get beat up by Irish trash, or lynched. That was the lesson of the Draft Riots. Heh-heh. Nothing like seeing a luckless darky hanging from a sweet gum tree on Broadway and Spring to make one think, 'No, sir, I doan want to be *that* visible.' Heh-heh-heh."

His chuckles were a mirthless tic; he did not really find any of this funny. Jackson was a clean-shaven, mahogany-colored man, faintly feminine, where his wife was faintly masculine. He wore a white paper collar; his hair was flat with brilliantine.

"That's all slave talk," said Isaac. "Playing-possum talk. Congress is going to give us the vote. Then people'll have to respect us."

"Hoo-hoooo!" laughed Jackson, his hilarity genuine now, Lydia joining him from the sink.

"You would know about slave talk, Preacher!" she cackled. "You would know!"

"What a young man you are." Jackson was all of ten years older. "You're still full of Kingdom Come. For old folks like us, it's all Kingdom Come and Gone."

Isaac gave a quick grimace in my direction. He did not enjoy being laughed at, not even by fellow Negroes. And they called him "Preacher" much as Fanny called me "Professor." We were both oddities among our kind.

"Now, don't go sulking, Preacher," said Jackson. He leaned over and threw a friendly arm around Isaac. "We love you, child. We just want to share our hard-earned wisdom."

Isaac stiffened under the arm. In an age when men constantly touched each other, slapping backs and hanging on shoulders, Isaac did not like to be touched in public, not even by men of his race.

I thanked Lydia for the cider, told everyone good night, and left for work, feeling only somewhat relieved.

I had been worried that Isaac opened a side to the Freeborns that he didn't with me. He remained his argumentative, conscience-thorned self with them, but there was an intimacy in their argument that excluded me. I was strangely jealous, uneasy.

I remained uneasy even when, the next morning, while Isaac got dressed and I lay in my bed—I often woke briefly before he went out—he launched into a short sermon against the Freeborns.

"They're wrong, you know. Dead wrong. They've had it too easy up here. If they'd seen what I saw down south, they'd know the world can change. I've seen it change. It's just got to change more. A whole lot more."

But that wasn't what concerned me. "What do you tell them about us?" I asked.

"Us? What do you mean?" But he knew what I meant. "Oh, that I am your part-time servant. And that you're an easy boss and that, well, I got you wrapped around my finger."

"You don't tell them that we're friends?"

"Oh, no. I couldn't tell them that. They'd never understand."

He spoke as if I should be pleased that he kept our friendship a secret. And I *was* pleased, I am sorry to say, pleased yet worried. Secrecy might sustain a love affair, but could it feed something as social by nature as friendship?

It was an age of golden hypocrisies, a great time for masks and secrets, public lies and private truths. But a private truth can be quite fragile when neither party can name it in public, and you are both too shy to name it even when you're alone.

12

Like the saloons in that happy, depraved age, Roebuck's was open
on Sunday evenings. My one night off was Monday. I looked for
activities that Isaac and I could share, events where white and colored mixed: Quaker lectures, Abolition League musicales, the cheap
seats of some theaters. I cannot guess how we looked in the eyes of
strangers, a white youth and colored youth who didn't treat each
other as master and servant, and did not dress like criminals either.
But one saw all manner of freakish oddities in New York.

Isaac preferred words to music, instruction over amusement. We
crossed the river by ferry one Sunday morning to hear the Reverend
Henry Ward Beecher, the Conscience of the Nation, at Plymouth
Church in Brooklyn. I was impressed by Beecher's booming voice
and his gate—nearly a thousand people packed the floor and sweeping gallery—but Isaac found the religion tepid, a mug of warm
milk, the sermon no better than a self-improvement lecture.

We went to Cooper Union to hear the great Frederick Douglass.
An actual black man stood upon the platform, a noble, shaggy, iron-
gray lion. Isaac was moved by his words, and I enjoyed looking at
his face but was disappointed by his speech, a wordy baritone rumble
that took flight only toward the end.

We returned to Cooper Union a month later for Margaret and
Katherine Fox—the Fox sisters.

Spiritualism—talks with the dead, communion with ghosts—had had its day when I was a child but came back in vogue after the war. The seats under the low vaulted ceiling of the lecture hall that night were full of people wearing black for husbands, brothers, and sons lost in battle.

The houselights remained on. The platform was bare except for a plain round table and four ladder-back chairs. Two ladder-back spinsters in plain muslin dresses shuffled out. Their lack of theater surprised me. They had been doing this for twenty years, since they were children. I'd come to be entertained as if at a magic show, but they were deadly earnest.

Isaac dubiously folded his arms over his chest.

The sisters sat across from each other at the table and held hands. The audience was as hushed as people in church. Without a dash of hocus-pocus, no hypnosis or magic words, the sister on the right, Margaret, snapped to attention, went into a trance. She announced in a flat stage whisper, "I feel the presence of someone whose heart brims with grief"—an easy thing to say in a room full of widow weeds. "For a departed one who is trying to get through. Agatha? Agatha Church?" Silence from the audience. "I am sorry. There are so many spirits clamoring in the air tonight that I must strain to hear them. Agatha—Chappell."

A woman down front let out a sharp gasp.

"Someone who loves you very much wants to speak with you. A man in uniform. Oar? His name sounds like Oar?"

"Orestes!" cried the woman. "My husband Orestes!"

With so many peculiar names in the world, the Foxes had their work cut out for them.

"Come join our circle," said Katherine, the untranced sister, in a warm, courteous voice. And the woman stood up, stroked and petted by envious strangers as she made her way to the aisle. Dressed in black silk, in a great poke bonnet like a sail, she looked like a galleon in mourning.

She sat facing the audience, between the sisters. She closed her eyes and held hands with them. The sisters joined hands, too, so they formed a circle of hands. Margaret continued to stare blindly into Katherine's face.

"We need silence," Katherine instructed the audience.

"Orestes Chappell?" said Margaret. "You have no mouth with which to speak. I offer you our Table of Love as your palate. Knock once for no. Twice for yes. Do you understand me?"

And in that great hall, where several hundred people held their breaths, came two clear, audible cracks.

"Thou art with us tonight, Orestes?"

Two more cracks. They seemed to come from the table. The table was completely exposed, and we could see the hands joined above it, the square-toed shoes peeking from their skirts firmly planted on the floor.

There were no cries or whispers among the audience. People remained quite still, treating the miracle as something rare yet natural, like the sight of a rainbow.

"You want to speak to your wife, Agatha?"

Two more raps, quick and urgent.

"Where are you, Orestes? Are you in hell?" Silence. "Or in Summerland?" Knock, knock.

And so it went, question by question, yes and no, the dead man slowly knocking out his story. It was all in the questions, of course, and one might accuse Margaret of leading the witness, except she led him down many blind alleys. But eventually Orestes told his widow, yes, he had died at Gettysburg and was buried in the national cemetery. No, his suffering was of nothing now. He dwelt in Elysium. There was no hell, there was only heaven, what the sisters called Summerland. Orestes promised to wait there for Agatha until her own time came. Tears leaked from the woman's clenched eyes, but she was smiling, overjoyed to know that her husband still loved her. For now he advised her to sell their steamboat bonds and invest in railroad shares. Something else concerned him. A family member? Yes. A son? Yes. A mortal sin? No. It turned out that their little boy was snitching cookies again, which elicted a knowing chuckle from the audience. They enjoyed learning that the dead were not without a teasing sense of humor.

Other spirits followed: a son who died in a prison camp, a wife struck by a runaway wagon, a little girl drowned in a well. Margaret Fox was right; the air positively fizzed with spirits, all of whom yearned to communicate with loved ones.

I was impressed, touched, even excited. Oh, I was skeptical, too, yet my doubt focused on the hit-or-miss quality of the questions, wondering if the sisters understood the spirits as well as they pretended. But I had no trouble believing in the spirits themselves. Surely our wonderful, lively souls did not just disappear like soap bubbles when we died. I'd never wanted to believe in hell. I found myself grinning at the cosmic comedy of eternal life. And it did feel comic to me, the giddy hope that my own pretty self would not end in oblivion but could go on and on, and death would only increase my opportunities.

Isaac, however, much to my surprise, was coldly dismissive afterward. "The Lord does not knock on furniture," he declared as we walked home. "Jesus Christ does not speak in Morse code."

"How can you be so cynical? You of all people. You're a bigger believer in the afterlife than I am."

"It's because of my faith that I know those spirits were just trickery. Humbug."

"You can believe in hell but not Summerland?"

"That was no better than the mumbo jumbo of old conjure women back home. Field-nigger superstition." He could be as snobbish about religion as I was about music.

"Then how did the sisters do it? Tell me that."

He couldn't. The table had been wide open; a respectable institution like Cooper Union would never allow the sisters to hide an assistant under the platform; and the subjects had all seemed too genuine to have been plants. Isaac finally admitted that the spirits might be real. "But they must be devils."

"Maybe they're free spirits," I argued. "Liberated spirits who're no longer the slaves of God."

Isaac said I was being perverse and ended the discussion.

But the evening continued to ring inside me over the next days, the wonderful possibility of spirits. Why couldn't they come back to earth? And why shouldn't they knock on tables? It was a pity they didn't knock on something more articulate, like a piano. No, I had not forgotten the music that had come to me in a deserted house in Virginia. Who or what had dictated that sudden composition, if not spirits?

Late one night, after the last guest went upstairs at Roebuck's and the parlors were empty, I remained at the piano and tried to will myself into a receptive state of mind. I remembered a corpse in a wagon outside the door, a silent clock in a hall, a dazed emptiness of head and stomach. I toyed with a snatch of Beethoven. I followed it into a new key that sounded rich and strange. Here it was, a song from the Other Side! But then I recognized it: Schumann. My head had become too full of written music for me to hear the music of the supernatural.

Meanwhile, the back pages of newspapers began to fill with news of trouble in the South. While Congress debated over what to do with the conquered Rebels and freed slaves, there were reports of lawlessness, resistance, and riots. I paid no heed to politics, but an article about a street battle in New Orleans, where forty-eight colored men were killed, seized Isaac's attention. He was indignant and enraged, then despondent when he could do nothing with his rage. One night he confessed that he wanted to go down and join the fight.

"And do what?" I said in a panic. "You're not a soldier, you're not a politician, you don't write for a newspaper. All you could do is get yourself killed. What good would that do anyone?" I surprised myself with my passion and persuasiveness.

Because Isaac was quickly persuaded, as if he'd known all along that there was no practical purpose in his going south. "Yes, I am useless. And young. There will be time for me to do my part. When I am up in the world in a place where I can do something of value."

And so he stayed on. And so we continued, with work and life and friendship, our affection a quiet, deceptively smooth brook, so long as I didn't stick my hand in the rushing water.

The change did not begin until one afternoon when I went to work early to give a special performance for a Mr. Woodhouse. "If music be the food of love..." the man had said, offering to pay handsomely for a meal. There was extra money for Mrs. Roebuck, and for the lady, too. The only lady to jump at the cash was my friend Fanny.

Wearing my handkerchief as a blindfold, I sat at the piano and played Offenbach's Barcarolle, over and over, while they did their business on a divan at my back. I mastered the art of the nose-peek that afternoon—no blindfold is so tight that you can't peer down it—but I had no desire to watch Fanny get mounted. "I am your pasha, and you are my concubine," said Mr. Woodhouse, who was a high clerk at the Customs House. There was a rustle of crinoline, the thud of dropped shoes, the slap and squish of flesh. "Oh, you are a beast," cried Fanny. "A brutal beast." When Woodhouse's grunts became louder and Fanny began to peep like a sparrow, I pounded the sleepy repetition of chords even harder.

I had expected to be coldly amused. Instead, I became warm, nervous, envious. I knew what went on upstairs here, but in a dry, intellectual fashion, as though it had nothing to do with me. Now my body remembered the old joy of lewdness. I missed being lewd. The dirty deed that I'd shared with Uncle Jack did not seem so dirty now. Only I didn't want to do it with Fanny. I didn't want to do it with Mr. Woodhouse either. I simply wanted to do it.

Mr. Woodhouse commanded me to keep playing while he got dressed and Fanny helped him with his corset. Finally I heard the door close and could stop playing that stupid, tedious melody.

I pulled off the sweaty blindfold. And there stood Fanny, leaning against the door—in nothing but white stockings and freckles. I saw her little red beard, and the long, russet hair that hung to her shoulders. Her undone hair was as startling as her cream-and-nutmeg nudity.

"What a pig," she sneered. "Weighed a ton and took forever. While you just sat there, bang bang bang on your piano, sitting in judgment on me."

"I do not judge," I said and turned away. "You seemed to enjoy it."

"Oh, but he was a pig in rut. Flabby and grabby, old and sweaty." She plumped down on my bench and looked into my lap. "What's the matter, Professor? You didn't get any jollies hearing us?" She grabbed my flies.

I grabbed her wrist. "Don't," I said. But then I let go. I knew she wanted to bring me down to her level, yet I let her unbutton me. I was curious.

"Huh, a sleeping parson," she sniffed.

I had been stiff during the Barcarolle, but now, nothing.

She tugged and squeezed. Then her free hand took my hand and placed it on her sex. Still, nothing. We sat at the piano, coldly touching each other, until my apathy, my embarrassing lack of manhood, made my skin crawl.

"Here," I said, removing her hand and spreading the fingers on the keys. "Like this," I said, and I showed her a pattern of notes and set her playing. I started in with my right hand:

> All around the cobbler's bench
> The monkey chased the weasel.
> The monkey thought 'twas all in fun—

"Go on!" she cried, laughing like her old self. And she swung around and played "Pop Goes the Weasel" with me, banging at the keys and knocking my shoulder until we were both laughing, a naked whore and unbuttoned piano player as giddy as a couple of children.

Only I didn't want to be a child. I wanted to be a man.

Isaac was still awake when I got home that night, sitting up in bed with a newspaper. While I changed into my nightshirt, I told him about Mr. Woodhouse, without any lurid details. I knew he would disapprove. I spoke of the business contemptuously and didn't mention Fanny's skylarking afterward or my failure to respond, although that was why I needed to discuss this, hoping Isaac's moral disapproval would make me feel that my failure was actually a virtue.

He heard the wistful regret under my scorn. "You never give in to temptation in that place," he said. "Do you?"

"Oh, no. I don't even feel tempted." The floor was cold, but I lingered at his door in my bare feet. As I hoped, he invited me to join him under the blankets.

I had no intention of trying anything. But once I was stretched out beside him and his bare feet brushed mine, the Barcarolle began to play in my head again.

"Isaac? Do you ever think about women?"

"In what way?"

"Oh, a love-and-marriage kind of way," I said, safer than saying, "A cathouse kind of way."

"No," he admitted. "I can't afford to get married yet. So I don't think about women. But I will. One day."

"I don't either," I said. "But I doubt I ever will. I will spend my life alone. Well, I have one friend. For now." I rolled against him. I often used his chest as a bolster when we talked. Tonight, however, I pressed an extra bone against his hip. It felt wonderful in the warm flank glowing through his nightshirt.

Isaac felt it there. He stared at me.

"I am feeling so sad and lonely tonight," I explained. "It'd be nice to pretend that we're just boys again."

"I'm not a whore," he said sharply. "I'm your friend."

"If you love me as a friend, you'd want me to be happy."

He scooted back. "Our love is above sins of the flesh."

He actually said "love," but I was too bent on my flesh to be satisfied with that. "If love is a virtue," I argued, "then pleasure is no sin. Not if it's done from love." I don't know where I got that, but it sounded convincing.

He considered it, frowned, and shook his head. "Sophistry," he declared. "You're feeling blue tonight and saying things you don't mean. I will forget you even said them." He irritably took up his newspaper again and shook it open, treating my hard prick as no worse than a fart.

His chilling disapproval filled me with shame. "You're right, Isaac. You're a better man than I. A more virtuous man." And I guiltily climbed out of his bed, blushing over the snag in my night-shirt.

13

You must remember. I was only sixteen. The sexual instinct did not blow into full flame until now, which was why I had remained so pure despite where I worked. And because of where I worked, too, since sex seemed such a tawdry, commonplace act.

Suddenly, however, almost overnight, fleshly thoughts began to pop into my head and run around my brain like squirrels. I became morbidly obsessed with picturing the bare rumps and bearded coxcombs under the frock coats at Roebuck's. I disliked the men and considered only their parts, which was what made my thoughts feel morbid.

These squirrel thoughts did not attach themselves to the ladies, and they *never* swarmed around Isaac. I didn't dare think of him in that fashion, not after the night of my lewd request. I thought of him whole, his mind and soul and moral authority. As my secret obscenity increased, so did my admiration of his virtue. I craved Isaac's good opinion, his trust, his friendship. He pretended my proposal had changed nothing between us, yet he seemed cooler around me, more guarded and aloof. With his natural reserve, I could not be sure if the change were real or imaginary. Only he no longer invited me to join him in bed when we talked. And he carefully closed his door whenever he used the wide, shallow pan that served as our bath.

That shut door stung like a judgment. I did not burn to glimpse Isaac squatting nude in a platter of water—I'd seen that often enough. Yet I felt judged by his fear of me, as if my love had become a threat. And perhaps it was. My affection was no longer white and airy, but hungry, desperate, real. It had an impediment now, shame, and a hard-running brook of love swelled around my heart. Except I could not risk wanting anything from Isaac except daily doses of his company. When he went off one Monday night to a meeting of the African Temperance League, where I couldn't go, I was bereft. When he accompanied me two weeks later to see Edwin Booth in *Othello*, I was in heaven.

Isaac overcame his antipathy to theater for the sake of the Moor's tale. Seated beside him in the cheap mixed seats upstairs, careful not to brush his knee, I intently watched him watch the play. He sat up straight, his large, articulate, carpenter hands spread on his thighs, his handsome head craning upward as if another inch might bring him closer to the high, noble phrases. His trim black sponge of beard sometimes twitched when he repeated lines to himself, like a man who moves his lips when he reads. An earnest, self-improving fellow, he had never looked so wise or good to me. There were tears in his eyes when the play ended in its bedful of corpses.

My heart was full of virtuous love, my head was full of squirrels. I was a sensual crime waiting for the right criminal to come along.

New York aristocrats, the so-called Four Hundred, did not frequent Roebuck's. Too well bred and proper for brothels, they restricted their pleasures to mistresses or, it was rumored, each other's wives. So it was quite an event one evening when a pack of silk hats showed up, a half dozen sons of wealth out on a tear. They'd gone straight from the opera to a blind pig to a late-night "living picture" show—tableaux vivants of half-dressed ladies posed for a painter who didn't paint and guests who paid. The scenes were usually classical or biblical, and that night's picture, *The Wives of Solomon*, inspired a visit to Roebuck's. The young nobs were in their cups, yet their elegant manners, like a second suit of clothes, were only slightly rumpled by drink. They addressed the flirting ladies with the stiff if tipsy formality of royalty meeting their first Martians, while I couldn't stop thinking of the jiggle of clappers in the bells of their trousers.

Accompanying them as their guide to the fleshpots was an older, plump fellow with a glossy pink face and fluffy blond mustache. He dressed like his companions yet did not seem one of them. He showed no interest in the ladies but sat patiently in a corner, like a man who'd brought a friend to the dentist. After a time, however, as his young friends went upstairs with their new acquaintances, he began to notice my music. He stood up and came over. "What was that you were playing, sir?"

That he called me "sir" and not "boy" promptly won my trust.

"Schumann's *Forest Scenes*. With my improvements."

"Lovely," he said, gazing into my eyes. "Far too lovely for this place."

His name was Orlando Wilson. He was not rich himself but a chum of the rich, a society painter. Moneyed people collected artists much as they collected first editions, Sèvres china, and pedigreed dogs, and several families shared Wilson. He appeared quite old to me but was only thirty. He had remarkably small hands and a languid drawl whose laziness did not seem arrogant so much as philosophical, even Buddhist in its resignation.

He asked me to play something else, and I did. He lounged against the piano as if at a fireplace, perfectly at ease, his starched white shirtfront lightly cracking whenever he sighed. When I finished, he nodded appreciatively, glanced around the room, leaned over, and said, "Would you dine with me at home one evening, sir? I own an antique spinet that I'd love to hear played by a true artist. I recognize that your time is money, but I will pay you."

I was schooled enough in the ways of the world to know that it was not just my music he wanted to buy. Nevertheless, I told him I'd consider it. He gave me his card and returned to his chair to wait for his friends, treating me as invisible again.

I thought I might make a quick visit, just long enough to be shocked by his intent, take his money, and leave, with my purity intact. Over the next few days, however, I began to wonder if this plump artist might offer a cure for my plague of squirrels. It had been two years since I last performed the deed. Perhaps lust was like a boil and needed to be lanced now and then.

I arrived at Wilson's bachelor rooms on a Monday evening, sustaining my charade of innocence with a folder of sheet music under my arm. Wilson was more honest than I: He received me in a heavy silk dressing gown. But he actually did own a spinet, and an elaborate cold supper was laid out on a table in the parlor: oysters, quail, and several bottles of iced champagne. The gas jets were turned up bright, the chamber a posh stage set with a tapestry on one wall, a genuine Gobelin whose colors had faded to pastel, behind a Persian couch as long as a whaleboat and as wide as a bed.

We sat down to supper. The oysters were cold and firm, the quail meat as delicate as the yolk of a hard-boiled egg. Wilson politely asked after my opinions on art and music before he grew more personal. "Working where you do," he said, "I suppose nothing in the world of men surprises you anymore." He idly twirled the champagne in his glass. "Do you partake of the goods?"

I told him I didn't.

"Oh? Why not?"

"Because women don't interest me," I said.

His blond mustache bristled with the hint of a smile. "I should tell you, Mr. Boyd, that *you* interest me. Enormously."

My heart was pounding in my throat. I had to swallow before I could speak. "I hoped I would," I told him.

His eyes narrowed as his mustache rose over a full grin of healthy teeth. "Shall we continue this on the sofa?" he proposed.

We did, and a half hour later, when I hung backward and saw

my shoes and britches on the floor of an upside-down room, I found that Uncle Jack's invention was more widely known than I'd imagined, and not half as shameful as I remembered.

I visited Orlando Wilson twice a month. He was wedded to his work and put his appetite on a tight rein. I always spent the night, only we never slept. He kept the gas up bright, the fire heaped with coal. We lounged about in nothing but our dressing gowns—Wilson had an extra gown for guests—left untied and open like capes, worn not for warmth but for the cool, slippery caress of silk on bare hips while we ate cakes or smoked cigars or took turns at the keyboard between bouts. He was a cheerful, shameless sybarite, a fleshy voluptuary who resembled Rodin's statue of Balzac, without the goatee. He had a plush, pink bottom, and his body was dusted from head to toe in gold down. His sex was short and stubby, a fat plum that sat neatly in the mouth. Oh, yes, I gave as good as I got, and Wilson was so relaxed, persuasive, and clean that I wanted to try it all. I can feel quite fond of him now, grateful for what he introduced to me. He was always considerate and well mannered, even in the throes of passion. His own climax elicited nothing more than a delighted giggle. Mine were louder, more fervent, and twice as frequent.

I felt guilty at first, but that was merely psychological. I did not believe in sin, but I did believe in Isaac. He would see this as sin. Yet I didn't feel that I was betraying him. I was protecting our friendship, keeping my greedy sensuality in a separate box where it wouldn't harm our bond. I told Isaac only that a rich insomniac hired me now and then to lull him to sleep with music, which was why I didn't come home until dawn. Isaac indifferently accepted that, although it gave us fewer Monday nights together.

But after the third or fourth visit, he must've sensed the change in me, the way I looked forward to these sprees, or my sated, sheepish demeanor afterward. One evening, when I stood at the mirror fixing my cravat, brushing my hair, happily humming to myself before I went out, Isaac irritably asked, "What exactly do you do with this man?"

"I told you. I play the piano. Lullabies. Nothing but lullabies. Tiresome, but he pays well. And his food is quite good." I didn't want Isaac to suspect anything, but some inner demon made me say, "Why? Did you think I was his whore?"

His lips went pale and pinched. "No! I didn't!" He had to spit the words to get them out. "I didn't," he repeated. "I'm shocked such a sordid thing can even cross your mind!"

His disgust and temper terrified me—I was afraid to mention that the thing had clearly crossed his mind, too. "Well, I'm not," I lied. "But if I were, why should it concern you?"

"Because I love you as a brother. And I don't want to see you fall into—vicious habits."

"Don't worry about me, my friend. No, no, no. My soul's clean, thank you. Quite clean. Good night."

I hurried out, feeling ashamed of myself, wanting to cancel tonight's visit. And then it hit me on the street: Why did Isaac care? Was it from morals? Or could it be jealousy? Was there something unbrotherly in his love? It was a touching thought. But what good was such love if it didn't include my body? It was a tyrannical, possessive love, a dog-in-the-manger love that denied me physical satisfaction.

I had worked my way through remorse by the time I arrived at Wilson's building. The sight of the elegant façade was enough to turn me to stone in my pants.

"My word, but we're adamant tonight," said Wilson, sitting in his chair and watching me undress.

I saw him only in his rooms. Wilson never took me out, not even to his studio. He said little about his painting. He let me do most of the talking, in fact, although he sometimes spoke of his clients— Blisses, Roosevelts, and Choates—in the exasperated tone parents use about impossible children. The one display of temper I ever witnessed was after Mrs. Bliss told him she'd decided to have her portrait done by another painter, as if Wilson had spent countless hours taking her to galleries out of friendship and didn't need the commission himself.

I intended to get favors out of Wilson, but I was new at this game, did not know how to ask, and was usually too keen on the joys of flesh to risk spoiling my visits with business. He gave me occasional gifts but never any money, not even disguised as loans. He spoke of possibly taking me to Saratoga Springs or Newport when he visited patrons during the summer season, if we were still seeing each other.

Wilson warned me early on that he always grew tired of his sensual friendships and would eventually end ours. I managed to keep his interest all winter and into the spring, with sex and music, of course, and with stories. He enjoyed my tales of Uncle Jack and life at Roebuck's. He preferred spicy anecdotes but was much taken with my tale of the haunted piano. He asked me to reenact it for him, which I did, seriously at first, then turned it into a joke, pounding up and down the keyboard with my eyes closed, my mouth unhinged as if I were mad, scrambling together Beethoven, Schumann, and "Home, Sweet Home."

"My word," said Wilson when I finished. "You almost had me believing it. But you were faking? You have a gift, Fitz. A gift for what, I'm not sure. But it's definitely a gift."

It was Wilson who provided me with my first taste of Wagner. "All the rage in Europe," he announced one evening, taking out a heavy leatherbound opera score that a friend had sent from Munich. "They call it the Music of the Future. This one's the newest, premiered last year." *Tristan und Isolde.* I explored it at the keyboard, trying out a page here, a page there, looking in vain for coherent arias or melodies while Wilson lounged on the couch and smoked a cigar. Neither of us quite knew what to make of these rivers of noise. The spinet had no pedal, so the notes and chords were quite bare, without the woozy blurring that gives the Master of Bayreuth the illusion of mystery.

14

April arrived, the trees turned green, the streets turned to mud and manure, and Wilson declared that time had come for us to part. The fault was his, not mine, he claimed, but he was bored again. Besides, the Blisses were taking him to Europe next month, and he preferred not to leave any loose ends. I was disappointed, although hardly heartbroken. I even liked the idea that I might now become moral again. And Wilson softened the blow with a proposition. He so enjoyed our friendship that he wanted to do something special for me. "How would you like to be introduced to society? You and your magic piano."

He proposed taking me out as his newest discovery, not a young virtuoso—he did not think my playing exceptional enough—but a clairvoyant of the keyboard, a musical spiritualist. "Our little joke on the high-and-mighty," he said. "A most amusing prank. Only who knows where it might lead for you? What doors it will open?"

I didn't want to be a fraud, only what other chance would I get to glimpse the salons of the rich? I hesitated, until Wilson said he'd spring for a set of evening clothes as a farewell gift.

So one evening in early May, Orlando Wilson took an awkward musical boy to a supper party in an old brick mansion on Union Square. We went in a hired cab, my first, a coupe glassed in like a hearse. The new suit of black broadcloth fit me like a glove—better, in fact, since the white dress gloves pinched my fingers like dried paint. Wilson did not splurge on a silk hat but loaned me one of his, slightly too large, but my ears kept the ungainly shape balanced on my head.

That mansion was my first peek at true wealth. Walking past such houses every day on Fifth Avenue, I had imagined glittering fairylands behind the stone façades. But it wasn't fairyland. The rooms looked old-fashioned, even dowdy, large yet bare compared to Roebuck's. There were candles instead of gas and, as if to hide the lack of decor, flowers everywhere, lilies and gardenias, real flowers, not wax. The petals were quite pretty by candlelight, only I'd expected more ostentatious splendors. The women's dresses were disappointing, too: I didn't know enough to see that the fabric made up in cut and quality for what it lacked in mass. There were no diamond diadems, ostrich feathers, or nude shoulders, but then this was an intimate, "family" gathering. The men wore jet-black suits identical to mine, a masculine uniformity broken only by the variety of stickpins and configurations of whiskers.

Nobody was arrogant or curt with me; all were courteous and cordial, the men as well as the women. I said almost nothing. Wilson had suggested I'd make a better impression if I posed as a backwoods genius, an idiot savant, which was easy to do when I spent the first hour fussing awkwardly with my hat and gloves until a butler took them from me.

For the light supper at a long, candlelit table, I was seated beside a dour, clean-shaven, white-haired man named Strong, an elderly lawyer with musical pretensions. When he asked what I thought of Mozart and Bach, I feigned only the most superficial acquaintance with all the great composers. When he let slip his opinion that Schumann's symphonies were all right but his piano suites were only stunts for show-off pianists, "trashy and interminable, as bad as Liszt," I had to bite my tongue to keep from leaping to their defense.

Wilson was as smooth as machine oil, smiling and nodding at his end of the table, with a slight stoop to his posture that he didn't have at home, an automatic slouch of deference. His glances in my direction were quick and natural, betraying no fear that I might let him down.

After supper the men and women did not separate for coffee and cigars but moved together into a spacious music room. Wilson led me to the piano, an enormous black grand with its lid raised over a well-tuned rainbow of wires. The guests settled into the scatter of chairs and sofas with murmurs of mild curiosity. There was no explanatory introduction. Wilson had told everyone simply that I was a musical mystic. To say more would have spoiled the surprise.

I put on a blindfold, another of Wilson's suggestions. The silence at my back alarmed me; my music was so rarely the center of attention. Except for Strong, they did not seem a terribly musical bunch, yet the dilettante lawyer was sure to see through my imposture. Well, here it goes, I thought. I had nothing to lose. I'd never see these people again. If I'd been there as my real self, I might have been terrified, but I was safely padded in soft, plush thicknesses of make-believe.

I began with the adagio of the "Moonlight" Sonata. "This puts me in my trance," I called out, loudly, as if the blindfold made me deaf. "And the spirits love Beethoven."

There were no snickers or snorts. Everyone sat quite still for the funeral cadence of moonlit ripples over black water. Then, without warning, I broke it with loud splash, a major chord that shattered the Teutonic moonshine.

"The trance has begun," Wilson explained, for those who didn't know their Beethoven.

I continued to splash around the keyboard. "The spirits want to tell me about someone in this room!" I shouted. My right hand jingled a few high notes. "It seems to be lady." The notes became sweeter. "A beautiful lady."

And from the stew of bass rumbles on my left, bars of "Dixie" emerged, then "Casta Diva" and "Home, Sweet Home." Wilson had filled me in on the lives of several guests: I chose the most beautiful woman there, the young wife of the host's nephew, a former Southern belle dressed in summer white despite the season. She was adored by her philanthropist husband, devoted to her family, and deeply worried by a small son with asthma. I intended to turn "Home, Sweet Home" into a series of thwarted runs like strangled breaths.

Terribly crude, but this was my first go at musical mind reading. I remained full of fear and doubt. But suddenly I began to feel a change throughout the room, a sharpening of attention. I heard the creak of chairs as people recognized the subject of my musical portrait and turned to see if others recognized her, too. Without intending it, I'd brought human nature to my side. When people congratulate themselves on solving a puzzle, they immediately believe the puzzle must mean something.

And maybe it did. Because the strangest thing began to happen. The change in the audience produced a change in me. My playing grew more confident, more physical. I swayed back and forth at the keyboard, making faces in my blindfold, first for show, then for real. The keys galloped under my hands, and I arched my spine and flexed my buttocks, as if I were riding a horse; I worked the foot pedals like stirrups. I rode the music as if it were a horse, my body taking over, the music filling my body with emotions that reshaped the music. My mind stood off to one side and watched. Under the deliberate snatches of songs, I heard ideas and sensations that I hadn't intended. The "Casta Diva" came out in a new key that made it less fragile, more sincere: This husband really did love his wife. "Home, Sweet Home" turned into a joyful little fugue. In the double darkness of blindfold and closed eyes, I clearly pictured the woman, a summer angel at home with her pretty children, including a sad little gasping boy. Of its own accord the fugue came apart and broke into asthmatic runs. Then, when the runs resolved themselves in a melodic happy ending, they somehow became "Hail, Columbia," and I had a powerful premonition, a revelation: The asthmatic little boy actually would become president.

I swear it's true. That's what I felt, quite strongly. Yet I couldn't tell anyone that night for fear they'd know I was a charlatan for sure. Not until years later, when I better understood my gift and Theodore Roosevelt was president, did I realize that the beautiful lady in white had been his mother.

I let the piece die away. I sat perfectly still, then removed my blindfold and rubbed my face like a man waking from a dream. I turned around and saw them all, a roomful of pinched lips and blinking eyes. They did not appear awed, but intrigued, puzzled. They enjoyed being puzzled.

I translated my music into groping words: "I heard the presence of the South, South Carolina or, no, Georgia!"—the Fox sisters had shown how a dose of uncertainty makes a revelation more convincing. When Mrs. Roosevelt embarrassedly laughed, covering her mouth with two dainty hands, I acted surprised to learn that she had been my subject. I addressed the rest of my comments to her. "You are the angel of your household, adored by your husband"— the spirits enabled one to be impertinently frank with strangers— "beloved by your children." I closed with "One child's health gives you no end of worry. Rest assured. He will be fine. He will be very fine."

She laughed again, as if over a parlor trick, yet I could tell from her high color and moist eyes that she was genuinely relieved. I was pleased to have made her happy.

"Again! Again!" people cried, delighted by the performance. "Can you do me?" said an old woman in black. "Oh, please," she pleaded, wanting her musical palm read. I explained how I could not choose my subjects—I knew nothing about her—and Wilson said that my trances left me drained and might not happen again.

Men and women crowded around, asking for my card, giving me theirs, asking Wilson wherever had he found me. Even Strong came up to compliment my performance. "Savage yet moving. I don't pretend to understand. But I wish Liszt did what you did, instead of claiming his improvisations were art."

I basked in their attention, soared on the winds of their praise. Then I saw the amused glint in Wilson's eyes, the cruel hint of smile in his yellow mustache, and I remembered: None of this was real. I was only a joke, *his* joke. My performance had been nothing more than a society painter's droll revenge for years of slights, wasted favors, and deferential slouches.

Wilson withheld his scornful delight until we departed and got into a cab out front. "Those well-bred nobs and snobs!" he crowed. "So fine, so discriminating. They gobbled you down as quickly as any pack of bumpkins. More quickly, since they can't dream of anyone daring to put something over on them."

It hurt me that he could squash my achievement so easily, hurt and angered me. I felt I'd been tricked into prostituting my gifts, even though those gifts were purely imaginary. "Yes, I was just a hoax," I grumbled. "A practical joke."

"And a very fine joke you were," he said. "You understood that all along. Now, don't act put out. You have your name in their pockets now, and their names in yours. What you do with the opportunity is up to you, but we have sown your name on fertile ground." He tapped my knee. "Shall we go back and celebrate? One last time."

I shook my head and said, "No. I am not in a frisky mood tonight." I could at least retain command of that part of myself.

Wilson was not annoyed or even surprised by my refusal. "Ah. Applause has made our little musician haughty." He chuckled. "His first taste of cream has gone to his head. Very well, then. I won't beg. I have a full schedule tomorrow anyway," he drawled in his most indolent, Buddhist manner. "I suppose I should drop you off," he said. "What is your address?"

He had never been to my neighborhood, of course. We rolled down my street to the block where the streetlamps ended and the slums began. Wilson leaned over to look up at the red clapboard house next door to a grocery. "How sad," he said. "How squalid. Well, my boy. I've given you a foot up in the world. I'll be curious to see what you do with it. So. Until our paths cross again." He did not pat my shoulder or offer me his hand but waved me out of the cab with the backs of his fingers. "Good-bye."

I stood on the curb and faced the boardinghouse while his cab turned around on the last few yards of cobblestones. Only then did I realize that the borrowed top hat still sat heavily on my head. Wilson had forgotten to ask for it back—maybe he wasn't as dry and indifferent as he appeared. I refused to run after him to return this lending from a better life.

My house had never looked so drab as it did that night when I stood outside. There was squalor in the drooping roof, squat brick stoop, green washboard shutters, and dark windows. Only one light remained burning, in the narrow panes of the sleeping cupboard in my rooms.

Isaac was still awake when I came in. He sat up in bed, his heavy Bible open in his lap. He looked out at me through the doorway, not idly but with a cold, stern, worried gaze. He seemed to be waiting up for me. He closed the heavy Bible.

"That was *your* cab outside?" He spoke as if cabs were a sin.

"Yes, my insomniac brought me home," I said irritably, in no mood for Isaac's righteousness, not when I was so full of hurt pride. I flung the dishonest silk hat into my room; the hollow tube bounced off the wall and rolled on the floor. I hurried to my bed and lit my candle, staying where I couldn't see Isaac's chiding stare.

But he got out of his bed and came to the door. He filled the doorway in his nightshirt. His arms were folded across his chest, his bare feet set solidly on the floor.

"Those clothes," he said. "Where did you get such fancy-dress finery?" He'd been out when I put the suit on tonight; I had kept it hidden in its box under my bed.

"My insomniac bought them for me."

He took a deep breath, flaring his nostrils and lifting his beard at me, Jehovah in a nightshirt. His tone was cold and damning. "So you *are* his whore."

"Whore?" I said. "Whore?" My anger with Wilson instantly turned into anger with Isaac. "You think only whores have pleasure! Yes, I take my pleasure with him. For free! For the sheer pleasure of the body. You wouldn't understand, but it's no concern of yours." I was too proud to tell him that those pleasures were finished.

"Do you love this man?"

The question caught me by surprise. "No. Not at all."

The truth only fed his righteous scorn. "How can you sin with a man you don't even love?"

His scorn fed my rage, and I seized my next thought. "Because the man I do love is too damn virtuous to admit he's got a body!"

"That's your excuse?" He stepped forward, his hands closed in fists. "That's why you fornicate with this—whoremonger?"

"Yes," I sneered and defiantly faced him. He had the stern, indignant look of a father intent on beating a bad child. I wanted him to hit me, so that I might hit him back.

But he clutched the collar of his nightshirt with both hands. He hauled it over his head and hurled the shirt to the floor. He stood before me, angrily naked, scornfully nude. "If I sin out of love, will you end your double sin?"

I stared at his heaving chest, the eye of navel, his sex cowled like a monk. But his wrath was like clothing, and he did not seem naked. "Isaac. Don't mock my affections like this."

"No more words!" he commanded. "Just do it and be done with it!" His arms were at his sides, his palms turned out. He was actually offering me his body.

"No, Isaac. Don't," I said. My anger melted into pity and alarm. "You don't need to betray your virtue to prove your love," I told him, placing my hands on his shoulders. Then my mouth on his neck. Because once I touched him I couldn't stop. I was startled to find him only slightly taller than me. I, too, had been growing. I hadn't noticed that Isaac no longer stood as large in fact as he did in my mind.

When I had touched Wilson, he had stopped being Wilson and became simply flesh. But when I touched Isaac, he remained Isaac, and it terrified me. He kept his head high, his arms at his sides. His skin felt warm and dry; his heart galloped in his chest. I couldn't look at him. I closed my eyes and kissed his spongy beard, his scarred cheeks, the pink corners of his mouth.

Then he began to return my kisses, and they were as timid as mine. His arms closed around me, his carpenter hands callused like leather. "It is a sin," he repeated, in a whisper. "But it will save you from worse sins."

Religion did not make Isaac stupid. This was the language of his emotion, his psychology. I did not believe his talk of sin and desire. He was jealous, painfully jealous, I told myself, but he had to translate that pain into selfless sacrifice before he could give in to his body. I didn't even think to tell him that the cause of his jealousy was over.

One of us blew out the candle—it may have been me. He lowered us to my bed, shyly slipping his hands under my clothes, frightened to discover that he could love with his hands as well as his heart. But he could, and he did. As we timidly touched strange new continents of skin and hair, I believed that I finally understood his feelings for me. I was not just his habit, his haven, his friend. He loved me, body and soul, heart and limb, the sacred and profane. Isaac was not so skilled in the arts of love as Orlando Wilson, but he didn't need to be. I was in love with him.

I am sorry, Tristan. I keep forgetting that you are my scribe here, the audience in this private theater of memory. It can only disturb you to hear your father discussed in such an intimate manner.

PART

III

15

ENOUGH of my words. Let us leap ahead a few years, so that our story can be taken up by another voice.

Sunday, May 2

I go to bid Father good-bye after church today & set fresh flowers upon his grave. Who will bring him flowers after tomorrow? I depart Hartford tomorrow. Forever? I cannot guess what life has in store for me, only that the Bottses & their precious Isabella await across the ocean. One should be full of profound reflections on the eve of such a momentous journey, yet no great thoughts come to me. Only this: I will be fearless. I am fearless.

Monday, May 3

The new life begins not in adventure but vexations. The train was crowded, bad smelling & late. We arrived in New York at 1:15 instead of 11:20. I took a horsecar to the Inman Lines, resisting the expense of a cab despite my fatigue & dislike of the unclean press of strangers. I was aboard the City of Brooklyn by three & found I must share my second-class cabin with the chatty little maid of a banker's family from Albany. How I detest the gossip of servants, even now when I am a servant myself. If Father knew the kind of company his daughter would keep, he would not have died leaving only an estate of books and mortgages. Nobody can tell me if my trunks have arrived or not. Dinner was served in a narrow saloon to the passengers already aboard. First- & second-class dine together, but the copious gravies do not disguise the poor cooking & the service is execrable.

I should make note here of my fellow passengers. The Albany banker & his family appear to be as full of conceit as Penelope their maid claims, the daughters a trio of fashion-mad poodles. I daresay my Isabella will never stoop to such frippery. There is an old minister in the gaudy checked trousers of a college student, & a wife like an old pudding. A callow young couple on honeymoon gaze constantly upon each other in a shameless show of affection. Still more alarming is a smooth-faced boy of a man with long hair, a cape & *yellow boots*—apparently an artist or, worse, an actor—accompanied by a large, brooding, Negro servant. They dined apart from the others last night, at their own table.

I hurry back to my cabin without coffee, so that I might have time alone in these pages without my garrulous roommate jogging my elbow and smearing my ink.

Tuesday, May 4

We lifted anchor with the tide at ten this morning. The weather was excellent, the salt air delicious after the smoke & smuts of the city. I feel much better. (My trunks turned up last night, set in the wrong cabin.)

Everyone stood on deck as we passed out to sea, pretending to admire the sublimity of water and sky, but were too busy chattering among themselves to appreciate Nature. The little artist in particular, who is merely a musician, eagerly held forth to anyone who would listen in a high, piping voice. I bristle at the thought of being trapped on a long voyage with such an effete personage. This evening, however, he did not appear at dinner. His Negro dined alone & then retired to their quarters when the rest of us moved to the grand saloon. But talk there immediately turned to the absent musician.

The Albany banker had heard him speak of "the music of the spheres," which I presumed meant he tapped out tunes on water glasses, but Revd. Checked Trousers said he was a pianist & surmised he was a concert artist, an American Rubinstein bringing our national genius to the Old World. I sat apart & did not join this improper gossip. I thought I escaped it, but down in our cabin Penelope wondered if this were the piano-spiritualist whom she had heard of from friends in New York, a musical sorcerer who reads your thoughts & exposes them in sinister tunes. "It makes me flesh creep to think on't," she said.

Such a lot of nonsense. When I overheard this fellow on deck, I caught no evidence of a great artist or mystic seer, only the unmanly noise of a common little chatterbox.

How unkind. Yet how like Alice. I assure you that there was nothing common about me at this time. Still, it's amusing to learn that I was already a topic of conversation.

Read it all aloud, Tristan. I'll tell you what to mark for inclusion. But isn't her handwriting remarkable? That impeccable copperplate script. Business colleges stopped teaching it long ago. You transcribe your shorthand into something more orderly on your typewriting machine, but the handmade elegance is lost.

It's been decades since I once stole a peek at Alice's diaries, long before my eyes filled with smoke. I don't remember what I read, only an impression of years of swoops and swirls, as regular as sewing-machine stitches. Even her pen wore whalebone stays. With her upright posture and tiny niblike feet, Alice resembled a pen herself, a pen in petticoats and pince-nez "nippers." Alice Pangborn. Never was a woman named more appropriately.

This was 1875, and Isaac and I were going east. Not west with the American empire but against the current to Europe, seeking fortune and even fame. *The City of Brooklyn* was a sleek white ocean liner, sleek for that age anyway, a three-masted steamer with side paddles housed in two high wooden drums, the "bridge" suspended between with a pilothouse and smokestack. There was a simple dining saloon, a so-called grand saloon with a low ceiling and brass stoves at either end and, down below, a rabbit warren of second-class cabins and first-class staterooms.

The poetry in Alice Pangborn was buried quite deep: Nothing less than a sunset or a passage of Emerson could tap it. But she was right about the beauty of our departure. The wide, smooth bay was winged with sails, ivory white or parchment yellow, and smoke trails arched over the high blue sky and green shores. The world seemed to expand around us, a realm full of promise and freedom. Then we came out of the Narrows, and the ship trembled as the first ocean swell lifted the paddles from the water. We became a tiny object in the rolling hills of sea that carried us toward England. Up and down we went, up and down. Within an hour I was overcome with sickness, and it was ghastly.

Ocean crossings were so unpleasant in those years. The close quarters and tedium, the sour stink below, the endless vomiting. Memoirs and novels pass over the voyages in silence, much as they skip visits to the lavatory.

I stumbled up on deck that first evening, hoping the sea air would bring me round, only to gaze out on a heaving desert of waters as tedious as eternity. But what did I know of eternity at twenty-five? The pistons under my feet pounded away like a grim engine driving the universe.

Wednesday, May 5

The stormy ocean does my heart good, the dark sky & heavy seas. I apologize to myself for writing in pencil here, but the motion of ship is ruinous to pen while I sit out in the saloon & leave poor Penelope to her bucket. How I pity such weak wills. This is Nature at its finest & truest.

Yet a fly fell in the ointment of my contentment this morning. I went up on deck after breakfast to take the air & a brisk walk. I had the foredeck to myself, the others all laid low by their namby constitutions. I was enjoying a solitary reverie with Neptune, when I noticed I was no longer alone. The little musician's African manservant had appeared at the rail. He stood there in a tweed mack & a derby that sits oddly on his savage face—his barbered beard suggests a white man's beard pasted on a Negro countenance—looking at the sea. I had to pass him on my way back. He turned toward me & said, "Good morning, ma'am," with an insolent lift of that vulgar hat—& a smile! He actually smiled at me & then began to speak— words about the weather! I cut him with the curtest nod imaginable & hurried past. What must the officers on the bridge have thought? Who does this Negro think I am? His forwardness scalds my cheeks even now. Did my brother die at Cold Harbor so that such people could be insolent to American ladies? Why am I unable to shake from my brain the coarse image of a black face, thick beard, and round hat?

Thursday, May 6

The longhaired musician did not reappear at dinner last night— his man again ate alone at their table—but I encountered him below in the passage, looking quite peaked. I stopped him & told him, in no uncertain terms, that his servant was taking liberties with the female passengers. "But he is not my servant," he replied. "He is my friend." I suspect he was mocking me, yet he seems so Bohemian that he may be telling the truth. Before I could delve deeper, however, a fresh roll of the ship turned his face a new shade of green, & he fled.

Nevertheless, this morning I returned to the promenade, refusing to let the presence of an unplaceable Negro deny me my ocean constitutional. I cannot let my bowels be impacted with sedentary poisons. And he was already there, the haughty Moor. This time he merely tugged the brim of his hat at me, coldly, without a word, looking deeply insulted. His "friend" must have reported my complaint. I marched by him, with burning cheeks, feeling sorely offended that *he* was the one who took insult. I seized my nerve &

returned to face him. "Sir," I bluntly told him, "do not take that manner with me. My brother died in the war to free your race."

"I am sorry," he said with sincere gravity. "So if I were still a slave, your brother would be alive?"

I tried to explain I hadn't meant that, how he had misconstrued my meaning. Only what had I meant? Simply that he owed me respect. Too late, I had said too much & found myself in conversation with him. He expressed sorrow for my brother, then said he had seen the war on the other side, as a servant to his owner's son, & it had been terrible for the losers, too, albeit deserved.

He is a former slave, of course. Writing this down, I find myself picturing him in chains, or tied to a post for a flogging. Such images fill me with both pity and a strange thrill, similar to the flush I used to feel when I read Father's Abolition pamphlets. Yet on deck Mr. Kemp had the dignified dress and carriage of any white gentleman. Oh, yes, he introduced himself, & I had no recourse but to give my name in return. He is remarkably well spoken, his voice husky & humid, but he enunciates his words well, so white words seem to come from his black face. Only now do I remember his eyes, which had the sad curiosity of a spaniel. When dogs look at me as he did, I suffer the disquieting sensation that a human soul has possessed them. Mr. Kemp is a man, of course, not a dog, but I find this impression of soul oddly disturbing. I am surprised the Negro body is as unsusceptible to seasickness as that of us descended from maritime peoples. We spoke for perhaps ten minutes, standing several feet apart in perfect attitudes. The officers on the bridge could not possibly think there was anything improper in our encounter.

It may have been that night that Isaac said to me, apropos of nothing, "Miss Pangborn is certainly a dry stick. One can only pity such lonely spinsters. I am happy for her sake that she at least has pretty eyes." That night or the next. He was preparing for bed and stood with his backside to me in just his shirt, speaking over the soft roar of a thunder jug. I lay in a ship bed that was boxed like an open coffin, feeling so wretched that I wished I were in a real coffin. I paid no mind to his mention of this woman. I had noticed only a righteous old maid in steel-rimmed spectacles, a stiff-backed creature who did not so much walk as march, like a prissy grenadier. I should add that this sorry, lonely spinster was then an ancient lady of twenty-seven.

Friday, May 7

The seas run heavy & the ship bucks so that— Gosh! A sudden plunge took my breath away. The dining saloon was empty last night except for myself, Revd. Checked Trousers &, at his own table, Mr. Kemp. The Revd. asked after my church & appeared sorry I am a Unitarian. I was not surprised to learn he is Episcopal, a papist wolf in sheep's clothing. Yet I held my tongue & remained courteous.

Mr. Kemp, the African gentleman, turns out to be a great reader. He was on deck again this morning when a long plummet of steam was released through the smokestack, & he said, " 'Things are in the saddle, / And ride mankind.' " I was surprised to hear him quote Emerson & said so. We fell into a discussion of the author of "Self-Reliance," then of Carlyle, whom he respects, despite the Scotsman's views on colonial matters. We fell into a walk as we spoke, strolling side by side before I noticed our accidental familiarity. He has read the novels of Mrs. Lewes, admires them, though he did not know "George Eliot" was a woman. It would have been too forward of me to tell the sad nature of her "marriage" with Lewes. He agrees that Whitman is quite coarse, even vulgar, & shares my surprise that so many men of learning admire him. I so enjoyed our talk that I lost track of the hour, & forgot how we must look to the men on the bridge. I even let slip that I am going to Europe as governess to one of Hartford's best families, yet Mr. Kemp showed none of the leering forwardness men often display when they learn a young woman is to live among strangers. I was too shy to ask why he was crossing over.

Saturday, May 8

The foredeck was awash in spray this morning & I could not walk out for fear of getting soaked, so I took the air while standing beneath the bridge. Mr. Kemp soon appeared & boldly attempted a stroll, but soon came running back after a bucket of spray caught him in the face. I could not suppress a laugh at his loss of dignity, but he did not take offense. The waterwheel in the bulkhead made a great racket, but we entered a discussion of predestination, in which Mr. Kemp, I am sorry to say, believes, though he does not follow the doctrine so far as infant damnation. He has actually heard the great Revd. Beecher, while I have only read him, but he found the man's oratory wanting.

I confess to a sin of pride here, over my ability to enter into intercourse with a Negro. The good people of Hartford would be shocked, but the sea is a better Democracy & I feel safe in the company of Mr. Kemp, safer than I would with a man of my own race.

Sunday, May 9

We are in the Gulf Stream, the sea is calm, & the sun shines, of which I am glad, though the deck was crowded this morning & I did not feel free to speak with Mr. Kemp. Church services were held on deck, the sermon given by the Revd. Checked Trousers, a mealy ramble on the text of Jonah's journey to Nineveh. All faces were colorless & sickly after their days below, & the newlyweds no longer gaze at each other in rapt admiration. The Albany banker's daughters were in full fig, however, their ribbons & skirts aflutter in the breeze. Sailors rudely lurked about, no doubt hoping for a glimpse of shoe. Mr. Kemp was present without his longhaired friend. Nevertheless, the friend appeared at the noon meal, ate daintily, then went up on deck afterward, when I had hoped to meet alone with Mr. Kemp—I only wanted to recommend that he read Emerson on predestination. But Mr. Kemp brought his friend over & introduced him. He is called Dr. August—Doctor of what, I cannot guess, but such a music box of chatter, so unlike the manly Mr. Kemp. He held forth at length about the sea, the Mother of Life & Death, he declared, & I thought he was being poetic, until he explained how his own mother first took sick on ship when she & his aunt crossed over from Ireland, & she died two months later, soon after giving birth to him. Mr. Kemp interjected that the sea was his mother too, an even crueler one: His forebears were brought in chains across these waters. The men fell into a mild bicker over which had suffered more at the hands of the sea, a peevish banter like a squabble between man & wife, somewhat comical though it made clear that they aren't master & servant. Then what are they? "You are a musician?" I asked Dr. August. "And more," he said. "I play the music of the spheres," then smiled like a tomcat & added, "I perform at the piano, pieces dictated to me by spirits." I thought he must be taunting me, only Mr. Kemp did not correct him but stood by with a look of inscrutable calm. "Come along, Isaac. Show me the high points of our vessel," the chattering boy declared, & Mr. Kemp bowed to me & followed Dr. August.

Oh, yes. Not only had I changed my hair, which I now wore long and straight like Liszt, but my name as well. "Boyd" had such a flat, ugly sound; it did not do justice to my talents. So I chose the portion of my name I admired most, the imperial Augustus, only I would be an emperor whose domain was not bound by earth and circumstance but was all light and air, an empire of the imagination. I threw in the "doctor" for a modern, scientific flourish.

How curious that I told Alice about my mother. I spoke so rarely of that beautiful, departed songbird. Why did I tell her? Did my Metaphysicals intuit that this voyage would not be our only encounter? Go on. Go on.

Monday, May 10

I went up on deck tonight after dinner for the sunset & found Mr. Kemp there, of which I was glad, since we no longer have the deck to ourselves in the morning. He stood like a prophet against the crimson sky, smoking a pipe, which he put out when I appeared. We examined the sunset together, then the stars, & made small talk about infinity. It was all quite proper yet pleasant, to take in the sublime with a companion. Then we spoke of Europe, & I asked Mr. Kemp why he was going there, & he said his friend had been invited to perform his music in England, "his sonatas for spooks and piano." So his music *is* dictated by spirits? "Oh, yes," Mr. Kemp replied, with a bashful, uneasy look. He could not explain, he said, but would bring me some reading matter that would make it clear. His hesitance gives this music more mystery than it deserves. Truth be told, I do not care two whits for Dr. August or his spook sonatas. I told Mr. Kemp about Isabella, & he said he was certain I would be a wonderful tutor. I regret to say that I did not blush.

Thursday, May 13

Nothing is what it seems, the world is full of traps & snares.

It has taken me two days to recover & open this journal again. I remain in bed, still struggling to compose myself & understand what happened.

Mr. Kemp came up on deck after dinner on Tuesday, as before, & we were alone, as before. We spoke about the sunset, as before, but ran out of words. Then Mr. Kemp said, "Oh, I remembered to bring this. About my friend's music," & he reached into his coat & brought out a small, yellowed newspaper. On the front page was an article, "A Marvelous Musical Medium: The Spirits Sing in His Hands," with an illustration, a crude engraving of a boy playing a piano while an old Negro laid a hand on his head as if to bless him. Neither figure looked remotely like Mr. Kemp or his friend. I had not read a word & was about to make light of the illustration, when I saw what paper it was: *Woodhull & Claflin's Weekly*. The organ of the vile Victoria Woodhull, "Mrs. Satan" herself. Who denounces the family & praises free love & libeled the great Revd. Beecher as an adulterer.

"Your friend knows Mrs. Woodhull?" I said. Mr. Kemp admitted

that they both did, without a trace of shame. He was actually proud
that they were in her newspaper, sorry only that the picture was so
poor. "She is a Communist," I said. "A Christian Communist," Mr.
Kemp replied, as if that made a difference. "She espouses free love,"
I said, & he answered, "She wants equal rights for women, Negroes
& workingmen." "Free love!" I repeated. "Free love! Free love!" I
heard myself repeating that obscene phrase, putting all my indignation there. It had never sounded so obscene, but I had never said
it aloud. "And what is love if not free?" he replied, in a startling,
pleading manner. I looked up & saw a Negro standing before me,
stiff & bearded & in a domed hat, gazing into me with spaniel eyes.
Suddenly, though the sea was calm & the ship steady, my abdomen
filled with sickness. I rushed to the rail & ————. It was as though
God chose that moment to punish me for my lack of sympathy with
other people's illness. When I had finished, & my mouth was vile &
my throat burning, I found Mr. Kemp *at my side*, holding out his
handkerchief. He had seen me in my distress, & it was awful. A
white gentleman would have turned away, but he stood very close,
with the shameless regard of a dog who catches his mistress at a
necessary function. I turned from him, shouting, "Thank you, no!,"
hurried to the entry & started down the stairs. I heard him pursuing
me. "No!" I cried. "You are not to see me like this!" But when I
reached the foot of the stairs & looked back, he was not there.

Friday, May 14

The weather stays fine, the sea calm, yet I remain in my cabin.
Penelope is puzzled I am seasick now when she & the rest are enjoying the sunshine. She pretends to be kind, but I know she is
secretly laughing at my distress. Yet it is not my body that is full
of nausea, it is my soul. I remain full of shame and humiliation over
letting Mr. Kemp witness my animal distress. That is what agitates
me now, not his association with Mrs. Woodhull. She *is* Mrs. Satan,
but knowledge of her strange opinions was not what made me ill
Tuesday evening. I do not know why I responded as I did; the body

has laws that the mind cannot fathom. But I have learned my lesson. Now that I am alone in the world, I must watch my every step, guard every encounter. It is not wise to become acquainted with strange men, Negro or otherwise.

Poor Alice. Poor Isaac. I knew their shipboard acquaintance had ended abruptly, but nothing about an unladylike puke. How embarrassing. The name Victoria Woodhull means little now, yet it once carried quite a charge, needless to say.

What a remarkable pair. One cannot help smiling over a flirtation disguised in talk of infinity and infant damnation. And they *were* flirting with each other, without a doubt. But when his spiny governess did not appear on deck or in the dining saloon for the rest of the voyage, Isaac expressed neither surprise nor alarm. "These New England bluenoses," he grumbled. "Such an effort to know. So high-strung and fretful inside their hard, righteous shells. I don't understand why I even bothered to strike up an acquaintance with that one."

16

WE steamed into Liverpool on a cool May morning through dingy wedding veils of fog. My first glimpse of the Old World was of dark phantoms emerging from a soft gray chowder, tall shapes that slowly resolved themselves into masts, factory chimneys, and warehouses. When our engine shut down after twelve days of incessant drumming, the silence was unearthly, as if we had come to an Isle of the Dead. Then strange English voices called out across the black water; there was a clank of chains and timbers groaned as we squeezed against the pilings. A whistle loudly blew, and all at once, ship and shore burst into life.

Isaac promptly took charge when we disembarked, snapping commands at white men, ordering porters about before they could order him. I was not much help. The earth still bobbed under my drunken sea legs in the gaslit murk of a customs shed. "There goes your friend," I told Isaac, pointing out the prissy grenadier as she hurried through a mob of black hats, sticking close to her new escort, a burly American with a handlebar mustache. She pretended not to see us. "Did the two of you argue on the boat?" I blithely asked. "Not at all," sniffed Isaac. "Miss Pangborn took a turn against me. I do not know why. Perhaps she finally noticed my race."

We arrived at our hotel, and I had to go through the usual nuisance of requesting a room for both myself and "my servant." Unlike in America, however, the sallow clerk did not suggest we place my man in the attic or a nice colored hotel down the street but treated us as equals, *two* American freaks.

A hotel was a hotel, even in that strange land, and I began to feel more myself among the shabby furnishings and stained wallpaper. We ordered up a bath, which we both badly needed after twelve days at sea. You might have thought the English had not heard of the practice, it took the staff so long to bring in a tub and kettles of hot water. We took our turns in the oversize coal scuttle, sharing the bathwater as we shared so much else. While I soaked, Isaac sat in a chair wrapped like a Roman senator in his towel, smoking his pipe and gazing intently at the coal fire that warmed his bare feet. When I got out of the tub, he knocked his pipe against the fender and came over to rub me dry, without my asking.

As in any marriage, one loses count of intimacies, and we'd shared a bed for seven years now. Yet I cannot forget our first embrace in Europe, the fog in the window, the coals in the grate, the mattress swaying underneath me like the ship. This man who smiled so rarely in public was full of secret smiles in bed, grins in his hands and tongue and loins. I am trying to be discreet, Tristan, but you must understand: The physical was part of our bond. He was more affectionate than usual that afternoon, gripping me in his arms, scrubbing me with his beard, and I thought he was making up for the celibacy of the voyage. I held on to him with my arms and legs, feeling enlarged, radiant, as if heaven itself were shining in my bowels. He closed his eyes, ecstasy filled his face, and we shared a staggered chord of bliss.

He gave me a quick kiss, then lay beside me, happily catching his breath like the winner of a footrace. He was silent—I was in love with Isaac's silences. Yet his silence that day grew heavy, confused.

"This is nice," he suddenly said. "Very fine. And yet—I wish it made something. I wish it made life. Children."

I laughed. He could be so earnest, so innocent. A rock of stern, masculine certainty in public, he became someone else in bed. "But we make life," I said. "Spiritual life, afterlife. They're our children."

"You make them," he replied. "I don't."

"I couldn't do it without you," I claimed.

He frowned and shook his head, then said that corporeal offspring might be nice as well.

But my mind was too concerned with higher, more ethereal things to pay much attention to Isaac's changing attitude toward the spirits, and toward me.

What were we doing in England? What brought us to Europe? Very well, then. I should fill in some of the history that I skipped in my rush to learn what was in Alice's diary.

Orlando Wilson had been right: The Roosevelt dinner party opened doors for me. Within a week the shabby green baize of the Kuntzler front table began to fill up with large, square envelopes: invitations to call on big names. Oh, I was intimidated at first, but success in love made me bold, even cocky, so to speak. I went to their homes, drank their tea, and arranged future engagements. I began as a postprandial entertainment at dinner parties, then went on to provide private sessions for families, couples, or solitary individuals. I charged, of course, like a doctor making a house call, and, like any doctor, I made no promises: The spirit might or might not come. As I visited more households, however, and picked up more gossip, the spirit appeared more frequently. Meanwhile, I said goodbye to Roebuck's, where the gay ladies bade me a tearful farewell. Fanny Gaskins disguised her envy in a few last sisterly insults. "So Professor Mouse is off to play lapdog to the rich. Well, if you can do it, so can I. And I won't have to sing for *my* supper."

I was briefly the rage of society, but only for a season before my novelty wore off. Then came "the new people," however, the nouveau riche, more plentiful and more gullible. Women were my specialty: widows, of course, and wives who wanted to know if their husbands were faithful, and wives burning to hear if their tender,

chaste regard for a bachelor cousin or brother-in-law was recipro-
cated. My music was an opportunity for grown-ups to indulge in
games of make-believe about lives mired in logic and propriety, to
vent their hopes and fears in private fairy tales. I offered the same
service that Gypsy fortune-tellers provide the poor. The rich were
more comfortable with such fancy when it wore the swallowtail coat
of high culture. Their attitudes could be quite mixed and contradictory. Mrs. Tarbell, for example, a wealthy widow from Pitts-
burgh, treated my improvisations as pure humbug, shaking with
laughter when I translated my tunes into words for her. Yet she
continued to ask me back, continued to ask about the future of her
bachelor son, Titus, and unmarried daughter, Ellen, both of whom
lived at home. She did not want to hear about her late husband. "I
am well rid of Horace, thank you. I don't need his long face peering
over my shoulder from the Great Beyond." Mrs. Tarbell was a pagan
cynic of another era, a connoisseur of scandal, a reader of Balzac.
She was the one who suggested I grow my hair to my shoulders in
the style of Abbé Liszt. I amused her, yet under her laughter were
serious frets about her family that she preferred to address in the
guise of nonsense.

What did Isaac make of my new career? Well, he was mighty
glad to have me out of the whorehouse. When I began to earn
enough to support us both, however, he refused to leave off his
carpentry work. When I proposed we use my windfall to leave the
boardinghouse for grander digs, he argued against that, too, pointing
out how my good fortune was built on sand and we should save my
money. But he did speak of "we." And he began to handle my
finances—our finances—putting the cash in a bank, then in bonds.
He had an aptitude for money, a disinterested love of numbers. He
also enjoyed the respect that even a colored man could get when he
put on his best suit and entered a stately marble bank with a wallet
full of cheques.

But yes, Isaac was uncomfortable with what some would call the
element of deceit in my new trade. You might think that his dis-

covery of love in the flesh would make him more flexible in his morals, but no, Isaac remained just as scrupulous about everything else, perhaps more so. I told him that my performances were more about music than chicanery, the spirit only a gimmick, my compositions a foggy mirror where listeners could see whatever they wanted. Was it my fault that they believed what they heard? I had to tell them what they'd just heard, of course, but it was their decision to believe. Oh, I contradicted myself constantly in my efforts to explain. Yet my music, too, remained a mystery in Isaac's ear. He was nearly as tuneless as President Grant.

But he wanted to understand my art, wanted to see me at work. So I asked him along one afternoon to be my "starter" when I went to visit a philanthropist widower, Theophilus T. Lowe.

Most clairvoyants use an assistant of some sort, a hypnotist to put them in a trance or a partner to mumble a few magic words, someone to make the experience less subjective and self-willed. All I needed was a well-tuned piano, but I had another reason for enlisting Isaac. Theophilus Lowe was an anomaly among the rich. A white-haired Yankee merchant who had made his pile late in life, he was a thinker, a reformer. He was a scientific spiritualist, a *skeptical* believer, with a reputation for sniffing out frauds. He was also an old-school abolitionist, a believer in the black man. Not only would he welcome Isaac into his home, Isaac's presence might soften his doubts about my music.

Lowe was overjoyed to meet Isaac. He shook his hand and even slapped him on the back, more taken with the manly Negro than with his willowy, longhaired friend. We went into his study, where Isaac followed my instructions. He tied on my blindfold, then stood behind me at the piano to rub my shoulders. It was the first time we had touched in the presence of another: The invisible hands seemed enormous, galvanic. I snapped to attention, with such a jolt that Isaac let go as if I'd just caught fire. And I began to play. I had done this so often now that I simply let the music take over, yet I found myself performing not so much for Lowe as for Isaac.

I wanted to prove my worth to him. It did not cramp my flow but set my horse galloping off in new directions. In the patchwork quilt of song, a lugubrious hymn turned into the Prisoners' Chorus from *Fidelio,* the solemn joy of men climbing from a dungeon into sunlight. Then the freed men put their hands on each other's shoulders and stepped into a merry waltz.

When I took off my blindfold, I promptly looked at Isaac. He stood against the wall, scowling, blinking, kneading his beard with one hand. Lowe, however, sat in his chair nodding sagely, treating my performance as both convincing and natural. "I heard the chains of the South," he declared. "Giving way to the song of freedom. Yes, you read my heart quite well," he said. "Quite beautifully." He mistook my portrait of Isaac for a portrait of himself. "And you cannot do this without Mr. Kemp? Wonderful. That a white man and a Negro make such music together. You gentlemen are an allegory of equality. A living allegory."

I expected Isaac to take pride in that, yet he lowered his head, only pretending to nod in agreement. He said nothing until we were out on the street.

"I did not like that," he confessed. "It was all for show? All a trick on that man?"

"Yes and no," I claimed. "I felt every note I played. What it means, I don't know, or where it comes from. But I did feel it." I did not tell Isaac that I'd been musically sketching *him.*

"Well, I was a fraud," he declared. "You could have done that without me. I was a sham in there. And I was ashamed for you. Embarrassed to see you playing the piano like that. You looked so ...undressed." He lowered his voice and angrily whispered, "You were making the same faces that you make in bed."

Was I a fraud? That is what you're asking, isn't it, Tristan? That's what everyone wants to know. Well, one can argue that I was no more fraudulent than any artist. A good actor, for example, who begins in feigning but goes on to plumb real emotion and truth.

Only I did not hide my truth in the dishonest pretense that it was merely art.

But to be honest, despite what I told Isaac that day, I thought I *was* a fraud. In my heart of hearts. It took time for my make-believe to turn into full-fledged belief. Oh, there were little sparks and flickers, like my premonition that a boy with asthma would become president. I considered them idle fancies, whimsical imaginings, not yet understanding that the imagination is a higher faculty of knowledge. And that it was not my own doing but came from another place.

This understanding did not come about until a few months later, in Troy, New York, when Mr. Lowe took Isaac and me as his guests to a convention of the American Spiritualist Association.

The idea of such an event must conjure up visions of bedlam, a hotel packed with lunatics and con artists, a gathering of longhaired men and shorthaired women. And yes, many queer types sat in the rocking chairs on the hotel veranda after supper, yet it was all quite earnest, serious without being solemn, like a church conference. And it was scientific, too, with tests and experiments during the day and public meetings at night.

The big controversy that year was over Materialization. A new generation of mediums claimed that they could call up spirits who did not just knock on tables but made themselves visible. Isaac and I attended a demonstration one afternoon, in a curtained room with a red lamp that cast a crimson monochrome like a disease of the eye. But the mediums, a lean husband and leaner wife, failed to bring forth any floating heads or nightgowns in that darkness visible, only a smell of sulfur, which may have been the brimstone of hell sticking to the spirit's feet, as they claimed, or just its fart. The spirit itself was apparently made shy by the scientific observers who guarded each door and window.

None of this was as absurd as it now sounds. It wasn't. If I had announced fifty years ago that airborne spirits would one day speak inside electric cabinets in any home, I would've been dismissed as a quack. But it came to pass, and we call it radio. In another fifty years I wager that these radios will give us even more, and we will hear voices from the past and, perhaps, the future.

Mr. Lowe waited until after the failed demonstration to spring his real reason for bringing me and Isaac to Troy: He wanted the scientists to test *us*. He proposed they explore our "gift" under hypnosis. Isaac refused, angrily, with a blaming look at me. His refusal suggested we had something to hide. So I promptly said, "I'll try it alone," assuming I could fake a trance, remain in control, and nobody would be the wiser.

The curtains were drawn again, but there was no red light this time. Isaac, Mr. Lowe, and a few earnest men and women took their seats in the shadowy room. Dr. Calgary, a physician from Chicago, sat me at the piano, placed a clammy hand on my shoulder, and swung a little ivory elephant on a chain before my eyes. Back and forth, back and forth. This is ridiculous, I thought, this is too easy. I closed my eyes when he told me to. I opened them again when he said to open them. I took on a blank, placid expression that I'd seen on mediums, opium smokers, and dairy cows. And then, without a command from my brain, my hands fell on the keyboard and began to play.

I had actually gone under. I was hypnotized, a most curious sensation. I was both there and not there, like falling asleep in an armchair with a closed book in your lap and dreaming that you are in an armchair with the same book in your lap, only now the book is open and you can read it. The hard keys seemed as soft as pillows, as pliant as playing cards. The notes became a deck of cards that I shuffled into musical phrases. I wore no blindfold but played with my eyes shut, except I could see through the lids to a set of black-and-white stairs. I arranged the cards into staircases in different major and minor keys, flights of crystal stairs that shared steps with other flights. And then, as I climbed a new stairway, in a key I'd never heard before, I saw him, for the first time. My familiar, the spirit who occasionally told me things. He loomed over the staircases like a judge, a puppeteer, a composer. I suddenly knew: My fancies were not my own inventions but came from him.

What did he look like? I prefer not to say. It will only sound ridiculous. Most spirits take conventional forms, a bearded man in flowing robes or a baby's head with wings. Mine was ... well, a father. Not the father I never knew, and certainly not God the Father, but a brooding, paternal presence. Only this presence did not look like a man. It did not look like anything at all. Very well, if you must have an image: He looked something like a horse, and something like a piano. It's absurd to picture him, since my spirit was neither a piano-playing horse nor a concert grand with mane and hooves. He was something else entirely yet could be best represented in my head by a horse and a piano, like a rebus or Egyptian hieroglyph, with queer echoes of a remembered beast and instrument standing together in a haunted mansion in Virginia. My first Metaphysical, he did not have a name. He did not need a name until there were others.

I don't know how long I played before Dr. Calgary clapped his hands and broke my trance. I clumsily banged one last chord as I opened my eyes and understood where I was. I looked over my shoulder. Lowe sat up front, beaming like Christopher Columbus. Isaac hunched behind him, perfectly still, perplexed yet calm, coolly puzzling it out.

Calgary and the others instantly questioned me about what I had felt and seen. I answered them truthfully, mentioning a fatherly presence, though not the horse and the piano. I asked what the music had sounded like, but they weren't a terribly musical bunch. They didn't know how to describe it, though one man said it reminded him of a power loom with a loose bobbin. They called Isaac over and questioned him, then came to the conclusion that his touch must affect me like hypnosis. I agreed, pretending that today's performance was identical to the others.

The stairway up to our room seemed as strange and elastic as the musical stairs in my trance. I climbed them on metaphysical sea legs. When I closed our door, I turned to Isaac and said, "I did not fake that. Not a note. None of it was in my control."

He only said, "Ah?" with his eyebrows skeptically coming together.

"Isaac," I insisted. "He was there. I felt him. The spirit never showed himself so clearly to me." I grew more breathless with the truth of it. "But you see? My spirit is real. I have not been dissembling."

His skeptical look was replaced by surprise. "I never thought you were," he said. "I don't understand it but trusted that you did." His faith in me was both touching and alarming.

"Well, sometimes I must dissemble with others," I confessed. "In order to convince them I am real."

I asked him what the music had sounded like, but Isaac didn't have a language for it either. "Quick," he said. "And clean. Like numbers. And like nothing I'd ever heard you play before."

I performed that night in the hotel ballroom, with Isaac as my starter. He swallowed his own feeling of fraud for the sake of the "allegory of equality." Dr. Calgary introduced us and vouched for my authenticity. Neither Isaac nor I spoke. I sat down at the piano. Isaac rubbed my shoulders—it was exciting to be touched by him in front of such a large public. I made my jolt, fell into my music, and Isaac withdrew. I played as I usually did, holding the audience for a good half hour without a peep from my spirit.

Afterward, a handful of music lovers approached me in the hall— me, not Isaac—asking if I were in touch with the ghosts of Mozart, Beethoven, or Stephen Foster. Certainly their favorite composers continued composing while they decomposed? Then a female voice cried, "Capital! Simply capital!" A pretty woman in a shawl and dinghylike hat came forward, her arms outstretched, not to embrace me but to announce herself: "I am Woodhull!"

Yes, Alice's dreaded "Mrs. Satan" herself. She'd not yet earned that sobriquet but had already led quite a life. Beginning as Commodore Vanderbilt's personal medium, she had become a mystic

stockbroker—both the spirits and Vanderbilt gave good advice—
then founded her weekly newspaper with her sister. A smart, tough,
feminine little beauty, a fearless flirt when she dropped her podium
manner, she was Fanny Gaskins with brains. I can well believe the
rumor that she was once in the trade herself. She had come to
address the spiritualists and enlist their support in her bid for office.
Women did not have the vote, but Victoria Woodhull was running
for president.

She called Isaac over, praised us to the skies, admitted she preferred sopranos to pianos but agreed with Lowe that we made "a
capital allegory." She introduced her husband, Colonel Blood, who
managed her paper. She wanted to help us with a few articles,
admitting that it would also help her. She hoped to bring the new
Negro vote to her Equal Rights Party and had already approached
Frederick Douglass to appear on her ticket as vice president.

"You should speak," she told Isaac. "A handsome, strapping fellow like yourself. You'd be glorious onstage." And she rushed off to
work the room like any cigar-smoking politician while her dour,
muttonchopped husband arranged an interview with us.

Nothing much came of Woodhull's campaign for president. She is
completely forgotten now. I half forgot her myself until we read
about the violent response of Alice's viscera. Woodhull got her name
in all the papers, but not in the ballot box. And she put me and
Isaac into her paper, the infamous *WC*, before her career went
smash. I regret that we have no copy of the newspaper from the
boat. We carried our last copies to England, for what they were
worth. The piece was all purple assertion and few facts, the scratchy
illustration more a cartoon than a portrait. I looked like Peck's Bad
Boy with a string mop doodled on his head; Isaac had been drawn
from a cheap edition of *Uncle Tom's Cabin.* After all, we were only
an allegory.

I was too full of my own life at this time to pay much attention
to the news of the world, so I cannot give a full account of Wood-

hull's fall. Our meeting in Troy was our only encounter. I seem to remember her campaign ran aground on her belief in "free love." She took her revenge on the nation of hypocrites by reporting in the *WC* that the Reverend Henry Ward Beecher, the Conscience of the Nation, was the adulterous lover of his best friend's wife. The paper sold like hotcakes even as everyone reviled Woodhull. Not that they believed Beecher was innocent. They hated his deceit almost as much as they hated the effrontery of the woman who exposed it. Isaac, however, expressed surprising pity for the man's ruin, a sad sympathy for the preacher's feet of clay.

There was a bank crash around this time, which had nothing to do with Woodhull or Beecher, except both morals and money became very tight. Isaac had invested our funds in railroad certificates, so we lost little, but his carpentry work grew scarce. People were reluctant to hire a Jew and a Negro when there were so many nice unemployed white men who worked for less. Now and then Isaac acted as my starter at a public performance, but there was not much call for us outside radical circles, and radicals, too, grew scarce after the fall of Woodhull. When I called on the rich, I always performed solo. Oh, yes, I still kept my thumb in that pie, a fortune-teller to the carriage trade.

So times were slow, though not hard, when a theatrical agent asked me to meet him in the lobby of his hotel one winter afternoon to hear his proposal: He wanted to book me on a musical tour in England. American spiritualists were all the rage, he said. He had not caught my "act" but had heard about it, including reports that I sometimes used "an Ethiopian" assistant. He thought that would go over swell with English audiences, who adored minstrel shows. When I told him our music was more like Liszt than "Jim Crow" Dan Rice, he said that was fine, too, so long as it had novelty. His name was Uriah Darling, and he would pay our passage and handle our bookings and promotion in exchange for half of the profits.

I was immediately tickled by the proposal, tickled and tempted. But I was certain that Isaac would say no. He was more practical than I, more toughly realistic. That night, after we finished our supper and sat on either side of a banked fire in our cold rooms, our dirty plates on the floor, I told him about Darling's scheme. He listened in silence, his chin on his chest, his lips drawn tight. His jaw began to chew the proposal as if it were a plug of bad tobacco. When I finished, he continued chewing in a long, slow silence.

Then he said, "Yes!" With a vehemence that surprised me. He looked surprised himself. "Another country!" he declared. "Over the ocean! We *could* go there, couldn't we?" And he smiled, a startled, giddy smile—well, giddy for Isaac. He wanted to cross the ocean, he said, and see the strange, alien land that he knew from the secondhand books he bought at street stalls, tracts by Carlyle and Samuel Smiles, novels by Walter Scott and Dickens—I don't remember him reading George Eliot yet. "New York has grown as old and confining as Norfolk," he said. "I need to go out in the world, as I intended when we were young."

As for appearing onstage, he disliked being a fake but thought this might be his chance to try his hand at public speaking. "That Woodhull woman said I'd be good on the platform," he explained. "I have wanted to do something for the Negro question. And it should go easier with foreigners. Who will see me differently than narrow, hidebound Americans do." He'd been told race was a matter of small importance over there, looser, less confining.

So the decision was Isaac's as well as mine. This was the first I'd heard of any secret dreams about travel or the podium. I hadn't guessed that his hard practicality now housed a bright-eyed romantic. In fact, I was the more practical one. On the outside chance that Darling didn't know his trade and there'd be nothing for us over there, I insisted we put our savings in a letter of credit that could be cashed at the Bank of England. Between that and the families who I knew would be summering at the gaudier watering holes on the Continent, we wouldn't starve, whatever happened across the sea.

Isaac and I had been together for eleven years when we left New York. We'd been bedmates for seven. We were business partners, of a sort. He might be called my manager or my assistant, depending on whom you asked and the man's mood at the moment. But I arrived in England believing our private life rested on bedrock, and any unpleasant surprises could only come from the cold world without or the fickle spirit realm within.

17

WE went straight to London from Liverpool. Surely the sun came out sometime during our stay in England, yet I remember only a constant pall of rain, fog, and smoke. London was an underwater city where gaslights floated like jellyfish at noon and herds of carriages clattered like crabs over a seabed of streets. One inhaled raw fog as if through gills.

My assumption that England possessed a nobler, less commercial civilization than our own was swept away for good when our train rolled into the station at Charing Cross. A solid wall of placards filled one side of the high shed, notice atop notice, a newspaper page three stories high and a city block long, full of advertisements for coal oil, cough medicine, boot polish, eyewash, and a hundred brands of soap. Uriah Darling met our train and proudly pointed out our placard—way, way up there in the dim haze, where only the sparrows could read all but the largest red letters: THE MUSIC OF AMERICAN SPIRITS. DOCTOR AUGUST AND CO.

"Coming to the Rosegarden Theatre!" Darling proudly sang out, waving his bamboo cane at the little square, pretending he could actually make out the words. "Also appearing," he added and sang the other names. We were not the only "act" on the bill but part of a musical evening, with an American singing family, *two* sopranos, and—shades of Uncle Jack—a solo violinist. Darling's plan was that we would open here and earn notices that would enable him to sell us in Manchester, Bristol, and the rest of the country. A short, plump, bouncy Scotsman, Darling was a rubber ball of a man, hope springing eternal in a derby and orange-plaid suit.

He took us to our tiny hotel and then by the Rosegarden Theatre. Tucked away on a back lane, it was more a music hall than the concert room he had promised. A duplicate of the placard was pasted out front, reading exactly as Darling had quoted.

"I hope ya doan mind 'and Company,' Mr. Kemp," he said. "I didna know how else to explain ya."

As part of his promotion, Darling had arranged an invitation for us to dine with the London lodge of the newly formed Theosophical Society, thinking such people would be useful in spreading the word. The society was the creation of Madame Blavatsky—the infamous Madame Blavatsky—and *her* consort, Colonel Olcott; the spirit world was top-heavy with colonels. Blavatsky lived in New York, when she wasn't in India, Tibet, or on the moon. I had heard reports back home of a Russian noblewoman bent on improving homely American mysticism with the wisdom of the East. She was in London that summer without Olcott. Whether she came over by steamer or spiritual osmosis, I cannot guess.

The society met in a crooked house on a crooked street behind Piccadilly. The fog was so thick the night of our dinner that the house had dissolved, and all we saw was a single bleary window. Then a bright door opened in the fog bank, and a gaunt Hindu servant in silk pantaloons and frayed dinner jacket nodded us inside. Darling, Isaac, and I followed him down a misty hallway to a murky dining room, where the party was already in full swing. Only it more resembled a wake than a party. The long table was lined with wax faces, wan smiles, and furtive glances. There were a dozen members: spiritualists, journalist-spiritualists, poet-spiritualists, doctor-spiritualists, and one defrocked minister.

An old woman with the face of a bulldog and body like a sack of grain sat at the head of the table: Madame Blavatsky. She did not stand when we came in but squinted at me with her unearthly ice-blue eyes. "You are Dr. August, yes?" she said in her unplaceable accent. "You play the automatic music, yes? It is like my automatic writing, I think."

Automatic writing was her invention, a trancelike scribbling of words "precipitated" by spirits. And yes, it was similar to my music, though I hadn't heard of automatic writing until that evening. I knew better than to tell her that.

"Yes, they're very close, Madame Blavatsky. I discovered the music on my own, but your bold example helped me understand it."

She took my flattery as her due. "And theez is your starter?" she said, gesturing at Isaac. "Your conductor? A dark soul, a black man? Yes, primitive peoples are more close to the fountains of wisdom than we in the West."

Isaac responded with a tightening of his jaw and a curt nod. This bulldog woman was more primitive than he'd ever been.

"Later you will play," she said. "Sit, sit. No, down there." She pointed out two chairs halfway down the table. "I fear our magnetisms are too strong for us to sit close. But you, Mr. Darling, you may sit at my right hand." She had more need of a good promoter than another medium.

This was Darling's first social encounter with mystics, and he took it in stride, with the smile of a man determined to show he could enjoy a good joke even if he didn't understand it.

Isaac and I found ourselves opposite a ruggedly handsome American with elaborate bobcat whiskers, dressed better than the others, a dapper dandy like a riverboat gambler. "Captain Marmaduke Cunningham," he said, shaking my hand and, after a slight hesitation, Isaac's. He was a spiritual adviser, he said, as well as an author and journalist. Perhaps we had heard of him? No, we hadn't. Yet I felt an instant, inexplicable dislike of this well-oiled fellow.

Only half the guests were English, the rest American or Irish. No women were present, unless you counted Blavatsky. Like a man among men, she addressed everyone by his last name. She distrusted other women. "You are friends with that whore, Woodhull?" she called down to me. "She is a fraud, August. All fancy dress and civet stink. You must come to us. We are the way." The spirit world was as rife with party and faction as New York City politics.

"Woodhull, huh?" Cunningham whispered. "She's a tasty piece. You had a helping, Doctor? No? Oh, I see," he added with a sneer. "The fair sex ain't your line."

The meal was served on tiptoe by the Hindu servant. It was a meager affair, a single potato and shadow of beef—Theosophists fed on shadows. Blavatsky ruled the table, dominating each turn of conversation like Queen Victoria in a court of ghouls. I missed the friendly noise and earnestness of American spiritualism. We eyed one another warily over our thin smiles, rival actors inspecting each other's wigs and false noses.

And they all eyed Isaac, surreptitiously, even the Hindu, as if they'd never seen a Negro. Whoever told Isaac that race didn't matter in England had been wrong. They found him exotic, strange, which was not much of an improvement over being seen as lowly. Isaac hid his discomfort in lofty composure and perfect manners. You might have thought he was a visiting duke or prince as he fastidiously cut into his shriveled potato.

A young Irishman had an incident to report. A few nights ago his wardrobe door opened and a hanger floated out. The next night it happened again, only now a coat hung on the hanger. The following night hanger and coat reappeared, with a hand poking from the sleeve. The hand held up two admonishing fingers. He wondered if anyone could shed light on this cryptic occurrence. He waited for a reply with a subtle twinkle in his eye.

"Rather!" Darling cried and burst out laughing. The others turned looks of scorn and pity on him.

"It is no laughing matter, sir," Captain Cunningham declared, "when the spirits have their fun at your expense. I remember my first visit from the other side, during the war . . ."

Cunningham's presence continued to annoy and gnaw at me, more than his insult of my manhood deserved. I wondered if I were irritated simply because he was another American, or by his hand-some masculinity. His name meant nothing to me. He was telling Darling about a midnight encounter with a pretty female ghost during his days as a captain—with the cavalry in the Army of the Potomac. And suddenly, in my mind's ear, I heard a sergeant shout, "Cunningham!" and I remembered: a clearing in Virginia, the bitter smell of gunsmoke, and the sight of corpses. And I recognized the handsome jaw and dandified side-whiskers. The whiskers had grown down his jaw and up over his upper lip, but it was the very man, the soldier thief. A murderer had gone up in the world and now mixed with spirits. I glanced at Isaac, but he had noticed nothing odd about this smooth fellow.

"August," said Blavatsky. "You will play now." She wagged her pudgy hand at an instrument in the corner. "Play, play."

"Go to it, Doctor!" cried Darling. "Show us your stuff!"

I went over and examined the instrument. It was not a piano but a melodeon, a small reed organ that you pumped with your feet, its keys like sticky teeth, yellowed and carious. I warned Blavatsky that I did not know how my familiar would respond to this machine. I took another look at Cunningham and called Isaac over. I did not bother with a blindfold. These people were professionals and would know their nose-peeks. Isaac rubbed my shoulders. I snapped to attention and commenced pumping.

The sound was awful, like a sick cow, but I did not need beauty to make my point. Chance had given me a golden opportunity, not only to expose a killer but to prove myself to Blavatsky. I played for a few wheezy minutes—"Just Before the Battle, Mother" fol-lowed by "Saul's Death March" and other nonsense—then stopped, sadly turned and shook my head. "I'm sorry," I said. "My spirit does not like melodeons. He's making mischief tonight, talking nonsense about a Captain Sly Pig. I know of no such man."

"Sly Pig?" said the Irishman. "Don't you see? It's a riddle!

Cunning pig? Cunning ham! He's talking about Captain Cunning-ham."

"Of course!" I said. "I'm sorry, sir. I'd forgotten your name. My spirit has a dreadful taste for puns."

"Your spirit spoke of me? Ha-ha!" crowed Cunningham, sharing a fearless grin with the others. "And what does your spirit say?"

"Well, sir. Let me repeat: He's in a mischievous, lying mood. He says you were in the cavalry but were never an officer. More malicious, he claims that you robbed the dead. You were a better scavenger than a soldier. He wants to know if you still rob the dead, *Captain* Cunningham?"

His cinched lips turned white. He glared at me. He tilted his head, straining to recognize my face from his past, maybe wondering if I actually had a spirit who could tell on him. "Stuff and nonsense!" he finally cried, then laughed, desperately. "Your spirit lies!"

"That is what I thought," I claimed, even as I let him know with a thin smile that we both knew otherwise.

The others turned to Blavatsky, waiting for her verdict.

She sat there, hands on the table, lightly rocking, as if thinking with her entire body. Then she looked up and said, "No, August. You must have more faith in your familiar. My elementals, too, have had doubts about Cunningham. Ever since the funds of Widow Jamison disappeared."

Cunningham slowly turned to Blavatsky, displaying his pretty white teeth in a clenched smile. "They did not disappear," he muttered, as if for the hundredth time. "I told you. They were never there. I showed you her bank sheets. The woman was deluded. She had no money to leave to the society."

"That is not what my elementals report," said Blavatsky. "Bank records can be altered. And now our new friend's spirit reports that you have a history of robbing the dead."

"Only dead Confederates," I said, pretending to defend him. "Their money and watches."

He stared at me again, frightened now, and his temper suddenly gave way. "You call me a thief!" he cried at Blavatsky. "Me? Marmaduke Cunningham? You will believe this fraud"—he pointed a trembling finger at me—"after all I've done for you?"

"Pish posh," went Blavatsky. "After all *we* have done for you. Taking you into our bosom. Introducing you to widows. I have long questioned the sincerity of your belief."

He looked at the others and saw that no one would come to his aid. He rose to his feet. "I will not be treated this way," he declared. "You have insulted my honor for the last time, Blavatsky. And you," he sneered at me. "You will regret this slander." He stormed out of the room.

My simple trick had surpassed my wildest expectations.

"My deepest apologies," I told Blavatsky. "I didn't mean to make trouble. If I had known there might be truth to his songs, I would've kept my spirit's comments to myself."

"No, no, August, you were right to share them. You have a most trustworthy spirit. Do not worry about that charlatan," she scoffed. "My elementals will protect you and your spirit."

We bade Blavatsky good night soon after that. She assured me she would send all of her disciples to the Rosegarden. Darling did not forget to hand around a few free passes before we left.

"Good show, Doctor," said Darling out on the street. "Ya raddled that fella good. How did ya guess all that?"

"Oh, but I didn't guess. My spirit told me."

Darling hesitated, then snorted and shook his head. "I doan pretend to understand, Doctor. But if ya say so." He said good night and, still chuckling to himself, turned off and disappeared into the muzzy night. The metaphorical fog of Theosophy had been replaced by the very real fog of London.

Isaac and I walked in silence toward the next smothered streetlamp. Then Isaac quietly said, "So it really was him? The thief at the ambush?"

"Without a doubt. I recognized his name and then his face. The very man who killed your—" I was about to say "master," then "master's son," but what did we call him now? "Tom Kemp. Whose corpse we hauled home to Norfolk. Fancy Dan back there was the one who put a bullet in his head." I hadn't considered Isaac's stake here, but he had one, didn't he?

Isaac only nodded to himself, slowly, dryly, then said, "The world is smaller than we imagine. To come across the ocean and encounter *him*." He was neither shocked nor indignant over meeting Tom's killer, merely philosophical.

"It doesn't concern you beyond that? You knew Tom Kemp. You grew up with him."

He mulled it over as we walked. "Yes. But it was so long ago. Another life. I have put it behind me. No," he announced after the next lamp, "I can feel no anger toward the man who killed my master. Nor gratitude either."

There was good sense in such an attitude, even wisdom, yet I was amazed that Isaac could wash his hands of the past so easily.

18

OPENING night. London. The Rosegarden Theatre. Oh, yes, I am playing "Casta Diva" again. The ubiquitous "Casta Diva." Even in England one could not escape it. On opening night *both* sopranos sang that damned Bellini aria.

I stood at the back curtain and peeked through the eyehole one more time, measuring the audience before Isaac and I went on. The hot sticks of lime in the footlights burned like sunlight on water, but I could see through the glare to the layer cake of class out front. The house lights were left on during the performance, and the prosperous businessmen and their wives in the stalls and boxes looked respectful enough. They might enjoy my music even if they didn't buy its source. The galleries, however, seemed a bit rowdy, the rails hung with giggling shopgirls and noisy young toffs who didn't even bother to remove their hats. It had been years since I last performed for a paying public. I'd forgotten how fickle they could be. They loved the sopranos, ignored the violinist—they chatted while he played—and merely tolerated The Diddles, one of those singing American families, ages six to sixty, who were as common in that age as "Casta Diva."

The soprano began her encore—each act had an encore, whether the audience wanted it or not. I went around to the wings where

Isaac stood with Darling. "Nervous?" I asked. "Excited?" My own stomach was a bushel of butterflies.

Isaac waved away my concern as pesky condescension. His white gloves made his hands look large and absurd, yet he was quite handsome in his cutaway, his hair shiny with pomade.

The soprano hurried offstage, giving us a broad, gap-toothed smile that declared, "Can you top that!"

We stepped out into the white light and roaring space.

There was applause from the stalls and happy hoots and hollers from the cheap seats overhead. That puzzled me until I realized that they were thrilled to see Isaac. They thought they'd see something new and freakish: a piano-playing African. There were mutters when I sat at the piano instead.

Isaac had spent hours working on his speech, writing and rewriting it on the boat, reading and reciting it to me in our hotel as he committed it to memory. I had advised him to keep it short, saying that what sounded rich and full in one's room could be interminable in public. But he had heard Douglass, Beecher, and a hundred other public speakers and was certain that he could do as well.

He marched boldly to the center of the stage, took his first look at the audience—and froze. We had performed for gatherings of a hundred or less, never more, and never in a real theater. The first glare of limelight and public left Isaac stunned. I could not see his face, but I heard his silence and saw the white gloves hanging dead at his sides.

"Dr. August and I," he finally began. "Dr. August and I . . . Dr. August and I . . ." His mouth kept going dry, and he had to stop to moisten it and start over again. "Our music . . . the music you will hear tonight . . . is original. Every performance is original. Dictated to Dr. August by his spirit. A spirit neither of us claims to understand."

"Speak up!" someone shouted from the gallery. "Can't hear a bleeding word from the Hottentot!"

"Dr. August and I," Isaac continued, "Dr. August and I..." He kept catching on that phrase. "...met in the great war to free my race from bondage. We passed together through bloody battlefields and an empty wilderness, forming a bond that—"

Instead of making him raise his voice, the shout from the gallery dampened it, lowering his bass to a bashful mutter. I could barely hear him myself.

A girl cried out, "Forget the speech, dearie! Give us a song!" Others picked up the idea: "Sing!" "Give us coon songs!" "Nigger songs!"

He went as dumb as a statue, his memory suddenly as dry as his mouth.

The conductor stood up in the orchestra pit to frown at me, threatening to start playing if we didn't start soon.

" 'Old Black Joe'!" people cried. " 'Massa's in the Cold, Cold Ground'!" " 'Camptown Races'!" A pack of office boys near the rafters began to sing, "Doo-dah, doo-dah."

"Pssst!" I went. "Isaac! Come touch me. Put on my blindfold and touch me."

He slowly turned around. I'd never seen such a look on his face. Isaac, the cool stoic, the fearless, manly Isaac, had gone ash gray with fright. Not stage fright, but the blood-chilling terror of public humiliation. The catcalls reduced him to an orangutan in the zoo, a freak at Barnum's Museum. My heart broke for him even as it filled with scorn for the mob who mocked him.

He staggered upstage toward the piano, without looking where he was going. I had to grab his elbow and tell him what to do. "Where's the blindfold?" I whispered. "Put on my blindfold. Rub my shoulders." As he fumbled through the procedure, I muttered, "I'm sorry, Isaac. I'm sorry. I tried to warn you. I did."

He seized my shoulders and shook me, angrily, as if he blamed me for his humiliation. I snapped into my trance.

That shut them up, although one card cried out, "Give the lad a drink! He's having an attack of the hypos!"

I slammed the keyboard in a loud, thunderous chord, the wrath of Zeus, as Isaac fled into the wings. I would give the bastards what they wanted: I launched into "Camptown Races" in a scornful, mocking harangue, chopping at the keyboard, then "Roll Over, Jordan" in an angry fugue. I tore apart "God Save the Queen" in an ugly, ear-splitting key. Schubert once said that he envied Nero, "who destroyed a detestable people with strings and song." Sweet, tender Schubert could say that, and many performers have felt the same, yet none could have felt it as strongly as I did that night. If music could kill, my piano would have blasted the house like a Gatling gun.

I played in a hot fury for ten minutes, maybe longer, without the fury subsiding. Finally I could find no way to end my wrath except to hurl myself backward from the stool. I slammed my skull against the floor, shuddered a moment, and feigned unconsciousness. I was not so full of wrath that I forgot to put on a show.

There were gasps out front and shocked silence. I heard Darling in the wings plead with Isaac to go back onstage and take care of me. But then Darling came out alone to slap my cheek and help me up. The house went wild with applause.

"Splendid," whispered Darling. "Ya ne'er told me ya did St. Vitus fits." He held me up and turned me to the audience so that I might bow. I stared at them through my snarled curtain of hair, enjoying their applause even as I despised them for their vicious stupidity.

Darling led me offstage, into the corner where Isaac sat numbly on a crate. "We should have a good long run once word gets out," Darling declared, then herded the others—sopranos, violinist, and Diddles—out for the grand finale. All of them, down to the littlest Diddle, gave me dirty looks for having upstaged them with such a cheap stunt.

"The public are fools," I told Isaac. "Stupid, insulting fools."

"They liked you well enough," he muttered.

"Because they're fools." I laid a hand on his arm. "I'm sorry,

Isaac. I forgot how cruel they can be. I should have prepared you for that."

He snatched his arm away, refusing to be consoled. He was too proud to be comforted. "I was a child to think I could speak in public. An idiot child." He spit on himself with words. "But I have learned my lesson. Never again. I will not cast my pearls before swine."

He actually said that. I'd heard his speech, of course, and there were no real pearls in it. But a public speaker has to start somewhere, and Isaac's speechmaking would've improved if he'd given it a chance.

We fought about it the next day, after I allowed time for his temper to cool and his burns to heal. But pain only covered itself in thick scars of pride.

"I was a fraud," he declared. "A fraud and a fool. I deserved to be humbled and punished. I will not go back. You don't need my presence. From now on you will have to perform without me." He plunged himself in a cold bath of humility but did it proudly.

"Damn it," I snapped. "I can make a fool of myself. Why can't you? You don't have to speak. Just come onstage and start me."

"No. That's a fraud, too. I was willing to be a fraud for the sake of my message. But I have no message. And it does not pay to be untrue to yourself. No matter what the purpose."

He blamed himself, he did not blame me, not in so many words. Yet I felt responsible for his pain: I had encouraged him to join me in fraud, I had exposed him to the mob. I could press only so hard before I guiltily gave in to him.

I went to the theater alone that evening, told Darling that Isaac was indisposed, and asked him to be my starter. The show must go on. It was a new house, of course, yet I despised them, too, even as I courted their applause. I'd spent years on the boards and could swallow my share of toads.

Defeat, however, stays with a righteous man, even when he walks away from it. Isaac fell into a deep melancholy in the week that followed. His proud anger gave way to sad anger, then plain sadness, a despondency that he refused to acknowledge or discuss. We went out during the day to see the sights together—the Crystal Palace, the Tower of London, Madame Tussaud's—but Isaac remained indifferent to it all. One might compare his listlessness to the stupor of snakes before they shed their skins, except Isaac was not a snake. I patiently waited for his mood to pass as if it were a fever.

He wandered the London streets alone at night while I was at the theater. He did not visit pubs, of course, but churches, reading rooms, and the lobbies of the better hotels. He wanted to come to understand the English, he claimed, only he never reported having any conversations with strangers.

19

AND what do we hear from our little diary keeper? Where is she at this time? The Botts family *was* in London, but only briefly before they crossed over to the Continent.

Tuesday, July 13

I expected Paris to be shameless, yet have seen nothing shameful—excepting the yard behind our hotel full of empty wine bottles. I have seen nothing much at all but what I see with Isabella. She, however, is shameless, a monster of appetite & vanity. I strive to cure her precocious love of mirrors, but to no avail. When I proposed a visit to the Louvre yesterday, she refused unless I promised a visit to a sweet shop afterward. I did not give in to her demand, & so we took yet another stroll down the Champs, where she kept pressing her nose to the windows of dressmakers. She continues to perch in my lap & smother me with kisses at home, excepting when she does not get her way. Then her caresses turn to pinches, in much the same way she tortures her dolls. When I talk to Mrs. Botts of this obstinacy, I am mocked & chided for being unable to master a nine-year-old child. I hope that Mrs. Botts, when she knows me better, will see me as a friend & sister. But for now she treats me as a fool. Mr. Botts remains a man of few words, but seems to look upon me with gruff fondness, excepting when his wife is in the room.

Sunday, July 18

We are going to Baden-Baden, for the cure. The heat of Paris & indulgence of its restaurants have taken their toll on Mrs. Botts. She wants only to repair her health, she says, but admits the presence of a casino might provide amusement for Mr. Botts. And this is one of Hartford's best families? Who would have guessed that moral city could harbor such secret depravity? Their depravity has infected my dreams. I dreamt last night that I was a slave & stood on an auction block. The auctioneer tore my nightgown to my waist & exposed me to the mob. It disgusts me to dwell on such lewdness, yet it was my dream & I merely record it.

Sunday, August 8

Rain. More rain. It has rained ever since we arrived in Baden, so I cannot escape this awful household & hotel. The mister & missus snapped at each other in my presence last night as if I were but furniture, until Mrs. Botts left the room by the door where I stood & said, "Can one never turn around & not see your moping face!" I had thought my isolation would pass once Mrs. Botts took the time to know me & see me as her friend. But she does not want to know me. I am but a servant. This morning she was more scornful than ever when she handed me a letter. "Are we now your post office?" Her words destroyed the pleasant surprise that someone had written me, even if it is only Mr. Kemp, the colored gentleman on the boat. His letter was forwarded from Paris. He was kind to write, & I will respond in a cool yet courteous fashion. I told Mrs. Botts his race in order to assure her this man was only a formal acquaintance. "You are friends with a nigger?" she sneered before she & Mr. Botts left for the casino. I will write him, thank him for his attention, but request that he not write me again.

"He was kind to write"? Kind to write? I learned about this letter soon enough without discovering its contents. Thinking of their secret correspondence brings back all my rage and hurt of the time.

You found his letter with her papers, Tristan? Very well, then. Let's hear what my dear friend, that monument of virtue, that tombstone of scruple, wrote behind my back in his time of woe.

My respected Miss Pangborn,

Forgive me the grave impertinence of taking the great liberty of writing to you in care of your employers' hotel in London. I trust this letter will reach you and hope it finds you in good health. You have perhaps forgotten our brief acquaintance on board the City of Brooklyn last month. If so, you may ignore this letter. If not, understand that I am writing to express my fear that we parted on a grievous misunderstanding. Let me assure you that I have the highest regard and respect for you. I meant no insult by showing you a newspaper which you consider obscene. I have carefully examined the publication again. The reputation of obscenity is quite unmerited, I assure you, as are the bad reputations of many things in the world. I was angry over this grave misunderstanding yet have overcome anger in order to write this letter and assure you I am an honorable man.

I trust this letter finds you in good spirits as well as good health. If you care to respond, letters addressed to my name at Wenn's Hotel in London are certain to reach me.

Respectfully yrs,

Mr. Isaac Kemp

That is all? You are not leaving anything out? Hardly my idea of a love letter. And it's peculiar to hear Isaac, whose spoken speech was so direct, tangle himself up in so much epistolary folderol.

And her reply?

Mr. Kemp, sir,

Let me assure you that I bear you no resentment or blame over your innocent display of a newspaper. Of course I remember our conversations on board the City of Brooklyn. They were literate, intelligent, and well bred.

I know that you mean no harm with your respectful note but must request that you not write to me again. It has created a misunderstanding with my employers, who are already unhappy with me. I hope you understand.

I will always bear a kind regard for our brief acquaintance at sea.

Yrs. truly,

Miss A. Pangborn

How extraordinary. They are oblivious, dumbly, sweetly oblivious. I should have guessed as much. Neither of them understood what their hearts were doing. They are like a lady and gentleman taking a morning ride on horseback, who coldly ignore each other while their animals sniff and rub muzzles.

I suspected nothing, of course. I spent my evenings playing musical clown to the crowd at the Rosegarden, only it did not go as well as it had that first night. It did not go badly, but I could not fake wrath every evening, and Darling was wrong about the English. They were not much interested in American spirits or melodic epilepsy. When I failed to catch fire with the general public, I was moved down the bill and the prettier of the two sopranos given the large red type. Darling insisted I persist, that I would catch on soon enough, even without Isaac. And maybe I would have, if not for a certain newspaper article.

Darling arrived at the theater one evening with his eternally cheerful face crimped in worry. He clutched a fresh copy of the *London Illustrated*. AMERICAN HUMBUG AND NIGGER MAGIC, declared a headline. It was about me, of course, and the author was "An American Captain," the pseudonymn of Marmaduke Cunningham. You must be very careful about whom you cross in a profession where truth is so malleable. Your enemies don't need truth to expose you in return. Captain Sly Pig did not denounce me as a fraud but took a more cunning approach. He claimed I wasn't the real medium. Isaac was the medium, he said, while I was merely "a nigger's marionette." As proof, ever since "the Ethiopian" had become ill, the magic was gone from my performance and I was just "another trained Chopin-zee." I was furious, even as I thought Isaac should be flattered. But I couldn't show the article to Isaac, because of something else in it:

> They make a most curious couple, this effeminate musician and black brute. There are rumors that they live as husband and wife, completely untrue, yet such unsavory thoughts cannot help but spring to our minds when we behold this peculiar pair.

Or words to that effect. I quote from memory. Cunningham was careful not to open himself to libel charges. Darling never mentioned that slimy insinuation. His great fear was that this article, combined with Isaac's absence, would kill what little interest I'd sustained with the mob.

Word traveled quickly. The next night at the Rosegarden, when I came out on the stage alone, the gallery began to holler, "Where's the nigger? We want nigger magic! You can't do it without the nigger!"

I played as well as I always did, but the audience was unconvinced. I did not dare ask Isaac to return, could not bear to see him humiliated again. There were boos the next night, and yawns the night after. The public is a fickle, flat-footed beast.

At the end of the week Darling announced that there would be no tour when I finished at the Rosegarden. Word was out on the circuit: The mystic pianist was box-office chloroform. Darling accepted defeat with surprising affability. "There is red wheat as well as white, and some prefer the lighter grain," he said, not blaming me or Isaac for the money he had lost on bringing us over. Since the tour was to be the cashmaker for everyone, I had to draw on our letter of credit to pay the hotel bill.

So there we were, stranded in London, marooned in Europe. I loathed the English with all my Irish blood and swore eternal hatred of that murderous weasel, Cunningham. But, I must say, I was glad the sorry business had ended. I promised myself that I would never again play for the great unwashed, only the genteel, the intelligent, the open-minded. I did not panic. We had enough money to return to New York, in steerage if not better, yet I had a happier notion. I took out the list of "friends" who were summering on the Continent. I fully trusted my ability to make myself amusing enough that they would not only take us in but take us back with them when they went home.

Isaac liked the idea, much to my surprise. Despite his grim mood, he was in no hurry to return to New York either.

We discussed the possibilities one morning at the National Gallery. We often used the vast halls as an indoor park on days when the fog turned to rain. The museum was open only during the week, so there was rarely anyone else there except foreigners, artists, and an occasional servant playing hooky.

I went through the list of hosts to whom we might offer ourselves. The Cantwells were in Paris, the Winterbournes were in Rome, Mrs. Horace Tarbell was in Baden-Baden.

"I think you should start with Tarbell," said Isaac.

I was already considering that and expressed pleasure that he would suggest it, too.

"You've said she enjoys your company," he explained. "And Baden is in Germany. I speak German. German music is your passion." He paused to clear his throat. "I think Miss Pangborn might still be in Baden-Baden."

"Miss Who?"

"The lady on the boat."

She'd made so little impression that it took me a moment to remember her. "The bluenosed spinster?"

"The governness, yes."

We were standing in front of a Bathsheba by Rembrandt, a robust nude under brown varnish that reduced her to a smoked herring. I am surprised I remember the painting so clearly. I was not alarmed by Isaac's mention of a woman, only puzzled. "And how, pray tell, do you know she is in Baden?" I asked.

He did not lie. That is what amazes me now. A few questions were required to get the full truth, but he did not lie. "I wrote to her. And she wrote back."

"How did you know her address?"

"I visited a few hotels. Until I found the one where her employers had been staying. They told me their hotel in Paris."

I blinked at him. "But why, Isaac? What does this woman mean to you that you'd go to so much trouble?"

"We had a misunderstanding on the boat. I did not want her to think badly of me."

"Why should *you* care what a prickly old maid thinks?"

"Because— I think I might be in love with her."

He said it as blithely as that. A lie would have been more plausible, more sane. I turned away from Bathsheba and stepped very slowly to the next painting. I remember that one, too: a sunny Poussin with two male figures, Apollo and Marsyas.

Isaac reappeared beside me.

"Love?" I said. "What do you mean, love?"

"I don't know exactly. A strange attraction. A desire to see her again." He spoke of love with an ignorance so deep it was like innocence. "I can even imagine marrying her."

I stared at him, wondering, Is he joking? But Isaac never joked. He has gone mad, I thought. He mentioned love as if my own love were a small, unrelated matter. Part of me wanted to laugh—and it *is* comical—even as I felt stung, slapped, dismissed.

I looked around the overcast room, saw other art lovers set about like mannequins. Their presence prevented me from losing my temper. "We cannot talk here," I muttered and hurried out, more quickly than I'd intended. I marched down the corridor toward the front entrance, hoping the fresh air would enable me to think clearly. Once I was using my legs, the desire to laugh became very strong. This is rich, I thought. This is ridiculous.

I heard his boot steps in the distance as I stepped out on the high stone porch overlooking Trafalgar Square. I went to the balustrade, where Isaac caught up with me. He stood calmly at my side while I took in the chill, damp air and gazed out on the shiny square crawling with black umbrellas.

"This woman," I said, "she has encouraged you?"

"Not at all. Miss Pangborn doesn't know how I feel."

"No? But she's given you some sign of her own interest."

"None. Our letters are models of tact and courtesy. We've made no mention of possible affection."

And my desire to laugh began to seem like wisdom. I didn't laugh, but I did grin. I faced him with my grin. "Isaac," I said. "Your feeling is absurd. Ridiculous. You barely know her."

"I realize it sounds strange," he admitted without apology. "But it's what I feel."

"She's a spinster, Isaac. A parched old maid. She's not the marrying kind." I did not point out that he wasn't either.

"I'm sure you're right. But it doesn't change how I feel."

"Do I need to point out that she's white?"

"I'm well aware of that. Which is why I am certain nothing will come of it."

He made no mention of the fact that I was white as well. He seemed to see no common ground between my love for him and his interest in Miss Pangborn. But then, neither did I. There was no way on earth, I told myself, a woman like that could fall in love with a black man, or any man at all.

"Who have you talked to?" I asked. "What have you read?" Had he seen the article that insinuated we lived as husband and wife?

"I read only what's in my heart," he said. "I want to go to Baden. I need to find out what my feelings for this woman mean." His eyes grew very large and wide, a moist look of hunger or maybe fear. "Please, Fitz. I beg you. I have never before felt this way about *anyone*, ever."

And I felt slapped again. I stared at the pleading eyes in an opaque mask of face. I did not know this man. I wondered if I'd ever known him. He suddenly looked so unknowable.

"You actually expect us to go to Baden? Even now when I know why you want to go?"

It took him a moment to understand why I spoke so sharply. "This has nothing to do with my love for you, Fitz. It does not take away from that. I would love a woman differently than I love you. I think. I don't know yet."

Again I wanted to laugh, but it was no laughing matter.

No, here is something I did not make clear in my rush over the years. Perhaps I didn't want to. Two men can be so physically intimate together, so amiably shameless, and still have things they will not say to each other. Isaac and I had no name for what we were. I thought we were above names and what we had was as good as marriage. But what I believed was marriage, Isaac thought was only friendship, one that happened to share a bed.

I looked out at the vast stone square half dissolved in a glaucoma of drizzle.

"If I refuse," I said, "would you go to Baden without me?"

Confusion swept into his face. He was stunned. "No," he said. "I can't imagine going anywhere without you. Ever."

Alarm subsided again. He was so innocent—so stubborn, selfish, and innocent. "Oh, Isaac. My poor Isaac. You don't know what you want, do you?"

He did not take offense. He smiled. A thin, shy smile, as if to acknowledge the absurdity in his heart. "No, I know," he said softly. "I want to go to Baden. With you." The smile tightened, the fearful, hungry look returned to his eyes. "Please, Fitz. I have never begged you for anything before. But I need to discover what this feeling in my heart means."

And I understood. He seemed unknowable to me because he no longer knew his own self.

20

WE returned to our hotel, and that very afternoon I dashed off a letter to Mrs. Tarbell, telling her I was available for a visit if she had room for a guest and his servant. I gave in to Isaac. I granted his request. I would like to claim that I did it out of selfless love, yet my generosity was reluctant, irritable, and more than a little calculated. If I'd thought he might succeed, I would never have agreed. If Miss Pangborn had been black, for instance, I would have refused. Yet Isaac needed to know, and I loved the man and wanted to teach him a lesson. Nobody in the world could love him as I did. I thought I might even enjoy the comedy of this wild-goose chase, the spectacle of two overly earnest people, neither of whom had a shred of humor, clomping around each other in a misunderstood courtship.

During the fortnight while I waited for Mrs. Tarbell's reply, Isaac became more himself again, less despondent, more alert and alive. He became affectionate again, too, perhaps out of gratitude or even anticipation, yet I gave the change my own interpretation: His mind might like the idea of Miss Pangborn, but his body remained in love with the fact of me. I began to feel safer and more amused with the prospect of Baden.

Mrs. Tarbell replied by wire: DELIGHTED. COME SOON. AM BORED TO TEARS.

Obedient to her every whim, Isaac followed Alice's command not to write again, not even to tell her that we were coming.

And so, after a day by boat and another day by rail, Isaac and I crossed the Rhine into a lovely valley on the edge of the Black Forest. Our train climbed up through birch trees and fragrant sprays of pine, and I eagerly hung out the window, elated to be in the land of Schumann, Brahms, and Beethoven—his "Pastorale" Symphony played in my head while a ruined castle appeared and disappeared on the green mountainside. I did not dwell on what had brought us here. The town announced itself up ahead with a gold cupola of a church rising from the trees.

Baden was a quaint toy town of steep roofs and winding streets. The famous resort lay just across a little river, a lovely park of hot springs, expensive hotels, and the Kurhaus—it sounds like German for doghouse, but English speakers called it the Conversation House, the home to restaurants, meeting rooms, and the spa's notorious casino.

As our carriage rolled past the grounds, Isaac sat coolly beside me, showing no excitement, never glancing at the pretty ladies in the dogcarts and landaus that trotted past us.

Mrs. Tarbell had taken a whole villa on the edge of the Kurpark, a huge cuckoo clock stuffed with white silk and chintz. The old tomahawk-faced pagan received us in her drawing room on a throne of pillows, a bandaged foot propped sadly before her, a stack of new French novels bound in yellow paper at her elbow.

"Mr. Boyd!" she cried. "Welcome, sir! You are a sight for weary New York eyes." She knew me by my old name, and I didn't correct her. She had put on weight over the summer, and the thinning hair under her lace cap was refreshed with a macaroni of artificial curls. The bandaged foot that looked like gout was actually an ankle sprained at the swimming baths. "Your man speaks German!" she exclaimed when Isaac exchanged words with the dour housekeeper. "I know only *français*, you see, which the servants claim to have forgotten since Bismarck unified their country. Your man will come in most handy."

Mrs. Tarbell insisted that I stay and talk while "my man" settled our baggage upstairs. "I am starved for good talk," she declared but then proceeded to do all the talking.

"This is your first time in bad old Baden? Oh, a wicked place." She laughed. "There is the gambling, of course. I so enjoy the spectacle of fools being parted from their money. But there are the waters, which are excellent. They produce a glow in the stomach, a vitality in the bowels. You could get the same benefits from a good laxative, of course, but then you wouldn't meet such extraordinary people."

The people, however, were less interesting since the war with France, which had made German vacations unfashionable for the losers. "A French family owns this house," she said, "which is why I was able to rent it on the cheap. But I so miss the French. They brought the most wonderful scandals." She sighed wistfully. "That's why I'm overjoyed that you are come, Mr. Boyd. I am starved for amusement. There is nobody here but rich Germans, richer Jews, shabby Russians, and one pesky family of Americans."

"Oh?" I said. "Anyone I might know?"

Mrs. Tarbell burped one ugly syllable: "Botts."

"Never heard of them," I replied. I was glad that Isaac wasn't present to hear the news. But I would tell him they were still here. When the time came.

Mrs. Tarbell immediately wanted music, not magic music but something gay and French. I played her some Offenbach and tried to enjoy the cheap champagne that purled under my fingers.

A young man entered the room, attracted by the music, a large fellow with a pear-shaped body, small head, and wispy beard. "Have you met my son, Titus?" asked Mrs. Tarbell. I never had, although my spirit had discussed him constantly with his mother. He studied me coldly and glumly mumbled a greeting. I wondered if I'd inadvertently spilled the beans on his private life, but the only vice

Mrs. Tarbell ever ascribed to either of her children was dullness. Her great fear was that people would marry them for *her* money.

"Oh, Poodle," she chided. "Can't you be sociable? He's been so gloomy ever since his sister got married," she explained. "Now he has only his shocking mother for company."

To prove her impropriety, she insisted "my man" dine with us. "We are all Americans," she said, "and he can tell Cook how I like my beefsteak." So there were four at dinner. Again Mrs. Tarbell did most of the talking. She addressed Isaac as "Mr. Kemp," spoke through him to her servants, and asked if he knew the rumors about the parentage of Alexandre Dumas. She seemed quite pleased with herself, tickled to have a Negro at her table.

After dinner Titus proposed that they take me to the Kurhaus. "F-F-For the m-m-music." He had a terrible stutter whenever he was nervous. I wondered why he feared the Kurhaus.

"You take him, Poodle. I've had my music for the day. I'd rather not hobble among Hebrews and Prussians tonight."

I invited my valet along. "To translate," I explained.

I thought Poodle must be warming to me, but he said nary a word as we strolled through the park to the Kurhaus. Isaac walked a few feet behind us.

The white building with colonnades looked more like a royal palace than a house of chance. We went up to the wide terrace beside it, a sandy space full of well-dressed water-holers, hundreds of them, loitering in an open-air salon surrounded by mountains. On a smaller terrace above ours, under a pagoda roof, a full orchestra performed an exuberant Strauss waltz. Nobody danced but only stood or sat in their elegant clothes, making small talk as the sunlight faded to a warm glow of candlelight. The men wore timeless black, except for a few officers in blue-and-gold uniforms, but the women wore violent new colors—chartreuse, vermilion, or mauve—in superfluous swags of silk that were rucked or pleated in front and gathered in back for bustles and trains, suggesting a herd of brightly painted snails.

I wondered if they were why Poodle had wanted to come here: The awkward boy was smitten with a pretty baroness or rouged courtesan and couldn't mention it to his mother. But he did not appear to know anyone and only stood by the far side of the terrace, gazing now and then at the casino, which was closed for the night, its stained-glass windows glowing like mammoth playing cards. Isaac and I stayed by him, and I surveyed the gaudy fashions and flat German faces, looking for American forms, listening for a tell-tale twang among the polyglot jumble of German, Italian, and languages I'd never heard. When Isaac didn't bring up the obvious question, I finally asked Poodle, "Your mother mentioned an American family. Are they here tonight?"

Poodle drowsily looked around. "Naaaw," he said. "Though I sometimes see the husband at the r-r-roulette wheel."

"Ah, you're a gaming man, Mr. Tarbell?"

I said it only to make conversation, but Poodle's sleepy eyes snapped open. "Do not tell M-M-Mother. But yes. I am working out a system. A p-p-pattern." He swallowed hard and said, "Your sp-p-pirit? Can he foretell n-n-numbers?"

So that was why Poodle wanted my company. Well, it was good to learn that he had another demon besides dullness.

"Alas, Mr. Tarbell. As your mother must've told you, my spirit is a vague, undependable creature. It is useless for something as precise as the destination of a roulette ball."

"You sure? Ah. Hmm. Pity." He began to mumble to himself.

"I take it that your mother doesn't want you to gamble?" I said. "That surprises me. She's such a connoisseur of vice."

Poodle frowned. "Other p-p-people's vices. Not her own b-b-blood."

Our terrace parapet overlooked a sweep of lawn, with a dark hill looming above it. From the corner of my eye I caught sight of a little girl in white far below, skipping along a gravel path. She was followed by a lean woman in brown. The woman did not glance up at the terrace, at least not while I watched, but I recognized her prim little march. I considered keeping the sight to myself but dutifully smiled at Isaac and nodded at the lawn.

He looked over his shoulder, gazed a moment, and faced the crowd again, without any change in expression. Then he took a long, deep breath. I could almost hear the thudding of his heart.

He didn't say a word about her, and neither did I, until we were back at the villa and "my man" and I unpacked our clothes. "Your friend is still here," I said dryly.

"So she is," said Isaac. "She most certainly is," with a note of giddiness that made me want to kick him.

Monday, September 6

A most irksome development: Mr. Kemp, the man on the boat, is here in Baden. I saw him on the terrace of the Conversation House this evening when I took Isabella for her walk. He was far off, & my first thought was only that any gentleman of color made me think of him. But there was no mistaking the longhaired fannikins at his side. I hope Mrs. Botts will not learn of his presence, or she will think that he came here for my sake or even that I suggested a visit.

21

THE next day, while I entertained our patroness after breakfast, Isaac did not go off to hunt for his beloved, as I expected, but remained in his room, which was on the floor above mine, in the servants' quarters. When I finished reading Mrs. Tarbell's musical palm—she wanted to know if her daughter was happy with her new husband in New York, but only laughed at my spirit's "Home, Sweet Home" variations—I went upstairs and found Isaac stretched out on his bed, mooning unhappily at the ceiling.

It took him all morning to work up enough nerve to make the first move. After lunch he idly declared that he might take a stroll around town. He asked me to come with him.

"Oh, yes," I said. "Let the old horse get a look at the new one. Get his opinion before you make your purchase."

"Don't mock me, Fitz."

"Was I mocking? I meant only friendly banter."

"I don't even know if I'll run into her."

"But that's why you're going, isn't it?"

"Well, yes."

Of course I went with him. If Isaac ran into Miss Pangborn, I wanted to be there to measure the temperature of her courtesy, the coldness of her smile, and perhaps get some inkling of what the devil he saw in her.

We walked first to the Hotel Royal, then the Trinkenhalle—the Pump Room—and over the creek they called a river into town.

"I'm sorry to treat you like a servant with the Tarbells," I told him. "I hope it's not too humiliating."

"Not in the least," he replied, much to my disappointment. I had mentioned it only to rub his nose in his reduced status.

The winding cobblestone streets were sprinkled with elegant spa snails out in their summer poplins and parasols. We circled the Friedrichsbad, more like a cathedral than a swimming bath, and passed the pawnshops, which appeared to do a very brisk trade, without a glimpse of governess.

"You don't want to leave a note at her hotel?" I asked, not a suggestion, merely a question.

"No. I need to run into her by chance. I don't want Miss Pangborn to suspect that I knew she was still here. It will suggest I came for her sake. Which would be much too forward."

I was glad that Isaac expressed no burning impatience to see the woman of his dreams, as if she were more whim than passion. And a leisurely wild-goose chase seemed as good a way as any to see Baden. We crossed the river again and walked along it, away from the Kurpark down a long, shady avenue of chestnut trees. There were villas outside the trees, and an abbey, dozing prettily in the summer afternoon. Then I heard a piano playing. Softly chiming notes drifted through the warm air, a scale of notes, three-steps-forward-two-steps-back, that quietly gathered into something like a tune. Up ahead in the avenue, as if part of the tune, I saw a sphere like a spirit, a spirit like a balloon. Another followed, and another. A series of fairylike globes floated from sunlight into shade, glossy, pearl gray, solid. When one brushed a bough and popped, a small milky cloud uncurled in the air. They were soap bubbles full of smoke.

Curious, wanting to learn the source of both bubbles and music, I stepped through the trees. A house stood beside the avenue, with French windows that opened on an arbor. A shadow played a piano in a shadowy room, while out in the sunlit arbor a middle-aged man with longish hair sat at a table with a large cigar, a dish of suds, and a bubble ring. I was too thrown by the sight of a grown man blowing bubbles to recognize him at first. The famous bald brow was still framed in hair, and he had not yet grown his unmistakable haystack of beard. But I slowly placed the smooth, placid face from his portrait in the shop window at Schirmer's back in New York. It was the apostle of Beethoven, the friend of Schumann: Brahms himself. Remembering how I saw the great composer when he was still clean-shaven, I now feel that I glimpsed grandeur in its underclothes. But there he was, half listening to a friend at a piano while he idled away a summer afternoon with bubbles and cigar. I was embarrassed to have caught him at such a childish occupation. When Isaac came up behind me, I shooed him back and hurriedly returned to the chestnut trees before the Titan caught us spying.

"Brahms," I whispered reverently. "Johannes Brahms. I didn't know Brahms lived in Baden."

"The Lullaby Man?" said Isaac. He could be with me all these years and know the world's greatest living composer as only the author of a music-box tune. "You didn't want to speak to him?"

"No, I can't. I don't speak German."

"I could translate for you."

"Yes?" I liked the idea of speaking with Brahms through Isaac. "But not today. Not while he's blowing bubbles. We'll meet him again under better circumstances."

I wondered what I might say to Brahms, if I even had the right to speak to a real artist, as we resumed our stroll and I actually forgot what we were chasing today.

But Baden was a small, tight affair. There was not much to do with a young child except take her for walks. Sooner or later we were bound to run into our wild goose.

We had returned to the Kurpark when we finally spotted them. They were outside the Hotel Royal, on a stretch of lawn as green as a billiard table, a little girl in white and a woman in brown.

More sparrow than wild goose, Miss Pangborn faded into the landscape, but the child stood out like a chrysanthemum. She had a hoop and stick, only she did not roll the hoop but used it like a jump rope. Miss Pangborn appeared to disapprove of this misuse.

Isaac struck off across the lawn, and I saw the governess turn and see him. She looked startled. She turned as if to run, but then stood her ground and faced him.

"Oh! Oh? Oh," she said as we approached. *"Mr. Kemp?"* she declared, as if finally recognizing him.

I came up behind him.

"And Dr. August. Ah. You are in Baden?"

Isaac said, "Uh, yes. We are."

"Hello, Miss Pangborn." I smiled. "Fancy seeing you again."

She actually convinced me that she didn't already know we were here. But she did know, didn't she?

She did not shake hands with either of us. She betrayed no hint of sentimental interest in Isaac. And believe me, I was looking. But the pale face in steel-rimmed spectacles and flat hat did not seem as dry and pinched as I remembered. Her hardness was softened by a new sadness in her eyes.

"What a splendid surprise to meet you again," said Isaac.

"Oh, not so surprising," she factually replied. "Americans abroad travel such a small compass." She refused to play catch with the ball he had tossed her. "And what brings you to Baden?"

Her matter-of-factness left Isaac dumb, so I answered. "We're the guests of Mrs. Horace Tarbell."

"I don't know her. But I know nobody here. I do not go out."

The little girl came over and poked her rabbity nose at us from a nest of blond curls. Miss Pangborn put her hands on the girl's shoulders to assure her we were all right, though the child stared at us fearlessly.

"What a pretty little girl," I said, to fill the silence.

Isabella gave her curls a proud toss. "I certainly am."

"And not too spoiled." I laughed, but nobody laughed with me.

"Do you come here every day at this time?" asked Isaac.

"No. Oh. Sometimes. It depends on Isabella."

"How long will you be staying in Baden?" he asked.

"That depends on Isabella's parents. And yourselves?"

"Uh, we don't know yet," said Isaac. "No. We don't." His purpose for coming here was as dry as a desert, and he went silent again.

Miss Pangborn saw her opportunity. "If you will excuse us, sirs, Isabella and I should return to the hotel for supper. In case our paths don't cross again while you're here, I hope you have a pleasant stay." She did not shake hands with us but kept her hands locked on her charge's shoulders.

"And you, too, Miss Pangborn," I said with a happy lift of my hat. "Come along, Isaac."

We went twenty yards before Isaac stole a last look at her over his shoulder. I looked, too, but the governess kept her brown back to us as she shepherded Isabella toward the hotel.

"She barely knew me," he said. "Even with my letter. She hardly remembered me. I was sure I made an impression. As she did upon me." I didn't believe for a minute that she'd forgotten him—one did not forget Isaac—but there was no need to tell him that. "What a dreamer I've been," he said. "What a fool. We came all this way for nothing."

"Live and learn," I said. "And no harm done. After all, it got us to Baden. And I, for one, am happy to be here."

And I *was* happy now, perfectly content, my only worry that Isaac might fall back into his London melancholy. He was sad that night, but with a bitter amusement about his disappointment. "You were right, Fitz. It was absurd. Utterly absurd," he said when he came down to my room, ostensibly to put his master to bed. "The woman I painted in my mind was pure make-believe. A delusion."

The next day, when Mrs. Tarbell went down to the Pump Room for her daily pint of warm salty water, she invited us along so that Poodle might take me and Isaac, as our translator, over to the Kurhaus casino. "Poodle's never been, so it will be a chance for all of you to visit those lurid velvet stews."

At the Pump Room, Poodle tenderly helped his mother out of her carriage into a wheelchair handled by a German white jacket, bade her a loving good-bye, and raced us eagerly down the path to his secret pleasure dome.

We entered a high-ceilinged room full of bright chandeliers and gilded ulcerations. Even in the morning it was busy, a hive of sighs and murmurs over the clack of roulette wheels, fitful ringing of coins, and dry recitations of croupiers. The croupiers still spoke French, the language of chance as well as love, and they looked French, too, with the feline whiskers of the defeated Napoleon III. There was a greater human variety here than on the terrace in the evenings—English tradesmen, Cuban grandees, shabby Russian ladies and their shabbier men—all standing at the long green tables in a trance. The scene combined the agitation of a stock exchange with the strange, reverent hush of church. But if Providence is a higher form of chance, we were all very close to God.

"There's your American," said Poodle, pointing out a businessman with a handlebar mustache and plaid waistcoat. He stood at a baccarat table with glum hands stuffed in his pockets.

Isaac gave the man a quick, cursory glance. The Bottses meant nothing to him now.

I was in a celebratory mood, so I found the place more amusing than sinister. We strolled from table to table, looking over shoulders, watching people arrange their stacks of coin, mark their notepads, then bet by impulse or calculation, losing either way. Poodle explained the rules to each game.

"You don't want to t-t-try one?" he asked me. "Your spirit is n-n-not making suggestions?"

"My spirit speaks to me only at the piano," I replied.

"In c-c-case he does speak—" He placed a large gold coin in my hand, a new ten-mark piece. There is nothing like foreign currency to bring out the magical thisness of money. I turned the smooth, stamped weight around in my fingers, a gold wafer like a small, flat watch—I could almost feel it ticking in my palm.

We stood by a roulette table with a grid of red or black numbers painted on green felt. The wheel began to spin, and a flurry of hands, like a flutter of pigeon wings, rapidly distributed coins over the checkerboard.

Isaac frowned at me. I enjoyed his look of concern, his brotherly regard. He was all mine now.

"Lucky in love, unlucky at cards," I declared and set my coin on the nearest vacant spot, a happy sacrifice to love.

As the silver ball skittered and bounced around the wheel, an orbit against an orbit, a call went up through the room: "Doktor August. Herr Kemp. Doktor August. Herr Kemp." A bellboy in the livery of the Hotel Royal strolled through with a silver dish in his hand, dryly repeating our names as if he'd been saying them for hours. German rendered my name unrecognizable.

Isaac called the boy over, took a little envelope from his dish, and opened it. I looked over his shoulder.

Dr. August & Mr. Kemp, sirs,

Mrs. Phineas D. Botts requests that I invite you to join us to-morrow for a picnic in the mountains. The invitation is also warmly extended to your hostess and her family. If this is suitable, the carriage will pick you up at noon. I have advised my mistress that you might not be available, but she will understand if you decline.

Formally yours,

Miss A. Pangborn

There was a great moan all around the table, as if the other players had read the note with us. The croupier irritably called out to me.

"Boyd!" said Poodle. "Wake up! You won!"

A wooden blade on a long handle shoved a loose clatter of gold coins to my side of the table. The silver ball rode silently in the wheel, around and around, lodged neatly in my number.

22

VERY well, then. The story behind the note? Let's hear it from the wild goose's mouth.

                                        Tuesday, September 7

As I feared, I have encountered Mr. Kemp. He & his friend happened upon me & Isabella this afternoon in the park. We were most polite & made no mention of Mrs. Satan or her newspaper. Afterward I asked Isabella not to mention these men to her mother, or she might think we were rudely accosted. A futile request. We were no sooner back in our rooms than Isabella declared, "We met a nigger in fancy dress & a man whose hair is longer than mine! And they know Alice ever so well." Mrs. Botts demanded to know who they were. I could not successfully lie, so I admitted that these were the men from the boat. "If you want to mix with trash, that is your business," she declared. "But you are not to expose my child to your riffraff." She ordered me to avoid these men, & I assured her I would. Truth be told, I am glad to follow her command, as it takes a confusing situation out of my hands. Who would have guessed idle intercourse at sea would lead to such bother?

Wednesday, September 8

I cannot win. I am caught in snares whichever way I turn. When the Bottses returned from the café last night, Mrs. called me out & said, "You silly girl. Why didn't you tell me your friends were the guests of Mrs. Tarbell?" When I said I didn't know what that would alter, she said Mrs. Tarbell was a famous New Yorker, a society woman who had taken a whole house for the summer. Her friends must be very important. "We have wanted to meet her since we arrived, but she only puts us off." She considered it further during the night & this morning proposed that I invite these men to tea. "Or no, a picnic. A picnic would be a finer occasion, & perhaps Madam Tarbell will join them." When I repeated that I hardly knew these men, she said, "Don't play the milksop with me, missy." She stood by while I wrote the note, so I couldn't tell them the truth behind this invitation. After she gave the note to a bellboy, she called me an ornament to the household, which emboldened me to suggest I would not be needed on this outing. "Of course you'll come. They are your friends." Mr. Botts, however, refuses to join us, claiming he has better occupations than courting snobs.

Ah, the ironies acccumulate. Fashionable New York refused to have anything to do with Mrs. Horace Tarbell, but the Bottses didn't know that. When I told Mrs. Tarbell about the invitation, she said, "I didn't come to Baden to mix with nobodies from Hartford. But you should go. I understand the mountains are beautiful. And they invited your valet? How curious. They must do things differently in Hartford."

Of course Isaac wanted us to go—"This is her idea," he insisted. "She wants to make amends"—and of course I gave in. The win at roulette was a bad omen, yet I put more trust in what I knew of human nature than I did in superstition. And besides, my good luck had been at roulette, not cards.

The next day at noon a hired landau drew up outside the villa, an open boat of a carriage with four white horses, a uniformed driver, and a footman. Mrs. Botts and Isabella sat in back in matching white dresses with the dour little governess in brown. I made my excuses for Mrs. Tarbell, who was no doubt watching from a window. When Mrs. Botts suggested that Isaac might be happier sitting with the driver, the driver let fly with *"Nein, nicht"* and words only Isaac understood, although his meaning was spelled out when the footman held his nose. "What airs these Germans put on," said Mrs. Botts. "Oh, very well. There is room for you with Alice."

Isaac sat beside his delusion, the two of them facing us with the picnic basket between. I faced forward in the seat of honor between Mrs. Botts and Isabella.

"Such a pleasure to meet you, Dr. August," declared Mrs. Botts as we trotted off. "I have heard so much about you."

Alice's censorious frown made clear that Mrs. Botts had heard nothing from her.

"Mrs. Tarbell must be thrilled to have her own pianist at her command. Music is the key to the soul, don't you think? Isabella, dear. Don't crowd the good doctor."

Mrs. Botts was not the gorgon one might imagine from Alice's diary. She was quite beautiful, an American Gainsborough, and young. In their white ruffles she and her daughter resembled a pair of coconut cakes. She was, however, an unhappy woman. She didn't know she was unhappy, but I could tell. I'd made a career out of reading women's hearts. She was one of those wives who work at pleasure in order to hide unhappiness from themselves and can be a wonderful company so long as they get their way. I might add in her defense that the irritable new governess would have been a thorn in any household.

We did not go very far, only five miles or so up into a vista of piney mountains, but it could not have been a pleasant ride for either Alice or Isaac. They were unable to so much as glance at each other without the rest of us noticing, so they sat there stiffly, side by side, staring at the dust swirling behind the carriage.

We came to a mountain lookout, where we got down and stood

on the rocks, looking out, while the driver and footman arranged rugs and pillows and dishes in a grassy clearing under white birch trees across the road.

When we sat down to eat, Isabella stood behind Isaac and bathed her hands in his hair. "Oooh, like a sheep," she said. "Baa, baa, black sheep, have you any wool?" Isaac suffered her with a sickly smile before Mrs. Botts took out a handkerchief and told her daughter to wipe her hands before she touched any food. Alice said nothing.

"Another sandwich, Miss Pangborn?" Isaac offered, and Alice shook her head. "More lemonade?" Again she refused. After ten excruciating minutes of this deaf-dumb-and-blindness, Isaac excused himself to take another look at the mountains.

Meanwhile Isabella turned her attention to me. "Rapunzel, Rapunzel," she murmured, running her hands through my sheaves of long hair.

This time Mrs. Botts let her daughter maul to her heart's content. "I regret that I have not heard you perform," she told me. "The mister and I rarely get to New York. Will you be offering a musicale while you're with Mrs. Tarbell? Please ask that good lady to invite us."

I assured her I would as I pretended to cuddle her darling in an attempt to grip the brat's wrists and stop her pawing.

"We so love good music," she added and proceeded to tell me about an excellent brass band in Hartford.

I was too involved with Mrs. Botts and her octopus child to notice that Miss Pangborn had slipped away.

Thursday, September 9

I am returned from our picnic. It was even more confusing than anticipated. I was forced to sit with Mr. Kemp on our ride into the hills—of no matter to me, yet Mrs. Botts placed him there because she thinks so little of my station. I was most glad when we arrived at our view & could climb down, though I was too wrought up to note the mountain wildnesses. I made myself as small as possible while we took our lunch in the grass. Mrs. Botts & Dr. August prattled endless nonsense at each other—they are so alike—& when Mr. Kemp went off to look at the view again, I saw my chance to escape & went off *in the opposite direction*, requiring a breath of solitude to steel myself for more of this company. But I had not gone fifty yards when I heard someone loudly break the brush behind me. As I feared, it was Mr. Kemp in his bowler hat. He was most polite— "Pardon me if I intrude on your reverie"—as was I, yet I confess that I was frightened to find myself alone in the woods with a man of his race, despite his tweed suit & good manners. I gently moved us toward the clearing, where I could see the others, but stopped, afraid they might see us in conversation. It was *he* who brought up his letter and apologized for writing. I assured him I knew his intentions were good & thanked him for his concern. And then, I know not why, perhaps because we rode a tide of apology, I said, "I am sorry if I seemed brusque yesterday. But I am always occupied when I am with my charge." The spark of interest in his look made me fear I had said too much, but all he said in reply was that Isabella appeared a delightful child. "Oh, no," I told him. "She is a vain little monster." "Like her mother?" he said. I cannot describe how it gladdened me to hear him say that. I peered through the foliage to ensure Mrs. Botts could not hear us before I unpacked my heart about my situation. He was most sympathetic. But he would be, he who suffered a far worse servitude than mine. I found myself warming to him as I had on the boat during our literary chats.

When it came time to rejoin the others, I added, with a smile, that the world was indeed a small place for us both to be in Baden. "I would like to say it was chance," he replied. "But I can't. Because I came in hope that I might see you again."

My heart leaped into my throat, but I quickly swallowed it. "But why?" I said. My look of alarm appeared to frighten him, & his face turned apologetic, & he said, "We came for other reasons, too. But I did hope to renew our acquaintance."

"Whatever the cause, I am glad of it," I rapidly replied, "because there was a book by Emerson that I had wanted to recommend but did not get a chance on the boat—" I had led us back to the clearing as I spoke & put on my most proper, disinterested voice. The others made no comment on our absence, though Dr. August did give his friend a chiding, schoolmarmish look.

I had hoped that writing this out would end my confusion, but it only deepens it. I know that I should feel insulted a Negro is drawn to me. Yet I don't. Instead I feel—what? I am confused & alarmed, but what alarms me most is that I feel—not flattered, no, but noticed, & pleased to be noticed. This is how seducers work, of course, only Mr. Kemp appears much too shy to be a seducer. What does he intend? Only friendship, I am certain. We are both alone in a wicked world & need a friend. The thought that a man of his race would think of courting me is inconceivable.

Yet she has already conceived of it.

Most romances begin in flirtation or fights. This one began in apologies. It was a courtship between two mice muffled in enormous courtesies like suits of armor.

Yes, I'm sure I gave Isaac a dirty look when they came out of the birches, but I remember Alice appearing as cold and stiff as ever. I was confident that there'd been no attempt at a kiss. When we returned to the Tarbells after the picnic, Isaac reported only a courteous yet brief exchange with Miss Pangborn. I took him at his word and went back with Poodle to the casino that afternoon, where I made a single bet: ten marks, this time at baccarat. Again I won, which is to say I lost. My luck held at the gaming tables, which should have warned me that it was running against me elsewhere.

23

Friday, September 10

Mrs. Botts remains pleased by yesterday's picnic & awaits an inevitable invitation to the Tarbell villa. "Your friends will tell her what genteel company we are." But I have put yesterday out of my thoughts. When I took Isabella for her walk this afternoon, we returned to the park outside the hotel where we encountered Mr. Kemp & his friend the other day, but the gentlemen did not appear. I had not even considered the possibility until Isabella declared, "No fancy-dress nigger today." I reprimanded her sharply, telling her the man had a name & it was Mr. Kemp.

Evening, 11 P.M.

Shortly after I made the above entry, an invitation did arrive—addressed to me! Mr. Kemp & Dr. August asked if I were free to join them for the evening concert at the Conversation House. *"You!"* cried Mrs. Botts. "After *I* took them on that hideously expensive picnic!"—Mr. Botts had had words with her when he saw the bill. I pointed out that there was no mention of Mrs. Tarbell & perhaps they were saving her, Mrs. Botts, for a more prestigious occasion. When I offered to decline, Mrs. Botts said I should go & press them to remind her to their hostess. I waited for her to express concern over the unseemliness of a lady appearing in public with two men

& no chaperone, but she didn't. And the truth be known, I wanted to go. I surprised myself with how badly I wanted it. Yes, it would be nice to see Mr. Kemp again, if not his friend, though the chief reason is, night after night, I have heard the distant music & regretted an unattached young woman could not attend those concerts.

They were waiting for me in the lobby, Mr. Kemp looking quite distinguished, Dr. August glum & out of sorts. Neither gentleman offered me his arm on our walk to the Conversation House, of which I am glad, but they did not walk on either side as I expected, but with Mr. Kemp in the center—how odd what the mind singles out for comment—saying little except words on the mild evening. I regretted bringing my umbrella. I managed to be brave despite my fear & excitement, until we arrived at the terrace & I saw ladies & gentlemen dressed in the finery of a society ball. "I thought this a simple outdoor concert!" I exclaimed in a whisper. "I am dressed so plain. People will stare at me!" And Mr. Kemp, in his kindest, most considerate voice, said, "I am sorry. I did not think of that. But then people are always staring at *me*." That made me ashamed, & I steeled my will to stay, even as I looked around for ladies dressed as plainly as I.

The chairs were not set in rows but scattered hither & yon. We took three near the bandstand—again Mr. Kemp sat in the middle—& Dr. August asked for my favorite composer. When I said I loved all music, the little musician sniffed that such love was no better than indifference. I had been striving to think kindly of him, yet decided it not worth the effort.

I was delighted, however, when the music started. I have never heard so many instruments playing together, loud & full & rich, such a transcendent sound that I didn't need to know its name. To sit in front of such beautiful noise as the night settles in, with a considerate new friend at your side, was a fine experience. "Very nice," I said when I thought it was over, & the little artist sneered, "That was only the first movement, my dear. There are three more." I hated his tone but decided to be pleased there was more. Halfway through the next "movement," however, I had lost my rapture, & my attention began to wander—to the stars & people. I told Mr. Kemp how lovely it all was, & he said he was pleased I enjoyed it. "Shush," went Dr. August, glaring at us, though people all around had been chatting all along. Refusing to be shushed, I asked Mr. Kemp if he came every night, & he said no, only when Dr. August— "If the two of you must talk," the little man hissed, "will you do it elsewhere!" I would have been furious, but Mr. Kemp bowed to his friend & gestured toward a corner of the terrace. I nodded and stood up with him. "Is your friend always so rude?" I asked when we were out of earshot. Mr. Kemp defended him, explaining that music was to him what prayer is to others.

Needless to say, my temper was not just over their talking during the music, which did have a name, thank you, Schumann's "Rhine" Symphony. I had agreed to ask Miss Pangborn to join us that evening only because I was certain she'd refuse, and Isaac would finally get it through his skull this was a lost cause. That she actually said yes was the first indication her stiff little spine might be more flexible than she pretended. When I watched her and Isaac on the terrace, prim and proper yet clearly at ease with each another, I finally understood that this sparrow in spectacles posed a real threat.

I told him his friend seems to treat him badly. "Not at all," he replied. "He treats me as an equal, a brother. My situation is not like yours." We talked about that again. Mr. Kemp appears to enjoy lending an ear to the sorrows of life with the Bottses. We stood by a stone rail, where we could listen to the music or talk as we pleased. It was quite dark, & yet I felt perfectly safe with Mr. Kemp, what with other persons standing by, also in pairs.

When the concert was over, Mr. Kemp took me back to his friend so they could escort me home. Dr. August was more polite, but with a sting in his manner. "I am not feeling well. If you will excuse me, I must return to the Tarbells. Isaac can walk you back without me."

His challenging look made me suspect this was a punishment: He thought I would be humiliated to return to the hotel alone with a Negro. Such a petty man to strike at me for failing to share his reverence of music. But I accepted the challenge, curtly told him I hoped he'd feel better, & left with Mr. Kemp. Walking in the dark with the glow of hotels all around us & other couples strolling on the path, I felt no shame over being alone with him. He did not offer his arm but did offer to carry my umbrella. I told him this had been a fine evening & thanked him for his conversation. "Yes, I enjoyed it, too. I hope we can do it again." I told him I took Isabella for her walk every day at eleven & at four, & he said he would keep that in mind. "But you are greatly occupied when you are with her," he said. "Do you never go out alone?" I told him there was no place for me to go, though I was free from one to three when Isabella took her nap. "Would you care to see the cathedral?" he said. "I understand it's quite important. I could meet you there tomorrow, & we could look at it together." We were nearing the porticoes of the Royal & would soon lose our privacy in its glaring light. So I said quickly & thoughtlessly, "Yes. That might be nice. I will try to be there." He broke into a grin, & the grin alarmed me. But he set it to rights again by asking if we should say good night here or did I want him to escort me into the lobby? He understands my delicate situation. "This is fine, thank you," I said & held out my hand for my umbrella. He misunderstood & took my hand in his. He shook it, very gently, but the warmth of his palm in mine seemed to run up my arm into my heart & b———. "Good night, sir," I said, took my umbrella, & went in.

It is after one, & I have stayed up much too late writing this out. I will be in a poor state tomorrow for Isabella's morning lessons & will need a nap myself when she takes hers. I doubt that I will be able to meet Mr. Kemp.

Meanwhile, in a cuckoo-clock villa on the other side of the Kurpark, "the friend" lay in bed, unable to sleep, waiting for Isaac to return. How curious to hear Alice's account of that very hour. It makes one feel omniscient, if only about the past. And she was right: I deliberately abandoned them after the concert as a challenge, a hostile act. She was wrong only about my reasons.

I finally heard Isaac come in, but he did not stop by my room on his way upstairs. It was not a good sign. And the little bluenose was not as cold as she pretended; only the coldest heart could put a stop to Isaac's stubborn infatuation. I lay there another hour or so, wondering, worrying, wondering if I should be worried. Finally I could think of no way to put my fears to rest except to visit Isaac.

I did not put on a robe or slippers but went upstairs to the servants' floor in my nightshirt. The narrow hall was lit by one flickering lamp and full of German snores. I opened Isaac's door without knocking, slipped in, and closed it. His room was dark but small, and I could feel my way around as my eyes grew accustomed to the shadows. I found his bed and sat on it. I placed my hand on his warm chest. He woke up. He showed no alarm to find me there but lay perfectly still.

"Isaac," I whispered, "I need to be with you tonight."

"No, Fitz. I can't do that."

I was afraid to ask if he meant "tonight" or "ever again."

"Very well, then. Can I kiss you while I do myself?" I moved to climb into bed with him.

He blocked me with his arm. "Please, Fitz. No."

I'd anticipated that, but it hurt more than I'd expected, hurt and angered me. I snatched the matches on the table by his bed. His face flared into view, and he covered his eyes while I lit the candle. "Can I at least look at you?" I demanded.

He didn't understand what I meant until I hitched my nightshirt up around my waist.

"I need to look at you while I do myself," I said.

He covered his eyes again: The sight of my privates hurt him as much as the light had. And it was obscene. I wanted to hurt him with my obscenity.

"No, Fitz. Stop it," he whispered. "Now!"

"Why? You used to do it for me. Remember?" And I pulled my nightshirt over my head so he could see my entire body—long hair, bony chest, sable crotch—and remember everything he'd ever done with it.

He yanked his blanket over his face. "No, Fitz! Stop it!" he hissed underneath. "Do you think so little of me! Have you no respect for what I want!"

"This is what I want tonight! This is what I need!"

But nothing was happening there. I was too upset and only jiggled a limp pizzle.

"Very well," I said. "If it's so awful for you."

He lowered his blanket, saw I'd obeyed him, and was relieved, even though I still sat naked in the candlelight.

"So. Did you kiss her tonight?" The nude demon on his bed dared to speak of his pure ideal.

"No."

"But you say you love her?"

"Yes."

"What good is love if you can't kiss her?"

"I want to help her. I want to rescue her. She's in a dreadful situation."

"If you want her so badly, take her into the woods, kiss her, and have your way with her. See if you still love her then."

"It's not that kind of love. I want to save her. I want to marry her."

It was like talking to a wall. "She'll never marry you."

He didn't hear that either. "I want a wife, Fitz. I want a family and children. Can't you understand that?"

"No."

"It's different for you. You have your music, your piano, your spirit. I have nothing."

He had me, but that wasn't enough. "You could be a public speaker. If you gave it a chance."

"No. That was a lie. I need the truth. I want a true life, the life that God intends all simpler men to have."

When he dragged God into it, I knew there was no reasoning with him. I felt like crying yet didn't. If I had burst into tears and sobs, would I have persuaded him of my love? Probably not. He knew I loved him, and it didn't matter.

"And this?" I said. "Remember this?" I flipped myself at him. "This doesn't mean anything to you now?"

He didn't even look at it. "I loved you that way because I love you as a friend," he said. "And *you* wanted me to love you that way. But I can't love your way now. I have found someone I love in my way."

You cannot imagine how shattering it is to be told that seven years of embraces were only a favor, a kindness, a lie. I was devastated. He had said something similar in London, yet not so bluntly: I love you as a friend, I would love her as wife. I could no longer dismiss such talk as innocent confusion. He knew his heart quite clearly now.

I gathered my nightshirt off the floor and shook it over my pathetic, rejected body. "You are making a mistake, Isaac. You will not only break my heart but your own as well." And I left, pulling the door shut before he could answer me.

24

THAT'S one gloomy tune your spirit's playing today," said Mrs. Tarbell the next morning. "I hope it's not for me."

It wasn't. When I shuffled through my musical tarot cards after breakfast, a new nocturne turned up, unbidden and unexpected, a forlorn thing of unresolved chords and dying bass, with one thin phrase piping in the treble distance, growing happier the farther off it went, a song of farewell. The message was for me, of course, my spirit announcing Isaac wouldn't break his heart, only mine. He would win his love, and I would lose him.

You ask why my spirit didn't warn me sooner? No, it's a perfectly reasonable question. If he were truly omniscient, he would have warned me off Baden altogether. But Metaphysicals can be as fallible as mortals, as fickle in their silences, as obtuse as village gossips. Maybe he'd tried to tell me before, but I'd been too cocky to hear. My spirit spoke loudest when my spirits were low. Crushed by last night's visit to Isaac, I finally heard the terrible news. It was bizarre how quickly my sunny confidence gave way to grim resignation. But all the signs were against me: the gaming tables, Isaac's certainty, and my own music.

Now it was my turn to become despondent and withdrawn. In the days that followed, I played for Mrs. Tarbell in the mornings. I went to concerts in the evening, alone. I continued to visit the casino every afternoon with Poodle, hoping against hope to lose there, because it would be a sign that I might not lose Isaac. But cards and spirit were both against me. I tried other games besides baccarat and roulette, but I continued to win. I did not wager huge amounts, only ten marks a bet and one bet a day, but I amassed several hundred marks that week. Poodle began to bet exactly as I did, with larger stakes, so he got rich off my misery.

Meanwhile Isaac met with his governess. I didn't want to know what went on between them, and he didn't volunteer any reports. But he continued to confuse me. The day after our argument he invited me to come with him to see the cathedral. Knowing his feelings about the Romish religion, I could well guess what this visit was for and told him no.

Saturday, September 11

The Cathedral of Baden is most impressive. I had expected a cold & gloomy place, like the cult itself, but found instead a white interior of light & air, which I learn is the style in this part of Germany. Oh, yes, I visited after all. I was alert & restless once I put Isabella down for her nap & walked into town with no qualms except that anyone seeing me enter the church might think me a papist. Mr. Kemp was in the vestibule with a monk who was to be our guide. He spoke to the monk in German & had removed his hat. I wondered if he were papist himself, but he put my mind at ease by commenting that so much gold leaf could only blind one to God. "One must stand free & alone before God," he said, "without priests or masters." The monk, whose breath smelled of brandy, I am certain, pointed out crypts & such in chapels along the walls. A mass of limbs brought a blush to my cheek, before I understood they were babies, a cloud of plaster cherubs floating over an altar. Mr. Kemp gazed at them most fondly. I found myself frowning at a figure of Our Savior. The Germans tend to treat the Crucifixion as gruesome, but this one was quite—there is no other word—licentious. The glazed plaster was rendered with unbecoming attention to musculature, the artist ignoring the sorrows of the spirit to dwell on its flesh. It did not help that Our Lord's garment was no bigger than a handkerchief.

When new visitors arrived, our monk took his shilling from Mr. Kemp & left us to explore on our own. We walked a few paces in silence before I said, "What was it like? To be a slave?" I do not understand why I chose that moment to ask, but Mr. Kemp knew about my life, & I knew nothing of his. "Forgive me for asking, but did they whip you?"

He said they hadn't. "I was caned, but no more than Tom, my owner's son. My owner did not believe in the lash. So my body was never whipped, only my soul." I wondered if he thought I was too delicate to hear the worst, or if the memory still humiliated him. I am now ashamed for asking. I don't know what I hoped to gain, unless it were knowledge that his life had been worse than mine. And different.

As we walked in & out of chapels, Mr. Kemp told me more. He did not know his mother or father. His mother died in childbirth, & his father, people said, was from the next farm & sold down South. He does not even know what year he was born, which seems to me the deepest injury, something that reduces man to animal. I told him so, & he replied, "Yes, they saw me as an animal. A pet. A child. An idiot child. Which I did not know when I was a child. But then I grew to manhood, & they refused to see I had changed. Fool that I was, I hoped to persuade them & went off with Tom to prove myself by fighting the men who wanted to set me free."

I told him he must hate his owners very much now. "Yes. I hate them, but it is not a simple hatred. They treated me as an idiot child, yet they taught the child to read. They denied me the freedom to practice my skills, yet they gave me those skills. The life was soul-killing, yet my soul wasn't killed."

I said he was too kind & made slavery sound no worse than a bad marriage. "A hellish marriage!" he declared. "One I was born to & didn't choose for myself. But there can be good marriages," he added. "There are good marriages." Confused by the shift of subject, I assured him I knew such things existed, rare though they were. He nodded gravely, took out his watch, & said I no doubt wanted to get back to my charge. I wondered if I had said something wrong as we went toward the door. He said tomorrow is Sunday & there are Protestant services at the English church. Would I attend? I told him I might, & perhaps we would see each other. Wanting to make amends, for what I do not know, I thanked him for trusting me with his story. He bowed his head & said, in a solemn, quoting manner, " 'She loved me for the dangers I had passed, & I loved her that she did pity them.' "

I laughed, most nervously, & told him I didn't know the quote. "Shakespeare," he said. "Good day, Miss Pangborn."

Quotation often leads people to say things they only half intend, with words that don't fully apply. And yet— I will say nothing more on the thoughts & questions & fears that come over me while I write this.

Oh, say it, Alice, just say it. One can die of old age waiting for you to admit what was happening. And Isaac, too. He certainly took his sweet time with the approach indirect. How strange to learn that I was already more certain of the outcome than they were. But that was *Othello* he quoted, the hero on his wooing of Desdemona. I must admire the accuracy of Isaac's selection. Their love was built on mutual pity, a terrible foundation for romance, though a common one for marriage.

Sunday, September 12

Mr. Kemp is in love with me. He declared it this morning in the Protestant Cemetery.

We were both at the services, though we did not sit close by. Mrs. Botts was scornful when I declared I was going to church, thinking it a judgment on their slackness. It was an Anglican ritual, yet the sermon was rigorous enough, on Revelations—a strange choice for spa visitors, or maybe not so strange if you think on it. But I temporize. When it was over, I visited the cemetery attached to the church, a shady place separated from the street by a high wall. Mr. Kemp soon joined me & asked what I thought of the sermon. How we got from the Lamb & Seven Seals to his declaration I cannot remember, only that we stood by the mossy marker for an entire family that had passed away in a typhoid epidemic. He removed his bowler hat & said, "You realize, don't you, Miss Pangborn, that I am in love with you?"

"No, Mr. Kemp. I suspected no such a thing." But I had, hadn't I? I had suspected & feared it all along.

"And what do you say?"

"I don't know. I am so taken aback. I cannot give you an answer." But it is not as though he asked a question. If a gentleman of my own race had said this, I would know that he was asking me to marry him. Is that what Mr. Kemp intends? No, he must know it is an impossibility.

"I am most fond of you, Mr. Kemp," I finally said. "But not in that degree. I do not wish to lose the pleasure of your company. So I must ask you not to speak to me again in that manner, if you want to maintain my friendship." He hung fire a moment, like an unresponsive pistol, then said, "I do & will obey." We shook hands on it & then had nothing further to say.

He did not seem hurt when I told him good day. I did not flee him, no, but cannot remember how I departed, only that we did not arrange a future meeting.

I now find myself furious with him. He has spoiled all the pleasure of our friendship. I feared a feeling like this lurked underneath yet could overlook it so long as it remained unsaid.

I spent the rest of the day in a foul temper. When I combed Isabella's hair after her nap, she screeched that I was hurting her, & I suddenly hated her curls & wanted to cut them & shear her of her vanity. I had taken up the scissors when Isabella ran to her mother. I pretended to Mrs. Botts that it had been a practical, well-considered idea, but she was shocked by the intention.

That churchyard conversation surprises me. I never suspected that Isaac's courtship ever hit a solid refusal. He implied no such thing when, that afternoon or the next, he invited me to go with him to the Friedrichsbad.

"Why?" I said. "Do you have something to announce?"

"No. Not yet. It's just that you seem low, Fitz. I thought you might enjoy a swim." It must have been the next afternoon, when he needed a distraction for himself while he let Miss Pangborn stew in her refusal.

I didn't want to know, but during our walk into town I came right out with it. "So. Have you asked her to marry you?"

"No. It's too soon."

"I wish you'd hurry up. We're not going to be here forever."

"I know. But I did tell her that I'm in love with her."

"Oh?" My heart shivered. "And what was her reaction?"

"She was—flummoxed. But she'll overcome that. In time." He seemed serenely confident of success. Then he caught the look on my face, lowered his eyes and frowned. "I am sorry, Fitz."

"Sorry? About *what*, pray tell?"

"That I cannot love you the way that you love me. I don't intend to hurt you. But I am put together differently." He spoke without glibness or insincerity but with *some* sympathy, which only made it worse.

We arrived at the men's swimming bath and were issued bathing drawers by the attendant, who hesitated over letting Isaac in until Isaac spoke the language as haughtily as any Prussian. We changed in separate cubicles and met under the marble columns of a great indoor pool. There was a faint smell like molasses, which must have been the sulfur, and patches of steam fogged the yellow-green water. The architect meant to evoke the grandeur of classical antiquity, but there were no nude Apollos present, only fat, bearded bankers in sopping drawers. The baths were segregated by sex, but a fashionable modesty was creeping into the upper classes, or a pretense of modesty. The damp linen, trimmed in blue at the knees and tied with string at the waist, clung to every crevice and root.

The Germans all stared at Isaac, but with curiosity rather than disgust. Nobody jumped from the pool as he tiptoed down the steps into the hot soup. He eased himself in, wagged his hands underwater, and smiled. He no longer let me see his body in private but thought nothing of displaying it among strangers. Needing to get away from him, I pushed off to the center of the pool, my long hair trailing after me.

It was like swimming in hot tears. The water changed me, melting away my anger, then my body. Floating on my back under that high, echoing nave was like levitating in a cathedral. I dissolved into pure sadness. And the sadness deepened, becoming a soft, round feeling of conclusion, of completion, as when an elaborate piece of music ends in the return of a melody from the first bars, transformed into a tender farewell. Only when I looked up and saw Isaac still by the side, immersed to his neck in green, did I recognize the source of the emotion. He no longer sat on the shore while I swam with the soldiers but had joined me in the water. Theme and variation. Return and conclusion. Let's throw in a few bars of "Träumerei" for good measure. We were indoors now and wore bathing drawers—the world had grown more civilized—but Isaac and I had come full circle. We were finished. We were done. It was time to say good-bye.

I swam back to him.

He remained hunched in the milky green ripples to his brown shoulders, his black hair and beard softened by the warmth. He wore the pool like a vast robe. He looked pleased by my return, thinking my swim had cheered me.

"When you win her?" I said. "When she says yes? Where will you take her? Back to New York?"

"Why, wherever we go next."

"*We?*" I said. "You mean us?" This was the first I'd heard of it. "You expect me to come along?"

He looked surprised that I didn't already know. "I told you, Fitz.

You're my friend. My partner. We need to stay together." He gave me an apologetic, pleading look. "I love you as a friend. I will love her as a wife."

I hated hearing that litany again. "The three of us? No. She won't want to share that life." I certainly knew I couldn't.

"If she can accept me despite my race, our footloose existence should be of no matter to her."

Love had addled his brain, I thought. Happiness had turned him into a selfish, callous, anything-is-possible fool.

"Will you tell her about us?"

"I already have. I told her that I love you like a brother."

"Did you tell her I love you like a husband?"

He frowned. "No. She wouldn't understand. I'm not sure I ever fully understood it myself." His love for a woman made him willfully stupid about me.

There was that solution, of course: I could tell Alice the true nature of our "friendship." I'd already considered it. It would require much explanation—I seriously doubted that sodomy was in her vocabulary—yet Isaac would never forgive me, and I would lose him that way as well the other. An anonymous note might have done the trick, but it seemed like cheating, and I still lost Isaac, body, heart, and soul. Oh, he might give me his body again, but it would be table scraps without the rest.

"But you see," he said, "winning her does not exclude you."

"Oh, yes, I see perfectly."

I saw that I had lost. But I could not bring myself to say good-bye just yet, as if I wanted to consider his proposal. Then he climbed out of the water, setting both hands on the edge and hoisting himself up, the whole unobtainable length of him. His middle showed through the whitewash of linen. I did not feel lust but a reverse lust, a counterlust. To see what I'd lost—what I'd never really had—only gave me pain. I must say good-bye to Isaac, I decided, and let him go his own way to marriage and perdition. I could never share him with a wife.

Monday, September 13

I went back to the cemetery today, while Isabella took her nap, but Mr. Kemp was not there. We did not agree to meet, but I expected & wanted to see him again, in order to stop my foolish second thoughts & fancies. I spent an hour looking at tombstones & feeding my foolish fear that I have made a grave error.

But I was right to tell him what I did. I do not know him, & he barely knows me—it is foolish for either of us to talk of love. We cannot pursue it further. Besides, there is his race, no small thing, yet I often forget it when we are alone. When we are with others, however, the little musician or even that monk, I cannot forget his alien skin & hair & nose. It is morbid to think so much on a friend's body. It causes a sensation similiar to my sudden sickness on the boat, only now the sensation is not in my abdomen but ticklishly dispersed under my skin.

Away from him, however, as I was today, I can feel fondness for him, & gratitude for his fondness of me, which might be akin to love. Yet it is an impossible love. I should learn to enjoy it as such, a private impossibility that will never be acted upon.

If only I were not so unhappy here & isolated & had someone with whom I could discuss these inappropriate emotions. But there is nobody in the world with whom I can discuss this, excepting Mr. Kemp.

25

I wanted to leave Baden after my swim with Isaac, alone. I had no reason to stay in that unreal city of baccarat and bathwater. I'd said good-bye to Isaac, in my heart if not to his face; it would be easy enough to say aloud. I no longer needed Mrs. Tarbell's noblesse oblige, but had plenty of money from the gaming tables. And yet I stayed, hoping for what, I do not know. I was like the Confederate army in its final year, when it knew the war was lost yet continued to fight. Except I did not fight.

Instead I attended the Kurhaus concert that evening, alone, though music seemed awfully trivial to me now, mere snatches of pretty noise. But it had been announced that Brahms himself would perform. I had forgotten all about Brahms. There was no orchestra in the pavilion that evening, only the composer at the piano—short, square, and babyfaced—and a quartet of string players. They performed his Piano Quintet in F Minor, spacious and dramatic. Brahms disliked concertizing, and his arpeggios were a bit rusty, but it was of no matter. I can be quite nasty about other musicians, yet I did not sneer that evening. His quintet was all of a piece, the instruments equal, their playing unmarred by showy displays. They wove a single skein of changing colors, emotional, thoughtful, intimate, the short musical phrases combining into long, elaborate sentences. It spoke to me as the work of Schumann once had, which was no surprise, since Brahms had been the protégé of Schumann and the friend of his wife, Clara. The audience, however, grew restless: A symphony was an event, but a chamber piece was something you could hear at home, and this one contained no catchy tunes. Brahms had the worst luck. For the longest time his music was considered too advanced for the common ear, all shifting textures and mixed rhythms, his melodies evaporating just as they revealed themselves. Then, almost overnight, after Debussy, Richard Strauss, and the rest, he went from being considered too modern and cerebral to seeming sentimental and old-fashioned.

He swayed like a bear at the keyboard, tensing into each transition, making endless faces. He was notorious for being critical of his own compositions. I sat close enough that I could actually hear him grumble and groan as he played. The other musicians swarmed and blended around him, intensely alert to Brahms and each other, a coven of musical conspirators.

They came to the slow movement, *"Andante, un poco adagio,"* and I recognized the wander of notes: It was the passage I'd heard during my walk with Isaac, when Brahms blew smoke bubbles and I thought my world was solid. I sank back into my own troubles again, yet the music continued to move me, not just the music but the situation of its making. Five people made it together, a family of friends, a sonorous little utopia. I, however, played alone, and would always play alone. And once Isaac left me, I would live alone as well, with my art, pianos, spirit, and the rest, until I died.

There were the racing rhythms of the finale, a descent into a home not quite a home, and the piece ended. Brahms and his friends took their bows and applauded each other, the string players thanking the composer with a grasshopperish tapping of bows against music stands. The audience hurried off to cafés and restaurants. I remained in my chair, stranded under stars and mountains, thinking about music, thinking about life. Art seemed a beautiful consolation, but could it set right all that had gone wrong in my life?

I needed to think at a piano. A keyboard would concentrate my thoughts. The terrace was empty now. I fearlessly climbed the steps to the abandoned pavilion, where the instrument had been covered with a dropcloth. I lifted the cloth, sat down, and opened the lid. The keys were still warm from Brahms's touch. I played a few notes. If my emotions were too deep for tears, they were not too deep for a piano.

It began in self-recrimination. Had I not loved Isaac well enough? Had I not understood him and deserved his love? I had mistaken his kindness for love. But it was not just kindness. He had enjoyed our seven years in bed—that was not merely a favor on his part— but in much the same way I had enjoyed my months with Orlando Wilson. Isaac liked sex and he loved me, as a friend, only the two had little to do with each other—while for me they were one and the same. But our years in bed had been only a way station for Isaac, a rehearsal, a time-killer before he began his real life.

What right did I have to deny him the life of marriage, wife, and children, the things that all good men wanted? It was not in my power to deny them. I should accept them. If he were serious about the three of us traveling together, me and him and her, I should accept that, too, despite the pain it would cause me. Or maybe *for* the pain it would cause, because then I would know love in its fullest: as real as a thorn, as solid as earth. More important, I would not be alone.

Such grim, mournful thoughts. But just as the saddest music, when played well, can be a joyful expression of sadness, so my hour of resignation achieved a formal beauty. This mental calculus was hardly the stuff of a tone poem, yet my music was part of my thoughts, a searching thing of groped chords and tentative resolutions, all played *andante, un poco adagio.* Much of it seemed to come from my lugubrious spirit, my horse-and-piano familiar, as solemn as Beethoven, as reckless as Liszt. He did not possess me but only engaged me in conversation. Yet there was a new presence in this shrouded piano, a light, flippant, careless voice. Like a boy, a mischievous, impertinent boy, fourteen or so, who did not argue with my familiar but ignored him and sang his own song. Hearing him in my head, I tossed off his giddy phrases with my right hand: He seemed to thumb his nose at all the heavy sincerity. This was my first encounter with a new familiar, a second spirit, one whom I would name later. He continued to chirp like a syncopated bird, until the very end, when a deep, oceanic chord declared it over.

The piano cooled in the night air, and I remained perched on the stool, sorry the fantasia was over, wondering if I should keep any of these ideas. They were all fine and good for music, but did they make sense in life?

Just then a voice called out: *"Mein Herr? Sie, lieber Herr?"* I jumped back from the piano before I realized the voice had come from the terrace. The sandy space remained deserted except for the scatter of gaping chairs. Then I saw two red eyes glowing in a dark corner, a pair of burning cigars. "Excuse me!" I shouted. "Forgive me! I thought I was alone. *Nein sprechen sie Deutsch."*

"Ah? *Engländer?"*

"American." I started hesitantly down the steps toward the twin cigars.

"Come here. I speak the English. In a fashion."

I approached and could make out the man who spoke, a heavy fellow with a long beard. The other man remained a silhouette, until he sucked his cigar: A round, pink, clean-shaven face blossomed in the dark. It was Brahms again. He had caught me playing his piano, just as I'd caught him playing with bubbles. I came around and could see him more clearly in the glow from a window, his face framed in a cottage roof of center-parted hair. He studied me with the same mild, curious look that he gave his cigar. There was a half-empty beer stein at his feet.

"We are wondering," said the bearded friend, "if you find your lost chord."

I laughed nervously. So that was how my music sounded? I introduced myself. "Dr. August. And you are Herr Doktor Professor Maestro Brahms?" I was not sure of his official title and threw out all the possibilities. The friend translated, and the two men laughed together.

The friend's name was Billroth, Dr. Billroth. "A medical doctor," he explained. "Of surgery." He asked me to join them and offered me a cigar. "What you are playing?" he said after he lit my stogie. "That is your composition? Much too loose, much too loose, if you don't mind our saying so. But with nice passages."

Billroth did all the talking, translating for Brahms whenever I said anything of interest. The great man knew little English. When I began to praise his music, he winced and held up his hand to stop Billroth's translation. Yet he did not take his eyes off me. He had serious eyes, dark, hooded soul-windows, misplaced in the smooth face of a well-fed boy with a sensual mouth. No wonder he later grew a beard, so he could look as old as he felt. His tone was gruff, but with a falsetto gruffness, like a lad who talks low to hide the cracking of his voice.

They wanted to know who I was. I did not play backwoods idiot savant but told them the truth, which was barbaric enough. They probably thought that Americans banged on their pianos in tepees. I explained how my performances were never composed in advance but always improvised, then blithely added that my best music was dictated by a metaphysical spirit. Billroth laughed, until he realized I was serious. When he translated for Brahms, however, the composer solemnly considered it. He replied at length, and I caught a phrase: "*mein Freund Robert.*"

"Brahms is not surprised," said Billroth. "After all, angels dictated music to Schumann, but only after he went mad."

I assured them I was not mad.

"But you make the living off this?"

I told him I did, for the most part. People assume that artists must talk about art and beauty and the sublime whenever we get together, but no, we usually talk about money. I gave them a comic account of my fiasco in London.

"*Die Engländer,*" Brahms grumbled. "*Die Philister.*" Philistines.

The two men conferred a moment, Brahms puffing thoughtfully on his cigar. Then Billroth said, "Our friend recommends you forget the English. Try Brussels. Brussels is a most curious city at present. Very new, open to new ideas. He knows a useful man there. He likes your music. He wants to write you a letter of recommendation."

Brahms had already lifted a leather case into his lap. He took out a sheet of foolscap, unscrewed a pen, and wrote, humming to himself as if he were composing. We no longer have the original of his letter to M. Héger of Brussels, only the key paragraph, translated and reworked, again and again, whenever I needed an advertisement:

> This raw American youth is a rare being, a primitive who combines originality with sweetness and grace. He performs chords no man has ever heard before. Whatever the source of his compositions, be it angels, demons, or his own genius, here is the true "Music of the Future."
>
>   —J. Brahms

We later deleted "youth," of course, and some phrases are translated more freely than others. There are those who claim I made it all up, or that this was a Jack Brahms, a grocer or barkeep. But no, it was the real Brahms, and he truly wrote it.

He blew the ink dry, passed the letter to Billroth, who read it over, chuckled, and passed it to me. Both men wore the smiles of cats with mouthfuls of canary.

Why did he do it? Was it only a jest? "The true 'Music of the Future.' " That was a dig at Liszt and Wagner, of course, whom Brahms saw as the enemies of beauty. It was not the first time someone had given me a leg up in the world out of mischief. But I believe there was warmth as well as drollery in his gift, that this genius from the slums of Hamburg, this eternal bachelor married to music, saw a bit of himself in me, a hungry, solitary youth making his way up the slopes of Parnassus.

Whatever the reason, I got a famous man's recommendation, like a musical letter of credit, and a destination. What might happen in Brussels, I did not know, but I had somewhere to go, once I finally told Isaac good-bye and departed.

Wednesday, September 15

To the cemetery again, with no expectations. But Mr. Kemp was there, waiting for me. I told him I had come the day before. "I did not know if you wanted to see me again," he said. I assured him I did or I would not have come today as well. I told him we must be frank with one another. "When you said that you were in love with me——" He broke in & declared he was still in love. "Were your intentions serious? Or do you only toy with my affections?" "My intentions could not be more serious. If you felt anything similar for me, I would ask for your hand in marriage."

I did not blush or smile or weep. I told him, as gently as I could, that such a thing was impossible. "I would be lying if I said I did not feel affection for you, Mr. Kemp. But there are conventions, realities. Two such as we cannot marry." I feared he would ask me to enumerate, but instead he said, "So what shall we do with our love?" He actually said *our*, & I did not correct him, but suggested we should enjoy it as a beautiful but impossible thing, a pure thing. And he said yes, assuring me he could be pure. I wanted to thank him with a kiss on the cheek, but checked the impulse, even as I wondered if his beard feels as coarse as it looks, & noticed for the first time a sad pattern of pocks & scars between his beard and cheekbone.

Thursday, September 16

Strange distress: Last night, in the middle of the night, Isabella woke me up & pleaded, "Where is the candy? Please. Share the candy with me." She dreamt I have been slipping out our window every night to meet a Negro in the bushes & eat a wonderful new candy with him. It hurt her that I didn't share it. I put her back to bed, assuring her there was no Negro & no candy, but if there were I would certainly let her have some. Where did the child get such a disturbing notion? She told her mother about the dream this morning, & Mrs. Botts blamed me for exposing her child to Negro bogeymen, though I claimed I had not seen Mr. Kemp since the concert.

I was afraid to visit the cemetery this afternoon, but did. I told Mr. Kemp only that the Bottses treated me more miserably than ever. He said, "You don't have to stay with them. There is another way." "No, Mr. Kemp. We cannot talk of that. It is impossible." Why? "If I marry you, I can never return to Hartford." "You do not need to return," he said. "We can live in New York. Or stay over here." "No, Mr. Kemp. I am sorry. I am not as brave as you. I do not dare go against realities. You see, I am unworthy of your affection." He is unconvinced, yet it is certainly the truth.

And *that* was where things stood? How odd. How very odd. What with Isaac's certainty, my spirit, and the rest, I was sure they had progressed much further.

26

MY last day in Baden began like all the others.

We took our breakfast in the dining room, I performed for Mrs. Tarbell in the drawing room, and she went down to the Trinkenhalle for her cure. The air was crisp, the sunlight warm. The foliage on the mountains had begun to turn, but here in the valley it felt as if the mellow late summer would last forever.

Over lunch, however, after her return, the old lady was full of bottled mirth. Her gray eyes glittered. Her dry lips kept pinching in a smirky beak as she cut into her beefsteak. She couldn't look at Isaac without her jaw going taut and her crepey neck quivering. She resembled an old snapping turtle with a wig and a secret. Only after Isaac left for his daily walk into town did she confide the cause of her delight to me and Poodle.

"I heard the most wonderful gossip at the Pump Room today. About your valet, Mr. Boyd. Your valet and the Hartford governess. The priggish girl in brown holland and specs? I had no idea your man was a rake. He seems such a wooden Indian. But I suppose they can't help themselves, can they?"

To what exactly was she alluding?

"Your valet and the tutor!" she laughed. "Don't you know? They've been tête-à-têting every afternoon on the sly. In the Protestant Cemetery. Imagine. A nice way to pay one's respects to the dead. But I would love to drop those Hartford people a note and tell them, 'My black ram is tupping your white ewe.' "

More *Othello*. Everyone had some Shakespeare on hand for any occasion. I listened in cold silence while she tittered on.

"Oh, it is rich. I'm just glad that he chose her, or I'd be worried about the maidenhood of my chambermaids. There'd be an epidemic of dusky German babies here long after I'd gone home."

I kept my temper. I was surprised I had so much temper to keep. "Mrs. Tarbell. Please. Do not speak of Mr. Kemp in this free-and-easy manner."

"Pshaw. Don't 'Mr. Kemp' me. I don't care that he's seduced a pathetic little drab. I'm amazed she has it in her. She looks such a dry thing. But surely she's not the first flower your man's plucked. Does he always prefer white blossoms?"

"No!" I declared. "No! Stop this talk! Isaac Kemp is a good man, a moral man. He's more moral than I, and a damn sight more than you."

The snapping turtle coughed an uncertain laugh. "Mr. Boyd?"

I tried to contain my words, but they came pouring out. "You have no right to sit here smacking your lips over a pack of lies. I will not have you slandering my best friend."

I knew it was untrue, yet the idea that their meetings might not be chaste added jealousy to my indignation.

"Your friend?" scoffed Mrs. Tarbell. "You call your servant your 'moral' friend?"

"Yes. While you, madam, are a debauched old bawd."

Her tomahawk face snapped backward.

Poodle finally jumped in. "B-B-Boyd. You will not talk to Mother like that!"

But I couldn't stop. The stillness that I mistook for resignation was a tightly wound spring of fury: It all flew out at that foolish old woman.

"It's indecent," I told her. "The obscene way you gloat over perfectly proper relations between two innocent people. Two souls who've never done you ill. The girl is a timid sparrow who's all alone in the world. You should want to protect her, if you had any heart, instead of snickering over her fall into vice. But it isn't vice, madam, it's love. Isaac, my good friend Isaac, cares for the girl and wants to protect her."

"Indecent, am I? Debauched?" said Mrs. Tarbell. "You little hypocrite. I indulge you in your charlatan music, feed and keep you, and this is how you thank me?"

"Oh, yes," I said. "You sit here on your bags of money, with your French novels and worldly pretensions, tossing a few coppers to the rest of us. You treat us as a show, an amusement, a circus of vice. You are decadent, madam. *You* are the hypocrite."

Poodle said nothing, and a good thing, too, or I might've told her about vices closer to home. But inside his stupid, hangdog look, Poodle appeared to enjoy the tongue-lashing I gave his mother.

Her cheeks turned apoplexy pink in her face powder. She got up, slowly, proudly, tottering on her lame foot. "Mr. Boyd," she declared. "You no longer amuse me. I will not have you under my roof one more hour. Poodle, my cane. Give me my cane!" she snapped. "You are to send this mountebank flying. Throw him and his oh-so-proper coon out on the street. They no longer amuse me. I will be in my room. I will not come out until this trash is swept from my home." She hobbled toward the door but turned for a parting shot. "Maupassant was right. To bring an artist into a good home is like a grain merchant opening his store to rats."

She slammed a door. Poodle let out a sigh. "Sorry, B-B-Boyd. I know she had it coming. Still. Couldn't you have d-d-disguised it in j-j-jokes? Well, too late. You heard her, old man. Hard cheese. Sorry to see you to go."

That's all it takes with the wealthy: One snappish bark, and the beloved lapdog is tossed into the gutter. But I was glad to go. I was overjoyed. Suddenly, after days of stalemate, paralysis, and brooding, I'd set myself free with that outburst. It broke my stupor, and I could act again. I became drunk on action, intoxicated. I do not know how else to explain the change of heart that came over me while I tossed clothes into my trunk upstairs. But I wanted to continue to act, impulsively, generously, without self-interest. Defending Isaac and his sparrow had put me on their side. I gave in to the fate that I'd heard singing in the Kurhaus piano. I cast my lot with the lovers.

Isaac returned from his walk—the Protestant Cemetery, of course—to find me busily packing.

"Get your things together," I said. "We're leaving. The old lady has thrown us out."

"*What?* But why? What did you tell her?" he said accusingly. He didn't wait for an answer. "Where are we going?"

"Brussels."

"But how? We have no money."

"Yes we do." I jangled a purse of casino gold at him—I'd turned most of my winnings into banknotes, but kept a fistful of coins for their sound.

He didn't ask where the money came from. No, that was not what concerned him. "But what about Miss Pangborn?"

"We'll take her with us." There. I said it.

"*Today?*" He looked shocked.

"Yes. There's no time like the present. If she loves you, she'll come. She does love you, doesn't she?"

"Yes. But—but—"

"Hurry up, then. There's a train for Aachen at six."

He obeyed me, in the dazed, uncertain way you obey anyone who knows what he wants when you don't. I did not think our hurried departure would end the Alice business. I honestly didn't. No, I expected action to be contagious, that my urgency would drive Isaac and Alice from their leisurely courtship into the final leap.

The German servants took our bags and dumped them unceremoniously on the porch. They were happy to be getting rid of us. Poodle sent for a buggy. "Sorry it had to end like this, Boyd. I really am. I'll miss you and your spirit at the casino."

I asked him to send our bags on to the station when the buggy arrived and told Isaac to come with me to the Hotel Royal.

"Now?" he said.

"Yes! When else did you intend to tell her?" I took off walking downhill toward the Kurpark. Isaac caught up with me.

"No, Fitz. No. It's too soon for that."

"Do you want her or don't you?"

"Oh, I want her. More than life itself. But she's not ready yet. Can't we take a room in town and stay a few days longer? Let me tell her we're going and give her time to adjust her mind."

I thought he was still hung up on good form and romantic etiquette, the all-the-time-in-the-world proprieties that were not for the likes of us. "No," I said. "I despise this place. I can't stay another day. And what will a day or two change? If she wants you, she'll take you now." And another day might change my mind again. All right. Maybe part of me did hope that forcing the issue would end it, even though my spirit declared it a foregone conclusion.

27

W_E entered the Hotel Royal, and Isaac nervously asked at the desk for the Bottses. I thought we would send up a note requesting Miss Pangborn to come down, but no, a bellboy appeared and took us upstairs, assuming we were expected. Isaac was too busy rehearsing phrases to himself to pay much attention to where we were going. The bellboy knocked on the door, Mrs. Botts answered, the boy bowed and departed.

Mrs. Botts was as beautiful as ever, as pretty as a painting in her at-home dress, a bit of lace around her slender throat. She recognized us and smiled, assuming that we'd come from Mrs. Tarbell. Then she noticed our traveling clothes, Isaac in his plaid ulster, me in my cape.

"Mrs. Botts," said Isaac. "I hope you will excuse the unannounced visit. I beg a word in private with Miss Pangborn."

She'd been looking at me, expecting the master to speak, not his servant. "What?" she said. "Who?"

A man called from inside. "Don't stand there jawing at the door, woman. Ask them in, whoever it is. Close the door."

Mrs. Botts stepped aside, uncertainly, and we entered the parlor of their apartment. The Bottses were having a quiet hour *en famille* among the hired cushions and ferns. It was still light outside, and no lamps were lit. Mr. Botts, the paterfamilias, lounged on a couch with his newspaper and waxed scowl of a mustache, his belly un-buttoned from his waistcoat.

Isabella sat beside him in a white pinafore. She leaped up as soon as she saw Isaac. "Did you bring the candy?" she cried—and I had no idea what she meant.

Mr. Botts was startled to see a strange white man and Negro in his apartment. "What's this? Who are these men?"

His wife hesitantly explained. "Mrs. Tarbell's friends. The pic-nic?" She sensed that something wrong was afoot.

Their governess shyly appeared at the door to the next room. She had a paper sleeve guard on one arm and still clutched a pen. She must have been making her diary entry for the day. Her lenses were askew. Her face turned pale as milk when she saw Isaac.

"Excuse us, sir," said Isaac with a slight bow. "I came only to ask a minute of Miss Pangborn's time. In private."

Mr. Botts stared at us and glanced over at Alice. He had no idea what was going on but refused to admit it. IIe drew himself up in high paterfamilias fashion and announced, "No. I cannot allow that. The young lady is my responsibility. Anything you have to say to her must be said in front of me."

This family head who had played absolutely no role in any of this suddenly insisted that *he* was in charge.

Isaac turned to me, to Miss Pangborn, back to me. He was not prepared to speak his piece in public. He held his hat in both hands, slowly turning it around by the brim. "Miss Pangborn," he began. "Due to an unexpected change of plans, we must leave Baden today. I came to say good-bye." And he stopped, as if that were all he had to say. But hearing himself say it, the fact hit him, struck him hard: He would never see her again. The hat stopped turning. He leaned forward—and *dropped* to the carpet on one bent knee. "Miss Pang-born," he said. "Miss Pangborn. I must ask you one more time. Will you marry me?"

The whole room drew a single breath. I expected Alice to faint. But nobody fainted. A few jaws fell open.

"Mr. Kemp," she began. "Mr. Kemp, I told you——"

Mrs. Botts snapped to life. "You've been spending time with this man? You've encouraged this nigger? Hussy!"

"No, I——" She faced her dreaded mistress, then back to Isaac at her feet. Her eyes were wide, her lips thin and straight. But no, she could not deny him. "I am friends with this man. Yes. He has become very dear to me, only——"

"You insolent harlot!" cried Mrs. Botts—the pretty painting turned vicious. "You play high-and-mighty with us, but go sneaking off with this—orangutan!"

Isabella began to chant: "Alice is getting married, Alice is getting married."

Isaac remained down on one knee, hat in hand, a penitent at an altar, a squire hoping to be knighted. He seemed deaf to the noise around him. "Miss Pangborn? Please. What is your answer?"

Without intending it, we had put her in a dreadful spot, a humiliating trap. Like a cornered deer, she swung her eyes left and right—her shocked employers, her chanting charge, her pleading lover of the wrong race.

"Give me the word, Miss Pangborn, and I will leave you in peace," said Isaac. "I will trouble you no more."

I was confused. I didn't know he'd already asked her once and she'd refused him. But I had set my coin on a number and could only watch the ball fly around the wheel, waiting for it to hit its slot, baffled that it didn't hit sooner.

"Woman!" Mr. Botts shouted at his wife. "What's the meaning of this? What the devil has been going on in my household?"

"I don't know!" Mrs. Botts shouted back. "If you spent time with us instead of at cards, you would've caught wind of this!"

A small white hand fluttered by Isaac's shoulder, Alice wanting to touch him yet afraid to touch. "Stand up, Mr. Kemp," she said in a very small voice. "I beg you."

"Alice! Get to your room!" Mr. Botts commanded. "I will deal with this man. We will deal with your conduct later. Alice! Do you hear me? Leave this room at once. Take Isabella with you. My daughter has no business being exposed to this kind of thing."

But the child remained delighted by the sensational melodrama being performed in her own parlor.

And the order produced a sudden bit of fight in the governess, a stiffening of back. "No, Mr. Botts," she said, without taking her eyes off Isaac. "This is between Mr. Kemp and myself. Please. Allow me to step outside and talk with him in private."

"You will not!" cried Mrs. Botts. Disobedience increased the fight in her. "You go out that door, hussy, and you can consider your employ with us over."

"Don't be fools," I told them. "She's not your child or slave. Let her deal with this on her own."

"Don't tell us what to do!" Mr. Botts shouted. "Who are you anyway? Who are you?"

"The piano player," said Mrs. Botts. "Tarbell's musician."

"Aha," went Mr. Botts, as if that explained everything. "We are not your bohemian riffraff, sir. This is a Christian household where things are conducted accordingly."

While we bickered, Isaac and Alice remained perfectly still, Isaac on his bent knee, Alice bowed over him, as if gazing into his eyes, only I saw that her eyes had closed.

And then I heard her whisper, so softly that I wasn't sure I'd heard it the first time. "Yes," she went in a soft seethe. "Yes." The startled look on Isaac's face made clear that she had actually said it.

"You will come with us tonight?" said Isaac.

She opened her eyes, clutched her hands together, and nodded.

"No!" cried Mr. Botts. "No girl in my employ is running off with a nigger! I will have you arrested. I will call the police."

"And do what?" I said. "She's of age. We're Americans in a foreign country. It's none of their business."

Isaac slowly climbed to his feet, not taking his grateful eyes off Miss Pangborn. Botts abruptly shut up, startled to see his opponent's size.

"You'd better pack," I said. "We want to catch the next train to Aachen."

"You hussy," said Mrs. Botts. "You foolish tart. Stay or go, you're finished here."

"Wait a minute!" cried her husband. "Not so fast!"

"No," said his wife. "I am sick of her moral sass, her righteous snits. But she's made her own bed. Let her lie in it. Take your things and go, hussy. You are dismissed. You can sleep in the fields tonight, for all we care."

Alice only stood there, looking at Isaac, slowly understanding what she had told him and what it meant.

"Can I keep your green pig?" cried Isabella. "The calico pig with flowers?"

"Yes. You may," Alice murmured. She blinked at Isaac, attempted to smile, then turned and marched from the room. Mrs. Botts followed her, sputtering about a petticoat, a borrowed garment that was theirs, not hers. Isabella skipped after them.

"You have ruined that girl," said Mr. Botts. "You've destroyed her. I don't know what sweet nothings you poured into her ear, but this is a fate *worse* than the fate-worse-than-death. I demand that you leave our quarters. You can wait for her downstairs."

"No, sir," said Isaac. "We will wait for her here."

Unable to fight us or his wife, feeling helpless and foolish in the presence of these men stealing his employee, Mr. Botts fumed a moment, then left the room and joined his missus, whom we heard scolding Alice while she packed.

"There," I told Isaac. "Was that so hard?"

"No. Not at all," he muttered, with a note of surprise that surprised me.

When Miss Pangborn reappeared, she looked plainer than ever in her squashed hat and rubberized overcoat. Her face had a hard, determined set. She carried a single carpetbag, stuffed very full, and her umbrella.

"Just go!" cried Mrs. Botts. "I will send you your trunk, after I go through it and see you haven't stolen anything. If you have a place where it can be sent," she sneered. "But don't think you can come back when you find out what kind of men these really are. Because we are finished with you, hussy. Finished."

Isaac took Alice's bag for her. I opened the door for them. He did not place a loving arm around her shoulder, and she didn't look at him as they went out. The Bottses stopped their shouting, afraid of what anyone in the corridor might think. Then Isabella called out, "Bye, Alice. Good-bye. Have a nice honeymoon."

The door banged shut, and Isaac and Alice walked ahead of me, side by side, down the long, silent carpet. From behind they looked as inevitable as any married couple, as if they were only doing what they had long intended to do.

And what words had Alice been writing? What thoughts did we interrupt with our rescue?

Friday, September 17

Today in the cemetery we sat while we spoke. All previous intercourse has taken place standing up, but today Mr. Kemp & I sat side by side on a sarcophagus. Mr. Kemp has experienced so much more than I. He is wiser. I do not know what I want, but he wants me. Why cannot I accept that? Why do I resist? Because it is impossible, the world being what it is. I shall let this dream end when one of us leaves Baden. There will be letters, but love will fade in ink & sealing wax, & I can later look back &

And what? No dash where she left off? Not even a blot?

Is that where she was? That's what she'd decided? Oh, my.

It *wasn't* a foregone conclusion? If I had let things go and not forced the issue, it might not have happened?

No, I cannot believe that. My spirit told me otherwise. And the prophecy came true. It came true with a push from me, of course, but— It was all my doing? I had imagined it, yet my imagining made it real?

So that was why Alice remained silent, even after we left the hotel: She had expected nothing like this. She remained pinched and silent even when she sat with Isaac in the swaying second-class compartment bound for Aachen, the orange dusk dying away to blue in the window. I sat opposite them on a thinly padded bench, surprised that they did not hold hands. You might have thought Alice was going to a funeral rather than a wedding. And Isaac, too, did not look like a proud hunter who'd just bagged a prize deer but like a slightly guilty thief. Then, when her eyes began to flow—tears of joy, I thought—Isaac took her small white hand in his great pale palm and timidly stroked the knuckles. After a few minutes she swallowed her tears and faced him. She looked like she might kiss him. Instead she only reached up with her free hand and tentatively touched his soft, dry sponge of beard.

28

VERY well, then. Very well. Let's wrap up this sorry business. After the high drama of elopement, the gray prose of consequence—I still cannot believe the outcome wasn't already guaranteed.

We arrived in Aachen late and checked into a hotel. Two rooms, one for the lady, one for the gentlemen. There were two sagging beds in our shabby chamber. Isaac and I undressed with our backs to each other, much as we had during our first year together. Hearing his buckle clatter on the floor, I suddenly hoped he might propose climbing into my bed for one last toss before matrimony, so that I could tell him, "No, you love Miss Pangborn." It would be a beautiful renunciation, a perfect slap to his face. But Isaac got into his own bed, blew out the candle, and said, "I can't believe it. I won her. She's mine. After tomorrow she'll be mine forever. Thank you, Fitz. Thank you. It wouldn't have happened without you. How did you know?"

I thought at the time that he was only being rhetorical. "My spirit told me it would happen."

And down the hall, Alice was all alone with her diary.

Saturday, September 18, early A.M.

My crowded hour. I need not write it down because I will remember it the rest of my life. In sorrow or gladness I cannot guess. Tonight I am afraid, but it is too late to turn back.

I could spin a whole chapter on the dreary comedy of finding someone to perform the marriage the next day. We went to the American consulate, but the chaplain there, a hoary old Methodist from Ohio, refused to wed a white woman to a black man. He scolded Alice as if she were a child until she drew herself up and, with the same note of fight she'd shown the Bottses, declared, "This is what I want. I choose it freely." He scornfully suggested we visit a Roman church, whose priests didn't care whom they married if they could nab more souls.

Back on the street, Isaac proposed we go on to Brussels, which was two hours away, and try the embassy there. "And so we won't be refused again, we'll tell them I am only the witness and Fitz is Isaac Kemp."

"*No!*" Alice and I cried in unison. My self-abasement did not go that far.

Nevertheless, when we arrived that afternoon in Brussels, that's exactly what we did. We told them I was Isaac and Isaac was me, but he signed his own name in the proper place on the certificate when the minister wasn't looking.

During the ceremony the bride looked stiff, the groom annoyed, the best man unaccountably happy. When the minister said, "You may kiss the bride," he was surprised the groom only pecked her hand.

We checked into a hotel where Mr. and Mrs. Kemp took their own room. We dined in the restaurant, all three of us. I toasted the newlyweds with soda water. Isaac and Alice ate little and could not glance at each other without blushing.

The full awful meaning of my surrender did not catch up with me until that night, when I lay in a cold, narrow, solitary bed. I was an idiot, a man in moral pain who'd stupidly stuck his hand in a fire so that he could feel real pain. And yes, I couldn't help imagining what went on in the room down the hall. After all, I knew what Isaac's embraces were like. I tried to be patient in my misery.

I'd heard enough wedding-night tales about terrified virgins or clumsy grooms that I was not without hope. Even now.

They joined me downstairs for breakfast the next morning. Watery sunlight washed over islands of white table linen as they entered, side by side, Isaac's hands clutched behind, Alice's clutched in front, as mute and prim as two dressmaker dummies. Then he drew out her chair, and she glanced at his face as she eased herself down, and I saw the truth in their eyes.

Sunday, September 19

Words fail me. Only— It was strange & confusing & upsetting, but afterward, when we lay in the dark & I lay in his arms—I nearly wrote "Mr. Kemp's arms"—in *Isaac's* arms, I found myself full of peace, trust & some hope.

PART

IV

29

WHAT a queer bunch we Victorians were. Or rather, *are*—and I include you in our lot, Tristan. All that principle, appetite, and anxiety, our hunger to succeed in eternal war with our desire to be good. And all those *words*! We suffered a constant itch to explain and justify ourselves yet were so fearful of certain topics that our talk regularly spun off in irrelevancies. The important things were left unsaid or hidden in stale formulas: "country matters," "the fate worse than death," "a delicate condition," "the unspeakable vice." But three of us had entered a life too original for those ill-fitting euphemisms to come even close. We would have looked insane in the eyes of the world, if the world had known even half.

But my own grand renunciation was not so mad as it must seem. It wasn't. Its abruptness was a surprise, though my spirit had prepared me for it. And my spirit expressed the spirit of the age, which was not a bad spirit, I hasten to add. To renounce flesh and pleasure and love, to rise above the selfishness of self: Such sacrifice is a beautiful deed, a noble purging. Any wife of the time would have understood perfectly.

But can the sacrifice of one's own happiness ever guarantee the happiness of others?

Forgive me, my boy, for speaking of your mother as I have. You assured me that you could take the brunt of all that I remember

feeling and thinking back then, the full, irritable truth. If I sometimes put made-up words into our mouths for the sake of the drama,
I remain true to the essence of what happened and what I knew of
our hearts. Later, when we go back and expunge the dirty parts
from this tale, we could always change the names and sell this
account as a historical romance, a sentimental fiction.

At the time, however, I took no pleasure in my sacrifice, not even
of the hair-shirt-and-thorns variety. I felt only heartsick and stupid
in Brussels.

"The White City" was a new city, an imitation Paris of alabaster
façades and muddy, half-finished parks. Isaac and Alice saw little of
it our first week there but disappeared into their room, their bed,
their marriage. They came down only for meals. Conversation in
the hotel dining room was a matter of much small talk and many
silences.

I tried to put a good face on my misery. I can't say that they
rubbed my nose in their happiness. Their joy, in fact, was quite
discreet. They did not bring dewy eyes and pussycat smiles to the
dinner table, whatever transports of bliss they shared in their room.
Isaac's posture remained as straight as ever, Alice's neck as stiff. Yet
they overdid the decorum, like a pair of drunks pretending to be
sober. More accurately, they suggested two young actors in their
first play, reciting the right lines while their eyes betray their excitement over being onstage. And there was something like stage
fright in Alice's gaze, as if she were alarmed to be so happy. By the
second day of marriage, she began to enter the dining room on
Isaac's arm, gripping it with an expression of both belligerence and
pride. She was training herself to appear in public with her husband.

What does she say in her diary?

Monday, September 20

What a curiosity to see a man shave. Father never let me watch,
of course—I cannot count the undertaker's razor.

Wednesday, September 22

We read aloud to each other today, our favorite Psalms. My dear husband's is 32—"Thou art my hiding place; thou shalt preserve me from trouble"—which surprises me, as he is surprised that mine be 131: "Lord, my heart is not haughty, nor mine eyes lofty."

Friday, September 24

My husband continues to amaze. He can sew, & much better than I. He mended the rip in my ———.

And how was it torn, this unmentionable? No, we shall leave that be. But her entries are all like that? Gnomic half notes? One wonders why she even bothered. Not only had she lost her privacy, she had no need to confide thought to paper when she could pour it into the pillowed ear of a husband every evening. How quickly marriage ruins a diary.

So it was not as though marriage transformed Alice overnight from a dry stick to a leafy bough. But there was enough of a change to show up the drabness of her wardrobe. Alice owned nothing but brown clothes—sparrow-brown, dog-brown, mud-brown—skirts, vests, and jackets that had fit Miss Pangborn like a glove yet looked all wrong on Mrs. Kemp.

"More coffee, Mrs. Kemp?" "Could you pass the salt, Mrs. Kemp?" "Do you think, Mrs. Kemp, that it will rain today?"

Isaac never tired of using her new name, repeating it like a magic word. His happiness shone more brightly than hers, a shine in his eyes like fresh paint. His chin often rose of its own accord when he sat still, as if his head were inflating with the thought, "I am a husband." He had always been proud, but now he relaxed into his pride, looking comically cocky, terribly smug.

I was not jealous of their physical satisfaction. No, I didn't dare think of that. What did hurt, though, were Alice's allusions to incidents that had once been solely mine and Isaac's. They seemed to do a lot of talking in bed. "That was a vile saying your Hebrew carpenter taught you," she chided him one morning. " 'Silence in a woman is even more becoming than good clothes.' I would not care to be *his* wife."

"I repeated it only as a sample," Isaac said uncertainly. "I do not believe it myself, Mrs. Kemp."

"I never thought you did, my dear."

Hearing their banter, I felt shut out of a tender mystery. Children must feel something similar about their parents.

Alice attempted to include me in their life, but you could tell her heart wasn't in it.

"So you and Isaac once lived in a barrel," she said one evening. "In Virginia. How miserable that must have been. Unclean and foul. I'm sorry you both had to experience that."

"To be sure," I said. "We might be living there still, if I hadn't been taken up by two old panderers and their bevy of—"

A boot in my shin cut the sentence short. Isaac kept his head down, pretending to be busy with his dumplings. Here was something else that he did not want Alice to know.

"If I hadn't found work through my music," I quickly added.

"When will I get a chance to hear you play, Dr. August? I have never heard you play, you know."

"You will have the opportunity soon enough, Miss Pang— Mrs. Kemp. You will have the chance."

The extra cost of two rooms and a third mouth nibbled at our purse, making clear that my windfall would not last us forever. But I could not bring myself to look up the address given to me by Brahms, even though I went out every day and wandered glumly among the white buildings like monstrous wedding cakes. My spirit had fled. It had done its mischief in Baden but did not come to Brussels. My playing would be a cold, bloodless thing.

Then one night I had a vision, a dream: I stood on a beach, a wide, endless beach like a desert. And the ocean caught fire. A forest of blue flames roared up like a church organ, towers of burning gas, gyres of combustion. There was no heat from the blaze, only the sense that this fire burned like ice. It threatened to ignite the sand and earth, and the whole world would be destroyed. Then way off in the distance, down the beach, the fire began to flicker, subside, and die. The burning ocean snuffed itself out at the approach of three figures coming down the shore: a boy, a horse, and a piano. The boy led the horse. The piano rode the horse. The piano was wrapped in a white cloak and hood, and you might have thought it was a man or woman, but I knew it was a piano even before I saw the brass pedals of its feet. The boy, however, was carelessly naked, mischievously nude, a larky, long-legged lad of fourteen or so, with a smooth belly, a shock of brown hair, and forget-me-not-blue eyes. I recognized him immediately. It was the boy who'd sung to me in the pavilion at Baden. He did not sing now—there was no music in the dream, only a silent cadence of the sea, still smoking after its organ chord of fire. Yet the scene moved me like music. The noble horse with a gloomy glower like Beethoven trod the sand under its heavy rider—my nebulous piano-horse had neatly divided itself. The boy tickled the horse's ear, whispered sweet nothings, and stroked its snout. Then he saw me, and he smiled, a warm, welcoming smile in F major. Or no, with a touch of insolence, so F-sharp major. Gladness filled my heart, and I suddenly knew his name: Eusebius. I cannot say where the name came from; it was simply there.

I woke up happy. The fire was out. And I was no longer alone. My spirits were back, augmented, multiplied.

Over breakfast that morning I told Isaac and Alice about my dream. I was not ashamed of it. After all, it was only a dream and beyond my control; I was glad to have something to discuss with them besides the weather. I recounted it in a jocular, waggish manner, as if it were a joke. I did not mention the boy's state of undress. "But you see," I told Isaac, "it was my spirit. Only I now have two, maybe three. I don't know where the boy came from, but I am pleased to have his company."

Alice looked confused, to say the least. She stole a look at her husband, wanting him to laugh off my tale. Isaac only looked down and smoothed the napkin in his lap. So she took it upon herself to laugh: Alice's laughter was never very convincing.

But my spirits had lifted my spirits, and I went out that very morning with my letter of introduction.

Brussels looked less grim and oppressive now, more lively and absurd. I found M. Héger's address in an arcade off the rue du Syndicat, a glass-roofed corridor of import and brokerage houses. The upper story was lined with statues of the local deities: Commerce, Industry, Agriculture—all female. Héger's offices were upstairs, behind a naked figure of Art. Her chalky rump peeked in at the window where I played a grand piano for a handsome, one-armed gent dressed like a banker. Henri Héger had been a concert pianist himself before a railway accident reduced him to an impresario, a dealer in musical horseflesh. But he knew music and still loved it and was not entirely cynical. Halfway through my set—improvisations on the sad thoughts that Brahms had overheard, yet played today with a lighter touch, a flippant, sarcastic brio inspired by Eusebius—I heard his chair creak as he leaned forward, growing more attentive.

"*Très amusant,*" he said when I finished. "*Très exotique.*" His shoulder twitched as he tried out one of my finger movements with the hand that was no longer there. "I am surprised that such Liszting excess gained the approval of our classical friend. But I might be able use your, shall we say, talents?"

He had contacts throughout Europe and a request from an American piano manufacturer, Decker Bros. of New York. They needed a virtuoso to puff their product in Europe. American pianos had come into their own, and a piano war was under way, Steinway versus Chickering versus Johnny What-Have-You, each firm with an artist under contract, a human advertisement who played with his sponsor's name hung on his instrument like a shingle. Steinway used Rubie—Anton Rubinstein—Chickering used von Bülow. The

Deckers, who preferred novelty to genius, had a woman, a Latin beauty named Teresa Carenno, touring in America. Later they would use infant prodigies—children were an even greater draw—but they now needed a similar novelty for the overseas trade.

"I do not do concerts," I told Héger. "My music is too intimate for large audiences."

But Héger liked that limitation, thought it would add to my appeal. Little soirées would make me and their product appear more exclusive. My being an American was a selling point as well. "If this rawboned hayseed can produce beauty from our instrument, just think what a sophisticated being like yourself might do"—that would be the unsaid message of my public appearances. Héger suggested I cut my hair so I would look more American, less cosmopolitan. Unlike Brahms, however, he saw I was no bumpkin, but as full of dead composers as any European musician, only their heritage was disheveled in my rough hands.

"And my spirits?" I said. "They create no difficulty?"

"Oh, let us go gentle with *la clairvoyance*," he said. "No mind reading or séances. But a little mystery concerning the source of your improvisations will not do badly for us."

The deal was this: Decker Bros. would pay me one hundred dollars per appearance, out of which I must handle travel and hotel expenses. I was free to make my own engagements on the side. I would also need an advance man, said Héger, someone to serve as both manager and salesman. "I think I can find you a fellow who speaks all the necessary languages."

"Oh, no," I told him. "I have my own man already. I prefer to use him." Fluent in German, Isaac should have no trouble picking up French and any other tongue.

That evening after dinner I told Isaac that the honeymoon was over, we had business to discuss. I expected Alice to excuse herself, but no, she remained at the table, as if this concerned her, too. While I laid out our future as piano shills, she listened with her head cocked to one side, a little dog pretending to understand human speech.

When I finished, she announced, "Why, I speak French. Quite well, if I do say so. What exactly does advance work consist of?"

Did she actually expect to work with us? I refused to consider such a thing. "Fine," I said. "You can teach it to Mr. Kemp." It would give them something useful to do in bed.

"It's not work for a lady," Isaac loudly declared, then added, "my dear."

Alice frowned. "I wasn't proposing that. I just thought— Oh, never mind. Yes, I can teach you. I will enjoy teaching you French. The good moral French of Pascal and Molière."

Isaac discussed the advantages and pitfalls of the proposal, in his usual practical manner, until the question of my spirits arose. "And you will still use your . . . um, other gift?" he asked.

"Of course."

He stole a sidelong glance at his wife, then changed the subject, asking me about the quality of Decker pianos.

The next day the two of us went to see Héger. The manly new husband displayed a manly new arrogance with the one-armed impresario, demanding better terms for us and a larger commission on sales. I was afraid he might spoil the offer, but Héger was impressed with Isaac's business sense and by his race—what could be more American than a Negro? They worked out good terms, and Héger toasted our success with his best cognac. Isaac, of course, abstained.

I was quite pleased as we walked back to the hotel. We had a fresh future. We would remain together. And I was glad to be alone with Isaac again, the first occasion since Baden. It was almost like old times, Isaac looking quite handsome in his bowler hat and cock-of-the-walk strut. Then he spoiled it all by announcing, "Mrs. Kemp is asking after your dictated music."

"Yes. I suppose she would."

"She doesn't understand the spirit part."

"No, I suppose she wouldn't."

His chin rose in his absurd new I-am-a-husband look. "I was wondering," he began, "if we might tell her that your spirit is all make-believe. A gimmick for the public. It would be easier for her to understand."

"What? No!" I said. "Absolutely not!"

"My wife will find it odd that you believe such things."

"So you'd rather have her think I was a knave than a fool?" It suggested that he didn't believe my spirits himself. "No, I refuse to lie about my spirits, and certainly not to protect *her* delicate mind."

He spoke scoldingly. "We are no longer alone, Fitz. It's time that you learned to take other people into consideration."

"Other people? Other people? What about me? If I pretend to be a liar, I will feel like a liar. I will *be* a liar." I angrily shook my head. "Marriage has certainly made you all high-and-mighty."

His hauteur began to waver. "I didn't mean to suggest you lie. I meant only— I don't want to upset Alice."

"So her feelings are more important than mine?"

"No. I just—"

"Do I need to remind you, Mr. Married Man, that it was my spirits who brought you and your beloved together?"

He winced. I had him. His pomposity gave way to raw uncertainty. "Oh, Fitz," he said sadly, "I am sorry. I love Mrs. Kemp. I want to protect her. But you're right. I have no business suggesting you be untrue to your . . . religion."

He wanted to be both a good husband and a good friend. He never forgot he was a husband, but sometimes forgot he was a friend.

"If you like," I offered, "I'll sit down and explain it to her. Every bit."

"That won't be necessary," he said, catching the note of mischief in my tone. "I should do it. In my own way."

One week later I had my debut as the Decker virtuoso with a free concert in an elegant piano showroom. A dozen different pianos crowded the floor, like a pianist's nightmare, but I was required to play only one.

"Decker Bros. of Boston is proud to present—" Héger's flyer featured the squib from Brahms as well as one from himself. "Dr. August's improvisations are a cataract of emotion and invention, as American as Niagara Falls."

Originally my music had been art disguised as spiritualism. Now it was spiritualism disguised as art. People are more forgiving of art. I required no blindfold this time, no magic caress from Isaac. He sat up front with Alice, an earnest married couple as perfectly matched in attitude as a pair of figurines. Héger introduced me. *"Mesdames et messieurs..."*

I was more nervous than I thought I'd be, but Héger's French put me at ease. There is nothing like a foreign language to make one feel safely invisible. I did not fake a trance but played as I did when I was alone, toying with accident and intention, following Eusebius in and out of the different pieces of daydream that I'd played over the years.

When I finished and stood up, the applause was slow, but grew as the audience woke from its own dream. I bowed to them. And I saw Alice up front, her eyes wide as saucers, her face quite pale. What had she heard in my music? Had I inadvertently given away my feelings of love and jealousy?

I tried not to worry about it while Héger translated and explained me to the members of the audience who gathered around afterward, mostly women. They were fascinated, intrigued. "Yes, I think you will do," Héger whispered when we were through. He told me to bring Mr. Kemp to his office tomorrow so we could draw up our itinerary.

I found my companions just outside the door, in a corner of the dripping portico, where Isaac held and petted Alice's tiny white hand. She remained deathly pale, despite the words of assurance he whispered. When he saw me, Isaac said, "You must excuse Mrs. Kemp. Your performance left her at a loss for words."

But Alice had lost none of her words. "Dr. August!" she declared, snatching her hand from Isaac. "I am sorry. The fault is mine. But I found your display in there disturbing. To see you behave so in public—" She saw we were still in public and lowered her voice. "It was unseemly. Unbecoming. You looked so . . ." She drew her waterproof around her shoulders. "Physical. Yes. Your state of abandon. It has upset and confused me."

All she'd seen were the palsied hands, bouncing rump, and frantic grimaces of any performer at a keyboard, but Alice had never witnessed anything like it, except maybe her husband in bed. I am certain that is what upset her. After all, Isaac himself once complained that I made the same uninhibited faces during both acts.

"When Mr. Kemp told me about your spirits," she continued, "I thought he was speaking in metaphor. Now I don't know what to think. I don't believe in witchcraft or demons. But you looked bewitched in there. Possessed."

"So I am, Mrs. Kemp," I said, smiling meekly. "Possessed to the tips of my fingers."

Isaac shot a blaming look at me, followed by an exasperated look at his wife. "We accomplish nothing by discussing it!" he snapped at her. "You must take it on faith! It has brought us this far. And it puts meat on the table."

A pinch of distress crossed her face, as she wondered—what? That her husband was bound to a madman? That her own beloved might be mad himself?

He took her by the arm and led her down the steps. "It is only music," he grumbled, in a more apologetic tone. "Fancy, foreign music. Understanding will come later."

She fired a look at me over her shoulder, a blaming, worried look. But all she said was "I do not mean to impugn your talent, Dr. August. I do not judge. But I do not understand your music. I found it mighty disturbing."

What does she say in her diary?

Tuesday, October 19

Our French lessons continue. My husband struggles with the rules of grammar, but his pronunciation is impeccable. I struggle to understand A's music, which I found alarming at the "recital" last night. It was a savage noise, with no pretty tunes, & embarrassing to see a man carry on like a wild animal. They attempted to explain, & I suppose I will understand in time. But it is of no matter. If my husband can accept it, so shall I.

Did my spirits mean so little to her? Or did she not dare ask any dangerous questions about her strange new existence?

30

WE began our new life of foreign parts. It unfolded not so much over time as in places: Antwerp, Bruges, Paris, Monte Carlo that winter, Nice and Marseille, then back to Paris and on to Holland. We passed down a long, narrow landscape of hotel corridors, second-class railway carriages, and miles of black-and-white keys. They say that travel broadens the mind, but too much travel can dissolve the world, reduce it to glass.

The Decker Bros. engagements gave us an itinerary, a bass line upon which I could improvise other jobs and private sessions. My spirits were a secret, but a very public secret, one that people asked us about constantly. I performed in piano showrooms, concert rooms, and elegant salons. Admission was free and by invitation only, except we invited everyone. Isaac served as manager, sales agent, introducer, and translator. He picked up French more quickly than I did, yet my inability to speak added to my mystery, enveloping my art in the light-headed dizziness of incomprehension. Music is the most mysterious of arts, erratic, irrational, nebulous. Yet our logical century of machines and money treated it as the king of art.

I fell deeper into my music, fascinated with the strange new grammars of sound that Eusebius shared with me, delicate off-key shimmers and pastel fragments. My audiences knew the old music already and wanted something fresh and exotic. The European moneyed classes were as bored as spoiled children. I grew less mindful of my audience. Oh, I never forgot they were there, a shadowy mass of evening clothes wearing wax masks of candlelight. I'd throw them a bone now and then, a showy hand-over-hand fugue or demonic variation on a popular song, but only as a transition to the gentler, subtler inventions that were my real meat. And I would finish with whatever phrase I'd used to begin, which created an impression of structure and purpose. It's the oldest trick in the book: The end is the beginning, the snake bites its tail, the circle is closed.

Isaac had no difficulty speaking in public now. A foreign language provided him with a disguise, a suit of armor, and he no longer spoke just for himself, or even for me, but to support a wife. He even sold quite a few pianos.

I'm not exactly sure how Alice occupied her days that first year. Hotel life reduces a wife's duties; she did not need to cook or clean house or wash clothes. Her chief chore was writing out the scores of invitations that Isaac delivered by hand. I often found Alice soaking her ink-stained fingers in a cup of vinegar while she read aloud to her husband in the evening. They were big ones for reading: Emerson, George Eliot, Walter Scott, and more sermons than I care to remember. They invited me to join them, and I often did, although I preferred livelier literature, Dickens or Twain or, when available, a good lurid penny dreadful. Alice read clearly and precisely, but she did not do voices. The name George Eliot remains pickled in my memory with a sharp aroma of vinegar.

One would expect a good New England Protestant like Alice to need to confront the business of my demons, yet she carefully tiptoed around them. She loved her husband and wanted to love his friend. I loved my friend and tried to love his wife. She accompanied us to performances and accustomed herself to my rapturous seizures. She even grew used to being mistaken for my wife. She developed a thick hide against the disdainful looks or amused smirks that appeared whenever we set people straight.

What does she say about all this?

Monday, July 24

Soap 1 franc

Boots (for A) 24 francs

Private item (female) 3 francs

Vinegar 3 sous

Oh, yes. She also handled our household expenses. I'm sorry that it crowds the personal from her diary. An occasional mention of something, even the weather, might help me to reconstruct that year better.

But there is a photograph. A studio photograph. I cannot see it, of course, but I don't need to. The image is engraved in my mind's eye. Photography ruins memory, filling our heads with mechanical reproductions, yet the tendency has benefits for a blind man.

But there we are, all three of us, in a studio in Amsterdam, posed in front of a painted backdrop of dikes and windmills. Isaac and I had never had our picture taken during all our years together. But he wanted—no, he needed—to be photographed with his wife. He insisted that I come with them. "How do we look, how do we look?" he kept asking when I stood beside the Dutch photographer burrowed under the black skirts of his camera. After four or five exposures Isaac invited me to join them for one last shot. I sat while they stood. And there we are, in black and brown and beige, no doubt, although my mind has tinted it and we're all in color, even the artificial landscape behind us.

We sat stiffly for the long exposure. There is nothing casual or natural about those old photos—the shutter speeds were too slow for smiles. But hidden truths float to the surface while you hold still, things disguised by the say-cheese of a kodak. Isaac looks handsomely majestic, his beard neatly trimmed, his forehead high and noble—his hairline had begun to climb. All doubt and uncertainty are buried in the virile righteousness of a good husband. He looks, in fact, like a bit of a humbug. Alice stands beside him, short, thin, pug-nosed, and bird-eyed without her specs—the little steel pretzel is pinned to her bodice. Her hand grips her husband's arm for balance. She focuses on something to the left, while her husband gazes to the right, so they appear cross-eyed as a couple. The young friend who sits in front of them, however—his short, pomaded hair and unfashionably clean-shaven face make him look much younger than they—gazes straight into the camera, with folded arms and a sly, winking aspect, as if throned in the catbird seat. He seems alone yet powerful, detached from the couple yet in control of their lives. I have always liked that photo.

I suppose the actual picture looks only antique and unreal now. If I could see it, however, it would still appear contemporary, as any old picture of yourself remains timeless despite the ravages of time. I was able to save it years later when Alice methodically went through our albums and removed each and every likeness of the man who wrecked her life.

We returned to Germany, for the grand opening of Richard Wagner's Festspielhaus in Bayreuth, the summer of 1876. Héger reported that the town would be packed with music lovers, great names, and crowned heads. I met the emperor of Portugal there, an old man with a white beard and no crown, only a red sash around his tux to let you know he was more than a banker. He'd just been to Philadelphia for the American Centennial. He came up to me after my recital to ask what I knew about the "talkaphone," the invention that his new friend Alexander Bell showed him in Philadelphia. He spoke as if all Americans knew each other and my music must owe something to Bell's wires.

My chief memory of Bayreuth was the mobs, as bad as Coney Island thirty years later. The restaurants were so crowded that it was hard to get anything to eat. I performed at a few evening parties, none of them attended by the Master of Bayreuth, although his hawk-faced wife came to one, no doubt attracted by reports that Brahms said I played "the true Music of the Future." She came up to me afterward, looked me up and down, and asked Isaac if I were a Jew. When he told her no, she appeared very disappointed and departed without another word.

We missed the premiere of the complete *Ring*—it had sold out months in advance—but were given three unwanted tickets to *Tristan und Isolde*. In a wide, dark theater like a cave full of bats, with much grumbling and whining from an orchestra hidden in a covered pit, two beefy singers drank a love potion that caused them to strike poses, for hours it seemed, until they happily expired in each other's arms. Alice was enthralled, much to my surprise, but then her poetic side always responded to the obvious: sunsets, sea storms, and Wagner.

I loathed it yet cannot say with certainty how much my dislike was for the music or for Alice's love of it. To tell the truth, I had been respectfully indifferent to Wagner until that night, admiring occasional passages and devices yet unsure what all the fuss was about. Alice's love forced me to take a stand. But I suspect she loved Wagner chiefly because I didn't. There was a secret war between us that did not find a way to express itself until we stood on either side of a great gray river of Teutonic noise.

We argued about it afterward, wading back to the hotel through a mob of moony, sleepwalking Wagnerites. "A musical gimmick," I said. "One long, woozy open chord. Infinity without melody, only snippets of tune repeated every half hour or so."

"Well, I don't know music, but I know what I like," Alice said defiantly. Only it wasn't the music she liked so much as the story. She loved the love-death.

"Sentimental foolishness," I scoffed. "Lovers dying for love. Only fools die for love."

"You have obviously never known love, Dr. August."

I bit hard on my lip. "That is of no matter," I said. "But the pain of unrequited passion is greatly exaggerated. To die of such pain would be idiotic. The notion can seem pretty only to someone who has never experienced unrequited love."

Isaac walked just ahead of us, looking for a café with a free table, betraying no suspicion that our argument had anything to do with him.

*   *   *

So, no. My fine renunciation, my selfless surrender, was not full of love and calm and the peace that passeth understanding.

I did not dislike Alice. Let me make that clear. But I did not like her either. I did not know what to make of this woman who had dropped into my life and remained there, like a gallstone in a cup of tea.

I had good days and bad days, kind moods and cruel ones. There were actually times when I was glad that Isaac was married. It took him off my hands. His bad moods were no longer my fault or responsibility. On other days, however, when I was feeling lonely, sad, or earthy, I hoped that once the novelty of marriage wore off, he might return to my bed, if only for a night.

You would expect a man of my tastes and situation to find a new friend, a fresh love. Yet it never crossed my mind. I still loved Isaac, not as he loved me, but I could not betray my love of him. I would be as faithful to Isaac as he was to Alice.

And I was not really alone. After all, I had my spirits, and one was a beautiful boy. Eusebius not only affected my music but continued to appear in my dreams, every month or so. The horse and piano always accompanied him, but the settings changed. Their favorite place was the seashore, but they also visited mountains, forests, gardens, and palaces. Once I dreamed that they were in a train station, racing through the crowd to catch the 9:15 to Ghent, a trotting horse with a cloaked rider and a bare-assed boy with wobbling wings. Eusebius was always nude, but he sometimes wore wings, stiff, springy folds of white feathers. He had to squeeze them through the door of the second-class compartment.

He continued to smile and wink at me, but we never touched, never stood closer than ten feet apart. Yet I was grateful for his company, moved by his beauty. He was a heartless boy, exuberantly, enviably heartless. He was only a spirit, of course, and had no body, but that was fine by me. A body can only get a person in trouble.

31

It was odd, however, to live in the shadow of a marriage, so close yet always outside it.

Good marriages are private mysteries. Only the truly rotten ones reveal their secrets in public. Unable to speak of sex, the old novels luxuriated in bad marriage. Alice's beloved George Eliot, for example, is full of husbands and wives naked in their misery, a pornography of nerves. The good marriages, however, remain clothed and whole, as solid as apples.

During that first year I had no doubts that Isaac and Alice had a good marriage. My moments of envy outside their magic circle seemed entirely justified. That happiness might contain a few contradictory tints crossed my mind now and then. They must have had their arguments but kept all disagreements to themselves. They settled into a solid connubiality like a perfect peace. I saw it as peace anyway, but then I was enjoying my own virtuous loneliness too much to notice any change in temperature.

We returned to Monte Carlo for the start of the winter season. We took a long stroll our first day there and stopped at an outdoor café high above the Mediterranean. It was a beautiful afternoon, the air alive with salt and pine, a single palm tree out of *The Arabian Nights* framing a sea painted in the blues and greens of a peacock's tail. The promenade squeaked with pretty ladies being pushed along in Bath chairs. We drank chocolate, I ate a plate of cream cakes, Isaac read an English newspaper. Alice sat gazing at the sea. She seemed in a wistful, quiet mood. "Dr. August?" she abruptly asked. "Do you ever feel homesick?"

"No, can't say that I do. The world is my home. If I feel homesick, it is only for the stars and ethereal spheres."

Neither she nor Isaac paid any notice now when I spoke in this flighty, whimsical manner.

"Europe is nice," Alice insisted. "I'm not saying it isn't. But I do feel occasional twinges of homesickness." She turned to her husband. "Do you ever feel that, my dear?"

"Homesick for what?" he grumbled.

"Oh, I don't know," she said. "The air, the light. People speaking the language you grew up with. The foods you knew as a child. Hotcakes and jam. Buttermilk. Apple pie."

"Table scraps," Isaac curtly added. "Rancid fatback. Stale bread." He lowered his paper. "People treating you like a dog. Scorning you for the color of your skin."

"Please," said Alice, wincing. "You do not need to remind me of that. I know your past was no church picnic. Neither was mine. I certainly do not miss how an unmarried woman was looked upon. Or no. There are times when I even miss that. Since here people do not look upon me at all." She frowned at herself for saying too much. "I do not mean to say that I want to go back," she claimed. "No. I meant only that I do feel mildly homesick. Now and again."

"I don't," said Isaac. "Never. Because—" He reached over and covered her hand with his. "*You* are my home."

Alice looked startled, hurt, hopeful, and skeptical, all at once. I would have killed to hear Isaac say something like that to me, but she only stared at him.

I thought she was being difficult and contrary, until Isaac removed his hand and returned to his paper, as if he had set everything right. Alice sank back and looked out at the sea again, avoiding my quizzical eyes.

It seemed that all was not right in heaven. I took a perverse thrill in the discovery, before I decided it was no business of mine and ordered another plate of cakes.

The next afternoon I went to the concert room where I would perform that night, to tune and test the instrument that had just arrived from Paris. It was like all Decker products, the key-and-hammer action crisp and clean but the sound pitched a bit thin. I still preferred the heavier, richer sonority of Steinway and Bösendorfer, our competitors.

I had finished tuning and was idly playing to myself in that breezy, open room over the sea, when I heard a clop of hard little boots across the floor. I turned and found Alice marching down the aisle, alone. She wore her best promenade clothes, meaning her usual brown habit was lightened with a gaily colored parasol, which she rarely opened, and a small hat like a slice of green velvet pie.

"Why, Mrs. Kemp," I said. "To what do I owe this—pleasure?"

"Fitz," she began. We still addressed each other formally, after a whole year together, but today she called me Fitz. "Do you have a minute? I need to talk. I want your ear."

Surprised by the request, and wary, I gestured at a chair.

"No, I do not need to sit," she said, but thought better of it and sat anyway. She had a furtive, guilty look. "It is wrong for me to come to you like this. But I am worried about Mr. Kemp. I wonder if you could shed some light on his state of mind."

"You want me to ask my spirits to read his thoughts for you?" I diddled at the keyboard.

"No, I meant only—" She frowned. It hurt her pride to come to me like this, but I did not make it easier for her. "Must you always play the fool?"

"I am only being myself."

"Not today. Please. I need to talk about Mr. Kemp. With someone who knows him." She began to stab the floor with the tip of her parasol. "Understand. This is not about my being homesick. I do not want to go home. It has nothing to do with what you heard yesterday. And I am no empty-headed schoolgirl. No romantic fool. But—" She couldn't look me in the eye. "Something has changed in my husband. My faith in him has— Is it my imagination, or is his heart turning cold?"

I was tempted to launch into the *Liebestod* theme from *Tristan,* but I was too interested now to mock her.

"Please, Fitz. Tell me. Have you seen it, too? I fear that he no longer loves me as I love him."

"What makes you think that?"

"Nothing that he says or does. It is only what I feel. Perhaps it is that the first excitement of marriage is gone. But no new feeling has risen to take its place. He is all tenderness and duty toward me, but it is only duty, even his tenderness."

There was no whine or whimper in her confession, only anger that she felt such things, and resentment that she had to share them with me.

"Something has gone off. Something isn't happening." She looked straight at me. "I fear my race is all wrong for him."

She actually said *her* race, not his. I wondered if it were not her race but her sex that was the matter.

"Has he ever loved a colored woman?" she asked.

"What? No. Not in all the years I've known him."

"Never?"

"You're the only woman he's ever been close to."

There was cause for worry there, but Alice only shook her head. "It makes no sense for me to dwell on my race. But I can find no other explanation for my fear. What has made his love an issue for me, Fitz, is that— He wants a child. And I hate to say it, but— I'm afraid to give him one."

Here it was, the real cause for her crisis of faith. Of course. But could a wife decide not to get pregnant? I didn't understand such things. I didn't dare ask how, only, "Why?"

"Many reasons. There is the mixed blood of the child, of course. But I am worried for its sake, not mine, the future of our child. I am sure I will love it as I love its father. I will not feel ashamed. But to give birth in a foreign land terrifies me. I don't know if my body will survive it. One hears so many stories. But I could master those fears if I believed he loved me. What worries me is that I will bear those risks for naught. That I will give him a child and find he is still cold."

I would be lying if I said that my soul didn't brighten with hopes for myself here. Their marriage would fall apart. I would have Isaac to myself again. And yet her predicament was so awful, so real, that I felt trapped with Alice in her sorrow.

"I don't know what to tell you," I said. "Except that Isaac has never loved anyone as much as he loves you." Which was true enough. And I'd experienced the same doubts about his love myself, yet we've seen that I was right to doubt.

"So there has been no woman of his own race?" she asked.

"Never."

"You do not think he would love me better if I were dark?"

I was tempted to laugh, it was such a wild hypothesis. "No."

Her fears over having a child, all valid, had become fears about her husband's love. But the only causes she could find for such a fear were dusky mistresses who didn't exist.

"So you and I are the only people that he has ever loved?"

"Yes," I said, "yes." Did she know how close those loves actually were? "His wife and his friend."

She gazed into my eyes, as if to see if I were telling the truth. Or see if there were another truth I wasn't sharing.

And I thought, wanting her to read the thought in my eyes, "If you are worried about me, be assured that he doesn't love me. We were lovers once, and I love him still, but he loves you."

I don't know why I thought that. If I'd really wanted her to know,

I would've said it aloud, only the truth might have ended their marriage. It seemed that I wanted to protect this marriage.

We said not a word as we gazed into each other's eyes, those delicate holes of quicksilver. We gazed as if in a glass darkly, two dark glasses reflecting a man we both loved. But all I saw in her eyes was "I do not know what I fear. I hoped that you could tell me, but you can't."

Her parasol suddenly jabbed the floor. "I have said too much," she declared and stood up. "I do not know what I hoped to learn. Perhaps I only wanted to test my fears by saying them aloud. But I thank you for your time. You will not mention to Isaac that we had this exchange?"

"Of course not."

"You have been kinder than I anticipated. I will be frank, Fitz. I do not always understand you. Sometimes you seem as mad as a hatter. And other times I think you're as moral and sane as Isaac or myself."

"And what makes you certain that both of you are sane?"

"Please. Don't spoil your kindness with nonsense. Good day." And she left, tucking her parasol under her arm like an officer's baton, an automatic disguise of her vulnerability.

I felt more irritable than moral once she was gone. I was annoyed with myself for being so kind. I should have ruthlessly seized the chance to recapture Isaac. Why had I taken her side? Because it was the honorable thing to do, and because, to be frank, I saw nothing here for me. I could have made Alice miserable, but it would not bring Isaac back to my bed.

My music that night was an angry, jangly, banging thing. Eusebius was petulant, as if furious with me for being nice to Alice. Afterward, watching Isaac negotiate with a customer, I found myself angry with him for not being a better husband. He was admirable now only in his role as a husband? My year as a tag-along to their marriage, a third leg, had warped my love into a lump of selfless perversity.

Eusebius appeared to me in a dream that night. We were in a deep green forest, all four of us. The boy did not smile but gave me a scornful, cursing look. He clutched the horse by the reins and stroked its snout, so lewdly I could feel the silky bone in my own hand. Then the boy made a fist and punched the horse in its muzzle. He struck again, and the horse reared up, nearly shaking the piano off its back. Eusebius gripped the reins tight and continued to beat the poor beast in its snout.

I woke up to a loud, furious knocking. It was morning, and someone was banging at the door. "Yes?"

Isaac entered. My heart leaped up—for an instant. I had wanted him to come to my bed, only not in daylight, and not fully dressed, and certainly not with such a fierce look on his face.

"Damn you, Fitz! You have no business discussing my marriage with my wife!"

"What? Who?" I was half awake. "Oh, yes. Alice asked if you love her. I assured her you do."

"Of course I do! She's my wife. I'm her husband."

I sat up, shaking myself free from my dream of Eusebius. "Alice told you we spoke?"

"It slipped out, and she had to admit it. She insisted you are my best friend and there was nothing wrong with the two of you discussing me." He had begun to pace the room. "But can't you imagine how that makes me feel? Like I was a child. A problem. To be considered and solved without my say."

"She wanted to know if you love her. All wives wonder that about their husbands. Sooner or later."

"I've told her I love her. What else does she want? Every time she asks, I tell her. But she doesn't believe me."

I knew exactly how Alice felt.

"What else does she want? What other proof?" He stood over me, waving his hands in the air. "Does she want tears? Does she want blood? What can I do to show——?" He suddenly sank to my bed. "Oh, Fitz," he groaned and clutched his head in both hands. "I am a terrible husband. I do not know how to love my wife."

"Easy there, old man," I said and patted his back. My legs were pinned against his rump. I could have grabbed his collar, pulled him down, and kissed him, but I merely continued to pat. "It's not so bad as all that."

"It is!" he cried. "She is falling out of love with me, and it's my fault."

They were so perfectly matched, two fretful mirrors of doubt. "She has not fallen out of love."

"She has. Because I have not given her a child."

"What?" I stopped patting. "She told you that?"

"She doesn't need to. I can see it. She wants children as badly as I do. But it has not happened. I know she blames me. But it's as if God does not want us to have children."

I cannot guess at Alice's method of contraception. Abortions were easy to obtain in that private age—any midwife, doctor, or phar- macist would have been happy to oblige. Yet I cannot believe Alice chose that remedy. I assume she avoided conception by carefully picking which nights each month were safe, a gamble, but with much better odds than a roulette table.

"She doesn't blame you," I said.

"She told you about this?" He looked horrified.

"Oh, no. Not a word. She said nothing about children." Honor prevented me from revealing it was her doing, however she did it. "But I feel it in my heart: She does not blame you."

"I hope you are right. Because if you are not, there is no hope for me, Fitz." He rubbed a hand over his beard and forehead, his face bare of its mask of pride. "What should I do?"

"I don't know. You might be more affectionate with her. Yes. Tell her you love her, even when she doesn't ask."

He didn't like that. "Love should show of its own volition, if it's sincere. Oh, I suppose one can force it a little. But you believe she still loves me?"

"Yes," I said. "So don't worry about the children. Fate or God or luck will give you children, when the time comes."

"One hopes," he said. "One can only hope." He slowly stood up. "Thank you, my friend. You are a very good friend, you know."

"Oh, yes. I know how good a friend I am."

"I will see you downstairs. Uh, you will not tell Alice we had this talk?"

"Of course not. I am the soul of discretion." As well as the soul of twisted, selfless love.

And that was the end of it. For the time being. That was all I heard anyway. They disappeared back into the sealed tabernacle of their marriage. It was all about them, of course. There was nothing here for me, despite what Eusebius thought. I would only have made a fool of myself if I tried to use their crisis to get Isaac back. There was vanity as well as pity in my goodness.

They were somewhat cooler toward me after our chats, ashamed of how much I knew. I didn't dare ask Alice what was happening. When I asked Isaac, he said only, "Nothing's wrong. Nothing ever was. Or if it were, it will soon pass."

We went to Barcelona after Monte Carlo, then Madrid, but the Spanish middle classes were too tin-eared and miserly for our jaunt to prove profitable. We went on to Lisbon, where I tried to contact the emperor of Portugal, but the old man, if he ever saw my visiting card or letter, had forgotten our brief acquaintance in Bayreuth.

On our last day in Lisbon, Isaac and Alice came down to breakfast arm in arm, with the beatific glows of two freshly minted saints.

"We have good news," Isaac announced. "Glorious news. Mrs. Kemp is—in a delicate condition."

"What a delightful surprise," I said. I don't think I sounded sarcastic.

I can't guess at the drama behind the deed, if renewed kindness from Isaac made Alice risk the wager, or she decided on her own, or the silver ball simply landed in the roulette wheel by chance. But whatever doubts and fears Alice had entertained before were swept away by Isaac's loving joy.

I cannot say that I was much overjoyed myself, but I was not heartbroken either, even when I recognized that a blessed event might be a holy nuisance in trains and hotels.

There was love in the marriage again, renewed interest and affection. Isaac fussed over Alice, which pleased her, though her patience was tried when he fretted over what she ate and how many hours she slept. She confessed surprise that pregnancy wasn't nearly as unpleasant as she'd been led to believe.

Eusebius reappeared one night and forgave me, in a fashion. He amiably shook his head and grinned, amused by my situation, while he lugged a melon at his stomach in mockery of Alice.

The first six months passed quickly. For weeks at a time I often forgot we had a loaf in the oven. When Alice began to show, Isaac refused to let her go out in public. There were arguments over that, until Isaac gave in and she suddenly changed her mind, confessing that it was too exhausting to walk the streets with a body like an overloaded market basket.

We settled in Paris for the final month, at the Hôtel Brittanique, waiting patiently as if for an unreliable steamboat. They discussed whether or not to use chloroform, another new invention, and Alice decided no, she should give birth as God decreed all women should since Eve, with pain.

I took a long walk in the Bois de Bologne one afternoon and returned to find Isaac seated in the corridor outside their room, petrified. It had begun. The midwife and doctor were inside. Isaac sat with his arms twisted around the arms of his chair, his jaw gripped so tight that I expected blood to spout from his eyes. The closed door barely muffled the loud moans within, yelps and gasps that made my piano antics seem quite tame, the experience so strong that even Alice lost control. I was shocked for her and filled with pity. Other guests coolly walked past our door, showing no alarm that their hotel had become a hospital.

The awful noises finally ended in sobs and murmurs, and then the high harmonica cry of a baby. Isaac let go in a great sigh.

Another eternity passed before a midwife opened the door and smiled at us. Isaac and I hurried in.

A French doctor in a top hat and croupier whiskers was pulling on his coat. He looked so matter-of-fact, so casual.

Alice lay in a gray bed, quite gray herself, bloodless and deflated. Her hair was undone, a chaos of hair spread on her pillow. I expected the sheets to be bloody, but the only sign of blood was a pink-filled basin on the floor. Alice gasped and sobbed, trying to catch her breath after running a hundred miles.

Isaac bent down to kiss his wife on her cold forehead. He then peeked at the tiny extra face by her side.

In all our sensational race novels and melodramas, this is always the moment of truth: Whose child is it? Will it live as white or colored? But what can one say about a new baby? They're such raw, red, squirrelly things. You cannot even be sure they're human. We saw only a life, a female life. It was a girl. We knew that much. I was moved, shaken, touched, not least because Isaac had promised that they would name a girl after me: Augusta.

He timidly gathered the bundle into his arms, stood up and held her. A wizened face no bigger than an apple lay on his coat sleeve. He gazed down at her, open-mouthed, rapturous. And all I could think was: He never looked at me like that. I glanced over at Alice, blaming her for this late flicker of jealousy. But I found her numbly watching Isaac with a curious gaze, as if she, too, were thinking: He never looked at *me* like that.

32

ENOUGH about Isaac and Alice. Whose story are we telling here anyway, theirs or mine?

And this was my heyday, my time of fame, the golden age of Dr. August. I had my vocation, my music, my art. If my personal life paled beside that of the Kemps, what is life for any artist but a mess of hindrances? For true artists there's no life, there is only art. Our friends can do our living for us.

What do the books say about me?

From *Monsieur Croche the Dilettante Hater* by Claude Debussy, newspaper columns, 1901–1903, published 1921:

"People grouse about the distressing new freedoms in work by Scriabin, Moussorgski, and yourself," replied Monsieur Croche as I watched his cigar form fresh fantasias in the twilight. "They blame the decadence of the new century. But artists have always needed to explore new shapes and sounds. I remember attending a recital twenty-five years ago, by an American named August, a fantasist who claimed to play music dictated by ghosts. Pure nonsense, of course, but a clever ploy, a sugarcoating for timid bourgeois who wouldn't have swallowed his original music otherwise. And it was very fine music, too, one of archaic modes and devilish tritones—

the *diabolus in musica*—much like the melancholy comedy of your eccentric friend, Satie."

From *The Letters of William James*, published 1920:

Bolton St. London, December 3, 1882

Darling old Father—

I am once more back with Harry after a flying visit to Paris.... My principal pleasure there was to meet a new kind of medium, an American piano player named Dr. August. You would have enjoyed him, Papa. My colleague M. Renouvier took me to hear the man perform at a party in the Faubourg St. Germain. He claims to improvise, but Renouvier knew the rumors that his inventions are spirit-borne would intrigue me. And his gently nervous tunes sounded quite unworldly to my untrained ear. I went up to him afterwards and slyly asked after his music. A pudgy, bloodless critter, like many uprooted American artists here, including our Harry, he retains nonetheless a good American grit. His mildly embarrassed joshing over his source convinced me that he is sincere about his spirits. He finally let go with the confession: "Yes, it does come from the other side. Dictated by a triumvirate of genies: a boy, a horse, and a piano." He laughed, as if he were having me on, and I laughed with him but continued to pursue this. I asked after his dreams and hallucinations, trying to guess at his subconscious. I even asked if he were aware of a subconscious, and he knew of no such thing, he said, only the spirits that some artists call The Muse. So he clearly believes them. His will to believe makes him of great interest to me.

Both Harry and our sister roast me for my fascination with such characters, but I trust you to understand, dear Papa. Most are charlatans, of course, but their metaphysical fakery is less rotten than the moonshine of our Hegelians. And now and then one finds those who open doors on worlds not yet understood by philosophy....

That was the Harvard philosopher, of course, then a doctor of
nervous disorders, but quite jolly, so jolly that I suspected at first he
was a Pinkerton hired to investigate me. His brother "Harry" was
the novelist, Henry James, who I gather was not jolly, merely prissy.
The doctor thought he was being so sly, yet I knew what he was
getting at, a confession that my spirits were only the misunderstood
dreams of my underself.

And they were dreams, but I understood them quite well, thank
you. When I faked my music, I used my brain, the part of me that
also produced words, arithmetic, and lies. But my spirit music came
directly from my body, the source of dreams, love, lust, and tears.
My brain only rode the process, steering it this way and that, as if
it were a horse. Now and then the horse would bolt, and the brain
could only watch helplessly as hands raced and scrambled and jug-
gled notes. But such occasions were rare. Usually I let my fingers
dreamily grope the keyboard, fishing up new chords and connections
from its depths, while my ears strained to hear what the spirits in
my body found, like eyes trying to see into the dark.

From "The Eltvey Home Organ," advertisement in *The Ladies
Home Journal*, 1883:

"I have long admired the rich and noble tones of your instrument.
My great friend Abbé Liszt agrees that the Eltvey Reed Organ is the
equal of a pipe organ in its range and sound."—Richard Wagner,
world-renowned composer

"A good organ."—Camille Saint-Saëns, chief organist at the Cathedral of Notre-Dame de Paris

"Such a glorious instrument. The music of the spheres can now become the music of the home."—Dr. F. W. August, American virtuoso.

I assume the Master of Bayreuth also got one of their wheezy
musical appliances in exchange for his squib. We sold ours to an
iron merchant in Rouen.

*   *   *

From *Journal de Goncourt* by Edmond Goncourt, fifth volume, published 1891:

Wednesday, 2 April 1884

Dined at Daudet's, where Mallarmé was as mercurial as ever, a perfect riddle. His latest foible is an American pianist, Dr. August, whose recitals are the Wild West Show of the season. Mallarmé would not stop talking about the man. What his overly exquisite sensibility takes from such a crude provincial is beyond reasonable comprehension, but the artful fox claims to believe the man's music is divinely inspired. Of more interest to me is the gossip about the American's family. He has a dry little wife and two children, a surprise for someone said to be quite a lady himself. But there is also a Negro servant, a strapping black majordomo, and the children have an Italian, even Creole aspect. Droll thoughts run through one's mind on the true state of affairs in this typical American household.

If the haughty snob had asked, we would have told him the truth. We never lied about who was married to whom.

Mallarmé must have been that cold Frenchman who kept coming to hear me play. He asked the most peculiar questions. I thought he might be romantically smitten, until one evening he presented me with a slim volume of poems, indecipherable stuff, at least as Alice translated them, all about satyrs and unicorns. He seemed to think I'd understand.

From *The Man Who Broke the Bank at Monte Carlo and Other Tales of Americans Abroad* by M. L. Cunningham, published 1904:

Wherever well-heeled Americans gathered to feed and play during that velvet age, one found not only threadbare dukes and out-of-pocket princes on the prowl for rich wives but charlatans preying upon the gullible. One of the most curious cases in my experience was the notorious Dr. August, the man whose name I myself made synonymous with infamy. He was a pianist, a purveyor of musical snake oil. A confidence man, his music inspired more uncertainty than trust, so perhaps we should call him a confusion man. I have spent my life exposing this dastardly fellow, ever since our first encounter in the insalubrious company of the shady Madame Blavatsky. His real name was Boyd. He was an Irish adventurer who claimed to be American, wrapping his dubious gifts in our glorious Stars and Stripes. He and his mongrel gang of musical mulattoes, including two pickaninnies, skulked into Monte Carlo whenever they needed to replenish their coffers. I have told the story of his most nefarious crime before and will repeat it here, but am saving it for a later chapter.

Yes, yes, let's save it for later.

You recognize our old friend Marmaduke Cunningham? He was still lurking about. He had dropped the "captain" and was a full-time journalist now, no longer dabbling in spirits, only lies and slander. I never encountered him in Monte Carlo, however. Our next meeting came years later, in another country.

From *Mémoires d'un amnésique* by Erik Satie, published 1912:

I admire Columbus for inventing America, which gave us such icy wit. The best sample of its wit was a comedian of the keyboard, Doctor F. W. August. His music was as hilarious as a train wreck in heaven. Angels flew from his smashed chords, God swallowed his beard, and Beethoven was knocked into a cocked hat. Debussy took me to hear him thirty years ago. His music was so much madder than mine that I seemed to have dreamed him. Or perhaps he dreamed me. Nevertheless, I am now awake, and he is gone. I can only call out to him in gratitude, wherever he may be: Hoopla.

The man is joking, of course, only I cannot tell if it's entirely at my expense. His name is one I do not remember. We might hunt up a few examples of his music. It sounds like he may have stolen some of mine.

That's all you were able to discover at the library? How quickly one sinks in the ocean of history. My fame was like my music: It evaporated in the air.

And yet, if you live long enough, you find yourself popping up now and then as a footnote to somebody else's story. I was there, wasn't I? I left a few footprints in the world, which is more than most men can say. Besides, the world is not our home. We are here only for a visit.

33

THERE'S still nothing but expenses in Alice's diary? I'm not surprised. She was a mother now and didn't need to measure out her days in ink, not when she had a living, growing two-footed calendar to mark the passage of time.

So we have only my memory to go on, and one remembers less of middle age than youth, less of peaceful times than turbulent ones. And this was a peaceful time, a good time.

We went from city to city. I played my music, Isaac arranged bookings and sold pianos, Alice raised their daughter, then their daughter and son.

They ignored Eve and used chloroform for their second child: Isaac Tristan Kemp. Yes, you, my recording angel. Since Isaac had named the girl, Alice named the boy. Why she named you after a fool who dies for love is beyond me, but Alice was full of surprises.

You were born in 1880. My God. I still think of you as young, but you're even older now than I was during this golden age. Time's wingèd chariot, indeed.

But there we were: the Kemps, their children, and me. Such a curious menagerie, a family of salamanders, only we did not pass from fire to water but from Lisbon to Oslo and back again.

If this book is illustrated, here's a good place for an evocative picture: We descend from a second-class compartment into yet another train station, wreathed in steam and foreign shouts. Alice's arms are full of a bonneted baby who grabs at the waxed cherry on her hat. Isaac, his own hat knocked askew, has a two-year-old girl draped over his shoulder, backward like a sack of grain, as he screws a tiny foot into a tiny shoe. The great virtuoso himself follows, struggling with four or five valises. He cries for a porter and dreams of the day when these infants are no longer luggage but old enough to carry luggage themselves.

There is nothing like children to make one aware that the years are flying. After all, they remind you how full time was when you were young and the year between your fifth and sixth birthdays seemed a joyful eternity. But you're an adult now, and you see *them* go from five to six in the blink of the eye.

The babies grew invisibly, like trees, from crawlers to stumblers to walkers. Isaac and Alice were like two trees themselves, slowly growing together, each remaking itself to the other. Isaac turned into the classic Victorian papa, a tough, dry businessman in public, a sentimental fool with his babies. Alice was the practical one. She lost some of her stiffness—living with children took the starch out of her manner. It made her more confident, too, hard-nosed without being heartless. Handling our expenses, she worried about money more than her husband did. I never thought about money.

Yet this straitlaced couple had hitched their wagon to me, a gentle lunatic. I am sure that Alice still assumed I was half mad. But she accepted it, as one accepts an addled grandparent or dotty aunt. She had to accept it, since our livelihood depended on my madness. People can live with almost anything under the right circumstances. I wasn't mad. Oh, I sometimes spent a morning comatose in bed, as if with a hangover, after one of my rare hallucinatory performances. And I could be terribly absentminded, forgetting what city we were in or even the name of our hotel. But I was not mad, not yet.

I assumed at the time that Alice and Isaac discussed me regularly, sharing doubts and theories. The worst aspect of marriage for friends is we can never guess what a man and wife say to each other in private. But the truth is that they spoke little of me. They had their children to think about.

Children fill up the heart and mind. And they open a window on the private intricacies of a marriage.

What I saw first were Isaac and Alice's caring, their patient love, their fretful concern, such a surprise for an orphan like myself, whose upbringing had been so blind and careless.

Any jealousy Alice had felt over her husband's love of Augusta quickly passed. The same love gushed from her heart. You cannot help loving a child more than a spouse. You have to. They need your love so much more.

I kept my distance during the age of nappies and teething rings. Babies are pretty enough, but not very good company. Afloat in their long gowns, wide-eyed and kicking, they resemble spirits, I suppose, but clumsy, stupid spirits. Isaac couldn't get enough of them, although he usually left the room whenever Alice had to change a diaper.

Your mother taught you to dress yourselves and go potty, then to read and write, with a patience one would never have expected from such a short-tempered governess.

Your father taught you morals, religion, the value of work.

And I taught you— Did Uncle Fitz teach anything of value?

I taught Augusta some music. I was awfully fond of Augusta. She was a coquettish little flirt, even as a baby. By the time she was four, she liked to accompany her father and me when we went to inspect a new concert room, quite the lady in her pink bonnet and white stockings. She would climb into my lap at the piano, and we'd play a duet, which meant she plucked or banged a few notes and I took the phrase, no matter how dissonant, and performed variations on it until it became a tune she knew, like "The ABC Song." She would squeal with delight and challenge me with a new phrase. I had fantasies of making her into a musician.

Tristan, on the other hand, was his mother's son, watchful and wary. He had to be carefully wooed. Since it annoys you so, I shall refer to you from here on in the third person. But I was fond of you, too, my boy. Don't imagine I wasn't. Although, being what I was, I might have been afraid of being too fond.

Your father, however, had no such fear. He was a doting, sloppy, sentimental papa.

He tried to be stern, but it wasn't in him. Oh, he could give his lectures—on duty, morals, and grooming. His idea of a bedtime story was to read to you from the Bible or, worse, *Poems for Infant Minds*, dreary, didactic rhymes about the rewards of good behavior and disobedient tots who suffer the most grisly deaths. Isaac didn't know how to be serious with children, but he knew how to have fun with them. He loved to play horsey. I remember many an evening when this solemn businessman went down on all fours in his shirtsleeves in front of the fire, and his freshly washed babies rode upon his back.

I enjoyed being Uncle Fitz—when the mood was right. I had the pleasures of children with none of the responsibility. Your parents trusted me with their offspring, although I had to watch myself. I remember one occasion when I crossed the line. We were in Paris again, and I visited a stall of English books by the Seine, where I found something I thought might amuse the little ones: *Uncle Remus: His Songs and Sayings*. Brer Rabbit looked far more entertaining than anything in *Infant Minds*. That afternoon, when Alice and Isaac went out on an errand and the children were left in my care, I opened the new book and sat on the sofa with Augusta to read it aloud. Tristan did not join us at first. A few pages into it, however, he clambered up beside me to peer at this mysterious thing that made Uncle Fitz talk so strange. I did all the voices: "Dis wuz in de time fore de animals had dere fallin' out and wuz still sociagatin' wid one annuder." The children were fascinated. They'd never heard anything like it. And the book was funny, so funny that it even made me laugh.

I heard Alice and Isaac come in. They stopped in the vestibule.

Only when I looked up and saw them staring did I realize that slave dialect would have a peculiar sting in this household. And their own children hung on me, happily drinking in trashy "coon talk." But I plunged ahead, refusing to admit I'd done anything wrong. Besides, the children were deep in the tale and needed to know if Brer Rabbit escaped the tar baby. When he finally did, I closed the book and sat back with an expression of pure innocence.

"Where did you find that?" said Isaac. "What book is that?" He held out his hand and I gave it to him, although the look in his eyes suggested he would pitch the book into the fire.

He inspected it, read the contents page, glanced at the pictures. "These are old stories. This man didn't make them up. I heard them when I was a boy. Joel Chandler Harris? Is he colored or white?"

"White, I think."

"It's not how I heard these stories." He returned the book to me. "Go on. Read another."

Alice was surprised that Isaac allowed me to continue. They both sat down and listened while I read, Alice paying more attention to the intent look on Isaac's face than to Brer B'ar's visit to the laughin' place.

Later that night, after the children were put to bed, Isaac sat by the lamp and read the book to himself, straight through, without a chuckle or smile, only the puzzled frown of a grown man visiting his own childhood.

There were many family readings of *Uncle Remus* after that, usually by me, sometimes by Alice, but never by Isaac. He would listen, but he refused to use slave dialect in front of his children, not even in the name of Brer Rabbit.

So yes, there was always that to consider, "the Negro problem," "the color line," under our very roof. When did you first realize that some of us are one shade and some another? Do you remember, Tristan, how you learned that your father was once a slave? You do not want to include your own memories here? Very well, then. Be like your father. As silent as the tomb.

You and Augusta were too much your own intricate selves for us to pay much notice to your race. Yet your parents must have caught themselves studying you now and then with concern for your futures. You both had your father's rich brown eyes and his tight, black, curly hair. "I don't know what's the matter with your hair," Alice would mumble as she wrestled a brush through her daughter's head. But she knew. Augusta's hair was woolier than yours, quite kinky, but her skin was lighter, paler. You had your mother's face, your snubby nose so like hers that I often pictured a little pince-nez on your infant scowl. It was her face, but deeply tanned, as if soaked in strong tea. I recognized early that Augusta might pass as white, but you never would. It's terrible when one has to look at children this way.

Children, however, invent stories to answer their questions, solving private puzzles with make-believe. Tristan, for example, became fascinated with Red Indians. He was five or so when he began to collect pictures of war hunts and powwows from the illustrated newspapers, carefully cutting them out with scissors and saving them in a box. He often played Indian alone in our hotel rooms, and his pretending went very deep.

You're surprised I remember this? But how could I forget? Especially when I woke one morning to find you sitting cross-legged on my bed, your face streaked with flour paste, your body clad only in a table napkin looped in a belt like a breechcloth.

"Tristy?" I said.

"No Tristy. I am Sioux. Kidnapped by palefaces. Palefaces are sorry people."

Being an Indian made you proud that you were different from other children. You were an imaginative child. And imagination can render children invulnerable, able to accept all kinds of oddity, so long as they get love.

And your mother and father loved you very much. They did. You were their lambs, their darling lambs, neither black nor white. They never saw you as a mistake or a trial. They worried for your future, but their love transcended their fear. And such a love. Especially your father's.

My sharpest encounter with his love was one Christmas Eve in Germany, when we lived in a palace. It wasn't our palace, of course. It belonged to the Herzog of Meiningen, a German kind of duke, Georg II, who had lost his kingdom in unification but kept his title, money, and palace. The Herzog adored my music, and he invited us to stay on when he and his family went off to their mansion in Berlin for the holidays.

Palaces are highly overrated, large, drafty, and difficult to heat. This one was like a huge hunting lodge, its halls lined with the glass-eyed heads of stag and boar. The Herzog loved a good hunt as much as he loved music, and I half expected to find the heads of a few composers mounted on the walls. We were snugly snowed in, the wooded hills in the distance looking like beards covered in shaving cream, but the fireplace in the main hall, as big as a hotel room, was always full of blazing logs.

An army of servants looked after us. They were thrilled to have children here for the Yuletide. They arranged the surprise without telling us. We'd gone up to bed when they knocked on our doors and said, "Wake up *der Kinder* and bring them. Quick. To see what the Christ Child has brought." Downstairs in the main hall stood a huge evergreen tree, tall and luminous, aglow with a hundred candles, a fragrant forest god. The children had never seen a Christmas tree before, and the adults had seen nothing like this one. We all sang "O Tannenbaum" around it, sweets were served, and Augusta ate a whole marzipan Jesus. Nobody told Isaac the plum cake was soaked in brandy. The celebration was so giddy that I didn't notice he was getting drunk.

Finally the candles were put out, Isaac carried his children back to bed, one on each arm, and the servants retired. Alice and I remained sitting in the haze of paraffin smoke. Even she was content, as who wouldn't be in such a circumstance. Isaac returned, fell into a chair with a tipsy grin, and helped himself to another slice of cake.

"Aren't they beautiful?" he said. "So beautiful. It breaks my heart to see them asleep. My children," he murmured. "*Our* children," he quickly added.

I'd never seen Isaac drunk before. I looked at Alice, wondering what she made of this, but she appeared only amused; she must have had some brandied cake herself.

"Blood of my blood, flesh of my flesh," Isaac chanted. "They are my heart and soul. It hurts me to look at them. So much that I sometimes wish they were dead and in heaven. Isn't that a silly thing to feel? But then my heart would stop hurting. And it won't be broken when they go out in the world and the world breaks their hearts." He smiled as he spoke, as if this feeling were only an emotional curiosity, a quirk of love.

"Come along, Greatheart," said Alice. "Time for bed." She was not upset in the least by this sentiment. She must have heard other, sober versions of it. She helped her husband to his feet and took him by his arm. "Good night, Fitz. Merry Christmas."

"Merry Christmas," I called after them. "To both of you."

I remained by the fire, thinking: How foolishly sentimental, how wonderfully foolish, for a man to love his children like that. I found myself genuinely fond of Isaac. And loving his love of his children, and his wife's love of him, I loved them all, and was full of love for my own life.

A common Christmas mood, one more wistful than true. But what is a good life? What do people mean when they say that they are happy? You live through the aggravations of a day, the chores, duties, bills, worries. And suddenly, in a quiet moment, you look around and think, "This isn't so bad. This is rather nice. I like my life." It's better to realize it that way than the other, when a catastrophe shatters your peace. Your ship breaks apart, you are plunged into a cold sea, you cling to a spar and stupidly tell yourself, "I was happy on that ship. I didn't know it, but I was marvelously happy."

What do you remember of those years? You were happy, weren't you? You and Augusta both. Two hotel children with loving parents, a dotty uncle, and all of Europe for their playground. You knew America only as a fairy tale, a dreamland of briar patches and talking rabbits.

We were happy, weren't we? In our fashion. For a time.

34

Then we went to Rome. It was 1886. I forget most dates, but I certainly remember that year.

We had not been to Rome before. We were in and out of Italy constantly—Milan, Venice, Florence—but the Eternal City had been a backwater, a poor place of barefoot monks and dusty ruins. Recently, however, it had begun to attract not just the unmusical English but rich new Americans, a whole colony of them.

Isaac and Alice arrived in bad tempers. Funds were low, which always worried Alice—Decker Bros. was two months overdue in monies owed us. The prospect of roomfuls of Americans always irritated Isaac. While Europeans treated us as exotic curiosities at worst, Americans were less kind in their condescension. And Isaac had come to dislike our country more of late, from reading the newspaper accounts of Negro life back home: the end of Reconstruction, the undoing of new laws, the riots and lynchings that had become part of the climate down South. I doubted things were as bad as the newspapers made them sound. They had never been good. Could they have gotten worse?

I myself was delighted to be in Rome. I loved any new city, and especially enjoyed the sun and heat of this one. Radiance seemed to pour into the body, lighting up internal organs like a magic-lantern slide. As soon as we settled at our hotel, I insisted we see the sights. Isaac and Alice frowned when I mentioned St. Peter's—our years abroad had not softened their mistrust of the Blatant Beast—so I proposed we visit the ruins. "Let's go to the Colosseum," I said. "Where the good Christians were thrown to the lions."

We put on our best clothes and strolled down a bright, dusty street toward a broken mountain of blood-pink stones. It looked like a mountain even when we stepped inside. Bushes and flowers and a few trees grew in the high, crumbling ramparts. We had the arena to ourselves; it was noon, and even the beggars were taking naps. Alice and I bickered over her Baedecker, unable to agree on which end of the Colosseum was north and which was south. Isaac stood beside us, gazing at the haunted circus, full of admiration for the people eaten here. He looked quite handsome in his green hounds-tooth suit, yellow waistcoat, and new soft felt hat. For all his pro-priety, Isaac still liked fashionable clothes, but there's nothing more proper than fashion. Even Alice had become less fubsy over the years, softening her browns with mauve or lilac. There were no lions today, only a sinister loiter of scrawny cats who scattered when Augusta and Tristan ran after them.

We went on to the Forum, where the sun-bleached bones of an-cient buildings spilled over the dry weeds. It suggested a city burned clean by a fire. Columns capped in twos and threes towered over the debris like music notes.

"You see, children?" said Isaac. "This is what comes of the wor-ship of idols. Tristan!" he called out. "Pull up your socks!"

I found the ruins quite beautiful. There is something soothing about the end of someone else's civilization.

We heard other voices across the baking stones, American voices, male and female. They came around the corner, a genteel, well-dressed gaggle. Their sunlit parasols glowed like luminous balloons against a shadowy Roman wall. I could feel Isaac and Alice tensing, until I noticed that these Americans were different: Some of their faces were dark. They were colored and white, mixing together. A white woman actually walked with a black man, an old gent with a silver mane and huge white beard. He made such a perfect Uncle Tom that I wondered if these were traveling players, an American company touring Europe with yet another production of Harriet Beecher Stowe's melodrama.

"Good Lord!" cried Isaac, and he snatched his hat off his head. "That's Frederick Douglass. Frederick Douglass himself."

"Here in Rome? What a small world." I knew what Douglass meant to Isaac. He followed him in the paper as intently as Tristan followed his Indians. "Let's go pay our respects."

"Oh, no," said Isaac. "We can't. He's with his family."

"And you're with yours. What's the fuss?" We'd heard the man speak twenty years ago, which should give us the right to address him. And wouldn't all Negroes want to greet each other? I started us over the ruins toward the lion and his pride of disciples.

They'd already noticed us, of course, and wondered who we were. Their silk parasols wavered as we approached. The sight of colored ladies in fancy dress struck me as novel; I'd never met a colored woman who wasn't a servant.

"Mr. Douglass, sir," I declared and held out my hand. "Forgive me. But I've heard you speak many times." Well, once. "Dr. F. W. August. And my manager, Mr. Isaac Kemp."

The hoary lion softened slightly when I introduced Isaac as an equal, then impatiently waited for us to finish our piece so he and his group could resume their stroll.

"Sir," began Isaac. "You have done much good for our race. I just wanted to say thank you."

"You are most kind," said Douglass in his deep, gruff baritone. He made a slight bow. "Thank *you*."

But I wanted more. "I'm a concert artist," I said. "I'm performing tomorrow night. Perhaps you and your friends would like to attend?" I dug into my coat for an invitation—I always carried a pack for my next event.

"Thank you, sir, no. I'm afraid musical debauches are not my style." He smiled at "debauches," but his smile was frosty. The fact he did not introduce his companions made clear that he assumed we were not in their class.

Isaac didn't notice the snub. "Sir, may I present my wife."

Alice came forward, shyly, reluctantly. "Mrs. Isaac Kemp," she said and made a little curtsy.

We waited to see how Douglass would respond.

His brow twitched, his white beard bristled around a frown. But then he bowed and said, "Madam? May I present *my* wife?"

And a lady stepped forward, the lady who'd been walking with him. I'd forgotten Douglass had remarried: His new wife, Helen Pitts, was as plain as rice, and as white. Yet Douglass was uncomfortable with Alice, perhaps afraid that he'd set a trend.

He quickly introduced the rest of his entourage, including their host in Rome, Miss Edmonia Lewis, a Negro sculptress. I missed the names of the white people. They were rather cool toward us, and Miss Lewis was especially aloof, as if afraid we'd camp on her doorstep if she were too familiar.

"And these are our children," said Isaac, drawing you and Augusta forward for the great man's benediction.

Douglass timidly patted you on your heads. "And where in America do you reside, Mr. Kemp?"

"We don't live in America," said Isaac. "We live over here."

"Yes? But a man of your obvious breeding and intelligence could do more good for our people back there."

"Yes, but this is where our work is."

"We have music in America."

"But it is better, sir, for my family and me over here."

"What is best for the individual is not always good for all," Douglass declared. But he looked at the children again, Augusta in ribbons, Tristan in a sailor suit. He frowned and said, "But things *have* gone bad back home. Very bad. I do not know what any of us can do." He didn't like the sound of that either. "If you will excuse me, sir. My friends and I—"

"Of course," said Isaac. "My apologies. We did not mean to intrude."

"No intrusion at all. A pleasure. Good day, Mr. and Mrs. Kemp. And Dr. August. God's speed to you all."

"And to you, sir," said Isaac. "This has been an honor."

The great man and his flock moved away with a dry rustle of petticoats.

"Mama?" said Tristan. "Was that Uncle Remus?"

"No, my lamb. He is a great man. A famous man in America. Your father admires him." She spoke in a detached, withholding manner. This meeting troubled her as much as it did Douglass.

"His skin is like Papa's. But not as dark."

Douglass, of course, had had a white father himself.

Isaac continued to watch the Douglass crowd drift off into the ruins. "He thinks we should go home to America."

"Yes, I heard him," said Alice. "Easy for him to say. He's Frederick Douglass. Nobody's going to say boo over *his* wife. It's not so simple for others."

"Mama, we going to America?" said Augusta.

"No, my pet. Not anytime soon."

When the children ran off in pursuit of another cat, Alice felt free to speak her mind. "What did he mean 'your people'?" she said indignantly. "We're your people, your children and I."

"*Our* people," said Isaac. "You married into us."

"The only *us* I know is us. Your family."

"We do not need to have this conversation," he said.

It was a familiar argument, one that Isaac and I had had years ago in New York, when he sometimes talked about going south. I was surprised this feeling still gnawed at him. Not even marriage and children had ended his irritable, wishful thinking.

I wanted Alice to know this was an old story and she should not be worried. "As I once said long ago," I told him, "it'd be different if there were something you could do. But you're not a lawyer, you're not a soldier, and you're certainly not a politician."

"I know all that," he said snappishly. "Yet one cannot help feeling what one feels. And I feel I'm shirking a duty."

Alice tried a gentler tack. She slipped her arm into his. "Your heart is much too big, my love. It's good to feel duty to others. But you must be kind to yourself. Be pleased that you've done your duty to your family."

"Yes, yes, yes," he grumbled and petted the hand in his arm. He did not like being indulged, but her words made him feel better, and he knew she was right.

We made our way up Capitoline Hill, away from the Douglass crowd. We could see them far below, a dainty cluster of parasols beetling over the brown grass and ivory ruins.

We returned to the hotel, and the concierge handed me a cable. From Henri Héger. REGRET TO INFORM YOU OF END OF DECKER BROS. DECLARED BANKRUPTCY LAST WEEK. WILL INQUIRE ON OTHER ENGAGEMENTS. CAN OFFER NO FUTURE FOR THE PRESENT. LETTER TO FOLLOW.

I showed the scrap of paper to Isaac. He showed it to Alice. And the three of us just stood there, staring at one another.

35

THERE was no panic, no anger, no tears. Alice calmly took the children upstairs to give them their dinner and put them to bed, then rejoined us in the lobby. We sat in a corner and discussed what this news meant and what we could do about it, keeping our emotions tamped down tight.

We had less than two hundred dollars. We were owed three hundred in commissions. Decker Bros. was often slow in payment, and we treated their debits as money in the bank, the closest we came to a savings account in our gypsy existence. We did not live hand to mouth but with a breathing space of a month or two. In the occasional lean time there was always another Decker Bros. engagement ahead to tide us over. Until now.

"It can't be as bad as it sounds," I insisted. "And something's sure to turn up. It always has."

"I knew it wouldn't last," said Alice with cool, matter-of-fact fatalism. "I always knew it would end. But it has lasted ten years. I am grateful for that."

"First thing tomorrow," proposed Isaac, "we need to give up this fancy hotel for cheaper rooms."

And he would make the rounds to the local theaters and music halls, if such things existed in Rome, and offer them "a world-class artist" who happened to be in town. I would write to "friends" in

Milan and Venice, asking if they'd like a musical guest. And we would wait for Héger's letter to find out if things were as grim as his cable suggested.

We moved the next morning to a simple pensione around the corner. We continued to take our mail at the hotel—we needed its distinguished address—and there was still no letter from Héger. I dashed off my own letters that afternoon at an open window overlooking a narrow courtyard full of wet bedsheets and clucking chickens. Isaac returned from his first day of hunting to report that the only music in Rome was opera and brass bands.

Yet we remained calm. We continued to consider other possibilities. It was May, and the season in Monte Carlo was over. Our best course, we decided, would be to return to Paris and see what might be arranged from there, only Paris was expensive. The children noticed nothing desperate about our sudden move, and they preferred a shabby pensione to a stuffy hotel. There were not only chickens to tease but a big dog who loved to be petted.

I decided to go ahead with my recital that night, even though I wouldn't be paid for it. A Decker Bros. piano had been sold months ago to an American family who lived in a palazzo near the Forum. I'd been sent to Rome ostensibly as a gift to thank them for their patronage but in fact to sell pianos to their friends. Only there were no more pianos. Mrs. Albert Coit, of the Philadelphia Coits, had invited all of us, but Isaac and Alice did not attend. Isaac would not be needed to translate, and the children had to be put to bed, they said. The real reason was that neither Isaac nor Alice could bear facing their countrymen, especially now when they had so much else on their minds.

I, however, was happy to get out, delighted to go to a party. The Palazzo Barberini was spacious and well lit, the food and drink excellent. The marble floors gleamed like water. The guests were Americans, with more women than men, and a single Italian prince. I enjoyed being among Americans again, the amiable buffoonery of the men, the fearless flippancy of the women. They had an easy life, and the most burning issue of the evening was where to go for the summer. "No, not Venice," a woman laughed. "Venice has become the vomitorium of Boston."

A spoiled, intimate, incestuous group, they were pleased to have a new face in their midst. I basked in their attention, enjoying myself so much that I postponed putting the attention to financial use. I was the king of the party, the cock of the walk, until a lady entered the room, alone, dressed all in black. A discreet hush passed in her wake.

She moved like a vapor in bone-stiffened bombazine. The breastplate of black brocade and large springy bustle seemed to carry her across the room of their own volition, the hems of her skirt just grazing the marble. She suggested beauty, even though her face was veiled in a moiré mesh that hung from her hat and reduced her profile to an ink silhouette. The veil trembled with a few puffed words shared with our hostess before the elaborate dress wafted into a corner and settled into a chair.

Instantly everyone wanted to tell me about her. It was Lady Ashe, they whispered, the tragic Lady Ashe, an American from a fine New York family. She'd married a lord, a Scottish one, but so wealthy that his family had given up Scotland for London and the world. He'd died several years ago while living in the Levant. Lady Ashe still lived there, in Constantinople, but had spent the past winter in Rome. Her mourning was not for her husband, however, but for a son who'd died only last year, a tender lad of fourteen. She had money, houses, horses, and another son, but none of it could lift her from this deep grief. She had been here four months but rarely went out. People were surprised that she'd come to hear me, surprised and impressed.

Their gossip gave me more than enough to work with. Sitting down at what might be my last Decker Bros. piano, I fell back on my old tricks. "As you have no doubt heard, dear friends, the music I play is orphic, dictated to me by spirits." I began to grope the keyboard. I no longer used a blindfold but could feign a trance by staring up at a corner. "What's this? Oh! They want to tell me about someone in this room. A lady? A beautiful lady." I rocked myself into oblivion and told a story with snatches of obvious tunes. "Yankee Doodle" married "Rule, Brittania" and gave birth to "Pop Goes the Weasel." "Weasel" grew, laughed, and played, then became ill in an off key. It died a wretched death. All was sorrow and darkness, a world bereft of light. And then, way off in the distance, like a child calling to its mother, we heard "Pop Goes the Weasel" again.

There was much applause, but lighthearted, facetious. People gathered around me, men slapped my back, and everyone grinned, not nastily but as people grin when they want you to know they appreciate a good joke. I'd hoped to move them with my portrait of a sad lady, but there were no earnest, table-rapping sorts here. Americans were more sophisticated now. Well, if they preferred to laugh, that was fine, too, and might still get us invited for a month in a cozy villa.

The laughter abruptly stopped, the smiles evaporated. The jocular herd parted as Lady Ashe stepped forward. She held out an unsteady hand gloved in black lace.

"Dr. August," she began, her voice muddy with tears. Her veil was streaked with tears. "It was him," she said. "It was truly him. That was his favorite tune. I could actually hear him laughing when you played it."

But "Pop Goes the Weasel" was every child's favorite in that age. Her hand was ice cold, her grief deep and sincere. I felt like a cad for having moved her.

"I am sorry," I said. "I didn't mean to upset you."

"Oh, no. These are tears of joy, sir." She lifted her veil to show me her tears, radiant, glittering trails. "It is good to know my beautiful boy is out there and still loves his mother."

Circumstance is everything, and twenty years had passed since I last saw this face. But there it was, glazed in years and grief, circled in costly widow's silk, the pert features of my frisky, redheaded friend of whorehouse days, Fanny Gaskins.

36

SHE didn't recognize me. Men age more quickly than women, and I'd grown heavy in my years of celibacy. I wasn't fat, not at all, but I was hardly the skinny lad who once played Schumann in a brothel. And I had a new name now, and a new vocation. Yet my leap was nothing compared to Fanny's. From a brassy five-dollar tart to this tragic, elegant ladyship.

Fanny gave no sign that she found my face familiar. She clutched my hand between her crusty lace gloves, beat her wet lashes at me, and said, "Thank you, sir. Yes. Thank you." Then she turned away, lowered her veil, and slipped out into the night.

I was too stunned to follow. Lady Ashe was Fanny Gaskins? I couldn't believe my eyes. It was wonderful, miraculous. I was so awestruck that I did not doubt the miracle until after I left the party myself, wondering if her title were real or part of a con.

I did not see Isaac and Alice until breakfast the next morning, a poor affair of bread and tea in a dingy dining room that stank of garlic.

"You'll never guess who I saw last night," I told Isaac. "Fanny Gaskins. Only now she calls herself Lady Ashe."

"Who?" said Alice. "Who's this?"

Isaac looked chagrined. "A friend of Fitz's," he muttered. "From New York."

"Fitz had a *lady* friend?" She sniffed away her surprise as a triviality. "So. Did you meet anyone else last night? Music lovers with houses in the country?"

"No. Not yet." I'd been so overwhelmed by seeing Fanny that I had forgotten to fish for invitations.

"Is this old friend in the market for music?"

I hadn't even considered that. "We haven't seen each other in twenty years. She didn't recognize me."

"Really? Not much of a friend, I must say." She gave up on me as completely useless. "Well, I hope we hear from Héger today. Let's have the worst and get it over with." As our crisis wore at Alice's patience, it brought back the brusque brittleness that motherhood had softened.

Isaac remained silent. He would not want his wife to know how we knew such a person as Fanny. They both disappointed me, being too full of their own troubles to enjoy the surprise of someone else's story. My own delight was disinterested. I did not see anything here for me but wondered how I could go about seeing Lady Ashe again.

I went straight to the hotel after breakfast, where there was still no letter from Héger. Instead, I was given a note that had been hand-delivered that morning.

"Dear Dr. August," it began, "or may I call you Fitz? Who would guess that two such as we would meet again. And in such changed conditions. Please call on me. Lady Ashe."

Her address was that of a palazzo by the Pincian Hill. I went there directly from the hotel, and an old man sweeping the courtyard pointed upstairs and said, *"La contessa. Sì."* She had the entire upper floor of one wing. Whether she was a real lady or not, little Fanny had done quite well for herself.

A servant in a black jacket and red fez met me at the door, a willowy, copper Negro with a beardless face. He was like no Negro I'd ever seen, but strangely ageless. "Lady Ashe eez expecting you," he said, with a French accent and the pure alto of a choirboy. And

I understood his strangeness. It's a myth that all eunuchs are fat or that they're imbeciles, as if gonads were wisdom. The knife, in fact, would improve the intelligence of most men.

He led me into a large shuttered room decorated in Italian draperies and Turkish carpets. Fanny, or rather, Lady Ashe, lay on a low couch, propped on silk pillows. She wore no veil but had a black choker around her neck, and her at-home dress was a dark cloud of crêpe de chine. The flame-red hair had faded to russet, and she wore it piled on her head with a half dozen sausage curls hanging behind like Medusa's snakes.

She smiled as I crossed the room. "Fitz," she said. "Dear, dear Fitz. My professor. It was so good of you to come." She spoke in the sad, low coo of a mourning dove.

"How could I refuse?" I took her hand, bare and cool. "It was such a surprise to see you last night, Fanny. Or should I call you Your Ladyship?"

"Call me Fanny. When we're alone. It will remind me of a happier past. Ismail?" she called to her servant. "Close the door. I won't be needing you."

She gestured toward the chair beside her divan, and I sat.

"Forgive me for pretending not to know you last night," she said. "I do not care what they think of me here in Rome. But I was so full of conflicting joys that I preferred we have our reunion in private. So. Tell me about your life."

"I'd rather hear about yours. You've certainly come far, Fanny. You always said you'd marry up in the world. You really are Lady Ashe?"

She sighed. "You will hear about me soon enough. Please. Tell me about Dr. August."

I told her everything, almost. It felt like everything but didn't come close. I told her Isaac and I had remained friends and business partners all these years, and that Isaac was married with children.

"A white wife?" she said. "That speaks well of him." It didn't shock her in the least.

"We worry about the future of his children," I confessed.

"That's a concern only in America. Such things are of no matter to us in the Orient. We are immersed in strangenesses."

Traces of the old cheerful Fanny lay under her tragic mask. I wondered if her grief were somewhat artificial, like the rest of her.

I proceeded to tell her about my Metaphysicals, how they'd come to me for years, but I hadn't understood my gift while we worked at Roebuck's. I even confessed that the spirits were fickle and I sometimes had to fake them.

"But that *was* my son speaking to you last night?" she pleaded. "Please. Tell me *that* was real."

"Oh, yes," I said. "Quite real."

There was a photograph of the boy on the table by her couch, framed in gold. He was a beautiful child, slim and deer-eyed, an oval face in a pretty lace collar. His name was Constantine, and he had died a year ago, of yellow fever.

Behind him were other photographs in plainer frames: her ladyship and her husband, an elderly, horsefaced man with mutton-chops. There was a portrait of the entire family—husband, wife, Constantine, and another boy, a homely child with enormous eyes and a sour little mouth, like a baby barn owl.

"Such a life I have had, Fitz. Such a rich, sinful life." She leaned back into her silk pillows. "Now I pay for my sins. I left Roebuck's soon after your departure, to be the mistress of a New Orleans man who said he was a banker. But he was only a crook, and we had to flee to Bermuda. We posed as brother and sister there, so that he could use me as bait for likely investors. Which was how I met Lord Alfred, a widower with three grown children back home. He adored me. I did not love him, but I loved his adoration. I played my cards quite well. I got rid of my partner by ratting on Bill to the Pinkertons, who hauled him off to the mainland before he could spill the beans. I refused to give Lord Alfred what I once sold cheap unless he married me. And he did, the poor besotted man, thinking he was getting a shy little spinster who'd lost her one great love in the war.

"Lord Alfred's children hated me, of course, and were quite cruel when he brought me home to England. But he took us off to the Bosphorus, where he was once attached to the embassy. He gave me everything: houses and clothes and affection. And then he gave me a child, a beautiful, beautiful son. It was as if God were telling me that I was a good woman now and all was forgiven. I loved the child as I've never loved anything, more than clothes, more than his father. I didn't care that the title would pass to his hateful half brother in England. But it was all a cruel ruse by God, a trick to unlock my heart. He took away my husband, and when I didn't grieve for Alfred, when I only gave more devotion to my son, He punished me by taking him away, too. So suddenly that I had no time to say good-bye."

She told her story with a faraway look and too many sighs, like a bad actress, yet she seemed to feel everything she said she felt, even if her words were stale and secondhand.

"You have another child," I pointed out.

"Oh, yes. Freddie. Poor Freddie. I left him at home in Constantinople," she replied. "I needed to get away from the scene of so much sorrow. But your music last night made me understand that I cannot escape it, I must give myself to it completely before I can find peace." She leaned forward on an elbow. "Which is the real reason why I needed to see you, Fitz. Will you help me regain contact with my son? I need to say good-bye to him. I have to assure myself that he loves and forgives me. Will you come back with me to Constantinople?"

I knew this kind of grief all too well from the widows and mothers I'd served in New York, this feeling of death as an unfinished good-bye. I was taken aback that someone as tough as Fanny could feel it. "I would love to help you," I said. "Nothing would please me more. But I have my own household to look after."

"Bring them with you. Isaac and his family. Yes. I should want to hear the laughter of children in my house again. I can take care of you all." Her face brightened. "I am rich, Fitz. It does me no good, but I have money. The Ashes paid me well when I signed away their name and agreed to stay out of England."

So there it was, the answer to all our problems. And I was moved by her sorrow and curious about her life. Yet I kept my cards close to my chest. I said I would have to think it over, look at our schedule, and discuss it with Isaac. I departed without ever being offered tea or lunch.

The letter from Héger finally arrived that afternoon. It was as bad as we'd feared. Without warning, Decker Bros. had gone completely bust. They owed Héger thousands. Bookings were bad all around, he wrote, and he'd be unable to find us anything before the fall. He suggested that we stay put in the meantime and consider the summer an extended holiday.

"A holiday!" cried Alice. "How lovely! How restful!" All the anxiety she had been able to suppress came pouring out in angry sarcasm. "What are we to live on in the meantime? We have funds to get us through the next two months, if we economize. But then what? Why should we believe times will be flush in the fall?"

I waited until now to play my Fanny card: "I saw Lady Ashe today. She's invited us to live with her for the summer."

"Yes?" said Alice. "She has? Why didn't you say so sooner?" Her anger subsided a little. "She lives here in Rome? She has a place out in the country?"

"No. In Constantinople."

Her face fell. "Why, that's at the ends of the earth!"

"Why does she want us?" Isaac asked suspiciously.

I explained how she was grieving over a dead child. She hoped to regain contact with him through my music.

"No," said Isaac. "We can't. Out of the question." But it was not from fear of Fanny or the need to keep our past a secret. "That poor woman," he said. "You're taking advantage of a mother's grief. Are you in touch with this dead child?"

"No," I admitted. "But it makes her feel better to think I am. And maybe my spirits will contact her child if we go there."

Isaac saw through my wishful thinking and scornfully shook his head.

Alice threw up her hands. "What does it matter if it's real or not? The lady offers us a roof. If she can get us there, wherever it is, we'd be fools to say no."

"How long do you expect us to live off her?" Isaac demanded.

"For the summer," I said.

"And then what?"

"Something will turn up."

"How will we turn up anything if we're off in Araby?"

There was Héger, of course, but Isaac no longer trusted Héger. He was afraid we'd be trapped in the Orient, dependent on a heart-broken woman. As a husband and father, he refused to put his family in such a humiliating position. But his stand made Alice even more adamant, demanding if he had a better idea.

They worried the issue around and around like a bone. Then Isaac said, "What about this? I propose this." He took a deep breath. "You and Fitz and the children go to Constantinople. I will go to Paris, Brussels, and the rest, see what I can arrange for the fall. On my own, I can live quite frugally. Then I shall send for you and the children." He said it with deep regret. He watched Alice, as if daring her to agree and hoping she wouldn't. "Will that make you happy?"

"My happiness is not the point," she said. "But it does sound like a practical solution."

Her choice pained him. "I will miss you," he said. "I will miss you and the children horribly."

"This is no time to be morbid," Alice replied. "We need food and shelter and a future. I see no other way."

I do not mean to make Alice out to be a nagging fishwife. She loved Isaac, and she loved her children, and she was fiercely practical. But she resisted sorrow as she resisted most strong emotions, by pretending to be colder than she was.

I visited Fanny the next day and gave her our answer. She was overjoyed. She could not wait to get back to Constantinople. In fact, she already had a steamship schedule in hand. It didn't trouble her that Isaac wasn't coming. "What's his wife like?" I described Alice as a quiet, subdued woman.

Her majordomo, Ismail, booked our train and steamship tickets. Fanny went ahead to Venice, arranging to meet us on board ship there. She and Alice had still not met when Isaac put us on the train in Rome.

"You will look after my family, Fitz?" Isaac gently commanded at the station. "They are the blood of my soul."

He kept touching and kissing his children as we settled among the velvet cushions and tasseled curtains of a first-class compartment. "Please," Alice grumbled when he kissed her again. "We're not saying good-bye forever. Only a few weeks at worst. People will think we're a pack of weepy Italians."

When our train pulled out, Isaac did not run alongside but stood on the platform. Tristan and Augusta happily hung in the window to shout and wave good-bye to Papa. He solemnly lifted his hat and smiled at us, the uncertain, guilty smile of a good man who fears that he has failed his family.

37

WE crossed the sea in a trim new steamship powered by screws instead of sidewheels. The voyage took four days, and the weather was perfect, the sunlit Mediterranean smooth and cerulean blue—wine-dark, I suppose, though I've never seen wine that color.

Lady Ashe spent most of the voyage in her cabin, joining us only for supper in the evening. Her first meetings with Alice did not go well. Wearing her grief like a crown, Fanny kept smiling at the children, a sadly wistful, regal smile, like a queen resisting an urge to pet her subjects like spaniels.

"What beautiful children you have, Mrs. Kemp. You must love them very much. As much as I love my dear departed Constantine."

Alice remained in a brittle, unsympathetic mood. "To be sure, Lady Ashe. Could you kindly pass the peas?"

I did not relish being trapped in a foreign city between two such alien female temperaments.

"Your friend is much too strange," Alice confided after she put the children to bed and we strolled the moonlit deck. "There's a selfish element in such overdone sorrow, selfish and insincere. But I am the last to judge sincerity. I wish I'd been kinder to Isaac when we parted. It's not his fault we are where we are. I had no business being so frosty with him."

I assured her that Isaac understood and that they'd been through too much for a few days of bad feeling to do any injury.

We passed through the Dardanelles at night, and the sun rose in the Sea of Marmara. Europe was a thin green line on our left, Asia a gray fold on the right. The horizon all around was nicked with the crescent sails of fishing boats, like Islamic moons, and the funeral plumes of other steamships. We spent the whole day on this sea, until late afternoon, when both shores came into full view and the sky ahead grew thick with smoke.

You might think we were approaching London, except the smoke was all from the ships crowding the entrance to the Bosphorus. The city on the left was clear and pristine, without a factory in sight. What looked at first like factory chimneys were minarets. They sprouted like beans around each domed mosque. The city was all domes, round mosques on round hills, a mass of globes rising from the trees and gardens to gather at one end in a great globe, the mosque that Europeans insisted on calling Santa Sofia.

We came around the point into the harbor called the Golden Horn, dropped anchor, and hung there while launches and lighters came out to us. The beautiful domed city on the left was Stamboul, the old city. On the right was the new city, Pera, with an ugly European waterfront of shipping and warehouses. Directly in front of us was a low iron bridge connecting the two cities, thick with people in red fezzes and white turbans.

Augusta, Tristan, and I hung on the rail, all three of us enthralled and delighted by the scene.

"Look! A camel!" cried Tristan, pointing at the bridge.

"Not a camel," sniffed Augusta. "That's a horse. Or a mule."

She'd never seen a mule either, but it *was* a camel.

"Look at the ghosts," she said. "Why're those people dressed like ghosts, Uncle Fitz?"—the Moslem women sheathed in sacks that hung from their heads to their ankles.

Over the murmur on shore, a thin voice began to sing, a high falsetto like a boy soprano. Other voices followed, other boys, the muezzins in the minarets calling the faithful to prayer. The different chants echoed and overlapped in a buzz of lamentation, a noise like a fly jar in a butcher shop. I expected the crowds on shore to halt, fall on their knees, and bow toward Mecca. I was disappointed when they didn't.

Alice joined us and stood there, frowning at the chanting city. "Come along, children. The eunuch says our boat is here."

We descended a shaky stairway into a steam launch moored to the side of the ship. Ismail was giving commands to the boatmen in a tongue I thought must be Turkish but was Greek. Lady Ashe sat in a cushioned seat toward the middle, hidden again in her fluttering black veil, a Christian version of the chador worn by the women on shore.

"You live in a very beautiful city," I told her.

"Oh, yes," she said sadly. "Constantinople. The city of my Constantine."

The city possessed other names, more names than I'd ever had: Istanbul, Stamboul, Byzantium, and, my favorite, the Threshold of Happiness, which they used on official decrees.

Lady Ashe owned a town house in Pera, but we did not land in Pera. Our launch chugged up the Bosphorus toward her summer residence. The swelling blue water was crowded with skiffs and sidewheeler ferries and sailboats whose lateen sails turned gold in the afternoon light. A palace on the shore glowed like a slice of Versailles, and I wondered for a moment if it were Fanny's place, but no, it was the Dolmabache Palace, one of the sultan's many residences.

Yali Ashe was a few miles farther north. The shore was lined with yalis, waterfront mansions of wood that resembled frame houses in New England, only larger and without lawns or porches. We swung out of the current toward a tall one of pure white clapboard. It climbed over us, row upon row of washboard shutters, the upper stories trimmed in latticework like starched lace, the eaves dense with shark-teeth finials.

While we tied up at the doorstep, a dozen people appeared on the narrow quay. I felt we'd arrived at a small town, but they were all Lady Ashe's servants, a hodgepodge of complexions and costumes. I noticed slippers with curled pixie toes. The household stood about, eyeing us and chatting among themselves, while the head butler, a Circassian dressed like Ismail in black coat and red fez, welcomed Lady Ashe and formally presented her with the keys of the house, which she then passed to Ismail.

Only Ismail and the head butler accompanied us inside. There was no hint of New England indoors. The walls and doorways were framed in hand-painted tiles, blue fantasias of curlicue and squiggle. The high ceilings were twilled in ribs of rosewood. The European furniture looked austere by comparison, a couch here, a table there. A fruity smell of beeswax permeated the hive.

We entered a large room at the rear of the house, where a low fountain plashed under French windows facing a park. Not a garden but a park, a smaller version of something you'd find in Paris, with flower beds, raked paths, and an open kiosk like a low bandstand under a spiny toadstool roof. The late afternoon glowed in masses of tulips, red, yellow, and violet, and upon two stately peacocks who dragged their emerald trains of quills over the golden sand.

"It's a fairy tale," I said with awe. "You live in a fairy tale, Lady Ashe."

She lifted her veil and gazed around her splendor. "I suppose," she said. "A fairy tale, not a home."

"Hello, Mummy."

The voice came from a pattern of tiles in the shadows. Not until he got up from his settee did the figure detach himself from the designs at his back. He had waited for his mother here, the boy from the photograph, the homely little barn owl with pollywog eyes. He stepped into the light in a velvet suit with a frilly lace collar. He seemed small for his age, but the large, red-haired head with cold eyes, hollow cheeks, and no chin looked quite old, too old for such a childish outfit.

"Hello, darling," said Lady Ashe, as if she'd seen him only that morning. "Did you miss me? Have you been good? I am sorry about Mrs. Wilcox, darling. I brought you a present. It'll arrive when they bring the trunks from our ship in the morning."

"Thank you, Mummy. Ever so." He watched her, studied her, his hands at his back, his shiny high-button shoes spread apart.

"Come," she said, pulling off her gloves. "Give your poor mother a kiss."

His eyes brightened, and he went to her. He did not run. She bent down, and he threw his arms around her neck. She stroked his velvet back. Then she abruptly drew away and stared at him.

"This isn't your suit," she said. "It's Connie's. Why are you wearing Constantine's suit?" She slowly straightened up, clutching the hand that had brushed the grainy velvet.

Freddie did not apologize. He did not look surprised or hurt by her reaction. He gave her a thin, knowing smile, as if he'd expected this response. "Because I wanted to wear something nice for your homecoming," he said.

"It was your brother's suit. You cannot wear your brother's clothes. You cannot take things from his room."

"Sorry, Mummy. I won't do it again." There was no hurt or regret in his voice, no emotion at all. "It's good to have you home, dear Mother."

"Yes. It is good to be home. Thank you, darling." Lady Ashe recovered from her upset and remembered us. "I brought us some guests. You'll like these people, Freddie. Dr. August plays the piano. And there are two children for you to play with."

Freddie said hello to each of us with the cold, perfect manners of a jaded diplomat. Augusta and Tristan stared at him, unable to decide if the boy were animal or vegetable.

"Ismail, show our guests to their rooms. We will have dinner in the garden tonight."

Alice hung back when we went up the stairs and whispered to me on a landing, "I don't know if we did the right thing in coming here, Fitz. This is a most peculiar household."

38

AND it was a peculiar household, in many ways. Five stories tall, Yali Ashe was a big as a hotel, but one that seemed all servants and no guests. I'd never seen such a mob of servants under one roof, a stewpot of nations: Turkish cooks, Armenian gardeners, Greek boatmen, and Circassian butlers, all commanded by Ismail, who was from Egypt by way of the Topkapi Palace—the new sultan had needed fewer eunuchs than his predecessor, and several took employment elsewhere. The only women on the staff were two Circassian maids, one of whom was married to the head butler, and Zoë, Lady Ashe's hairdresser. None of the servants lived in the main house but in a hamlet of outbuildings beyond the garden. The place was an elaborate plantation whose only crop was the comfort of Lady Ashe and her son. There'd been a governess as well, an Englishwoman, Mrs. Wilcox, who had left a month ago, reportedly because life in the Orient did not agree with her.

"I wish Wilcox had waited for my return," Lady Ashe told Freddie at dinner. "I hope you haven't been too lonely."

"Coxy was hardly company," he grumbled. "Just a dried-up old lady whose French wasn't half as good as she thought."

Sneering at a governess did not endear the boy to Alice.

But that was the most peculiar aspect of this house: Lady Ashe and her son. Homecoming only plunged Fanny deeper into mannered mourning. She remained distant and distracted around us, even with Freddie. She was kind to him but wary, without warmth. And one might have felt sorry for the boy, except he was such a forbidding child, a cold little man like a wind-up toy in short pants. His only sign of inner life was an occasional sour smile or comment. I hoped for Fanny's sake that Constantine had been as lovable as she said.

We ate dinner outside in the open kiosk, under oil lamps that swayed in a mild sea breeze. We had breakfast there the next day, a late breakfast at ten o'clock after Lady Ashe finished the elaborate toilette required for her curls and black-beaded bombazine dresses. The food at Yali Ashe was excellent: hearty American breakfasts of ham and eggs, biscuits and jam; light summer luncheons of vichyssoise and molded aspics; lavish late suppers of turtle soup, sturgeon, macaroni au gratin, roast beef, and asparagus, topped off with a rich torte or marrons glacés. There was nothing Turkish about the food, yet we could not forget we were in the Levant, not with that mob of servants standing in the shadows or the calls to prayer droned by a nearby mosque five times a day.

Our first dinner was a somewhat stiff affair, but breakfast was more casual. Augusta and Tristan came to life again.

"Do you play games?" Augusta asked Freddie. "Trissy and I play lots. Checkers and dominoes. And paper dolls. We make our own paper dolls. Great big fancy ones with Uncle Fitz."

And we did—I drew the figures and costumes, which they cut out and colored—but Tristan was ashamed to admit it in front of an older boy. He seemed quite taken with Freddie.

"Paper dolls," Freddie snorted. "Female rubbish."

"Yeah. Female rubbish," Tristan echoed like a parrot.

"Liar," said Augusta. "You like them, too."

"Do not," he said. Oh, the little betrayals of childhood.

"Children," said Alice. "I've told you not to call each other 'liar.' It's a very ugly word."

"Freddie, dear, do be kinder to our guests," said Lady Ashe, but shyly, as if doubting her right to correct him.

Her gift for her son arrived with the luggage that morning. The servants carried a large wooden crate into the garden, and we gathered around while they pried the box open and brushed packing straw from a strange, impossible object: a great round harp with brass antlers. A baby harp sat behind it, attached by a curved brass rod and ringed like its parent in solid rubber. Bicycles were the latest craze in Germany and England, but they were still luxury items, two hundred dollars each, and none of us had seen one up close. The servants were as intrigued as we were. Ottoman and infidel, we all studied the contraption with the same puzzled fascination. It was a simple complexity, more like an umbrella than a piano, but even an umbrella would be confusing if you'd never seen one.

Ismail held the brass pony while another servant formed a stirrup with his hands so Freddie could mount the leather saddle. He leaned back, holding the antlers like reins, his feet on the pedals. Ismail walked Freddie around the yard while the boy struggled with the pedals. Each time Ismail let go, however, Freddie began to fall, and Ismail had to grab it again. "Now! Let go!" Freddie commanded again, and Ismail did. The thing wobbled for a few feet and fell, pitching Freddie onto his back and elbows.

He jumped up, furious. "The damned thing doesn't work!" he shouted at his mother. "You gave me a broken machine! Oh, thank you. Ever so," he sneered and stormed into the house.

Alice, the children, and I were shocked to hear a child use such language. Lady Ashe only sighed and said, "I so hoped he would like it. But what can you do? What can you do?"

I gave it a try. I felt as if I were up on stilts, and pressing the pedals was like treading thick water. Then Ismail let go, and I, too, ended up sprawled in the sand. Our bodies did not yet understand that one had to go fast to keep from falling.

"Can I try?" pleaded Augusta.

"No, it's much too dangerous," said Alice. "And it's for boys, not girls."

"Me, then. Me!" cried Tristan.

"No, my lamb. Your feet won't even reach the thingabubbies."

Ismail banished the recalcitrant machine to a far corner of the garden. Later that day I saw two footmen trying to ride it and failing just as miserably.

I had my first session with Lady Ashe that evening before dinner. This always went better on an empty stomach. Her music room was on the very top floor, overlooking the Bosphorus. I had the bedroom down the hall, alone on this floor, the piano and I exiled from the others. Lord Ashe had played a little, quite badly I assumed, which was why the instrument had been stuck up here. It was an old German square piano, a Bechstein, painted gold, not in gold leaf but yellowy enamel. The cabinet and keyboard were well dusted and polished, but mice had nibbled at the damper felts so that even after I tuned it, the treble section had a slight twang like a banjo. I didn't mind. I'd learned my music on imperfect pianos, just as I'd developed my philosophy of life in the company of out-of-tune people.

I pulled the shutters closed, lit a candle, and sat at the keyboard. Fanny sat sideways on a settle by the window. She became Fanny again when we were alone. The piano faced the corner, but with a tarnished mirror above it, leaning from the wall so the room hung at a slope in its silver haze. I played a few scales to find my bearings in the warped aural landscape.

"How should we begin?" she asked.

"Tell me about Constantine. That will help me find the right music. The music will enable my spirits to contact him."

"He was a sweet child," she began. "He was affectionate. He was pretty. So pretty that it gladdened the heart just to look at him."

I eased into the adagio from the "Moonlight" Sonata, always a good beginning.

"Is that him?" she cried.

"No. I'm just trying to create the proper mood." I sincerely wanted to help her, one way or another. If I had to fake contact with her son, I wanted the forgery to be meaningful.

"I don't know why I thought it was him," she said. "That's such sad music. And he was a happy child. Until the end."

"Where did he pass away?"

"Here. In this house. Just downstairs. In his room."

No wonder she was so nervous and distracted at Yali Ashe.

"He passed away suddenly? Of yellow fever?"

"Yes. I thought it only a chill. There was no epidemic, no cause for alarm. We put him to bed, we gave him quinine. But then came the headaches. Awful, awful headaches. They made him cry. Then his skin turned jaundiced, and the doctor said it was—" Emotion flooded her throat and choked her words. "I cannot talk about it. Please. It's too painful to remember."

"Then, don't. Think quiet thoughts. Good memories. Lie down if you like." Glancing up at the mirror, I saw her stretch out. I continued with the sad music, hoping it would soothe her. It'd been so long since I'd done this. "Can I see his room sometime?"

"If it will help. But I can't go in. Ismail will take you."

People love their departed so deeply. And the dead are so lovable, far more lovable than the living.

"We had to bury him right away. That was the worst part. The undertaker took him that afternoon, so the contagion wouldn't spread. His little body was at peace, but I had no time with it. And he is alone in the cemetery here. The English cemetery. His father's body was shipped home to England to the family chapel, but we couldn't do that with Constantine, even if his half brother had allowed it. So he is buried here. Alone. All alone. Until I join him."

Her grief was so deep and genuine that I felt a hot prickle in my eyes. Then new notes came to my right hand, insolent little plinks and triplets completely at odds with Beethoven. Eusebius was thumbing his nose at us, mocking either me or Fanny, I couldn't tell.

Fanny didn't notice. "Do you believe in God, Fitz? I used to have nothing but scorn for whores who turned religious. But I have become like them. The best thing about living among Mohammedans is that you are not surrounded by people who *pretend* to be Christians. But my God is not a Christian God. He is a punishing God, a crushing God. He does not forgive."

Which sounded awfully Christian to me.

"Your spirits appear to be more forgiving," she said.

Yet Eusebius didn't forgive either; he tittered and snickered at her theology. I took my right hand off the keyboard and continued with the bass line.

"God did it to punish me," she continued. "There is no other explanation. Because my boy was a good child, innocent and pure. He was spared the degraded life you and I led, the life that made me behave so corruptly. But Constantine was innocent, happy, and good. God hurt him to punish me. I deserved the punishment, but my child didn't. Why should he suffer for my sins?"

When I tried the treble again, Eusebius had not changed his tune. He was scornful of Fanny, thinking her foolishly self-important for believing that a child's death had been personally directed at her. But it seemed perfectly human to me: Grief for her son had become tangled up in remorse over her past.

"That is what I fear most," she explained. "They know everything in heaven. My baby now knows the bitter truth about his mother." We seemed to be reading each other's thoughts. "I was not a saint. I was a whore. A greedy, selfish whore. Without scruples or shame. He must blame me for his suffering. He would hate and despise me."

I stopped playing. I did not know how to respond to that. Finally I said, "I'm sorry. This isn't happening today. It often takes time. We will try again tomorrow."

"Fine," she said. "Yes. I can be patient." But she sounded relieved, as if she had suddenly realized that hearing from her departed child might not be such a good thing after all.

After dinner, before she went to bed, Ismail brought Lady Ashe a glass of what looked like milk. It was her laudanum, a syrupy white tincture of opium dissolved in water to help her sleep. "Yes, Mummy's milk," she told Freddie and drank it down in front of us, without a bit of shame.

I dreamed of Eusebius that night. He was riding a bicycle. The horse and piano were still with him, and he was still naked, but he rode a bicycle, around and around his solemn companions, laughing at them, without a shred of pity for their troubles.

39

I decided to forget Eusebius. I would have to fake this and tell Fanny on my own what she needed to hear: Your boy loves you, he forgives you. As for God, His eye might be on the sparrow, but He does not kill sparrows to punish their mothers. Yet I could not say that without including a bit of magic, some secret detail or half-forgotten memory that would convince Fanny we were actually in touch with the boy. I wanted to do the job well; I took more care with my frauds than my real encounters.

Ismail escorted me up to Constantine's room the next day after breakfast. The third-floor hallway was gloomy with black oak and heavy doors. Fanny's room was at the end of the hall, Freddie's directly opposite.

The room was dark and musty, the shutters sealed. There was a sweet odor of rotting wood that one only imagined was the smell of death. A richly carved armoire towered over a little bed, a forbidding thing of fluted columns and enormous clawed feet; it must have been terrifying for the sick child. I had hoped there'd be pictures or toys, something to work with, but the shelves were empty. I laid my hands on different surfaces to convince Ismail that my snooping was purely spiritual.

"He was a good boy?" I said.

"He was *un enfant admirable.*" The matronly voice from the

manly face still took me by surprise. "The house adored him. We believe Azrael took him straight to heaven."

"Azrael?" Did eunuchs have their own spirits?

"The Angel of Death," he explained. "Who removes the soul from the body. When you live a good life, the removal is clean and easy. When you have a bad life, the sins of the flesh stick to your soul. There is much pain in the process. Bloody torn souls go to hell. But Master Constantine's soul would come out as clean as the bones of a steamed fish and fly to heaven."

A pretty thought, yet it left the "admirable infant" so pure that he remained unreal, without the details I needed.

"Why're there no toys here?" I asked.

"Lady Ashe ordered his toys destroyed. Except for those that we buried with the child."

It was too sad to imagine: a coffin loaded like a toy box. "Thank you, Ismail. That will be all."

He left, and I continued to explore the room. There was a real toy box, as empty as a tomb, but clothes were still in the clothes press. I went through the drawers of the armoire, hoping to find some keepsake or trophy. He remained an anonymous yet well-dressed child. I found his linen drawer. I took out a one-piece set of underclothes and unfolded it, short sleeves and short legs, a gullet of buttons up front. I draped it between my arms, trying to imagine the boy who had filled the garment. I sat on the bed, holding it just so, like a pietà.

I began to feel something in the room, a warm, sad presence.

I looked up. Freddie stood in the door, his big eyes staring. He contemptuously turned away.

"Freddie! Wait!" I had to explain why I was pawing his brother's underwear. "Can I speak to you a moment?"

"What?" he said.

I nonchalantly folded up the garment, pretending it was nothing. "Do you know why I'm here, Freddie?"

He wrinkled his nose at me. "Yes. Mummy thinks you can bring Connie back from the dead."

"No. Not exactly." He didn't believe in spirits? "She only wants me to contact him. So she can tell him good-bye."

"She's been saying good-bye for the past year."

"Well, she needs to hear from him. So that she can finish saying good-bye."

He snorted. "She'll never finish with Connie."

Freddie was jealous. Of course. I should have noticed sooner. But I could use his jealousy to discover something real about Constantine.

"Did you love your brother?"

"Yes." He was instantly defensive. "Everyone loved Connie."

"Surely you didn't love everything about him. Was there nothing he ever did or said that annoyed you?"

"He never did anything wrong. He was Goody Two-shoes. He followed all the rules, did whatever people wanted him to do."

"He doesn't sound very imaginative."

"He wasn't. He was stupid." Freddie was pleased to find someone who might understand. "That's why he was so good. He was too dumb and cowardly to do anything on his own. He was a year older than me, but he was such a baby." He abruptly stopped and sourly twisted his mouth at me. "Do you really speak to spirits, August?"

"Yes. When they want to be heard."

"If you want to know about my brother, ask them," he said. "Can't they tell you what you need to know?"

I thought I was being cunning enough, but he understood exactly what I was doing. "They will," I said. "But first I have to prime the pump."

He looked unconvinced.

"This will be good for you as well as your mother," I told him. "Don't you want her to be happy again?"

"You think you can make her happy?" he sneered. "I don't care if she talks to Connie. Or he talks to her. Or you all talk to the man in the moon. It's nothing to me. All female rubbish. I want no part of it." And he turned and went into his own room and shut the heavy door.

That evening I played a new melody for Fanny, the song of the happy child. I faked a trance at the gold piano and spoke as I played. "Yes? You mean that? I will."

"Is it him?" cried Fanny. "You found him?" But I was deep in a trance and couldn't hear her, of course.

The happy song included snatches of "Pop Goes the Weasel" and the opening section of *Kinderszenen*, "Of Faraway Lands and Peoples," surprisingly similar, before I developed them into a joyful hymn of forgiveness. I could not paint a real child, only a universal child, but that was how everyone remembered Constantine. When I finished, I let my head drop, like a marionette with a broken string. I could actually hear the tears running down Fanny's face. I was close to tears myself.

I slowly turned around. "Oh, my," I said, and pressed my hand to my heart. "I have never encountered such a sweet spirit."

"He was," sobbed Fanny. "He still is?"

"Oh, yes. And he's happy. Very happy. He misses you, but he knows that you still love him. Meeting other spirits, thousands of them, he now knows that you gave him more happiness in fourteen years than most people experience in the longest lives."

"I have so wanted to think that," she said. "But it *is* true?" She lay back as her bosom heaved in great sighs and a well of tears washed her face clean. "Did he talk of my past?"

"I asked him. He told me the dead care little about sins committed before they came to earth. The only sin in their eyes is the absence of love."

"Oh, Fitz!" she cried. "Is that true? He wouldn't say that just out of love for his mother?"

"Isn't that enough?" I said impatiently.

There was a faint buzz outside. The evening call to prayer had begun, the sun turning into a chorus of singing spirits as it sank into the earth.

"Can we talk to him again?" said Fanny. "Tomorrow? There are things I need to ask. Or no, I just want to talk with him again."

"Uh, yes. Of course," I said.

I should have expected that. This had been much too easy. But Freddie was right. She did not want to finish with his brother, not yet anyway. I could have shut off the source, but the poor woman had so much sorrow to work through, and I wanted to be a good guest.

40

MEANWHILE Alice settled into her own life at Yali Ashe, a quiet, somewhat anxious life. She and Lady Ashe were polite to each other at meals, but a great gulf remained. While one woman mourned a dead child, the other brooded over an absent husband. Lady Ashe fell into a dreamy lassitude after the first message from Constantine, a sweet daydream, like a wife with a secret infatuation. You might think we were engaged in a different activity when we shut ourselves in the music room each evening. Alice nervously told Lady Ashe over breakfast one morning that she was glad my music was helping her but asked that we not discuss it in front of the children: "Talk of dead babies is much too morbid for their tender ears."

The first letter from Isaac did not arrive until our second week. After that there was a letter almost every day. Alice reported their contents to me—there was nothing in Milan, he was going to Monte Carlo; there was nothing in Marseille, he was going to Paris—but she would not let me read them. I was hurt at first. After all, I'd never been apart from Isaac in over twenty years. Yet I was surprised I did not miss him more. Oh, I missed his everyday reality, his gravity and presence, but not his bad moods or preaching conversation.

Alice wrote to him daily. Her letters would not catch up with his for another week. Meanwhile she had her children to look after, their morning lessons, afternoon games, and general well-being.

The children, however, thoroughly enjoyed Yali Ashe. There was the novelty of staying in one place, and life without father turned out to be surprisingly restful. Augusta explored the strange new house and garden. She was fascinated with the servants, who adored her. Tristan was fascinated with Freddie. He followed the older boy around that first week like a little dog. Freddie barely tolerated him. He wanted no part of any of us and spent most of the day upstairs in his room.

One day Tristan came to his mother and said, "Mama, am I a nigger?"

"*What?* Where did you hear that word?"

"Freddie told me I can't go to college because I'm a nigger and they don't let niggers in college."

"Ignore him. He's an ugly, mean-spirited child. And you'll go to college. You will."

"Mama, am I a nigger?"

"No, my lamb. That's just a nasty name that people give to those they think are lowly and stupid."

Alice told me about this later, adding, "I do not like that boy. It's not his fault that he has such a mother. But I do not trust him around my chicks. I'm afraid he means them harm."

In the blithe, matter-of-fact way of children, Tristan stopped courting Freddie and rejoined his sister. They made paper dolls again, incorporating a rich new array of Turkish costumes. They joined their mother after lunch in a wide green hammock hung outside the kiosk, where they lay on either side of her, mother and daughter taking turns reading aloud from a *McGuffey Reader*. Side by side, in a swaying checker of shadows cast by a lilac tree, they made a very pretty picture.

I noticed Freddie one afternoon peering down at them from his bedroom window, a scornful little owl in his gloomy aerie.

*　　*　　*

Lady Ashe's steam launch was at our disposal, as well as her horse and carriage. Alice and I took the children into Stamboul one day, accompanied by Yuri, the head butler, to see Santa Sofia. The old city was not so beautiful up close, the streets narrow, muddy, and crowded. Santa Sofia looked quite dingy outside, although the dark interior was magnificent. We left our shoes at the door and entered a high, murmurous, vaulted darkness, like God's train station.

There were carriage rides in the country, down long, dusty lanes lined with pastures and apple orchards, like New England, except for the mosques and donkey carts. There were boat rides in the evenings. Once a week a hundred little boats from the other yalis would float downstream toward the Dolmabache Palace, where a small orchestra played in a pavilion. It was always European music—the Turkish upper classes were mad for Donizetti and Verdi. Lady Ashe loaded us all into a caïque, and her Greek boatmen rowed us down to the floating party of bobbing lamps and waterborne voices. She never accompanied us. Despite her many years here, Lady Ashe knew few Europeans and no Turks.

Our other chief recreation was swimming in the Bosphorus.

Yali Ashe had a private beach, with a pair of dressing wagons like those on public beaches in the West, tall cabins on wheels. You entered in your street clothes and were rolled out in waist-deep water, where you could slip discreetly into the brine. After your swim you climbed back in, changed into your clothes, and were rolled ashore. These bathing machines had made sense earlier in the century when people still swam in the altogether but seemed only preposterous now that everyone wore heavy wool bathing garb. The age grew bizarre in its modesty, which reigned even here, where there was nobody to see us except servants.

When Alice and the children swam alone, they used only one wagon. When I joined them, Tristan would change with me in a second wagon.

One day Freddie announced that he, too, wanted a swim. He

didn't ask, he simply declared that he was joining us, which surprised me. The boy had decided to be friendly? No, he sat across from me and Tristan with folded arms, as sour and aloof as ever, while our mildewed cabin was rolled into the water. Instead of the horses used at the beaches in Britain and France, the wagons here were hauled by the yard boys, still fully clothed except for their shoes—Moslems, too, are terribly modest. We heard them outside, a mob of seraphim and cherubim laughing and splashing while our privy on wheels bumped along. After we came to a halt, the yard boys splashed back toward the beach.

Tristan was old enough to undress himself, although I had to hang his clothes for him on the high pegs. We changed with our backs to Freddie. I stopped to help Tristan step into his suit—he had it backward—and found Freddie still seated in the corner, fully dressed.

"Why aren't you changing?"

"I am waiting for some privacy," he said sharply.

But his owlish eyes were watching Tristan, staring at his middle. I didn't like that. Still in my shirttail, I put myself in front of Tristan to shield his coffee-colored infancy from Freddie's lewd gaze. "No, wait," I told Tristan after I buttoned him up. "You can't go into the water without me." I changed quickly, wanting to escape this cramped closet with its obscene owl. I turned to give Freddie a chiding, disapproving look, only to find him staring at *my* privates. I yanked up my woollies. "What's the matter, Freddie? Never seen a naked man?"

And the voyeur's face turned crimson. "I don't care about your—posterior," he spat. "I'm waiting for you to g-g-get out. So I can change."

I only laughed and shook my head. Embarrassment made the wind-up boy seem almost human. "Don't be too long," I said and opened the door, a magic door: Just outside the narrow closet was wide blue water and bright blue sky.

I went down the steps; Tristan squealed and jumped in. He rode on my back as I waded over to the other wagon, where Alice and Augusta were already bobbing in the scalloped waves.

Along the beach the half dozen yard boys sat in the sand, waiting for the barbarians to finish their exotic sport.

Freddie finally came out, in a bumblebee-striped suit that puffed around him like a balloon. He remained in the shallows by our wagon, keeping away from the rest of us.

"Look at me, Uncle Fitz," called Augusta. "I can swim. I can dog-paddle." And she could, so long as I supported her.

"Feels lovely out here," said Alice, floating on her back, her purple flounces fluttering around her so she looked like a large, myopic peony without her specs.

Freddie finished his swim before we finished ours. I saw him climb the steps of the wagon, shriveled and shrunken, a drowned bee. And I recognized what he was up to. He was going to get dressed and wait for us to put on another show. That was why he had joined us today, the little Peeping Tom. Only a boy, I told myself. Shy and curious, that's all. But I couldn't bear letting him have his way.

"You finished, Tristan? Let's go back. No, no, I'm cold." We waded toward the wagon. The current sighed loudly in the spokes of the wheels. "Ssssh," I said as we went up the steps. I threw the door open.

Freddie nearly jumped out of his skin. It was all he wore under his towel. He squeezed himself into the corner where he sat, keeping his lap well covered.

"Have a good swim, Freddie? You should've joined us. We had fun. Didn't we, Tris?"

I innocently strolled in, dripping on the floor, dripping on Freddie. He nervously tucked the towel around his hips. His wet hair hung in his face like angry rust.

I did not want to see Freddie nude. He looked so puny, pasty, and sexless. It was only because he was so determined we *not* see him that I even thought of it.

"Here, Tris, let me get the buttons." I squatted behind him, with my back to Freddie, so the boy would think he was safe.

Then I swung around and grabbed his towel. He gasped as I whipped it away, his white body petrified in an electric jolt of fright. Then his hands were everywhere, grabbing for the towel, at the air, his torso twisting around before he realized his bottom was as obscene as his front. "No! Don't! Give it back!"

"You can't see us unless we see you," I laughed, holding the towel over my head, enjoying his naked terror.

Tristan laughed, because I was laughing and because Freddie looked so funny when he was upset. He saw nothing unseemly in my horseplay. And you didn't, Tristan. It was innocent. Wasn't it?

The excitement lasted seconds before Freddie understood that panic only made him more naked. He drew his knees to his chest and hid himself behind his spindly legs; orange-fuzzed gooseberries peeked behind his feet. "Not fair," he gasped, struggling to catch his breath. "Why'd you do that?" he sobbed. He was crying.

He was fourteen years old but seemed all ages at once, a sullen adolescent, a bitter old man, a six-year-old crybaby.

"Oh, don't go on," I said. "I'm sorry. Here." I tossed him his towel. "I was just having fun. Nothing to be ashamed of."

"I'm not ashamed, I'm just—" He covered his face with his hands. "You frightened me."

I helped Tristan out of his garment, wrapped him in a towel, then unbuttoned my own suit.

"See," I said, stomping a puddle of wet wool to the floor. "The human body. Nothing frightening about it." I took a towel but used it on my head, letting Freddie look all he pleased.

And he did look, with a pinched, disapproving frown. When I began to dry off my middle, he stood to get dressed, pretending to have grown bold and unashamed, even though he stuck out like one leg of a wishbone.

Now it was my turn to be embarrassed. I looked away, telling myself this often happens to boys his age. It meant nothing. I glanced again, and there it was, a red-tipped finger in a downy smudge of copper. I did not understand why I was distressed to discover this sour soul had a flesh-and-blood body.

I dressed quickly and hauled up the flag to signal the yard boys that we wanted to be wheeled in. I felt foolish for exposing the boy and surprised at myself for being disturbed by the deed. But it was over. Freddie pulled up his worsted stockings, and everything seemed fine. Maybe he would be more human around us in the future.

But Freddie ashore was once again a stuffy, bitter little man. I now sensed the confused boy hidden in that cold disguise, yet it did not make him likable, only more curious and puzzling.

41

I continued my sessions with Fanny, though not daily. I told her that these encounters were exhausting and that the spirits, too, needed rest. When I ran out of messages from Constantine, however, I found I could just sit and play and let Fanny read her own messages in my musical tea leaves. One day, shortly after our swim with Freddie, she offered, "There's so much longing in his music. I can't help feeling that he wants to pay us a visit."

"Oh, no," I told her. "Definitely not. Materializations are very rare. Much too difficult for a new spirit to manage." And, needless to say, beyond my abilities. I didn't even believe that the spirits could make themselves visible.

But late that night, after I blew out my candle and fell asleep, my mind suddenly snapped awake to— Nothing, nothing at all. Streaks of shuttered moonlight lined the gray room like a blank page of sheet music. My door was snugly shut. Yet I sensed a presence, a presence like an absence. I could hear it in my heart. I listened with my ears. A soft beat of bare feet? No, it was only the beat of blood in the ear pressed to my pillow. The Bosphorus snored softly outside. I was alone on this floor. Alice and the children were one floor below mine, Fanny and Freddie on the floor below theirs. A footman kept guard on the ground floor, a sleeping watchdog who never ventured upstairs. But I could not shake the sensation that there was someone up here with me.

I lifted the covers, touched cool wood with my bare feet, and tiptoed to my door. I opened the door, slowly. The hallway was pitch-dark, long and empty. Then I saw it! A gossamer shape stood outside the music room! I blinked and looked harder. Man-high, man-shaped, it floated by the wall. "Constantine?" I whispered. It didn't respond.

I stepped toward it, ever so cautiously. The shape wavered a moment. Then, all at once, it turned, snapped back, and resolved itself into a fold of moonlight. That's all it was. A man-high spill of moonbeams fell from the music room to rest upon the wall. I stroked the wallpaper, chuckled to myself, and went back to bed, feeling quite foolish.

The next day I went into town, alone. This isolated country life was unhinging me, I decided, making me prey to all kinds of fancies. I needed the reality of urban strangers and noise. So, in my best clothes, a smart porkpie hat, and elegant ebony cane, I rode down to Pera, feeling like a lord in Lady Ashe's open carriage as it flew along the road, even though I had only a few coins in my pocket.

We came to a French-looking park, Taksim Park, where veiled Turkish ladies in the latest European fashions strolled under chestnut trees and gentlemen in frock coats and fezzes trotted around on horseback. I told the driver to tie up here and wait for me.

I was happy to walk in a city again, no matter how foreign. But Pera, the new city, was not so foreign. It was an imitation Europe, its main boulevard, the Grand'Rue de Pera, pure Paris. The shop signs were in French as well as Turkish, Greek, and a curious alphabet of brads and staples that was Armenian. As soon as one stepped off the Grand'Rue, however, one was deep in the Orient: narrow twisting streets of mud and turbans and sleeping dogs— Constantinople was famous for its stray dogs.

I wanted to explore the sensual wonders of the East, silks and perfumes and such. *"Danseuses, danseuses très belles,"* chanted an old man outside a café. The belly dancers of the East were famous for their grace and artistry, so I went in.

The little room was hung all around with carpets, the floor covered in rugs and pillows. Men, all Turkish, sat or lounged around drinking tea and sucking hookahs. Two musicians, a man with a string instrument and another with a little drum, played a jangly tune in a corner. The first performer came out, a boy. No, it had to be a girl, I decided, seeing the long black hair, a white girl, Circassian or Greek, enveloped in gauze. But then he danced, and there was no mistaking the bud that flared against the milky fabric. It was hardly a dance but the sinuous writhe of a man fornicating with his bedclothes, sex and round buttocks pressing the loose gauze. I was appalled, disgusted. I genuinely was. This boy was like my own Eusebius made obscene, coldly eyed by a roomful of sulky Turks. The lewd gurgle in their water pipes made my skin crawl. I left as soon as the dance ended.

I've been living too long with Isaac and Alice, I thought out on the street. I've become a prig, a prude, a moral person. I returned to the Grand'Rue and the safety of the familiar. Yet my unease stayed with me. When a middle-aged white man, a dandified fellow with bobcat whiskers, passed me and his eyes met mine, I felt a repulsive shiver. Was this a whole city of sodomites?

I hurried on. Five minutes later I spotted the dandified bobcat again, walking in the same direction that I did. Was he following me? I tested the possibility by stopping to look in a shop window, a display of antique swords and daggers. A transparent reflection appeared beside mine.

"Dr. August?" he said.

"Yes?" I turned around. I didn't recognize the bobcat but saw that his blue-black whiskers were dyed.

"M. L. Cunningham," he said. "We met many years ago. I'm sure you've forgotten me." He sounded so cheerful, so innocent.

My spine stiffened. I coldly smiled. "No. I remember you quite well. *Captain Sly Pig.* You published lies about me in London."

And he laughed! The son of a bitch laughed. "You hurt me and I hurt you, Doc. I'd say that we're even. It was many years ago, and besides, we're in another country. Let's let bygones be bygones. My card." He handed me a piece of pasteboard. "I am with the *Levant Tribune* here, the English newspaper."

"You're a journalist?"

"Yes, I've become legitimate in my old age."

"I'd hardly call the muck sheets legitimate."

He laughed at that, too. "I understand that you and your wife are the guests of Lady Ashe?"

The European colony was a small town, and as in any small town its gossip was often inaccurate.

"Not my wife. The wife of a friend. And their children."

But he did not care about that. "Lady Ashe is one of the finest enigmas of this enigmatic city. I wondered if you might introduce me to her. I've tried, but she plays hard to get."

"Why would you want to meet her?"

"I could do a very pretty piece on the lady. A whole book, in fact. *The Mysterious Lady Ashe.* A sad American beauty stranded in the Orient. The folks back home would gobble it up." This vampire of ink was shameless.

"I'd as soon introduce the devil into her house."

He laughed again. He was above insults, or beneath them. "Don't be so hasty, my friend. One should be kind to reporters. A man never knows when he'll need a reporter in his court. Perhaps there's a favor I can do you sometime? Think about it, sir. You have my card. Good day."

The gods of chance had a vicious sense of humor. Of all the old faces to encounter here. We hadn't dropped off the earth after all. I had no need of newspapers, or fear of them either, yet it was annoying to realize that people like Cunningham still lurked about, even at the Threshold of Happiness.

* * *

I returned to Yali Ashe in time for our evening session.

"What's that?" said Fanny. "That can't be Constantine."

It wasn't. Eusebius had taken control of both hands for a dance in the Phrygian mode, an Oriental thing full of chiming notes like tintinnabula. Too curious to stop, I let him continue until I recognized the music: the profane dance of the boy at the café. Meeting Cunningham had driven it from my mind, but Eusebius remembered the tune quite well.

When it was done, when I came out of my trance, I apologized to Fanny. "There are many spirits out there. And like a hello girl at a switchboard, my familiar sometimes makes the wrong connection."

"I'm so relieved," she said. "It sounded coarse and rude. I was wondering what had come over my boy."

We joined the others outside for dinner.

"Another letter from Isaac," Alice told me as I sat down. "There is nothing in Paris either. Everyone is gone for the summer. Poor Isaac. He only makes himself miserable. I am tempted to tell him to stop beating his head against closed doors and join us here. There's plenty of room. And plenty of time. He could wait here until September to resume his hunt."

"You can suggest that," I said. "But his pride will stop him from coming."

"Yes, you're right," said Alice. "It certainly would."

Freddie had listened in with his usual nasty frown. "This wonderful Mr. Kemp?" he said. "You're always talking about him, but one has to wonder. Does he really exist?"

I was in no mood for his insolence. I leaned over and whispered, "If you don't watch your manners, I'm going to strip you again. Right here in front of everyone."

He took a deep breath and sat very still. Then he snorted to let me know that I didn't frighten him.

* * *

That night I dreamed of Eusebius again. He walked along the shore, alone, without the horse and piano. Had he abandoned them? He was covered in gauze, a glaucoma of silk like the outfit of that Greek dancing boy. Then he saw me and smiled, as always. He walked toward me, still smiling, a nervous, nervy, defiant smile. And he kept coming, closer than he had ever come before, until he was near enough for me to throw my arms around him.

I had him, finally, and he felt wonderful. He pulled away at first, then clung to me, as tightly as I clung to him. The gauze had disappeared. And I kissed him, his cheeks, neck, eyes, mouth. He had a sharp, birdlike tongue. I was ecstatic. We were alone. We were in my bed, and nobody would know. Angels are said to be cold to the touch, but Eusebius was warm, a silky warmth that melted into my skin and slipped under my nightshirt. And his warmth took shape in my hands as I sculpted it into flesh. I hung on his tongue, a soft drill as stiff as a man's sex. I molded his wings into the smooth cheeks of a boy's bottom, and I began to suspect that he was not an absolute being but a lewd dream, a common succubus. Just then the angel strained upward, as if trying to fly away, let out a soft cry, and the tongue in my mouth turned to honey.

I was suddenly alone. My blankets were kicked back. My shirt was yoked up around my neck with one arm free. I looked down my moonlike belly and saw my own stiff sex. It had been only a wet dream, but what kind of wet dream left you dry? I could taste him on my lips. I seemed to be dreaming still.

I turned over and—there he was!

He lay with his back to me, now bare of wings, his rump a large white peach.

"Eusebius," I whispered. Because I still did not understand.

"No," he said angrily. "Not Eusebius. Not Constantine. Me. Don't you understand! It's me!"

I put my hand on his shoulder and turned his face toward mine. The shoulder was bird bone. The huge eyes were Freddie's.

I sat bolt upright. I was in my room at Yali Ashe. The door was closed. And Freddie was in my bed!

"Why're you here? How did you get here?" I still had one foot in my dream and actually thought Eusebius had brought him upstairs, a vicious prank on us both.

Freddie turned away. "I came up to—to look at you or just stand in your room or— I don't know why I came. But then you grabbed me and did things to me, and I was scared but—" His breathless fear gave way to hurt. "You didn't know it was me?" he cried. "You kissed me and didn't know it was me?"

"I was asleep, my boy, and dreaming and—"

"Can't *anyone* love me?" he demanded. "Do I have to die before anyone will love *me*?"

My heart swelled and shuddered. No, it was not *my* love he wanted but the loving attention of someone, anyone. "My boy," I began. "My poor boy. This wasn't love. It can be, but only with somebody who—"

"I don't care if you love me or not." He curled up on his side and hid again behind his bony shoulder. "I don't know why I said that. It's just dirty what you did, isn't it?"

"I wouldn't have done it if I'd known what I was doing, Freddie. I don't want to harm you."

"Well, you did," he said. "And it was disgusting." Yet he made no move to leave my bed.

"It was awful of me. I'm sorry. Forgive me." I touched his shoulder, sharp and warm. My thumb traced a porcelain saucer under baby-soft skin. I'd forgotten he was naked. "Why're you undressed?" I said. "Where's your robe, your nightshirt?" My own shirt was still twisted around my neck, but I made no move to cover myself.

"Down in my room. I took them off to walk in the dark."

"But *why*?"

"Because I like it. Because it frightens me. Because I like being frightened."

I pictured his pale, nude shadow tiptoeing through his mother's house.

"Like when you stripped me in the dressing cabin," he said. "I've done it every night since. It excites me. It feels so unearthly. It makes me supernatural."

Sex and necromancy were one and the same to him, sublime terrors. He'd been possessed, not by Eusebius but by his own changing body.

"That was *you* last night?" I said.

"Yes. You opened your door, and I thought you'd caught me, but I stepped into the music room and saw you talking to a corner. You thought it was Constantine. You looked so stupid." He grew more confident and taunting. "When I came in tonight, I was just going to stand by your bed, and you'd never know how obscene I was in front of you. But then you grabbed me and did things to me. Vile, rude things. What you did with your mouth?" he said accusingly. "Was that black magic? Was it evil?"

My remorse and guilt returned, tenfold, and prudent fear.

"Freddie," I said. "You can't tell a soul that you were with me like this. You understand that, don't you?"

"Will you get in trouble?" I could hear a smile in his tone.

"You will get us both in trouble. But it would ruin me." I took his hand in mine to plead my case. His stubby fingers felt very soft, cool and naked.

How much more should I say? You know what's going to happen. For all my fear and confusion, I was hardly Lancelot beside Guinevere with only an unsheathed sword between them.

Without thinking, I began to kiss his fingers.

He rolled over to watch a grown man kiss his hand. He looked amazed, fascinated, pleased. "I don't want to ruin you," he whispered. "Now."

"You can't stay here," I said between kisses. "You have to go back to your room."

But he didn't move. He was looking down at me. "Bodies are so ugly," he said. "Yours is even uglier than mine." And he used his free hand to grope and take hold of me. He looked both disgusted and fascinated, like he was handling a newborn chick.

I used my free hand to feel how he was feeling. There was no wishbone, only a wrinkled walnut and limp stem.

"I can do to myself what you did with your mouth," he said. "It's frightening when it starts jumping, but it feels good, too. Can yours do that?"

"All men can make their pricks jump." Did he know nothing about sex?

"You can—" His mouth was dry. He had to swallow the dryness before he could continue. "You can do to me whatever you want."

"No, my boy." My finger tickled the stem. "I don't want— You shouldn't— We can never—" And I leaned in to kiss him.

He stopped me with his fingers on my chin. "I'm Freddie," he said. "You know that I'm Freddie, don't you?"

"Oh, yes. You're Freddie. I know that you're Freddie." Just as I knew that this was wrong and I was making a terrible mistake, even as I pressed my mouth against an ivory gate of young teeth and pulled him into my arms.

42

THE next morning at breakfast the same old wind-up boy reappeared in the kiosk, neatly sealed in a Lincoln-green suit with knickerbockers and a droopy black bow. His rust-red hair was glossy and parted, his mouth squashed in its usual elderly pout. He sat beside his mother, opposite two real children, and calmly ate his eggs.

I was afraid to look at him. I watched the others, wondering if they could tell, then avoided their eyes as well. I feared the deed must show in my face. I hated myself for it. I was filled with guilt, my soul shaken open in remorse. Circumstance and a boy's spooky game had initiated it, but he was only a boy, and circumstance was no excuse. I could've stopped it. Why hadn't I stopped it? Guilt left me feeling terribly protective toward Freddie. More than protective, I felt nervously tender, fretfully affectionate. I seemed smitten with the very person whom I'd wronged. It had been so long since I'd been in love with a mortal that my remorse felt close to infatuation.

"I am going to try the bicycle again," Freddie announced when he finished his tea. "Dr. August? Would you help me learn?"

My heart jumped, my hands turned cold. "Oh, why not?" I said with a shrug and set my napkin on the table. There was a new pang of regret when we stood up and I saw I was a good head taller than he, older and more responsible.

Freddie seemed only annoyed with me as we walked toward the

garden wall where the harp-wheeled bicycle leaned. I held the seat support and handlebars while he climbed up. It was unnerving to stand so close to him, his waist level with my face, my nose perfectly tuned to his private scents of skin and hair oil. When I walked him around the yard, his thighs rose and fell, safely wrapped in knickers buttoned over his stockings. He did not press the pedals but let my movement carry him.

I was trying to think of a way to address my crime when he announced, "I had the strangest dream last night, Dr. August. Only I don't think it was a dream."

"No, it wasn't," I admitted. "I take full blame for what we did. That was awful of me."

"It was disgusting," he agreed. "And dirty. But you didn't just do it to me, I did it to you." He produced a cold little smirk. "You think you're such a brainy fellow. But I saw you on all fours, no better than a dog. Wagging his tail."

My remorse lifted a little. It had not been so disgusting that he couldn't taunt me about it, and as an equal, not a terrified child.

"You have no business prowling at night in your birthday suit," I told him. "There's no dignity there either."

"I will not visit you again," he said.

"Good," I replied. "You can't. I would not be able to live with myself knowing I'd introduced you to vicious habits."

"I will not visit you again," he repeated. "Unless you ask me to visit."

Was this a trap? A test? "I am fond of you, Freddie. But last night was a mistake. It can never happen again."

He considered that, weighed it, with his eyes aimed forward. "Very well," he declared. "I don't want to."

"If we can remain friends despite last night," I said, "then it will prove that we love each other."

"What makes you think I want your love?"

"All right, then. My friendship."

He frowned. "Why would I want to be friends with a man whom I've seen panting like a dog?"

He only wants attention, I told myself. Whether he gets it from insults or shared secrets or his prick, he didn't care.

"I saw you in the same state," I reminded him.

His frown tightened, his nostrils widened. He said nothing.

I remembered the bicycle. "Here," I said. "If I make you go fast, you'll be able to keep your balance and ride this thing."

He used his feet to stop the turning pedals. "Oh, piss on the bicycle," he snapped. "A child's thing. Just let me down."

"No. Let's give it a try."

"You're beginning to bore me, August."

Startled and stung, I let him dismount.

He regained his aloof little smirk. "Good day, Doctor Dog," he declared and headed into the house.

He was angry at me. Because of what had happened? Or because I wanted us to go on as if nothing had happened? Or because it would never happen again? He did not reappear until lunch. I tried to be friendly to him, in pointed smiles and idle remarks, but my attentions only annoyed him. He was cold with me, scornful and indifferent, which hurt more than I could have imagined. I wanted us to be friends, despite our sin.

Late that afternoon I proposed another session to Lady Ashe. "I feel that Constantine has something new to tell us."

We went upstairs, she lay on her settle, and I sat at the gaudy gilt piano. I improvised a Freddie song out of Schubert's piano trio, a mournful lockstep march of solitude. I hoped she'd hear Freddie there for herself, but when I was done, she said that *Connie* sounded quite lonely today.

"He seemed to be singing someone else's song," I suggested. "The song of someone living."

She still didn't understand.

"To my ear," I said, "it sounded like Freddie."

"Freddie? Why would Connie sing about his brother?"

"Because he sees that Freddie is sad. Lonely. You love your dead son very much. But you must also love your living son."

"I know," she admitted with a sigh. "But it's hard. I cannot look at him without thinking of the child who's gone."

"You need to try. He's lonelier than he seems." My concern was sincere, even as I worked to make amends to my conscience.

"No, he's strong," she insisted. "He has always been an old child. He does not like me to fuss over him. He's a very manly, masculine boy. Unlike his brother. He's not an easy boy to love."

Yet I found Freddie quite lovable, dangerously lovable, like any runt of the litter. Guilt had led me away from lust into pity, and I thought I was safe.

At dinner I noticed Fanny stealing looks at her son, but she spoke to him as she always did, kindly yet distantly. After dinner we sat indoors in the room with the splashing fountain, passing around a stereopticon and looking at views of Stamboul, the nearby city that nobody was keen on visiting again. Augusta settled on my lap while I adjusted the focus for her, working a double photograph up and down the brass slide until—there!—the sepia blurs merged in the eyepiece and Santa Sofia leaped into view, sharp and round and three-dimensional.

I passed the device to Augusta and—there was Freddie, sitting ten feet away, sharp and round and three-dimensional. He slouched low in a wicker chair, watching me, studying me. He did not look away when I looked at him. Whatever he felt toward me, he was not indifferent. I was surprised at how attractive he'd become since breakfast. He was not homely anymore, or no, his face *was* homely, but my knowledge of the friendly body hidden in the green suit and black stockings made his homeliness seem beautiful. I could be wise and moral only during the day, when my tanks had not yet refilled.

He bade us all good night in his usual courteous manner, shaking Alice's hand, his mother's, then mine. His fingers lingered in my palm, a clutch of cool, slim digits. He strolled out, then paused at the door to glance over his shoulder. The touch of his hand had already swept away my resolutions.

"Excuse me, my dear," I told Augusta, and lifted her from my lap. "Right back." I got up and went out to the hall.

He waited for me on the stairs, a few steps up, hanging over the banister. "Yes?" he said.

"Oh? I thought you had something to tell *me*."

He smirked again and shook his head, reading my thoughts.

I couldn't say it yet. "Were you intending to take another stroll tonight?"

"What business is it of yours?"

I had to say it. "Well, if you do, I just want you to know that— I've changed my mind."

He smiled. "Maybe I've changed mine."

"Fine, then. Don't. We shouldn't."

"But you want me to?"

"Only if you want to."

"I want you to want me to, whether I want to or not." His smile hung open after the playful patter of words.

"Very well," I said. "Very well. I want you to visit tonight. Please. Whether you want to or not."

"I'll consider it. Good night, Dr. Dog." And he climbed up the steps, slowly, without looking back, his short pants pulling taut on his hindquarters with each lift of leg.

I was certain he wouldn't come, now that he had what he wanted from me, a confession of desire. Good, I thought. Yes. It was better this way. He was too young, this household too close, and physical love was only a profane game to him. Nevertheless, when I went to bed, I sat up with a book in my lap, unwilling to snuff the candle, unable to read a word.

The candle burned down one inch, then another. Then I heard my door squeak open. He remained outside, a nude white shadow with a mask of eyes. He was frowning. "No," he whispered. "No light. I won't come in unless it's dark."

He closed the door. I blew out the candle. The hinges squeaked again. The knob clicked shut.

"Are you supernatural?" he whispered.

It took me a moment to remember what that meant. I pulled my nightshirt over my head and tossed it to the floor. "You should at least put on a robe. What if someone sees you on the stairs?"

"No. This is part of the magic, part of the ritual."

A cool darkness scrambled over me, a twitchy, bony phantom with a bare bottom. We became two mouths, four hands, two exclamation marks, and no brains. Or no, I had just enough brains to tell myself that I seemed to be kissing—not Eusebius but the fulfillment of what my dreams of Eusebius had promised me all these years. Curse or blessing, I was too excited to care.

43

So it began, our divided life of lurid nights and drowsy days, secret obscenity and public decorum. We fell into it so easily. Too easily.

In the harsh light of breakfast the next morning, I felt sad and guilty again, yet less agitated, more at home in guilt. Freddie looked only dreamy and preoccupied, much like his mother, in fact, but with an entirely different cause.

Augusta stole a taste of my coffee and spat it out. "What did I tell you?" said Alice. "It's for grown-ups."

Lady Ashe asked, for the hundredth time, if Alice were teaching her children French, and Alice replied that she was, in the weary tones one uses with a pesky child.

"Would you like another cycling lesson?" I asked Freddie.

"Not particularly," he said. "An insipid pastime. But I might like a walk in the garden. Yes?" He held out his hand.

I took a slow, fearful breath—and took his hand, right there in front of everyone. But they saw only a child leading a grown-up by the hand, not a debauched youth and his seducer. I can still feel his hand in mine, the slim fingers, plump palm, his knuckles light as shoelace knots.

He let go as soon as we were out of sight of the kiosk. "Fools," he said. "They can't imagine it, can they?"

"Be glad of that," I said and reached for his hand again.

He swung it out of reach. "We're not married," he muttered. "I'm not in love with you." He stuck both hands in his pockets while he tried to decide what he felt. "But I like you, August."

"Good," I said. "Because I like you, Freddie. Very much."

We strolled among the tulip beds, only the tulips had fallen to mold weeks ago and the garden was dominated by roses, every variety of rose imaginable, a licentious riot of roses.

"Do you still love Constantine?"

I was not surprised that he mentioned his brother. "I never loved Constantine. I never knew him. In this world."

"Connie wouldn't have done anything like this, you know. He was too scared. Too yellow."

"Whereas you're very brave," I said. "And fearless." And unpredictable, I thought, as unpredictable as a child.

"And you're old," he said. "And fat. And smelly."

He was smiling. It was a child's smile, with the doubleness children often have when they watch themselves say this or that, wondering what they'll get away with. Only after we'd entered into adult deeds did I begin to see the child in Freddie.

And it was very adult, our adultery, without romantic sighs or valentine gazes. Freddie hated anything that sounded "swoony," so there was no sweet talk. He seemed nothing like a child in bed but was as shameless as a Frenchman with his mistress. During his initial visits he would leave as soon as we finished. Then he found he could repeat the act—he could, I couldn't—and would loiter in the bedclothes until he was stiff again.

He always came to me. I never went to him, although one night, early on, he dared me to walk him back to his room. "No," he commanded. "You can't put on your robe. You must be like me. A dirty dog. Or are you too scared?" So we walked down the gloomy oak stairs in our bare skin, Old Adam and Young Adam timidly descending through beeswax-scented darkness. We held hands again, a nervous tangle of fingers. His body was paler than mine, as white as chalk. I heard the clucking of the clock in the front hall far below us, where the servant on watch should be fast asleep. We passed the floor where Alice and the children lay snug in their beds, but no door flew open. When we came to his room, Freddie refused to let me in or even kiss him good night. I hurried back upstairs, feeling foolish and weightless, a skittish ghost in a mansion of slumber.

What did we do? You actually want to know? This isn't shocking enough already? Or do you believe some acts are more brutish than others? Well, we would kiss and touch and stroke. We did what I've heard called the Princeton rub, only neither of us had been to Princeton. But what Freddie liked best, since you want to know— He liked to straddle my face on his knees and elbows. I don't know why he preferred that, what it meant for him to ride me with his thumb in my mouth and buck away like a little goat. I couldn't see his face. Maybe that was it. He never let me light a lamp or candle, but the moon began to wax full again over the following weeks, and more light poured through the slats. I once had him take me as Isaac had, face to face, but he didn't like having my eyes in front of his. Afterward he said only that the act was too unsanitary to repeat.

His lovemaking was never easy or innocent. He needed his fireworks and pursued each climax with cold concentration, somnambulistic fervor. He was not much interested in my pleasure but would try with me whatever I did to him. "Nebuchadnezzar," I thought when I watched him do that for the first time, as delicately as a cat eating a mouse. Then I remembered where I'd heard the joke: Fanny had given the nickname to one of her regulars at Roebuck's, and I was using it for her own child. Was this in Freddie's blood? It's in everyone's blood, of course, but he knew nothing of his mother's history. Despite his privileges and comforts, I was bringing him down to the animal life that Fanny and I had worked so hard to escape.

Nobody had told him anything about sex, so I taught Freddie the facts of life, without blushes or euphemism. He didn't know that this had anything to do with how babies are made, that all men and women did something similar and our necromancy was a universal sin. He asked if semen were magnetic fluid, and he may have been right. I sometimes wondered if, years later, when he grew up and married and took his bride to their bed, he would remember how he'd learned so much physiology.

I told him all the names and some of the myths. "They say that each man is allotted only so many shots for his lifetime and he'll go dry if he uses them up too soon. And then there's the myth that if you spend three times in one night you will die."

"Yes?" he said. "Three times?"

"But it's not true," I assured him.

He wasn't convinced until I coaxed and ignited yet another burst from his loins.

After each bout I could never be sure who he would be: worldly man or sullen boy, cool stranger or friendly pal.

"Don't lie on me. You're too fat and sweaty," he would grumble. Or "Yours is bigger than mine. It looks like a bull next to a deer." Or "I can say anything that comes into my mind to you, can't I? I like that."

And he would say anything. Once, when he lay beside me, idly fingerpainting in the spill on my stomach, he calmly observed, "It's like Mummy's milk."

"*What?*"

"Her medicine. Her laudanum. I've had it a few times. Just a taste. She keeps a big blue bottle in her bedroom. Blackwood's Nightingale. Extra Strong. I liked how it made me feel."

Opium. Morphia. Lethe. "You shouldn't," I told him. "It'll make you sick. It's poison."

"I know. And this is better. I like this better. That was like sleep. This is like being wide awake. For a few minutes."

At such times he seemed quite young—I could not have been so young when I was fourteen.

As he grew more at ease in my bed, more relaxed between bouts, he would occasionally doze off in the crook of my arm. I liked having him there, his heavy head resting on my shoulder, his owl eyes closed, his mouth half open, a faint whiff of milk on his breath. He looked so calm, so vulnerable, so trusting. His honeyed warmth poured into my flank. Once, just once, he held my hand in his sleep—I remember his hands more sharply than any other part of him. His soft fingers gripped my old knuckles like a dreamer terrified of falling. When I gently kissed his hand to comfort him, he suddenly shivered awake and pulled away from me. "That's disgusting," he muttered. "Licking me in my sleep."

I didn't dare fall asleep myself. As our sessions continued, I was prudent enough to ask for an alarm clock, explaining that I hated being awoken by servants. I always set it for four o'clock, a good hour before any servants were up.

I became more comfortable during the day, less fearful that the world might suspect anything.

"Is there any message you wish to send?"

"What?" I snapped out of a reverie, one I often fell into toward bedtime. "Beg your pardon. Message to whom?"

"To Isaac," Alice said curtly. "Whom else might I mean?"

We were alone in the library, Alice at a desk in the glow of an oil lamp, I on a wicker chaise with an unread book in my lap. The others had gone to bed. I was waiting for Alice to finish so I could be sure she had retired before I went upstairs.

"Just tell him we're fine," I said. "And we miss him."

"But are we fine? You've been in a strange mood of late. You seem lost in melancholy."

"Melancholy?" I said, feigning surprise and pausing to weigh my mood. "I don't *feel* melancholy. Only musical. Wistful perhaps. I can't imagine why. It must be the rich food."

"Hmmmph," she said and resumed scribbling. It was always letters now. She had filled up her last diary years ago and no longer even recorded purchases. Alice must have written fifty letters to Isaac that summer. I wonder what became of them.

"I am suggesting," she said over her brisk scratch of words, "that if he cannot find anything soon, he should join us. For the children's sake. They are going half wild here. I cannot keep them to their lessons. All they want to do is play. Surely their noise must be getting on your nerves."

"Not at all. I hardly notice them."

"House of the lotus-eaters," she grumbled. "Everyone seems to have eaten of a root that's put them in a trance. Everyone but me. I appear to be the only one who's awake here."

But not so awake that she understood what was going on.

The children noticed nothing either, only that Freddie and I had become friendlier during the day. Or no, Augusta seemed to sense something, because she no longer sat in my lap. It may have been only my imagination, but I wondered if there had been a galvanic change in my body or if I simply no longer touched her in the careless, carefree manner of before.

All Lady Ashe ever said was that her son seemed less testy since our arrival, that he must enjoy the presence of other children. She remained sunk in her bombazine oblivion.

No, the only people to suspect were the servants. I caught the maids eyeing me from under their bushy caterpillar eyebrows. Ismail must have heard from them about the state of my bed linen, because he began to stare quizzically whenever I was alone with Freddie. Then one day, in private, he quietly remarked, "Master Alfred is becoming a man."

"Yes, I suppose he is," I replied.

"It is good for him to have another man for company."

"What do you mean?" I said, a little too sharply.

"Nothing of bother, Monsieur Docteur. Only that it is good for a growing man to have ... the example of a fully grown man."

I couldn't tell if he were sarcastic and condemning, or if he found it perfectly natural for two bachelors to slake their needs in each other's arms. Were we even talking about the same thing?

"Have you mentioned our, uh, friendliness to Lady Ashe?"

"Monsieur Docteur!" he said. "Such matters are no business of women. I would as soon discuss with her the color of Master Alfred's urine."

So he did know—the servants knew the bodily functions of the house better than the bodies knew themselves—and treated it as a common phenomenon. But was a eunuch the best judge here?

Our intimacies remained nocturnal. Except once, when we went swimming, just the two of us. We stepped into a bathing machine, closed the door, and the yard boys rolled us out. The cabin sat in the low, purring waves for half an hour, with no bathers ever emerging. Then the little flag went up, and the yard boys came out and rolled the wagon back in, and two wan figures sheepishly stumbled out.

We were friendly enough during the day, but in the shallow, bantering manner of two cousins. I wanted our nights to spill into our days, not in kisses but in openness, trust, warmth. We should share more than our spume. I began to invite Freddie up to the music room after lunch and played for him. He would lie on his back on the cretonne settle, like his mother, only I left the shutters open so there was no séance gloom. A bright square of sky and water hung beside the reclining boy.

Freddie did not like Schumann, and Brahms put him to sleep. But he enjoyed Offenbach, whose gaudy tempos sounded good on that gaudy piano. Looking up at the mirror on the wall, I could see two leather soles happily wag to two-four time galops, codas, and cancans, tawdry stuff, but I gladly gave up Schumann for Freddie's sake. He also liked the sulky, dreamy repetitions of the Barcarolle. "Play that sleepy-sleepy tune again," he commanded one afternoon. Only when I was well into it did I remember how I'd played this for his mother many years ago while wearing a blindfold.

"August?" he suddenly said over the music. "Are you truly in touch with Connie?"

I continued to play. It was as if he had heard his mother in my thoughts. We shared such a huge secret already, what did one more secret matter? I wanted to give him more power, as proof of my affection, as a show of my trust. "No," I said. "I'm not. I am only pretending with your mother."

"Yes?" he said. "Truly?" He sounded amazed, astonished I would confess such a thing. Then he began to laugh. "So you are a fraud, August! A fatuous fake." He laughed like one boy teasing another, but I was hurt.

"I'm in touch with some spirits, Freddie. Eusebius for one. But I have had to feign communication with your brother. Because it makes your mother feel better. I genuinely want to help her."

Freddie smiled to himself and rattled the coins in his pockets, as if he suddenly had great wealth.

I feared I had just made myself dangerously vulnerable.

"What's this Eusebius like?" he asked.

"Oh, he's young. He's beautiful. And he has wings."

"Wings? Go on! And a halo, I bet, and golden slippers."

"No, it's true. He doesn't always wear wings. But when the proper mood is upon him. Like dove wings. Quite beautiful."

"If he's so beautiful, how did you once mistake me for him?"

"Well, because— I sometimes find *you* beautiful."

He irritably shifted on the settle. "I'm not. Not in a hog's eye." He rattled his coins again. "I'm not like your spirit. Just ask him. Next time you chat."

"I will. But I already know that he likes you."

"Yeah?" He laughed, but in a pleased, secretly flattered way. "Go on."

"I think he might even be in love with you."

Freddie was suddenly silent. "I don't know if I like that," he said. "Being loved by a mushy ghost."

"He's not a ghost. He's a familiar. My familiar."

"Even so." He made a face and shivered.

One could say "like" to Freddie, but not "love." He feared the word, mistrusted it, even when attributed to a spirit whose very existence he doubted.

Eusebius, however, was gone. He had disappeared from my dreams as well as my music. The horse and piano still came to me now and then, trudging along the shore, looking sadder than ever without their friend, who seemed to have gone off on a brief visit somewhere. I did not believe for a minute that Freddie was Eusebius—Eusebius had blue eyes, Freddie's were green—or that Eusebius had left my dreams to take possession of Freddie. I cannot blame Eusebius. I was not his puppet; my Metaphysicals were not Fate. No, they only pointed out opportunities, chances, probabilities; they were markers on the highway that I could choose to follow or not.

My sessions with Fanny continued, chiefly me playing while she wool-gathered aloud. Without Eusebius to guide or interrupt, the compositions were all mine.

I played the Freddie song again. "It sounds sweeter now," she said. "Less lonely. You see, my boy doesn't need me. He knows I love him. In my fashion."

"Perhaps. But you really should pay him more attention." I did not press too hard, however, for fear that too much attention would enable her to understand the change that had come over him. Or was I afraid that more love from her might mean Freddie would no longer need mine?

Was it love that I gave Freddie? I *was* in love with him. I will not deny it. My feelings changed as our nocturnal acts continued, from repentant love to love of pleasure to a love of Freddie himself. But romantic love must be mutual to function as love. Otherwise it is only a bother, a humbug, an assault. And I knew that Freddie was not in love with me. He was too young to feel much love for anyone, including himself. This was about the discovery of his own body, his hunger for attention, his buried feelings about his brother and mother. Or if he loved me, it was only as a lonely child loves any adult who pays him attention. That was why he came to me every night. A happier boy doing this with a boy his own age would have visited more erratically, guilt and gooseberries vying with each other for the upper hand. Freddie overcame his bad feelings for the sake of repeated doses of my attention.

I am not speaking from hindsight. I knew all along that there were bad feelings. This was not innocent. It did not feel like the sin of sins either, but I'd been such a boy myself and remembered the mare's nest of emotions that accompanied fireworks below the waist. Yet I was far kinder to Freddie than Uncle Jack had been to me, more considerate and affectionate. Freddie did not hate me as I'd hated Uncle Jack. But then hatred can be a kind of armor that protects you from more vulnerable emotions.

I protest too much. I admit it. Even now, forty years later, I protect myself by dwelling on qualms rather than joy. Because both were there, side by side, only the joy seemed so elastic, a mysterious force like air, like time, with the rubbery not-quite-there-ness of a piano pedal pressed to sustain a chord. I knew it could not last.

One night, when Freddie lay across the bed with his head on my hip and I was feeling wistful, I timidly explored our future.

"You understand, don't you, that this can't go on? I have to leave here one day."

"You don't want to stay? Be my tutor, August. You've taught me so much already." His sarcasm was more flippant than bitter.

I wanted to be serious, so I treated his words literally. "A pretty idea, Freddie. But the Kemps need me."

"You don't want to take me with you? I could be your valet. Your errand boy." He remained taunting, teasing.

"Our life isn't easy. Your life here is far more comfortable. Besides, your mother would never let you go."

"Her?" The brightness went out of his tone. "Oh, she'll get rid of me soon enough. When she sends me off to school in England. If not this year, next year."

"You see," I said. "It'll end anyway."

He sighed and tugged at himself, as if that would give him the answer. "Well, I don't want it to last," he said. "Because it is shameful. Evil. It's fun to be evil. But only when you know it's going to end and you can be yourself again."

I was hurt that he still found this evil. Yet it was for the best, wasn't it? Because this *would* end, one way or another, when we heard from Isaac and departed, if not sooner, when Freddie grew tired of our sport. A return to virtue would be a consolation prize for us both.

And yet, now and then, at night when he dozed on my shoulder—Freddie was most lovable when he slept—or during the day when he first entered a room and I saw him from afar, so sharp and round and three-dimensional, more real than anyone else in the room, I imagined taking Freddie away with us, my own companion, my own helpmate. If Isaac had Alice, why couldn't I have Freddie?

A pipe dream, of course, a lovely impossibility, something I could consider only because it was impossible. But for so long now all my loves had been ethereal or secondhand, experienced through spirits or the love of others. Here was my own corporeal love, a sad sweetness, a beautiful confusion. It was sure to end in a broken heart, and I assumed the heart would be mine.

44

I T seemed to last forever, even as it passed quite quickly, like a sleep full of dreams. It went on for weeks; the weeks became a month. And I awoke one morning to a dull thudding at my window like a muffled thunderstorm.

The room was streaked with sunlight. There was a damp indentation in my bed where Freddie had been. He always returned to his room with plenty of time to spare.

I heard a squeal of children outside, Augusta and Tristan. I got up and opened the shutters. A sailboat stood in front of Yali Ashe, its slack lateen sail flapping loudly from a spar level with my window. Alice and the children stood on the dock far below, where a barefoot Turk passed a leather grip-case ashore. Then a squat, foreshortened figure covered by a soft felt hat stepped from the boat and was surrounded by his family.

I knew that Isaac was coming, that he had agreed to give up his quest and rejoin his family. I had even been present the evening when Lady Ashe offered to wire a steamship company and arrange his passage. But I had put it out of my mind, treating his arrival as only a vague, sometime-in-the-future matter.

The soft felt hat hugged his children, kissed his wife, and never looked up, which was just as well, since I stood bare-shouldered at the window, my chest still splotched with Freddie.

I rang for hot water, I washed myself off, I shaved, I dressed. A dozen different thoughts and emotions shifted inside me like iron filings responding to a newly introduced magnet. I was glad to see Isaac again. I was. And yet—

He was seated in the kiosk when I came down, happily enthroned at the breakfast table with Augusta in his lap. He did not stand when I came up the steps but broke into a grin and held out his hand. "And here's Fitz!" he cried. "A sight for sore eyes!"

"And you," I said, gripping his heavy, leathery palm.

I was startled by how vivid he looked. He had been absent only two months, but we'd never been apart before. Looking at his face was as confusing as looking into a mirror and seeing a whole new man there. His colors were stronger, his eyes velvet brown, his pink lips bursting from his umber skin like the interior of a broiled beefsteak. The grooves of his scarred cheeks, forgotten over the years—the permanent mark of a slave boy's attack of shingles—had resurfaced, along with two unnoticed sets of crow's-feet. And I saw for the first time a gray patch in his beard, a few white threads in his hair.

Alice sat across from him, contentedly hugging herself in her folded arms, gazing through her bright lenses, drinking him in with her eyes. I had not realized how dry she'd been until I saw her come alive again. "Now, let your papa eat," she told Augusta. "He's come a long way. He must be famished."

"Oh, no, this is my breakfast." He laughed, and buried his face in his daughter's frizzy hair. She giggled in delight. "My breakfast, lunch, and dinner."

Lady Ashe was pleased to see him again, quite giddy, in fact. "What a joy to have you, Isaac! You're as changed as I am. What a man you've become." His masculinity awakened something in her that the rest of us hadn't touched. "Your wife is a darling," she told him. "Your children are jewels. And Fitz, dear Fitz, has been a godsend. But now we have you, and the picture is complete."

Freddie sat at his end of the table, frowning as he ate, belligerently indifferent to the new guest.

*   *   *

The first day passed peacefully enough. Isaac was relieved to be back in the bosom of his family. The children eagerly took him on a tour of the house and grounds, accompanied by Alice; he claimed to be impressed. He moved in a happy fog, repeatedly touching his progeny, stroking their hair, even setting his hand in the small of Alice's spine, something he rarely did in public. He was gracious to Fanny at luncheon, and at dinner, too, repeatedly expressing thanks for her generosity, asking again if there were any inconvenience in our staying until October. Not at all, she said. She enjoyed our company and was glad we'd be here long enough to move with her to their town house in Pera. It was now the first week of August.

The only indication of discontent was the look of distress that creased his brow each time a call to prayer floated over the trees. We'd stopped hearing the muezzin buzz weeks ago, but Isaac winced, as if insulted.

After dinner, while Alice put the children to bed, Isaac remained outside in the kiosk with me, under the flickering brass lamps, to smoke a pipe of what smelled like cheap shag tobacco.

"One of my economies of the road," he explained. "It has a taste of humble pie." And he dropped his mask of contentment. "I was a disaster as a drummer, Fitz. It was misery. Two months on the road, two miserable months of bad hotels, third-class carriages, solitude, and loneliness. And all I could get for you was a three-week engagement in Monte Carlo in October."

"Times are hard," I said. "You can't blame yourself."

"Maybe not. But it made me see how superfluous I am without Decker Bros. You're the goods, Fitz, not me. No matter what I showed them—clippings, Héger's brochure, the letter from Brahms—theater managers didn't take me seriously. And without my wife and children at my side, strangers saw only a lone wolf, a low-life darky, no matter how well I spoke their language. The cheaper the bed, the poorer the meat, the more the people serving me made clear that I was only a nigger. Nothing but a nigger in a necktie. Step a few rungs down, Fitz, and the Continent can be as bad as America."

He spoke without self-pity or anger, and it hurt me to hear him sound so defeated. His face had the forlorn, empty look of a shoe without its laces.

"I'm sorry it was such a bitter pill," I said. "But it is summer. We'll do better in the fall."

He didn't seem to hear but reached into his coat and took out a folded square of paper. "Look at this," he said.

A piece of newsprint, I opened it and saw a yellowed picture engraved from a photograph. A corpse hung from a wooden bridge, a Negro with a cruelly bloated face. At his limp feet stood two constables looking thoughtful, as if this were a mystery that needed to be solved. A caption said the dead man had been a schoolteacher.

"That is what's happening back home," said Isaac. "Lynching, riot, and murder."

"Terrible," I replied. "Simply awful." I held the gruesome clipping to the light, then returned it to him, not knowing why he showed it to me or why he carried it. The scrap looked months old. Did he keep it as a reminder of who he really was? Like a tender scar that one cannot help touching now and then?

"So my troubles are as nothing," he admitted as he refolded the clipping. "And yet being spared the sorrow over there only adds to the pain of my uselessness over here. I cannot even support my own family."

"Don't be so hard on yourself, Isaac," I insisted. "You tried. You deserve a good rest. And you can recover here. Life is lovely at Yali Ashe. You can have anything you want."

He surveyed the dark garden, the illuminated house. "Yes, I suppose," he said. "Everything except peace of mind. Except pride and self-esteem." He released a heavy sigh. "I never thought that my family and I would have to live off a ... fallen woman."

Even in defeat he remained the good, moral prig.

"Let's be grateful," I told him, "that our fallen woman fell into a jam pot. And is happy to share her jam with friends."

"I know. I know. I hear how ridiculous I sound." He tried to smile. "One cannot look a gift horse in the mouth. But this is such a strange household, Fitz." He lowered his voice. "A whoring hussy is now a wealthy lady? And has all these servants? They're no better than slaves. That gelded overseer in the red cap—?"

"Ismail."

"Yes. A she-male?" He shook his head. "How could any man let that be done to him?"

"He had no say in it. It happened when he was a child. His family did it to him so he could work in a palace and have a better life."

"A heathen family like that is worse than no family at all," he muttered. "But I shall accustom myself to all this. I will. I must say, Fitz, you seem quite happy here."

"Well, yes. I suppose I am." Did it show? A light in my eyes, new color in my face? "It's very comfortable. And I've been helping Fanny. I am glad of that."

"Whatever the source, you have a tickled, satisfied look that I haven't seen recently." He did not make it sound like a compliment.

"Oh, just the satisfaction of a job well done," I claimed.

Did the secret life of my body actually show? If so, only Isaac noticed, but then he had once shared that secret life.

Ismail came out to ask if we'd like tea or sweets. As I thanked him and said we were fine, I caught Isaac suspiciously eyeing the man.

"I'm sorry," Isaac confessed when Ismail was gone. "The fellow makes me uncomfortable. But you seem quite warm with him."

"No more than I am with any other servant," I said. Isaac thought there were something going on between me and Ismail? That was a laugh. Why Ismail? Because he was black? Or did Isaac think that I, too, was a kind of eunuch?

Isaac resumed his discussion of business matters—the engagement in Monte Carlo, possible futures beyond—and I stopped wondering what he might suspect. After all, I was the clairvoyant here, not Isaac.

Freddie came to my room that night, in his usual state.

"Please, Freddie. You should put on a robe from now on. Mr. Kemp doesn't sleep as soundly as the others."

"Pshaw on him," he muttered. He was already annoyed with me for staying up late to talk with this stranger. He grew more annoyed when our kisses and pricks did not work in tandem.

"The hell with it," he finally said. "Lie down. Do me."

And the little goat straddled my face and went at it, quite fiercely, until he arched his back and opened his throat. He was very loud, but my mouth was full, and I tried to silence him with my hand. He jerked his head away, jigged harder, and let out even louder final yelps.

He fell over on his back, gasping for breath.

"Damn you!" I whispered after I emptied my mouth. "He might hear us up here!"

"He? Him? It's always him now?" He was still breathless. "What's so important about this nigger of yours? Just a fancy-dress coon."

I grabbed Freddie's arm. I nearly hit him. "Don't call him that! He's my best friend. He means more to me than anyone else in the world."

"More than me?"

"No," I said. "No. But as much as you."

Yet that didn't satisfy Freddie.

"Did you ever know him the way you know me? Like a dog?"

I could not afford to make Freddie jealous. No. There were now secrets that I could not trust with this unpredictable boy.

"Never. He's not like us."

And I lay on top of Freddie to prove myself to him. He was convinced enough to stay for seconds.

45

AUGUSTA," said Isaac at breakfast, "your mother tells me your lessons are not coming as well as before. You are having a very nice summer here, but you cannot forget the nose and the grindstone. Books are the road to knowledge. We need knowledge to get on in the world."

"Yes, sir," said Augusta with lowered head. "I know."

By the second day Isaac was acting like a father again, and the children became reacquainted with the bitter as well as the sweet of Papa's presence.

Freddie ate breakfast as if nobody else were at the table, then tossed aside his napkin and stood up. "August? Shall we go for a walk?" And he held out his hand, daring me to take it.

I could not refuse him, not even with Isaac present. I grabbed his hand, clenched it hard, and led Freddie down the steps, without looking at him. Nor did I glance over my shoulder to see what Isaac made of us, for fear a glance would betray me.

Freddie let go as soon as we were among the roses. He almost never held my hand except when others were present. "What a pompous fool your friend is," he said. "But you act all pious around him. Like he's your father."

"We've known each other a long time. He's a man with strong

principles. He's had to be principled to come as far as he has. He was born a slave."

"And now you act like *his* slave."

"I act like his friend. And as his friend I know that he would not understand my friendship with you."

We came to a bench under a lime tree and sat down, a good three feet apart.

Freddie folded his arms. "You must choose," he declared. "You cannot be friends with us both."

"Why not? Friendship isn't like marriage. As you said yourself, we're not married."

Freddie frowned and was silent for a moment. "Do you rather I stop my visits?"

"No," I replied, even though I did. "But you might consider visiting less regularly."

"If I don't come every night," he said, "I might get my morals back and never come again."

But I didn't really want him to stop, not yet anyway.

"Lilies. Roses. Dahlias. More roses. Tea roses. I don't know what this fluffy flower's called."

I heard Tristan chattering, as if to himself. He came around the corner, followed by Isaac. The child was showing off to his father all that he'd learned about the garden.

Isaac saw us on the bench and smiled, automatically. Then the smile wavered, as if he suddenly noticed our solemn looks, remembered our handholding, and understood that my being with Freddie was not the same as his being with Tristan. Or did I only imagine the waver?

"Your mother has a fine garden," he told Freddie and strolled on, looking off as if he'd just stumbled upon a friend making water in the bushes.

He spent the rest of the day with Alice and the children. They went swimming that afternoon, just them. Neither Freddie nor I was invited along. I watched from the window of the music room as two bathing machines were rolled into a watery meadow of blue-green furrows. A father and son appeared, then a mother and daughter, a happy, splashing family costumed like circus clowns. Their holiday hoots and laughter carried clearly over the water.

No, I decided, Isaac had too much else on his mind to pay much notice to me and Freddie. After tea he and Alice took a stroll in the garden, arm in arm, sharing smiles and whispers.

Yet at dinner, when we were all together again, Isaac noticed Freddie and seemed perturbed by him. There were no covert looks between me and the boy, or none that I remember, but Isaac was abruptly attentive to him, in an idly noisy manner: "You have tutors, Freddie? You don't go to school? Then how do you meet girls? You don't have a sweetheart? Pity. Every young man needs a sweetheart."

Freddie was as curt and monosyllabic with him as he'd been with me my first weeks here. Was Isaac trying to flush the boy out? No, I told myself, he could not possibly understand what was going on, not so soon. My suspicions were only the product of my guilty imagination.

After he kissed his children good night and Alice took them off to bed, Isaac asked Lady Ashe if he might use her skiff. "I need a spot of evening exercise, an aquatic constitutional. Fitz, why don't you join me? No, please. I'd enjoy the company."

He wanted a private talk? What could be more private than a skiff in the middle of the Bosphorus?

Freddie watched me go with the pouty look of a young lady watching her swain go off with the men to smoke cigars.

A boatman met us on the dock with a lantern and set of oars. I climbed down into the stern. Isaac sat facing me and fitted the oars into the locks. I pushed us off, and Isaac dug into the water, awkwardly at first—he had not rowed a boat since his time in Virginia—but then he found his rhythm, and his body began to bend in and out of the speckled glow of the lantern at our feet, the locks creaking loudly. I anxiously awaited the worst.

"That poor woman," said Isaac, and took another pull. "She has come too far too fast. With no moral ballast to keep her upright. She's every bit as mad as Alice said in her letters."

I relaxed, relieved to discover this was about Fanny, not Freddie. "She isn't mad," I said. "She's unhappy. Very unhappy."

"She hides in unhappiness like madness. She uses it to shirk all responsibility. It seems to me that your music only makes her unhappiness cozy, Fitz."

"Not at all. I am helping her face her grief."

"It must hurt terribly to lose a child," he continued. "I can only imagine the depth of her pain. But she barely knows that her living child exists."

"It's true," I said. "And sad. Which is why I try to give the boy some attention."

Isaac stopped rowing and drew the oars half into the boat, letting the blades stick out like stumpy wings. We were a ways out, and Yali Ashe was a cluster of shore lights with snakes of light wiggling on the black water. A steamboat passed in the channel, a candlelit cake under a mammoth tree of black smoke.

"So peaceful out here," I said. "There's a water concert tomorrow night at the Dolmabache Palace. We should all attend it." I turned back to Isaac and found him with his head down, his forearms propped heavily on his thighs. Then he looked up at me. The glare of the lantern burned in his righteous beard and flared nostrils.

"*What* is going on between you and that boy?"

I'd been right. Here it was. My mouth went dry. I tried to stay calm.

"Freddie's fond of me," I said. "That's all. And I've grown quite fond of him."

"And *why* are you so fond of each other?" he demanded.

I opened my mouth again, and no words came out.

Isaac closed his eyes in pain. When he reopened them, they were full of rage.

"You've fallen back into old habits! You are fornicating with that boy!" He kept his teeth together so as not to shout, he was so angry.

I had feared his anger but never guessed it would be so strong. "You've introduced a child to your vice."

I did not panic. I did not lie. His anger made *me* angry, too angry to lie. "It's no worse than what you and I once did."

"That was wrong, too. Very wrong." He frowned. "But this is far worse. He's a child, he's innocent."

"I did not trick him into doing anything he didn't want."

"He's a child! He doesn't know what he wants."

"He's the same age I was when I did it with my uncle."

"And you hated your uncle. Remember?"

"I did. But Freddie doesn't hate me."

"Are you certain of that?"

"Yes." Was I?

He never asked what we did, where or when, but instantly assumed we did it frequently.

"He's nothing like we were, Fitz. He's genteel, he's educated. He comes from a better class. We were crude and tough. He isn't. He's soft. One can already see a debauched look in his eyes and mouth. You are introducing him to habits he will never break. You are destroying his future. If I thought anyone were doing that with Tristan, I'd kill him. You're lucky the boy's father is dead."

I was speechless. Isaac feared for his own son's safety? It was too awful to deserve even a denial. He looked like he wanted to strike me, but sitting in a small boat kept us both still.

"When I think of what is happening back home," he said angrily, "all that pain and suffering. While I sit here, surrounded by easy living and vice."

I was shocked and confused to hear him use lynchings and riots against me.

"I can do nothing there," he declared. "But I will not sit by and do nothing here."

"What do you propose to do?" I fearfully asked.

"I want you to break off with that child. Set him straight, put him back on the righteous path. If you don't, I will have no recourse except to tell his mother what you are doing."

"What will that achieve? She'd throw us out. All of us."

"Exactly. And it'll be on your head, Fitz. Because I cannot remain in this place while you take advantage of a boy's sensual appetites to use him like a whore."

But each argument I tried out in my head—"Like mother, like son," "He is using me as much as I am using him"—sounded hollow and beside the point. I didn't know what to say except what I should have said earlier: "I'm in love with him, Isaac."

"This isn't love."

"It's the same love that I once gave you," I snapped.

He looked down at his boots, but only for a moment. "Does he love you? Not as a child loves anyone who gives him a sweet, but as a friend loves a friend? Selflessly?"

Isaac knew the ways of the flesh better than he pretended.

"I don't know," I offered. Then, "No, he doesn't. He loves what we do. But he does not love me."

"You see, Fitz. It isn't love." He spoke more softly. "It's only lust, and you know it's wrong. I know you too well. I know you because of *my* love for you." He placed a hand on my knee. "But it hurts to love a man who could fall into such vile behavior."

His voice was sad and injured, his hand warm and heavy. And I suddenly wanted his love and approval back.

"You feel no remorse?" he said. "Are you so stupid with sensuality that you cannot understand what I'm saying?"

The cat of pride gripped my tongue; I did not want to give in to him.

Then he removed his hand, shook his head, and bent down to take up the oars again.

I could fight his words but not his silence. I could not bear his cold look of disappointment.

"There would be no repercussions?" I said. "No punishment of me or Freddie? You only want me to end our . . . lewdness?"

"There is no need for anyone else to know your sin. So long as you break off with him."

"It was going to end sooner or later," I said, half to myself. "Can I tell him in my own way?"

"So you agree to end it?"

"Yes," I said. "Yes." As simple as that. "I've enjoyed being with him, but I've felt bad, too. And it's not been good for him. He enjoys what we do. But it does not make him happy. No, I should break it off. I can." And instantly I experienced that lightness of heart and simplicity of conscience that makes one believe a decision is the right one.

"Oh, Fitz," said Isaac, and let go of one oar to clamp my shoulder. When that gesture didn't feel strong enough, he drew us together and pressed his forehead against mine. "I knew I could make you understand. I could not believe you were beyond moral reason. Thank you."

I felt reborn, right with Isaac, back on solid ground.

Isaac released me and took hold of both oars. He turned the boat around, pulling on one oar, pushing on the other. Yali Ashe was nowhere in sight; the current had carried us downstream. Then he began to row, pulling with such vigor that I half expected him to break into a hymn, only Isaac never sang.

"I want to be there," he said.

"When I talk to him? But why?"

"So that I can help you make him understand how wrong this was and that he must put it behind him."

Isaac only wanted to make sure that I did it. I hated the thought of Isaac being present, knew it was a terrible idea. Yet I wanted to prove my worth to Isaac.

"Very well, then. Yes. You should be there."

His presence might even help, I told myself, enabling me to convince Freddie that I was not rejecting him, only our unclean deeds. Otherwise the boy would think I was turning elsewhere for my pleasure.

"When?" I said.

"The sooner the better."

"Very well, then. Tomorrow."

I was already having second thoughts, but my second thoughts had second thoughts, and I knew that this was the right decision. Yes, my trysts with Freddie were wrong. I'd known all along that they were wrong, although not so criminal as Isaac thought. Love had been no excuse. Once I renounced lust, however, love seemed less sincere, a trick of conscience, a justification of lust. Or no, I still loved Freddie, but as a child, a responsibility. It was a simpler love. I was glad that Isaac had forced my hand. I was gladder still that he forgave me. A lesser man would have condemned me forever, but Isaac loved me again, now that I repented and vowed to set things right.

Yali Ashe reappeared over Isaac's pumping shoulder, lit up like a church at Easter.

I thought there would be one last visit from Freddie, and I could quietly prepare him. But he did not come upstairs that night. He only intended to punish me for going off with Isaac, I decided. He could not know that our supernatural games were over.

46

THE next morning was warm and overcast, close and humid. It
began to rain after breakfast, an English drizzle that did not clear
the air but covered kiosk and foliage with a shiny coat of spit. Rain
was common enough in Constantinople that summer, yet I remember chiefly sunny days, except for this one.

Isaac allowed me only so much liberty before he pressed the issue.
He waited until luncheon, which we took in the gloomy wainscoted
dining room that faced the gray, rain-pocked Bosphorus. "Fitz?" he
said. "Wasn't there a matter you wanted to discuss with Freddie?"

"Why, uh, yes. Freddie? Could you join me upstairs in the music
room after lunch?"

"Why?" He glanced at Isaac, then frowned at me.

"Dr. August has a proposal to discuss," said Isaac, so kindly that
it sounded like an invitation to a birthday party.

Alice looked puzzled—clearly Isaac had told her nothing—while
Lady Ashe paid no heed at all to this request for a conversation
with her son.

Freddie agreed with a lazy shrug. He maintained a sullen, cool
indifference to the end of the meal, acting as though nothing remarkable were afoot, until Isaac followed us up the stairs.

"Do not mind Mr. Kemp, Freddie. I have asked him to sit in on
our interview."

We entered the music room, and I promptly opened the shutters, needing light and air for this, even though the light was gray, the air damp and listless. Rain hissed softly in the evergreens. I perched on the piano stool. Freddie sat on the settle. He nervously watched as Isaac closed the door and remained standing there, his back to the oak.

"Freddie," I began. "Freddie..." Seeing his belligerent face and slickly combed hair, I remembered less belligerent looks, the hair in wild disarray, his milky throat free of its floppy satin bow. I forgot the careful preamble I'd prepared and leaped straight to the heartless heart of the matter. "We have been having fun, Freddie. But it was wrong, Freddie. It was wrong. And it is time we stop."

"What? What're you talking about?" He looked at Isaac in a panic. "I know *not* to what you refer!"

"Freddie. It's no good to deny it," I said. "Mr. Kemp already knows."

The boy swung his eyes back at me, a hurt, betrayed look.

"The fault is all mine," I continued. "I take full responsibility. I am older than you and should have known better. But I let my pleasure in your company, my selfish pleasure, get the better of my moral conscience."

Freddie lowered his head and sat pale and rigid. I was stripping him again, as I had in the bathing machine, only this time in front of another adult. No, Isaac's presence did not help. Why had I let him join us? So that I might have his authority behind me? Or in order to get closer to *him*?

I feared tears from the boy, or red-faced shame and terror, but he just sat there, staring at the floor.

"We were doing things only a man and wife should do. Things that will spoil you for marriage. You should want your body to be pure for the beautiful woman you will one day marry...." I went on at length with this health-and-marriage cant, the liberal, medical approach. I wanted to turn around and play the piano while I spoke, so that I might speak better, but it seemed too frivolous. Glancing over at Isaac, I found him standing by with his arms folded, his beard crushed to his chest, patiently listening to my windy words.

"But more important, Freddie, more wrong," I added, "is that you have not felt good about this either. You called it evil, remember? You said you'd be glad when it was over and you could be yourself again. Well, the time has come. We should both be ourselves again. Our good, clean, moral selves."

Freddie remained on the edge of the settle, his head down, his feet on the floor. His fingers gripped the cushion. "Are you finished?" he said curtly.

"More or less. But I need to hear what you think." Which was a strange courtesy to offer a child, but I had surrendered my role as an adult with Freddie long ago.

He released an irritable sigh. And he turned to Isaac. "Why're you doing this, Kemp? Why do you want me pure? What business is it of yours?"

Isaac was startled to be addressed, and so insolently. "It's not my wish. It's what Dr. August wants."

"No. It's what *you* want. Why? You want him all to yourself? You hate the idea of him worshiping anyone but you."

"Freddie!" I said.

"You're not my father, Kemp. I'm not your slave. Neither is August. You're the slave, Kemp. Nothing but a nigger slave. No matter how high-and-mighty you act."

Isaac kept his temper. "We are all of us slaves, boy. The slaves of God. We obey His rules or we burn in hell. Do you want to burn in hell?"

It had been years since Isaac had spoken of hell. I'd forgotten that he actually believed in it.

"I do not want anyone to *worship* me," he continued. "I only want to save you and my friend from damnation."

"You can't fool me with your hell talk," said Freddie. "You're jealous of our pleasure. All the pleasure your friend gets from me and I get from him." He twisted his mouth in a cold, lewd smile.

"Have you ever had your body on top of his? Your tongue in his mouth? Or your prick?"

"Freddie! Be still!" I shouted, shaking my head at Isaac, trying to signal him that I'd told the boy nothing about us.

But Isaac was too shocked even to look at me. "You shameless whelp! You foul-mouthed viper!" He charged across the room.

"No, Isaac!" I jumped up to throw myself between them. Freddie was already on his feet, but he did not flee.

"*You* can go to hell!" cried Isaac. "But you will not take my friend with you!" He grabbed at Freddie's collar, and I pushed him away and his bow pulled loose.

"Isaac, he's a child!" I cried.

"A vile child. A hellion child. What would his mother think if she knew?"

Freddie blanched but was not silenced. "What does Mrs. Kemp's mother think of her marrying a nigger?"

Again I told Freddie to shut his mouth.

"You ugly devil," said Isaac. "You prevaricating little sodomite. That and this are *not* the same. A man must not lie with man as with woman. A man must not lie with man as with woman," he repeated. "It is an abomination. You are an abomination, boy. Have you no shame? No decency?"

Freddie stood his ground. His bow hung undone, but he remained fearless, utterly fearless, until he glanced at me. His face abruptly knotted into a squashed, ugly look that suggested both tears and disgust.

"You are lost, boy! You are damned! If you had an ounce of conscience left, you would get down on your knees and ask God to forgive you for your obscene words and immoral deeds."

I was full of remorse for exposing the boy to Isaac. I looked at Freddie in sorrow, but he promptly turned away from me.

"You are idiots," he said. "Idiots and cowards. Both of you. I will not waste my time with fools." He marched past Isaac to the door, flung it open, and went out.

Isaac did not go after him. He remained in the room, trembling with anger, breathing through clenched teeth.

And my first words to him were "I did not tell him about us, Isaac. He knows nothing about us."

The very idea took him by surprise. "Of course not. Why would you?" He regained himself with a deep, chest-bursting inhale of righteousness. "I am sorry, Fitz. I have been blaming you in this. I had no idea the boy was so depraved. Now I understand. He led *you* down the sordid path."

"No. He's no more depraved than I am." I refused to betray Freddie more than I already had. "He's unhappy, lonely, and young. We cannot blame him. I shall not blame him."

Isaac resisted, but only for a moment. "You are right. He is a child. But so unnatural that one forgets his age. I had no business letting my anger fly so strongly. I do not know why his shameless mention of—obscene acts made me so angry, but it did."

"This went badly, very badly," I said, "but I did break with him. It is over. You should be satisfied with that."

"I will not be satisfied until we bring the boy back to reason. Which can be done more subtly in the days ahead. This is not about my satisfaction, Fitz, it's about yours."

But I felt no satisfaction at all. The boy now saw me as a fool and a coward, which I was. He was a hard little nut, and I couldn't help admiring his toughness. But I did not admire him so much that I wished him back in my bed. Isaac's talk of God and hell had confused the issue, yet such crude public truths are sometimes needed when one's homemade morality grows too flexible.

Freddie disappeared into his room for the rest of the day. He did not come down to dinner. It was still raining and we ate indoors. When Lady Ashe treated her son's absence as a matter of no importance, Isaac began to lecture her on motherly love. "You should pay more attention to your son, Fanny. He is at a difficult age. He needs a firmer, more disciplined hand."

Alice indicated with a frown that this was none of his business, but he plunged on. Despite the afternoon fiasco, Isaac was on a crusade. I finally recognized the personal need in his righteousness. If he could not save his brethren from being lynched at home, if he could not even find work to feed his own family, he could still make the people around him clean their moral houses.

"It is his growing pains," claimed Fanny. "He is no longer a child and does not listen to me. He has not been the same since the death of his brother. He cannot guess how much I love him."

"You need to show him that love," said Isaac. "In a firm manner. Otherwise you will lose him, too."

It was a cruel thing to say, yet I was surprised when Fanny actually began to cry.

"Don't speak like that. He is all I have left in the world."

Alice told the children to excuse themselves and play in the fountain room. "I will call you when dessert is served." They obeyed reluctantly, an adult in tears being such a rare event.

"Fanny," said Isaac, "you need to spend more time with your son."

"But it hurts so to be around him. When I know he doesn't love me the way his brother did."

"You must swallow your pain and show him your love. Before it is too late."

"Isaac," said Alice, "you need not frighten her to make your point."

"No, no," said Fanny. "He is right to say these things. And I will act on them. In time. Excuse me." She got up from the table, saying she only required a fresh handkerchief.

"Husband," said Alice firmly, "I know you mean well. But we cannot stick our noses where they don't belong. You cannot take the burdens of others on your shoulders. Because your intervention might blow up in your face."

"I am only offering her some badly needed advice."

Alice examined the crest on her silver fork, idly, guiltily. "I do not have your enormous heart, dear. But you will only break it if you try changing what cannot be changed."

When I went to bed that night, I locked my door, more a symbol than a necessity, I thought. After all, Freddie had declared himself done with me, a fool and a coward.

I was still awake when the knob turned and the bolt clacked in its socket. The door shook again and proved itself locked. "Open up," Freddie said softly. "Let me in."

I got out of bed and went to the door. I bent down to the keyhole. "Freddie. You know that I can't."

"Why? Are you scared of me?" He hit the door. "Let me in!"

"Don't, Freddie. Everyone will hear!"

He continued pounding. "Open up if you're so afraid!"

I pictured him out there, a naked boy in a dark hall banging against a locked door.

"I need to talk to you!" he cried.

"Then we can talk through the door."

His fist gave the wood a final blow. "Damn you," he said. "Damn you." His voice came closer. He knelt by the keyhole. "Don't you love me anymore?"

He was taunting, sarcastic, but it was the first time he had admitted aloud that I loved him. "Yes. I do," I said. "And that's why we have to stop this."

"You think he's right? You love your bully preacher friend more than you love me?"

I could see nothing through the brass slot, but a warm jet of moist breath brushed my face each time he spoke. The keyhole itself was a mouth, with metal lips and a bulbous brass nose.

"This does not concern loving one man more than another, Freddie. It concerns loving what's right."

"Will we go to hell?" That, too, was sarcastic.

"I don't know," I said. "I'm not convinced there is a hell."

"What do your spirits say?"

"They say the only hell is here, on earth."

"Then what are you afraid of?"

"I am afraid that——" How could I explain this to a child? "I have been expressing my love for you in the wrong way. It has made both of us coarse, demanding, and selfish."

"And how will you show your love now?" he demanded. "With my bicycle? Your stupid piano? Paper dolls?"

"Yes. Why not? There are innocent pleasures we can share."

"They don't mean a fart to me, August. Not anymore. Now that I know the supernatural pleasure two men can make. Open the door. Please." He became plaintive, pleading. "I want to kiss you."

"No, Freddie. I can't. For your sake as well as mine."

"You don't trust yourself with me?"

"No. I don't."

"You can't love me very much, August. If you can't forget your preaching friend and your good clean conscience long enough to give me what you want to give."

"It's the same love that would prevent me from giving you a loaded gun or a bottle of sulfuric acid." It was not a happy comparison, but I didn't know what else to say.

"You don't love me either. Nobody does. Nobody." His voice turned blubbery, tearful. I had never heard him cry and wondered if he were faking. "I hoped you did, August. I was sure *you* did."

"I do, Freddie. Believe me."

"Pisspot!" he spat. "Pisspot," with a strangled whimper and real tears. The hard little nut was not so hard after all. Water began to fill my own eyes.

"Go to bed, Freddie. You'll catch a cold sitting out there." My own tears were like a cold, an ague of remorse, and I feared I would give in to him.

"What do you care? What does anybody care?"

"I care, Freddie. Very much." I had to swallow the brine in my throat before I could continue. "We do not need secrets and lewdness to love each other. You'll see."

"A pot of piss on you," he sobbed. "Pots and pots on you and everyone else. I don't need your clean, fake love."

I heard joints softly click and damp skin peel off the floor.

"Freddie. I do love you. Believe me." I kissed the keyhole, hoping he could hear a mouse squeak of lips through the brass.

But he was already on his feet. His fist struck the door one last time and he walked away, on heavy, bare heels.

I remained kneeling there in my nightshirt, feeling virtuous, cold and heartless, before I slowly got up and stumbled back to my solitary bed.

47

I did not expect Freddie to come down to breakfast the next morning. Yet there he was, sitting with the others in the kiosk that now resembled a birdcage without bars. There was no trace of the angry, humiliated child who'd sat outside my door. He looked like a little old man again, aloof and invulnerable. One could no more imagine him crying than one would expect a stone to weep.

"Good morning, Lady Ashe," said Isaac when he joined us in the cage. "Good morning, Freddie." He smiled at him and even patted his shoulder. He was determined Freddie know there were no bad feelings, but the boy glared at the white-palmed hand like he wanted to bite it.

When everyone was present and the food was served, Isaac proposed a trip to Stamboul. "You may have seen the sights, but I haven't." Lady Ashe said that Yuri could take us in the launch and show us places none of us had seen yet. She seemed glad to get Isaac out of the house for a few hours, a respite from his chiding presence.

I said, "Come with us, Freddie." I wanted his company and, more important, wanted him to understand that we were not finished with each other.

But Isaac said, quite firmly, "Freddie doesn't need to see his ancient town again. He should stay here with his mother."

"Oh, yes. I'll stay with Mummy," he replied, sounding quite ironic, but he jumped up and went to her. He threw his arms around Fanny from behind. She looked surprised, then pleased. Freddie was pleased when she didn't pull away. Then he kissed the nape of her neck and continued kissing it, clutching and kissing her with the same fervor with which I had once kissed him.

Fanny squirmed, frowned, and pushed at his arms. "Dear! Whatever has possessed you!" She pried open his arms, pulled free, and nervously fixed her collar. She tried to laugh, but it was too late.

Freddie looked hurt, stung. He caught me watching him and recovered with a haughty sniff, a scornful smirk. "You see," his wide eyes seemed to say. "Nobody loves me. Nobody." He angrily shook his head and hurried into the house.

And I suddenly felt: Something terrible will happen.

We rode in the launch toward Constantinople, the Threshold of Happiness. The air was clear and sweet after yesterday's rain, the water amethyst blue. Nothing bad could possibly happen on such a beautiful day, I thought. I sat up in the bow, alone, trying to get a grip on my sudden fear. I could not tell if it were real clairvoyance or only the work of a bad conscience.

Isaac stumbled forward and sat beside me. "You do not need to sit apart and chastise yourself, Fitz."

I was surprised my worry read so clearly, even if Isaac misread its cause.

"You did the right thing, the moral thing. He is only a child. You forgot that and needed me to set you straight. But it is done now. It is finished. Be glad."

"I know. But I am afraid," I confessed. "I don't know why. The only real cause for fear I can find is that Freddie might tell Fanny what he and I were doing."

"He'd never admit such a thing to his mother."

"Oh, no, he's capable of it. He's fearless. You heard him yesterday.

He would tell her in order to strike back at me. Or to punish her. He's unhappy, unpredictable."

"We will cross that bridge when we come to it," said Isaac with a sigh. "If Fanny expels us. Better to be a poor man in heaven than a rich man in hell. But nothing will happen. You did the right thing. Freddie will understand that in time. His shame will catch up with him, and he will know that this is right." He clutched my shoulder, and again I felt better.

We landed in Stamboul, made our way up the narrow, crowded streets, and I stopped worrying about Freddie. The chore of keeping together in the alien throngs kept my mind occupied, dampened my fears. I did not much enjoy the city, however. When we entered the Blue Mosque in our stocking feet, so bright and airy, so unlike Santa Sofia, I felt that we were only flies crawling around inside God's skull. We ate a picnic lunch in the grassy park between the twin craniums of the Blue Mosque and Sofia, a foreign family playing house under the scornful eyes of passersby, gaudily uniformed janissaries and bearded holy men in white robes. When a beggar boy approached us, Yuri shouted him away as if he were a dog.

We started back in time for tea and my evening session with Fanny. I had been remiss since Isaac's arrival and had promised her a session today. Exhausted, footsore, and lightly sunburned, we all sprawled on the cushions of the launch and said nothing on the way back, relieved that the day was over.

Yali Ashe appeared up ahead, its elaborate white gingerbread coming forward from the dark pines. A pack of servants stood out front. They were not waiting for us, however, but faced away, gathered around something on the narrow paved yard.

As we came closer, I made out a heap in the grove of trousers, a black heap like an enormous fallen crow.

Ismail hurried over to us as the boat docked at the stairs. "It is the mistress," he announced. "The mistress fell."

"She fainted?" I asked. Why didn't someone help her up?

"No, she fell," he repeated and pointed skyward.

At a window high above us, the music room, a pair of white curtains blew out and floated against the house.

"Oh, my God," said Alice. "Oh, my God." She clutched Tristan and Augusta to her side and covered their eyes with her hands.

Isaac rushed over and knelt by the crush of black cloth. He lifted an arm from it, a white arm twisted at such an angle that it appeared boneless. I noticed a patch of red but cannot say if I actually saw blood on the stones or only a shoe knocked off a foot by the blow of a body striking the earth. Had Fanny even worn red shoes?

The sight was like a blow to the head: I seemed to think everything at once, everything and nothing, my mind racing with a concussion of fears. "Freddie?" I said. "Where's Freddie?"

Nobody answered. Nobody heard me.

He told her everything, I thought, all my lies, the lie of my love, the lies about Constantine. Or worse, even worse—

I ran into the house. "Freddie!" I screamed. "Freddie!" I flew up the stairs, over the hard, wooden silence, knowing I'd find the answer in the music room, without knowing what the answer was.

The shutters over the settle were wide open. The curtains floated out like arms still reaching for the woman who had leaped past them. A seagull floated indifferently in the blue sky. And on the cretonne-covered settle under the sill lay a child in high-button shoes, knickerbockers, and a black bow. His eyes were closed, his mouth open. Freddie looked fast asleep but was very white, whiter than I'd ever seen him. One arm hung to the floor. Beside his half-open hand was a milk-stained drinking glass, a jug of soda water, and a large blue bottle of Blackwood's Nightingale, on its side, quite empty.

48

On a warm afternoon in August 1886, in the European quarter of Constantinople, a curious funeral procession was seen on the Grand'Rue de Pera. There were *two* hearses, each drawn by a pair of white horses, the high-riding glass cabinets filled by identical walnut coffins trimmed in silver. Old-fashioned black plumes trembled atop the cabinets; more plumes stood on the blinkered horses. This caravan of wealth and death was followed by the smallest handful of mourners: a half dozen Greek servants, a junior official from the English embassy, and, at the rear, an American family, three adults and two children. The embassy man wore full mourning and carried the proper silk hat upright in the curve of his arm, but the American visitors had to make do with simple dark clothes and crêpe armbands.

There was no music, only a grind of wheels, a jingle of harnesses, the steady *clock-clock-clock* of horseshoes. I walked with my chin lifted high, so that I might breathe more easily, my eyes fixed on the icy smile of a silver coffin handle in the etched-glass pane of the hearse up ahead.

Death. Idiotic death. And not one, but two.

There had been no suicide notes, no witnesses, only a grim circumstance of corpses. Ismail reported that Lady Ashe, shortly before the afternoon call to prayer, went upstairs to the music room to await my return. He heard a loud scream, followed by cries and sobs, then an unearthly gasp, like an inhaled shout, and the startling noise of an angel hitting the earth.

The inquest, conducted by Turkish constables and the English embassy three days later, was quick and perfunctory. A child had taken an overdose of laudanum, it was decided, an accident, the boy thinking the drug no worse than liquor. The mother, already grieving for the loss of one son, took her own life in a fit of temporary insanity. I did not tell the board that Freddie was already acquainted with laudanum, well enough to know not to drink it straight. The oblivion he once pursued in *petits morts* with me had been achieved in steady drafts of "Mummy's milk."

As I followed their matching coffins down a public avenue, my mind spun with desperate, angry thoughts:

What a foolish child to believe poison was a solution, that eternal sleep was preferable to unhappiness, that death was the only road to love.

What a stupid mother to lose another son and find no better way to show her love than to leap after him into eternity.

Idiotic deaths. Imbecilic deaths. I was furious with the dead. I had never guessed death would make me so angry. The charlatan who made his living off other people's grief now had his own dead, and he didn't know what to do with his pain except to shout at the dead and curse them in his heart, to stop from cursing himself. Yet death put the dead beyond all blame.

I held Tristan's hand. Alice held Augusta's. Isaac walked behind us, alone, taking up the rear of the procession. Once upon a time he and I had driven a hearse ourselves, a creaking wagon loaded with a dead master. Now we followed the dead. His boot steps at my back sounded as forlorn as those of a murderer on his way to the gallows.

Tristan tugged his hand from my damp grip and took his sister's hand. The children stole frightened looks at the people staring at us.

CHRISTOPHER BRAM / 360

The Ottoman throngs parted for our little parade and watched us pass. A few Westernized souls removed their fezzes. All were silent, yet they seemed more curious than respectful: Why were there so few mourners, where were the other servants? I saw a white man with bobcat whiskers pop in and out among the fezzes and turbans for a dozen yards. Then he was gone.

The official from the embassy walked ahead of me, looking quite solemn, as if *he* were the chief mourner. He used his silk hat to shield his hand when he reached into his coat and inspected his pocket watch.

We came to the English Cemetery, a gated yard beside St. Mary Draperis, the Protestant church beyond the English embassy. The hearses halted outside, and the Greek boatmen carried in the coffins. I forgot which was Fanny's and which was Freddie's. Stones of all sizes and ages crowded the yard. A white-surpliced minister in a black cassock stood waiting for us beside two raw holes gouged at the foot of a monument not yet black with smoke and soot. A beautiful stone mother sat on a pedestal, holding an infant in her arms. BELOVED ALWAYS. CONSTANTINE ASHE. 1871–1885. The beloved child was no longer alone but would have a mother and brother for eternal company.

Isaac stood apart from us while the minister chanted the ritual words. Augusta went over to him, stood at his side, and looked up, waiting for her father to see her. But he could not bring himself to look at her. He finally touched her, timidly brushing her shoulder as if she were fragile spun glass. He abruptly withdrew his hand and closed it, in pain. Looking hurt and confused, Augusta slipped away to rejoin her mother.

I was too deep in my own pain to make any sense of this. It seemed a movement of puppets, an incomprehensible dumbshow. When the first shovel of earth hit the lid of Freddie's coffin, I closed my eyes. The repeated thuds of dirt sounded as pathetic as an open hand striking a closed door. But I did not cry. Nobody cried at the funeral.

*   *   *

We returned to Yali Ashe that afternoon, a yali of the dead. The Moslem servants who'd refused to attend the funeral would not even enter the house, and the mansion had begun to die. The clock at the foot of the stairs had wound down: The face scrawled in turquoise Arabic letters wore a bitter smile of quarter to three.

I walked the empty rooms, not noticing what the others did or where they went. The fountain no longer plashed in the rear parlor. All around was the drone of a single fly caught behind glass, its buzz filling the silence. I climbed the stairs toward the music room, the death room. I don't know why I went up to that awful room. I moved in a trance of grief, an opium of death.

I sat at the yellow piano yet was afraid to play. I did not dare open the lid. I didn't blame my music or spirits. No, my sixth sense had failed me yet again, but the five senses can be just as fallible, and an extra can give you only so much. Without eyesight I am down to five again, but am not so much more stupid or helpless than before.

My fingers began to tap and drum the closed lid; I played a tune on coffin-hollow wood. All that came to the ear were raps and knocks, but I heard the music in my head, quite clearly, as if performed by an orchestra. It was Offenbach, a galop from a fairy opera, *Voyage to the Moon*, circus music, all rhythm and no melody, a piece I had played for Freddie only a week before.

You know the tune, Tristan. You loved it, you and Augusta both. The two of you had heard me playing the opening bars that afternoon for Freddie, a quick, light, two-four scamper of notes. You came running upstairs from your naps, burst into the room, and began to dance to it. You called it dancing anyway, a gleeful, formless hopping. I expected Freddie to be annoyed by the invasion, and he did look miffed. But when the piano erupted into the loud passage, a fierce, triumphant polka, he leaped from the settle and joined the dance. He imitated you, hopping on one foot, then both, bouncing with two happy children, laughing like a child himself. I'd never seen him so exuberant and giddy. He grinned at you and spun around, rocking his head from side to side, his jacket flapping like wings. The floor creaked and jiggled under three giggling, springing, spinning children.

Strange that I did not remember the scene where it took place in time. I remember only my remembering, when it brought me great pain. But when Freddie was still alive, I had not wanted to acknowledge that he was still a child. I could not admit that he might be foolish, innocent, ignorant, and vulnerable.

Tears ran down my face as I pounded and slapped the closed lid, until I was blind with tears. I kept beating the wood, wishing I could be deaf with tears as well.

He was a child, a goddamn child. He did not know what he wanted. Yet I had surrendered to him, surrendered to his body and mine. And then I'd surrendered to Isaac. My contradictory surrenders had ruined everything, driving a boy to self-murder.

I stopped hitting the lid and clutched my head. Scalding tears poured from my eyes. My whole body shuddered.

Had I killed Freddie? *No.* I knew I hadn't. Could I have saved him? *Yes.* If only I had let him into my room that night. If only I had insisted that he come with us to town the next day. If only I had believed in myself: first in my love of the boy, then in my fear for him. If only I hadn't listened to Isaac. Such a hornet's nest of ifs.

And Freddie had done the deed here, in the room where I once played for him. His death was directed at me; he had killed himself for me. What an idiot child to murder himself for a fraud, a coward, a nobody.

Needing to cut my conscience with the sight of the empty settle, I slowly raised my eyes to the mirror. But it was not empty. In the silver square of fog I saw a heavy shape seated there, against the closed shutters of the death window.

I swung around. I had not heard Isaac come in. He sat on the settle, bent forward, his head in his hands, his face caged in his fingers. He showed no alarm that I had been pounding a piano lid like a lunatic. He accepted as perfectly natural that I sat there blubbering like a teakettle.

"Get out," I said through my tears. "I have nothing to say to you."

He raised his head and lowered his hands. His eyes were dry, his face forlorn and twisted. "I have no right to be here. But my heart is so heavy with my crime that I needed to tell you— I am sorry, Fitz. I can only begin to suggest how deeply sorry I am."

"Your crime?" I said. "Oh, yes. *Your* crime." When someone opens a door for blame, you cannot help but rush in. "Why did I listen to you? I loved that boy. And no, I loved him the wrong way, but it was hardly the sin of sins. You convinced me it was. You forced me to break the one tie the child had with anyone, and look what happened!"

"Yes," he said. "I destroyed him. I did. And destroying him, I destroyed Fanny. Out of blind pride and foolish righteousness."

I didn't argue. Yet I was surprised. I wanted him to take some of the blame, but did not expect him to take it all.

"I wanted to be a master," he continued. "Of my life, my family, of you. But I am a monster as a master. Worse than the men who once owned me. A monster of virtue." He had to close his eyes before he could continue. "I charged in and seized control of what I did not understand. I made the boy ashamed, told him he was damned and not worth saving. And so he destroyed himself."

"He did not kill himself from shame." I was furious that Isaac understood the boy so poorly. "He did it out of anger, loss, hurt. Not shame."

But Isaac didn't hear me. "I was so blindly, arrogantly righteous," he said. "I have searched my heart for a reason, and found it. The boy was right, Fitz. I was jealous. I wanted you all for myself. Morally. On my terms."

"You were jealous?" I said and almost laughed, I was so confused to hear him say such a thing.

"I could not bear to lose you to another kind of love," he confessed. "My righteousness was a selfish, grasping thing."

"Yes?" I said. "Yes?" But his confession did not turn my anger into sympathy. "And I wanted that oh-so-moral love," I sneered. "Your dog-in-the-manger love. And I gave in to it. And we created a catastrophe. We produced tragedy." You see, I was willing to share the blame.

"How can you bear to look at me, Fitz? You loved someone, and I destroyed him." Guilt deepened his voice to a bleak, muddy mumble. "I do not deserve to be among people. I do not deserve the love of my children. It hurt me so much to be with them today. Their father is a monster. Their father is a murderer."

It was only words, I thought, rhetoric intended to express the depth of his pain. I had no patience for his words. "You're not a murderer," I said sharply. "And they don't know what happened. Alice and the children need never know."

"But I'll know! To the end of my life, I will know!" He struck his chest with his fist. "What I did to that boy, Fitz, a boy you loved, and to poor Fanny. Every time I look at you, I will know what I did."

"What are you proposing?" I asked in a panic. "What did you want me to do?" He wanted us to part, so that he might never have to look at me again and remember?

"No. The question is what I must do. And I do not know," he said. "We need to leave this awful place. But after that . . . ?" He slowly stood up. "Something," he muttered. "Something." He looked behind himself, at the fatal window with its closed shutters, as if he, too, could consider the ease of quitting life—the idea was a contagion in that mansion of mortality.

Then he turned away and started toward the door. "I need to be alone," he muttered. "I need to think this through and pray. But God, too, has washed his hands of me." And he left the room, with his head down, his heavy arms at his sides.

Oh, yes, God. At times like these you expect Him to come to your aid, or why bother to believe in His existence? But a God who could let a child and mother kill themselves was either too careless or too cruel to offer any solace or meaning.

Once Isaac was gone, all fight and anger and fear went out of me. I sat at the piano, numb with grief, empty of feeling, an emptiness so deep that I could not even feel the passage of time.

49

I do not remember how I passed that night, only that I did not go downstairs. I assumed Isaac rejoined his family and tried to convince the servants to return and fix dinner, or that Alice cooked something, but I had no hunger myself, no appetite, no physical being. I must have slept sometime, however, and slept late, because the next thing I remember is being awake in broad daylight and shaving at a basin of dirty water left from the day before.

When I finally descended, the house was deathly still, the clock still frozen at quarter to three. Even the buzz of the fly had died away. Was everyone gone? Had Isaac and Alice fled with the children and abandoned me? I experienced a terrible panic, a fresh, deep pain. I did not know I could feel new pain.

And then I saw a figure outside, passing through the wrinkles in a windowpane like a watery brown ghost. I had to blink before I understood that it was Alice, strolling in the garden, alone. I was so relieved to see her that I wanted to embrace her when I hurried outside.

"Good morning," she said brusquely. "Or rather, good afternoon." She kept her arms wrapped in front of her, a cuirass of forearms and elbows.

I nodded gravely and looked around. "Where're the children?" I asked. "Where's Isaac?"

"I sent the children on a butterfly hunt," she said. "I want to distract them. They are confused. They felt no great affection for Freddie or his mother. I will not force them to feel a grief they do not feel." She seemed to be talking about herself as well; her words were dry and businesslike, yet she clutched her arms at the elbows as if she were freezing in the sun. "Isaac has gone into town. He rode in with the solicitor, who arrived this morning to close up the house. The man had received a wire from the family in England and was surprised to find us here. He says we can stay as long as necessary but clearly wants us gone. And I want to escape this terrible place. Isaac went to town to arrange boat passage. I only thank God that our—benefactress paid our return fares in advance, or we would be stranded here."

She went up the steps to the kiosk, and I followed her. The floorboards were strewn with dead leaves, the table shrouded in a dirty oilcloth. We sank into the cushionless wicker chairs. Just looking at each other's careworn faces exhausted us.

"He took his three best suits," she said irritably. "He intends to pawn them. And yes, we need the money, but he needs his suits, too." She studied me a moment and took a deep breath. "What is going on, Fitz? It is terrible, what happened. Ghastly. But why does my husband go on so? What did these people mean to him? That woman was in love with death. She infected her son with her love. It is sad, it is awful, but Isaac behaves as if he were to blame."

"He feels partly responsible," I said. "After all, he once knew Fanny, and he tried to help her but failed."

"His little speech at dinner did not kill her. It certainly didn't kill her demon child." She narrowed her eyes at me. "You, however, spent much time with the boy. If anyone should know the cause of his death, and feel responsible, it is you."

"Yes," I said. "And I do. I don't know what I should have done, but I wish desperately I had done more."

I waited for her to dig deeper, and might have told her part of the story, but she abruptly turned away, as if thinking, "I do not want to know; it is awful enough already."

Isaac had not returned when it was time for dinner. We dined off tidbits found in the downstairs pantry—or rather, Alice and the children dined. My first bite tasted like a mouthful of dirt, and I could not take another. Augusta and Tristan seemed fine, showing no alarm or fear, enjoying the adventure of a meal improvised out of forbidden treats, jams and pickles and tinned biscuits. Only when Tristan asked when Papa was coming home and Alice snapped, "When he gets here!" did a nervous unease fall over them, especially Augusta. She became very stiff and proper for the rest of the meal, taking refuge in the good manners required by her absent father.

The daylight faded, and without servants, the lamps that had seemed to refill and light themselves remained unlit. The house grew dark and sinister. We had candles, yet it was ridiculous to live like shipwreck survivors in this mansion. After dinner, at Alice's insistence, I went out to the servants' quarters to find Ismail and learn what we must do to be looked after again.

The servants lived behind the estate, in the ring of roofs and chimneys just visible from the garden. I crossed the garden and entered a dirt yard. It was like a camp, with huts as shapeless as tents and open doorways casting the shadows of men, boys, and chickens over the ground. If any women were present, they were hidden.

I circled the yard, but I was invisible here. Men turned away or looked past me. Even when I asked them—"*Ismail, s'il vous plaît, le majordomo?*"—they pretended not to understand or even to hear me. Finally one of the Greek boatmen—they sat apart from the others—wagged a crooked finger at a large cottage at the end of the yard.

I knocked on the doorframe. A boy drew the curtain aside, a tall Circassian lad of sixteen or so, with blond hair and blue eyes. He recognized me and jerked the curtain shut. I heard voices inside.

Finally he reappeared, lifted the curtain, and nodded me in, keeping as far from me as he could.

The interior was hung with curtains and rugs and illuminated by spouted lamps straight from the Bible. "Monsieur Docteur," said Ismail in his soft, matronly voice. He sat on the floor among carpets and pillows. "You honor me with a visit. Would you sit, sir? May I offer you tea?"

I told him tea would not be necessary, I was here on business, but he insisted, and I understood I must accept if we were to speak as equals. He commanded his Circassian boy, the servant's servant, to prepare a fresh pot.

"Why will nobody come to the house, Ismail? Is it because you are no longer being paid?"

"Oh, no, sir. We trust we will be paid in time. It is because of the awfulness of what happened."

"Mrs. Kemp and her children are not to blame," I said. "They do not deserve to suffer."

"You do not understand, Monsieur Docteur. We are not alarmed by the living but by the dead."

"You are afraid of their ghosts?"

"Ghosts are of no matter. And we are not afraid. We are appalled. By what the dead did. The very worst sin. Unforgivable. Even when performed by nonbelievers. We have no choice but to avoid the scene of such unclean acts."

He spoke calmly, logically, without superstitious horror. I did not know that suicide was the Moslem sin of sins, *their* unspeakable vice.

"We do not blame you," Ismail continued. "Although, if you will permit me, Monsieur Docteur, many believe that your barbarous music drove them to their deeds. But I know better."

"And what do you know, Ismail?"

"Master Alfred died for his love of you. We write poems about such love. Beautiful poems. But such death must come of its own, without being willed. He must have loved you greatly."

"He did not kill himself for love," I said peevishly. "But because he was unhappy, foolish, and angry. What does a boy know of love?"

"True," Ismail admitted, stealing a look at the youth preparing our tea. "Their love is less pure than ours. Yet they do love. We cannot pretend otherwise. Even when it leads them to perform the worst sin imaginable."

I remained annoyed, wondering which sin was worse in whose eye. Ismail was as adamant about right and wrong as Isaac, yet their rights and wrongs were quite different.

I took my tea from Ismail's boy and sipped it. "You are a wise man, Ismail. A moral man."

He smiled and nodded. "I am but a worm in the eye of God."

I had my reasons for flattering him. "For the sake of Mrs. Kemp and her children," I said, "could you at least come to the house and show us where things are kept? The food and oil. We are stuck here until we can leave by boat, and we throw ourselves on your mercy."

Ismail held up his hands in helplessness. "Alas, Monsieur Docteur. I cannot. I will lose face with my company. However, I *could* speak to the Greeks. They have no religion, only superstition, and perhaps will be more pliant."

"Thank you, Ismail. I would appreciate that greatly."

When I finished my tea, I bade Ismail good night and left the servants' quarters. I promptly stepped back into darkness and grief. For as long as I spoke to Ismail, or anyone at all, the heavy numbness lifted. Now it closed around me again.

There was no moon that night, and the darkness was also literal, dizzyingly so. I felt my way with my shoe soles, distinguishing sandy path from pulpy flower beds, until the house rose up, a black shape against a few stars. The visit had taken longer than anticipated, and Alice and the children had gone to bed. As I came around the kiosk, however, I saw a light in the pantry window, a candle left burning for me and Isaac—yet Isaac had to be back by now. The door from the pantry to the garden stood half open, and sure enough, Isaac sat by the window, bent beside the candle with a pen and sheet of paper. He heard my footsteps on the gravel and looked up as I came through the door.

"Good," I said. "You're back. We were worried about you."

He remained seated at the table, looking at me with neither satisfaction nor alarm. He appeared different, changed. It took me a moment to realize that he wore workman's clothes, a drab jacket, red kerchief, and canvas trousers.

"You sold *all* your good clothes?" I said.

"Yes," he said. With two blunt fingers he tapped a stack of bank-notes and steamship tickets on the table, then dipped his pen again and resumed writing.

I took up the money and counted it, a hundred dollars in French francs, which seemed a lot for his clothes, but then I looked at the tickets. They were for Venice, second class instead of first, and there were only four: two adults and two children.

Isaac intended to leave me behind?

He heard the change in my breathing, my rapid recounting of tickets. He laid the pen down and looked at the window; he did not look at me. "The money should last until October," he said. "When the Monte Carlo engagement begins. The boat leaves in two weeks. I did not get as much for my clothes as I had hoped, but did well enough when I changed your tickets to second class, and more when I surrendered mine."

"*Your* ticket?" I said. "And how will you get to Monte Carlo? Are you intending to walk?"

He spread a hand on the table. He glanced at what he had written: It appeared to be a letter to Alice.

"I have failed at this life," he said. "I tried to live it, but it was a lie. The lie has done grievous harm. I am going back to America. Where I can be what I am. A common nobody. A faceless nigger. I signed on as a carpenter's assistant on an American merchant vessel that sails tomorrow."

He spoke with such cool, measured certainty that I wondered if I were a dimwit for failing to understand.

"What about your family?" I said. "Your wife and children?"

"My children do not deserve to live with a murderer. It hurts to leave Alice, and hurts still more to leave my darlings. But I deserve to be hurt. I deserve to suffer."

There were tears in his eyes, balanced on his lashes, the very tears that I once imagined had scored his cheeks like acid. How often had I seen him cry in all these years?

"Don't be a fool, Isaac. If anyone should leave, it's me," I argued, only to gain time while I struggled to understand his decision and find a way to dissuade him.

"That accomplishes nothing," he said. "You are the one who makes our bread and butter. I can do nothing for my family. Nothing at all. I ask you to take care of them. It is a grave responsibility, but I have failed. In so many ways. I deserve to suffer."

I felt faint, this was so insane. "You intend to leave tonight?"

"As soon as I finish my letter."

"You're not going to say good-bye to Alice?"

"How can I? I cannot even bring myself to go upstairs for one last look at my babies."

"You can't do that, Isaac. You can't abandon your family."

"I am not abandoning them, I am saving them. From a man who can do nothing but bring sorrow to others."

It was like any argument with Isaac once he had made up his mind, like debating a mountain or arguing with the sun. But if I couldn't persuade him, Alice could. Just seeing her should bring him back to his senses. "Very well," I said. "If that is your decision. You are making a terrible mistake. But there is something I want to give you before you go. Something to remind you of us."

"I do not need to be reminded. I will think of my children to the end of my days."

"No. Please. Wait here. I will be right back."

I hurried out, wishing I'd come up with a better subterfuge, but

I didn't know what else to tell him while I ran upstairs to fetch Alice. I raced up the dark stairwell, found their bedroom door, and pounded it.

"Alice," I whispered. "Quick, wake up!" I pounded again, not too loudly for fear Isaac would hear. Finally I threw the door open. "Alice! Come speak to Isaac! Before it's too late!"

She was already sitting up, her feet on the floor. "What, what?" she mumbled. "He's back? Finally. Where is he?" Then, "Too late? What do you mean? Let me get my robe and slippers."

"No time. We have to hurry. Before he gets away." I grabbed her arm and pulled her into the hall.

"Gets away?" she hissed. "What are you prattling about?" She yanked her arm free but then followed me. I heard her knock and feel her way along the banister; the stairs were darker for two people than they'd been for one.

"Hurry," I whispered and raced ahead of her, tumbling down the stairs, not caring if I fell or not. I reached the bottom and hurried toward the pantry. But it was dark up ahead; the candle was out. "Isaac?" I called. "Isaac?"

The pantry was pitch black, with a breath of night air from the garden. I groped the table for matches, struck one. The room exploded into view. The chair was empty, the door wide open. I lit the candle with a trembling hand. On the table was the pile of banknotes and steamship tickets, stacked on a letter with a glittering-wet signature.

Isaac had seen through me, finished his letter straight off, and fled into the night.

I ran to the open door. "Isaac!" I shouted. "Isaac!"

Alice came into the room, a scarecrow in a nightgown and specs, her undone hair stuffed in her cap. She frowned at me as if I were being cockamamy about nothing.

I ran out into the garden. "Isaac!" I shouted again. "Come back here! Don't be a fool!" All I got for reply was a dog barking in the night, a hapless yapping at a man fleeing through the gates. I considered running after him, chasing him down, but could I even find him in the dark? "You fool!" I shouted. "You can't do this to us! You can't do this to yourself!"

Alice did not join me outside. I saw her through the door, standing at the table, reading the letter. I went back in. "I tried to stop him," I told her. "But I couldn't talk sense to him. So I went to get you."

She stared down at the letter, her arms locked straight to hold her stunned body over the open sheet of words.

We do not have the letter. Your mother burned it when she burned everything else, any note or scrap of paper with Isaac's handwriting, and all the photographs. Do I dare attempt a reconstruction?

To My Dearest Wife,

These are the most difficult words I have ever had to write. I am not the man you believe I am. I am not the good moral man I pretend or want to be. In the name of principle and morality I committed a terrible sin of pride. It brought pain and death to two innocent people. Our friend, whom I love like a brother, loved Lady Ashe's child. I thought his love was wrong and intervened to end it. But my intervention was cruel and reckless and ended in the child's self-murder.

I do not deserve your trust. I do not deserve the love of my children. I deserve the worst punishment, and the worst suffering I can imagine is to give up you and our darlings. Because I understand now: My soul is as black as my skin. All my life I believed my soul was pure and I was as good as you. I need to return to my own people, where I will be looked upon as the lowly creature I am.

Or words like that, a single page of them, quick and terse, with two blue splotches, like eyes, where tears splashed the ink.

Alice looked up at me, through spectacles like glass tears. "Why?" she cried. "Why?"

And I told her, in a rapid, stumbling fashion: How I loved Freddie, how Isaac had understood and demanded we break off, how the interview ended in talk of hell and damnation.

She sank into the chair as I spoke, stealing new horrified looks at the letter, matching his words with my meanings. She looked disgusted, sickened. "Animals," she muttered. "You and that beastly boy. That vile, vile boy. What business did he have killing himself for *you.*"

I was stunned by her attack on Freddie. "He was a child, Alice! A confused, wounded child!"

"But not so confused as my husband! Oh, no! That martyr. That would-be Christ." She drove her fingers into her hair, pulling it from her cap. "What business was it of his that you were—*diddling* that boy! Why should he take the deaths of that stupid boy and his idiot mother on his oh-so-moral head?"

I expected coals of blame from her, but heaped on me, not on the dead or on Isaac.

"Damn him!" she cried. "How dare he love his conscience more than he loves us!"

I desperately tried to calm her. "He'll come back," I insisted. "He has to come back, when he comes to his senses."

"Oh, no. He is too proud for that. Too damned proud to swallow this wrong on top of that one. Damn his moral pride!"

She flung her arm across the table, knocking tickets and inkpot to the floor.

"I swallowed *my* pride! Again and again! I married a colored man! I had his children! I made myself a hostage to your musical claptrap! All for love!"

She jumped up and faced me, trembling with anger.

"But can he swallow *his* pride?" she demanded. "Can he live with his mistakes as I live with mine? Never!"

She plunged her arm into a shelf of plates and swept them to the floor, a crashing, clanging cascade of china. And she burst into tears, as if over the broken dishes.

"The bastard! Vain, black, stiff-necked bastard!" She stumbled backward and covered her face with her hands. She slowly sank to the floor, sobbing into her hands.

I leaned down to help her. She angrily twisted away.

"Get away from me! I cannot bear to have you here! I despise you for seeing me like this!"

I backed toward the door.

"Just go!" she cried. "Please! Leave me in peace!" she sobbed. "Please. *Please!*"

And I obeyed, so stunned was I to see Alice—cool, dry, factual Alice—utterly undone by pain. I intended to go only as far as the next room but found myself stumbling up the stairs, thinking, No, no. It isn't possible. Isaac is gone? No, he cannot be gone. Passing the floor where his children slept, I suffered a fresh stab of pain yet continued to climb the stairs.

I came to my room and lay down on my bed, thinking I would go back to Alice in a minute, when she was calmer, when she was herself again. But would any of us be ourselves again? Isaac would return, I thought. He would have to come to his senses and return. Tomorrow, or the next day, or the day after. It was too absurd otherwise. I had given up the boy I loved for the sake of the man I loved, only to lose *both* of them? No, it was too cruel to be imagined. I was beyond tears, reimmersed in that heavy numbness outside time, heavier than before. You think you have reached rock bottom and things cannot get worse. And then they get worse.

I suddenly heard someone in the hall. Isaac? He was back already? I sat up and listened. No, the step was too light. It sounded barefoot, even nude. Freddie, I thought. Freddie's ghost has come for a visit? But he passed my door and did not enter.

I went out into the hall. He had disappeared into the music room. I followed and saw only the gaudy gold piano, like a wing of light in the corner. There was light in the windows; it was already morning. But I sensed that Freddie was somewhere in the room, and that he wanted to hear the Offenbach.

I sat down at the piano and opened the lid. I spread my fingers and dipped my hands into a chord. The sound was startlingly loud and real. I intended to play the galop, hoping to make the boy reappear, but my hands produced a waltz I'd never heard before, dictated by Eusebius or maybe Freddie himself. It was a sad, light, lilting thing, more Chopin than Strauss, with a dissonant thread running through it like a tinsel nerve.

I glanced up at the tilted mirror, lightly fogged with a breath of light. And I saw him. He was stepping from a violent pattern of tiles on the wall, a nude white figure with pollywog eyes. I was overjoyed to see him again. I wanted him to forgive me, but he only looked at me with pity, an apologetic glance as if to say that I no longer mattered. Then he reached deep into the tiles with one hand and drew someone else from the wall, a veiled figure in sausage curls and a beaded black dress. Fanny came out of the pattern as neatly as if from behind an arras. She didn't see me. She had eyes only for Freddie. Her veil evaporated, and she gazed down at him with a tender smile. Freddie placed a hand at her back, used his other hand to take hers, and they began to step to my music, shyly at first, with a grace that I'd never expected from either of them.

They looked so beautiful together, so right. I drove the waltz into a stronger, more confident tempo. When I glanced at the mirror again, a third figure had joined them, a golden-haired child in a velvet suit. It was a coffin suit sewn in the back with white basting thread: Constantine. Constantine had returned, and they were together again, the mother and her two children gliding around the room.

More figures drifted across the mirror: Tom Kemp and Crawford and the other slain Rebs, still nude from their swim, each waltzing with a man in a muddy blue uniform, the killed dancing with the killers. And there was Uncle Jack, with Mrs. Tarbell in his arms, a tall grasshopper and a stout old lady. I didn't know either of them had died, but they were the right age, and their time had come, too.

I looked for Eusebius. He should be here, a dance master to this ball of the dead. But no, this was too large a crowd for his liking. My horse, however, stood in the corner, with my hooded piano perched high in its saddle. They towered protectively over the ghostly dancers sent spinning through the room by my music.

Shadows spun on the ceiling, like the toss of shadows from a fireplace. But the firelight came from the windows, which were full of twirling flames as steady as rain. Isaac was right. There is a hell, and we were in it. But hell did not burn as long as I kept playing the piano.

So I did not stop. I seemed to play for hours, for days, forever. The waltz no longer sounded joyful and superfluous but necessary, desperate. It went on and on, a rote rotation of phrases that threatened to last to the end of time. The dancers could not stop dancing until I stopped playing, and I didn't dare stop while the fires continued to rage outside.

I played against pain and sorrow, working to keep panic at bay with my music. I grew more exhausted over the years. But I did not stop, not even when I glanced over my shoulder and saw there was no hellfire at my back, only a haze of dust under dim electric lights, and a calm sea of straw hats, white shirtwaists, and pale faces.

I sat upon a stage before an audience in the Pavilion of Harmonia. I was in Dreamland, at Coney Island, in another country, another century. Twenty years had passed.

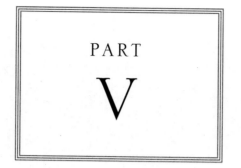

PART

V

50

AND that, Tristan, was how we lost your father.

You were only six at the time, too young to understand. But even an old man of seventy-five still cannot comprehend such a mad self-punishment. Isaac punished us all, of course, but meant only to punish himself. Because he did love you. With all his heart. You and Augusta were his sun and moon, his life, his soul.

And it was my fault. In part. It would never have happened if I hadn't fallen in love with a mortal.

If this were a novel, we could end the story here. People have died, other people have suffered, immorality has been punished, an experiment in unconventional living has failed. What more could the common reader want?

An uncommon reader might want the rest of the story. Because it isn't finished, is it? You and your sister and mother and I are still stuck in Constantinople. And in addition to the what-happened-next business is the music of it all. I have left us with a harmonic suspension, an open chord that hangs in the air, tentative, quivering, unstable, awaiting additional notes to be played alongside to modulate it into a homelike resolution.

I could illustrate better if I were sitting at the piano rather than stuck here in bed.

A touch of cold has knocked me flat. That is all. A cold exacerbated by history. The past can afflict us like illness. I did not know that these memories would hurt so much. I thought I could tame the painful old emotions by bandaging them in their story, but the story only heightened the emotions and brought back forgotten ones. What was once unbearable remains unbearable.

I cannot do this today. I do not know how to begin. I only ramble without a keyboard to help me gather my thoughts. I need to rest. I should sleep.

Did they miss their regular organist at church this morning? I assume old Miss Emily played in her usual emphatic fashion, pig-iron fingers on the keys, lead-soled shoes flooring the pedals.

What would they think, the good congregation of St. Philip's Presbyterian Episcopal, if they knew the biography of the blind white pagan who sustains their Sunday hallelujahs? Would my roaring anthems bring them so quickly to their feet? Would the widows who smell so richly of lilac water, fox fur, and hair straightener still pet and cosset me at the end of each service?

Perhaps. People will forgive you almost anything once you are old and harmless.

51

But the waltz in the music room did not really go on for twenty years. It only seemed endless, a dog of a tune chasing its tail, a closed circle outside of time. It had always been and always would be, ghosts without end.

And suddenly the musical circle broke, and I resurfaced in time and consciousness, as if after a blow to the head. I found myself in bed. It was daylight, and I lay in my own bed, the mattress soaked with sweat. My clothes were off. I wore only a day shirt. Had I merely dreamed the music? In a fever like Constantine's yellow jack? But my hands were swaddled in socks, the wrists bound tight with a twisted cambric scarf.

Alice stood over me in a frown of folded arms. She must have just shaken me awake.

My mouth was dry, and I couldn't speak. I lifted my bundled hands and asked her why with my eyes.

"You would not stop playing that blasted piano," she said.

"For how long?" I whispered.

"All day yesterday. From the crack of dawn to late afternoon. When I finally came up to demand that you cease, I thought you'd gone mad. You were like a sleepwalker I couldn't awake. I'd lift your hands off the keys, but you resumed playing as soon as I let go. So I stuffed your hands in socks and tied them up, and you became quite tame. I led you out and put you to bed, praying you'd sleep it off, whatever it was."

"The children?" I asked. "Did they hear me go on and on?"

"The children? Oh, yes, the children," she muttered. "You couldn't think of them sooner?" She shut her eyes and sighed. "Well, you seem sane enough now. I suppose I can remove these." She untied the scarf and pulled off the mittens.

I saw two hands, huge hands with red fingers and bruised nails, the thumbs and pinkies tipped with blisters. But they were not my hands. My body was too weak to own such heavy objects.

"I brought you milk and bread," said Alice, pointing at a tray on the bed. "One of the Greeks bought fresh food with the money that I gave him. You haven't eaten in days. No wonder you were ready for the asylum."

I stared at the glass of milk, the torn piece of bread, then raised my eyes to Alice. "Why are you still here?" I whispered. "Why didn't you leave me?"

"And go where?" she angrily snapped. "Do what? Oh, I wanted to leave. Don't think that I didn't. I do not relish being nursemaid to a lunatic. But running away was never *my* line."

So Isaac had not returned. There was not even a second of hope that things were whole again. Reality remained broken, like the pole of a circus tent. The heavy canvas lay over me, pressing my body to the bed.

"Eat," said Alice. "You're not doing anyone a darn bit of good lying here like Lazarus."

I struggled up and reached for the glass of milk. "Thank you, Alice," I said. "Thank you."

She only grunted and turned away, folding her arms again. We were like a dog and a cat who find themselves stranded on a desert island and must make do with one another.

I sipped the milk and chewed some bread. I had no appetite but took the food like medicine. Alice stood at the window with her eyes averted, as if eating were an indecent act. Her profile had the hard, worn look of a weathered figurehead at the prow of a ship. It was difficult to connect this wooden lady with the woman who had collapsed to the floor the other night in a fury of tears and undone hair.

"I am sorry, Alice. I know that you can never forgive me. But I am sorry for what I have done."

"You?" she muttered. "You?" She continued to stare out the window. "It was not just you. You only gave him his opportunity, his reason. He wanted to go back to his people. He wants to live and die for *their* cause. To suffer for us is much too trivial."

I did not believe that and doubted she believed it herself. But it was easier to blame the absent man than the one who remained. "He will return, Alice. When the wrongness of what he's done catches up with him."

She clutched herself more tightly and frowned, refusing to discuss the matter further. "Oh. I almost forgot. *You* had a visitor." She snorted at the absurdity. "An American journalist came by last night. He said he knows you. He would not say what he wants but promised to return today. He threatens to return every day until you see him."

Cunningham. Of course. Smelling blood, the vampire of ink had come running after the sensational tale. It was so ridiculous that I wanted to laugh, but all that came out was a groan. I explained him to Alice.

"Disgusting," she said. "Well, I'll send the vulture packing next time he calls."

Just then two small faces appeared at the door and warily looked in, a solemn little girl and her wide-eyed little brother.

"Augusta. Tristan. Hello. Come to see your Uncle Fitz?" I strained to sound cheerful, but the sight of a child, any child, split my heart in two.

"Is Uncle Fitz sick?" said Tristan. "Will he die?" You were so matter-of-fact about it, as if asking if it would rain. Death had become that commonplace here.

"Just a touch of the vapors," I said. "From too much music."

"Run along, lambs. Your uncle needs his rest." Alice went to the door and steered you out with her hands on your shoulders. Her fingers slipped up to your head, Tristan, and anxiously stroked the soft, sad, familiar wool before you scuttled off.

The collapsed tent of the universe fell back over me, heavier than ever. What had I done? What would become of the children? My crime lay on me like a heap of stones. But despair squeezed a fresh idea from my brain.

"What if we sold Cunningham a story?" I told Alice. "Make the bloodsucker pay for it."

She wrinkled her face in alarm. "You'd make this shameful thing public?"

"Not the true thing," I assured her. "A different story. An invention that will kill all rumors. We could certainly use more money." I was pleased to find I was not entirely helpless.

"I don't know," she said. "It's unseemly to consider such a thing, but— Oh, I don't care," she muttered. "You have a gift for lying. I don't. Do what you want. I'll take no part in it." And she took the tray off the bed and went downstairs.

Alone again, it all poured into me: Freddie was dead, Fanny was dead, Isaac was gone. I lay there red-handed and heartsore, wanting to stay in bed forever. I considered quitting life myself but couldn't think on it long, only a moment. Isn't that curious? That a man who made his living off the afterlife had no desire to cross over himself, despite his unbearable pain. Was it life I loved or death I feared? I do not know. But the extinction of a mother and son undid the allure of oblivion, and I'd visited death often enough and knew it was not an Eternal Rest, a Perfect Peace, only more of the same. Besides, there were two live children stranded in this haunted house who needed me.

So I forced myself out of bed, washed, and shaved, though I could barely hold the razor. I stole only the briefest looks at the tarnished mirror propped beside the basin. The blade trembled in my hand, but I gripped the wrist with my other hand and tenderly drew the steel over my cheek.

Cunningham returned that afternoon, as threatened. Alice brought him upstairs, and I received him in my room. Sitting in a chair in my dressing gown, I acted sicker than I was; playacted pain was preferable to the real thing. A newspaperman was grotesque here, yet I enjoyed the distraction, reveled in it.

"Ah, Cunningham," I croaked. "What brings you here? If you have come to interview Lady Ashe, it is too late. Much too late."

He stood before me, hat in hand, with a long face as false as his whiskers. "I come as your friend, sir. I heard of the terrible occurrence. I came to offer my sympathy. You look like you've been through the wars, sir. It must have been horrible. So what exactly happened? You can tell me."

I told him I would—for fifty dollars.

He was shocked—"I ask only out of concern. I wouldn't dream of writing this up, sir"—then tried to argue me down to twenty. We finally agreed on thirty, and he counted out its equivalence in French francs to Alice, then pulled up a chair and brought out a notebook and a pencil no bigger than a baby's finger.

I fed him a preposterous ghost story—with no mention of matters unfit for a family paper. Lady Ashe had been grieving for her son, I said. I tried to bring his spirit back with my music but conjured up a false child instead, a demonic changeling masquerading as Constantine. He terrified the household, appearing in dark hallways, grabbing ankles on the stairs, throwing dishes in the pantry. When I attempted to exorcise him with new tunes, he became more spiteful, producing visions of the boy's corpse in mirrors, calling out to us from keyholes. My family and I were well acquainted with wrathful wraiths, but Lady Ashe and her son were defenseless. They could find no escape from his reign of terror except by taking their own lives, which they did together, they loved each other so much.

Make-believe lifted my mood—it felt good to lie for a just

cause—even as I noticed the bloody gobbets of fact that stuck to the tale.

"So it is my fault," I said in closing. "I unleashed a demon in this house. And it destroyed Lady Ashe and her son."

Alice stood at the door, listening with a frown, then loudly cleared her throat and said, "The servants still refuse to enter the house, you know. If you like, I can show you the broken dishes in the dustbin."

Cunningham wrote it all down, smiling as he scribbled. Whether or not he actually believed this harum-scarum bunk, I cannot guess, but he knew a good story when he heard one, an unbeatable mix of the macabre and sentimental. He never asked about Isaac. Hardly noticing a colored man's presence, he paid no notice to his absence either.

"Thank you, August," he said when we finished. "Such a sad story. I will give it the full benefits of my literary arts." He looked like a cat full of cream as Alice led him out.

I wanted to feel better, wanted to think that my lurid fiction had insulated and muffled tragedy, making sorrow more bearable. Yet the satisfaction of lying vanished as soon as I was alone. The numbing melancholy returned.

Alice reappeared at the door. "So," she said. "It's done. You told your tale, and we got thirty pieces of silver."

The allusion annoyed me. "You're a good little liar yourself, Alice. Those broken dishes were a nice touch."

She grimaced even as she nodded. "I hated doing that. I despise myself for using those poor benighted people. But we will be gone by the time this story appears."

"And we need the money," I reminded her.

"Yes. We certainly need the money."

52

IT all came down to money. Money was all we could think about in the weeks that followed. Anything else was unthinkable, except our need to escape this awful place. We had our steamship tickets. I had my engagement at the Grand Casino of Monte Carlo. So we went, without thinking any further into the future.

We made our way back across the Continent, first to Venice by ship, then to the French coast by train. It was like crossing a country after a terrible war, the sunny landscapes looking forlorn and haunted. We had enough cash to get us to Monte Carlo and then to live cheaply in a nearby village until October.

Heartsick yet well enough to travel, I thought my numbness would lift once we were out of Constantinople. But the collapsed canvas lay as heavy on me as ever after we settled in a glaring-white village with a stark country inn. Alice now had three children to look after, the third a gloomy invalid, a weary old man. No, I exaggerate. I was not so helpless as that, but I felt tired all the time, bone-sad and exhausted. I went to bed early and always slept late, without a single dream. The cellar door that lets dreams into the head had been jammed shut.

I was here for the children, I told myself, yet there was nothing for me to do those first weeks except play dominoes with them at a table under the lemon trees behind the inn. The dotted squares of bone clacked against each other like loose piano keys and snaked across the table in elaborate silences. I patiently taught the game to Augusta and Tristan. Sorrow can be a kind of patience when one keeps it tightly reined. Alice, too, held everything in, keeping her voice low, moving with the clenched calm of someone holding her breath, while we waited, ostensibly for October.

We did not tell you about your father. Not yet. That was Alice's decision. We said only that he had gone on ahead to find me work again. Which would explain his absence if he returned.

Because his return was not impossible. I, for one, remained hopeful. After all, Isaac knew where we would be. He had time enough to cross and recross the Atlantic and find his way to Monte Carlo, once he came to his senses.

I assumed that Alice entertained the same hope, yet we did not mention it, did not discuss Isaac at all, as if talk of him might jinx his return. We did not talk about much of anything. Alice kept her own counsel, and I lacked both the energy and the moral right to press her. When she shared thoughts with me, she spoke as people speak to their dogs, without expecting an answer.

"Fifteen dollars left. That should keep us until your engagement begins. If worse comes to worst, I suppose we can ask Madame Tartine for credit. But we should avoid debt, since we cannot guess what the future will bring."

The children knew that their world had slipped its axis but hid their uncertainty, pretended everything was fine, although they sometimes behaved as if *they* might have done something wrong. Augusta became more polite, proper, and respectful, Tristan shy and silent. Alice gave you her full attention, continuing your lessons, lavishing you with hugs. Yet her moods were unpredictable, her affection fitful. When Augusta knocked over a bowl of cream bought as a treat to be eaten with the wild berries we had gathered, Alice flew into a temper as if it were the end of the world, until Augusta burst into tears and Alice covered her with frantic, apologetic kisses.

Finally October arrived. I put on my best clothes one morning and walked into Monte Carlo, a glum apparition in a black swallowtail coat and winged collar on a dusty country lane. I carried my patent-leather pumps under one arm, waiting until I reached town to change my shoes. But I was pleased to be in a town again, relieved to be among happy, well-dressed strangers. I entered the casino with a light step and introduced myself. The management showed me their music room, a satin-lined candy box with yellow silk chairs, potted palms—and a huge grand piano. A hand of ice clutched my heart. I stared at the keyboard, a long, cold grin of white and black. Would playing make me mad again? I hadn't considered such a possibility during my weeks without music. But I took a deep breath and sat at the piano. I had no choice. We needed the money. I gritted my teeth and played. Immediately the room at my back seemed full of waltzing ghosts. But there was no mirror nearby. I couldn't see my spooks. I played on, coolly ignoring their presence.

In the days that followed, my specters danced whenever I performed, invisible eddies stirring the air above the bald heads and feathered headdresses of my primly elegant audiences, until I found that I could turn them on or off at will. So long as I played deliberately, consciously, I could control my music and keep the dead at bay. Only when I let impulse take over did my hands produce that maddening waltz again. I did so now and then, just to see if the ghosts were still there. Without spirits, however, my music was mechanical, a mess of scrambled rhythms and abrupt key changes. It only confused my listeners. Without Isaac there to translate, my French was too poor for me to offer stories about anyone in the audience. There were no Americans that season.

I walked into town at noon each day and walked back to the village each night under a high dome of cold, glittering stars. I visited the gaming tables only once, placed a ten-franc piece on the painted felt, and lost. I could not believe that I was unlucky in love *and* cards, yet our finances were such that I did not risk repeating the experiment.

I hoped for Isaac's return, wanted it, needed it, so badly that I began to believe it was inevitable, as unhappy souls believe in the Second Coming. I needed him to reappear, not only so that I would have one less crime on my head but so I could escape. I wanted to leave. Life with Alice and the children was a terrible duty, an awful onus when I could do so little for them. Yet I could not abandon them, not when Isaac had played that card already. It would seem a cowardly imitation. I grew angry with him for doing what I now ached to do. It felt good to be angry with someone besides myself. I resented him for asking me to look after his family, as if it were in my powers, but that was not what kept me here. No, I stayed because a solitary future terrified me. It would give me more to grieve about, and less to distract me from guilt and sorrow and memories of Freddie. I might even go insane again.

Among the many things that Alice and I did not discuss was my continued presence. She did not ask if I would stay with them, or for how much longer. I was afraid to raise the question myself. We were like a Magdeburg sphere, two half globes held together not by bolts but by a vacuum so strong that teams of horses cannot pry the sphere apart.

October ended. Isaac did not reappear. There was not even a letter from him. The casino did not extend my engagement. But I had earned just enough money to buy us passage back to America.

It was Alice who seized upon the idea of returning. She had a cousin in Stamford, she said, a well-off relative who should be willing to help. Few prospects remained for us in Europe, but a mere cousin seemed a poor reason to cross the Atlantic. I had no ideas of my own, however, no desires at all.

"It's as good a destination as any, I suppose."

My indifference startled her. "If you prefer to stay," she said, "you do not have to accompany us. You have done plenty for us already."

I heard sarcasm there, and rebuke, but I did not argue. "There's nothing to keep me here," I said. "So I may as well come along. If you don't mind."

"Not at all," she replied. "Good, then. Fine." Her stiffness relaxed a little. "I know the children would miss you."

Neither of us could admit that we *wanted* to stick together.

But there was another issue I needed to raise. "I suppose that once we are there," I offered, "we might look for Isaac?"

She winced at his name. We spoke of "him" rarely, and never by name, as peasants avoid naming the devil.

"No," she declared. "I have no wish to hunt him down. And no hopes of finding him. Not in such a huge country. I want to go home. That is all. The only home left to me. I have no hopes of finding him," she repeated. "None at all."

On the edge of madness myself, I never considered that Alice might be a bit mad as well.

53

W E sailed out of Hamburg on a gorgeous new luxury liner but
were nowhere near its plush saloons, electric chandeliers, and six-
course dinners. Eighty dollars bought us four berths in third class,
a step up from steerage yet just as packed with emigrants. Everyone
was going to America. Alice and the children shared a cabin with
a mother and two girls who spoke a tongue none of us had ever
heard before. I was thrown in with five Jewish youths from Cracow
who carried a tattered copy of Wild West stories as their guidebook
to the Land of Dollars. I tried to correct their expectations and their
English but was soon too seasick to care.

The ten-day winter crossing passed like a year in prison. Our iron
cellar clattered with the beat of the engines, rocked and swayed
with the waves. The food was miserable, the washrooms filthy. My
cabin mates and I grew quite ripe, and one boy became as ill as I
was. I awoke each morning to the sight of his sad, lard-white foot
hanging from the bunk above mine. Any fears I may have had over
living so closely with these handsome young men were ended by
my sickness, and they were a discreet, modest lot. Now and then I
forced myself to join Alice and the children up on the deck, which
we shared with steerage, a section of the stern divided by a mesh
fence from the long, flat deck reserved for everyone else. We were
kept downwind from the better classes, in the rolling shadow of

smoke from the funnels. Despite the harsh wind and bitter cold, the enclosure was always dense with dozing peasants, card-playing city folk, and nursing mothers, too crowded for Alice to take a brisk daily walk. She remained impervious to the sea, strong and healthy, as if out of spite. She took to dressing herself and the children in their Sunday best so they could slip forward into second class for a breath of better air.

I remained too sick to join them. My melancholy turned to nausea, the seat of pain shifting from heart to belly. But it was a relief to be sicker in the body than the soul. I wanted to puke up my heavy sorrow. And after a week, when my seasickness passed, I did feel purged of grief but in its stead felt only empty, sour, and detached.

We arrived in New York harbor on a bright-blue December morning. Alice, the children, and I joined the mob along the rail, everyone staring through the forest of ships as a strange new world assembled itself in the scrolls of black smoke and white steam thickened by the cold. And it was a new world, even to me. I did not recognize this New York. A garish copper statue stood in the harbor, a dumpy pagan idol like an enormous piggy bank, still too new to be pretty or meaningful yet. The skyline of low roofs and high steeples from my youth had grown fat in my absence, filled up with stout ten-story buildings, solid brick strongboxes turreted like castles or crested like Renaissance palaces. And beside this wealthy city, peeking over and around it, was a long, gold harp, the high new cable bridge to Brooklyn.

It was as though I had stepped out of time for ten years, out of history. Yet I was back, and America had not stood still. The hush that came over the others was like the excited rapture of unborn souls getting their first glimpse of earth. All I could think was, Suckers. Fools. We're better off not being born at all.

I was quite bitter over my first glimpse of my homeland. But I was not alone. A little boy in the arms of his kerchiefed mother began to scream and cry as we approached the smoking monster.

Our own children did not make a peep. I held Augusta up on my shoulder, then set her down to hoist Tristan up for a look.

The ship docked first at Castle Garden—Ellis Island was not yet opened—and everyone in third class and steerage rushed down the gangway. I thought we should stay on board, but Alice thought otherwise, and I knew better than to argue when her mind was set. There were no porters, and we carried our luggage ourselves, the heavy wicker suitcases and overstuffed carpetbags. Augusta lugged a grip-sack in both hands while Tristan embraced a hatbox nearly as big as he was. We entered the round, cavernous barn of Castle Garden. Once a theater, the home of Jenny Lind, the Swedish Nightingale, it was now a human stockyard full of policemen with glazed caps, long blue coats, and nightsticks. You would think we were all under arrest. They herded us into a corral that ended in a gauntlet of officials and medical officers.

"But we're Americans!" I shouted over the fence. Passports were not yet standard, and we had no papers. "Americans! Let us in!"

"We've come home!" cried Alice, taking up my plea. "This is my husband, these are our children. We're from Connecticut!"

A cop with a beef-red face and whiskey breath strolled up to the fence. "American, huh?" he said in a low voice. "Gimme ten bucks, and I'll see what I can do."

Alice was suspicious, then indignant. I had to order her to pay the man. He stuffed the money into his own pocket. "We got citizens here!" he called out. "Americans! Let 'em through." He waved us around to a gap in the fence, and we came home.

But home to what? We stumbled out to a yard where luggage and bedding sat in heaps on the frozen mud and people stood blinking up at the city, waking from one dream into another. Buildings towered over the bare trees, elaborate cast-iron façades of a thousand windows. The sky was crisscrossed with wires, a crowded loom of telephone lines strung on poles like upended combs, suggesting a country of crazed spiders.

Men in drab American suits rushed forward to meet families still dressed in bright peasant garb. There was much weeping and embracing. But nobody met us. We were alone in this city, with less than twenty dollars in Alice's purse.

Alice had written her cousin from Europe. She now contacted her from the post office by that ubiquitous new marvel, the telephone. I remained with the luggage and children while Alice perched in a cubbyhole and shouted at a black horn on the wall.

"Is Mama talking to Papa on that thing?" said Tristan.

"Her cousin," I said nervously. "Who we are going to visit."

"Could she talk to Papa on it?"

"Perhaps. If we knew where he was."

"I thought so." You were at that age when children constantly ask questions and say "I thought so" no matter what the answer. "Will he know where we have gone? Can he find us?"

"Your father's a smart man. He'll find us, when the time comes." I glanced at Augusta, wondering what she believed. She only looked embarrassed, as if her brother were talking about Santa Claus.

We took a train out to Stamford, an American train with no compartments, only a long, open aisle of seats. The countryside was long and open, too, a rolling sea of gray fields dotted with stone towns. The children were fascinated, not least by the fact that everyone in the car spoke the same language that we used at home.

I did not know what to expect, if this cousin would take us all in or only Alice and her brood—in which case they'd say thank you very much and send me on my way.

The cousin met us at the station, a stout lady in a fur-trimmed coat and big hat; she resembled a well-dressed toadstool. "Alice!" she squealed. "Welcome home, my dear!" She pressed Alice to her bosom, and Alice *tried* to smile. "This is so exciting. We thought you'd fallen off the earth, Cuz. But here you are. Why, it's as thrilling as a melodrama!"

Then she saw the children, a gypsy-haired girl, a café au lait boy.

"These are yours?" she said, moving her hand to touch them but deciding against it. "And you're their father?" She stared at me, studying my face for a touch of the tar brush.

"No," said Alice. "A friend. Dr. August. Their father, my husband, is another." She stepped up to her cousin and whispered, "He is gone. I told you that in the letter. Which is why I had to return to America."

"And he was . . . Italian?"

Alice frowned. "No," she said, and lifted her chin and exposing her long neck. "An American. A gentleman of color."

The cousin looked ready to faint. She pressed a hand to her chest and glanced around the station in a panic. She recovered with a light laugh. "What an adventurous life our little Alice has led! You must tell me all about it." But she launched into her own story instead, about the renovations on their house and how everything was a shambles and she was putting us in the hotel by the train station. "You will be much more comfortable there. And I will speak to my husband about what we can do for you."

Alice expressed neither surprise nor hurt over this delicate snub. "Of course," she said, as if she had known all along that her life would appall her cousin. We went to the hotel, and Alice took the children straight to their room before I could ask her why we were even here. But I was too exhausted by travel to want to dig and delve yet. I had my own room that night, a bed that continued to bob and rock in the Atlantic.

The cousin met us for breakfast the next morning, bringing two winter coats for the children—her own children had outgrown them, she said—and a thickly stuffed envelope.

"I spoke to my husband," she sadly announced. "It will be months before our house is ready for guests. Stamford is such a dull little town. You would not be happy here. You should go to a big city. Like New York. But I hope you will accept this." She tapped the envelope. "Consider it a gift. Or a loan—until you find your feet."

I expected Alice to refuse the bribe, but no, she opened the envelope and counted the money, right there in front of her cousin. "Fifty dollars," she said coolly. "That's very generous. My children and I are most appreciative."

The cousin smiled guiltily but could not hide her relief that Alice understood and did not demand an explanation. These genteel Connecticut Yankees can be as subtle as the finest pocket watches. "If you need more," she said, "feel free to write. My husband and I will see what we can do."

"Don't think that I won't," Alice replied.

The cousin nodded, accepting the threat as her due. "Good. Very good." And she relaxed, glad that this was almost over. "We must keep in touch once you get settled, Cuz. It was so good to learn that you are not dead. We were never close, you know, but blood *is* thicker than water."

On the train back to New York, Alice sat quite still and rigid, her face turned to the window, the Connecticut of her childhood flashing pale in her glasses. It had begun to snow, a dry sweep of white blowing over the fields.

She looked so forlorn that I did not want to chide her. But when the children went off to explore the car, I said, "Certainly you knew something like this would happen. You brought us all the way across the ocean to be snubbed and bought off by that toadstool?"

"I didn't know," she said. "I never guessed that she would be so alarmed or disgusted." Her voice remained low and dry. "Not until I saw how she stared at my darlings. It broke my heart, and I could not fight her." She shook her head. "My cousin," she muttered. "So free and easy in her youth. She thought me a joyless prig. I should feel no shame in blackmailing her. No shame at all." And she smiled, a thin, bitter, sphinxlike smile. "I can just see it. Every month or so, when I need money, I will threaten another visit. And she'll pay. Out of fear of what her friends might think. How long can I keep that up, I wonder?"

As usual, she spoke as if I were the family dog, but this time the dog answered.

"We will manage," I assured her. "There are other ways. There's still my music to fall back on."

She said nothing for a moment, then, "I do not expect you to support us forever, Fitz."

"I can barely support myself. And it won't be forever," I added. "But for the time being. Until we all find our feet. And you happen to have fifty dollars now. While I don't have a cent to my name."

"Very well," she agreed. "I accept whatever help you can give. For the time being."

And so I stayed on. I never swore eternal support, and Alice did not pour forth a waterfall of gratitude. She did not even take my hand and say thank you. But there we were, still bound together, two people with nothing in common except our concern for her children, and the fact that we had both loved a man who was now vanished in the infinite desert of the world.

54

We found rooms that afternoon in New York, at a boardinghouse near Chatham Square. The landlady frowned at the little girl and boy but looked even more suspicious over our claim that Alice was my sister—we refused to pose as husband and wife. Nevertheless, she took us in, impressed by our clothes and trusting our ability to pay ten dollars a week. I remember little about money from flush times but here can report each and every expenditure.

The boardinghouse was temporary, only we didn't know yet if we would be moving up or down in the world. Alice shared a bed with the children. I slept on a couch behind a curtain. The place stank of cheap coal, steamed cabbage, and a swampy odor that was either leaking gas or unemptied chamber pots. Our ocean passage had prepared us well for New York. An elevated railroad stood at the end of the block, trains thudding and squealing past every few minutes. The trestles laddered the main avenue in black shadow, but the whole city was in shadow, an overcast gray-green sky that regularly refilled the streets with snow. Beyond the El stretched a neighborhood known as Jewtown, listing rows of tenements like rotting teeth. Not even a fresh snowfall could hide its poverty. Half the windows were patched with tar paper. Despite the cold, lines of wet clothes hung over the street, an airborne mob of frozen rags. I saw this slum each time I stepped outside, a daily glimpse of the abyss that opened at our feet.

I spent the first month slogging through the snow, going from agency to agency with my folder of clippings and letters of recommendation. Theater managers were skeptical of European fame, and the music world was no longer whole but sharply divided between art and trash. The high-art impresarios found my music rough and old-fashioned, while vaudeville agents thought me too "artistic." I might have tried a few brothels, since they were what I knew, but Roebuck's no longer existed, and nothing remotely high-toned remained anymore. Middle-class New York had become terribly virtuous. The whorehouses were all cheap, tawdry affairs off alleyways or over saloons.

Meanwhile Alice went out each day to look for better lodgings. She took the children along only on her first round. "These are your servants?" said a righteous landlord. "Slavery is over, madam." "No," said Alice, just as righteously. "They are my children." Which was even worse. The landlord said he did not rent to "darkies," and a woman who married a Negro was no better than black herself. After that, Alice left Tristan in Augusta's care at the boardinghouse and went out on her own. "I can expose myself to taunts and sneers," she told me, "but I must protect my lambs. And traveling alone, I can walk everywhere and save the nickels on horsecars."

Eventually she found a set of furnished rooms at the back of a three-story tenement on Bank Street, in the section of town once called Greenwich Village—it would be called that again a few years later when artists discovered the place. Now, however, it was a half-forgotten backwater, a motley neighborhood of Germans, Swedes, native-born Americans, a few Irish, and just enough Italians for tawny complexions to elicit little or no comment. Italians were considered no better than Negroes at the time—worse, in fact, since there were more of them. They were concentrated farther downtown, below Washington Square. Our block stood between the slums along the river and a few inland islands of gentility. We were on the second floor, with a back porch that looked out on more back porches, like stacked pigeon crates, and frozen strips of vegetable gardens. The rent was twenty dollars a month, which we could just afford, since I had finally found work. In a dime museum.

This was the age of the dime museum. Crude halls of amusement and oddity, the workingman's opera, they lined the Bowery and streets off Union Square. I turned to them only after I exhausted the other venues, and was hired at Huber's Palace Museum on East Fourteenth Street, a block from the old Academy of Music. Money had moved uptown, and the hoi polloi rushed into the vacant space. Union Square was now a gaudy, noisy district of cheap entertainment known as the Rialto. The ground floor of Tammany Hall contained Tony Pastor's Variety Theater; the Academy itself had become a vaudeville house. Around the corner from Huber's, facing the square, was the very mansion where Orlando Wilson had introduced me to society so many years ago, long since chopped into apartments, a grocery, and a butcher shop.

Huber's was not quite a theater but a long, smoky hall of straight-backed chairs facing a low platform. Performers worked the foyer and back of the hall during the other acts, all of us competing with one another for attention: jugglers, singers, magicians, and freaks. There were the usual midgets, a bearded lady, a six-legged cow, Shadrach the Transparent Man—an albino fellow so thin that one could see the silhouette of his beating heart—and Unthan the Armless Wonder. Hired for my spiritual improvisations, I had to speak for myself now and could no longer hide in being a foreigner or idiot savant. I stood naked and mumbling before the rabble. The gimmick of the blindfold helped; I didn't have to see all their gaping, gawking, leering faces. But my act was a total fizzle. I still played deliberately, without spirits—my spirits knew no tune except that damnable ghost waltz—and my improvisations were clever enough, yet meaningless to the common ear. The stories I concocted about departed loved ones—and everyone had their dead—pleased nobody. Huber's would have dropped me after a week if Unthan hadn't taken me in hand, so to speak.

"Come to dinner, Owgoost," he said to me one afternoon. "Ve must talk." His full name was Carl Hermann Unthan. He was German, a handsomely peasant-faced, flat-nosed fellow of my age who had been born without arms. His act consisted of doing things with his feet: relatively simple deeds like signing his name or threading a needle, followed by card tricks and a violin solo. He dressed quite well, in elegant trousers and sleeveless tailored coats that made his tapered torso look like an optical illusion. When we walked down the busy, crowded sidewalk together, the few people who noticed him only blinked a moment, uncertain what was wrong with the picture. We went to a nearby chophouse where the waiters knew him and seated us in a private corner. Carl promptly kicked off a slipper; a foot in an open-toed stocking appeared on the table. His toes were immaculate, the nails glossy and manicured.

"I like your music, Owgoost," he began, pointing his big toe for emphasis. "You are a serious artist. But much too serious for our vork. People do not come to us for the songs of dead babies. They vant jokes, nonsense, fun."

"Life is a solemn business," I told him. "I am not a light-hearted man."

"You must learn. If you vant to succeed in this world. Look at me. I am a serious musician. I luf good music. I play once for Franz Liszt! But art buys little salt here in America."

He spoke with such authority that I soon forgot his armlessness and thought of the black-gloved appendage on the table as a kind of hand, until the waiter came with our food. He set our plates down and began to cut up Carl's steak, with a fatherly kindness that was quite surprising in a waiter.

"Allow me," I said and took over. I sliced off a piece and held it toward Carl's mouth.

He angrily shook his head. "Just cut! I can feed myself, thank you!"

And he could, clutching his fork in his toes and spearing a piece of meat. His "miraculous performance" was also his daily life. He had a wife, a Czech woman, and I assume she helped him on with his pants in the morning. I cannot guess how he managed trips to the privy. But one could not spend any time with Carl without remembering the Persian proverb: "I was unhappy because I had no shoes, until I saw a man who had no..."

"I vant you to perform with me," he said. "Ve keep our own acts, mind you, but you assist me with mine. And in return I vill show you the ropes." He wagged his empty fork at me. "Vat do you say, Owgoost? Does my proposition interest you?"

It did. I had no choice. And he intrigued me, this man who spent his life in a body like a straitjacket.

So, under the guidance of the Armless Wonder, I developed a whole new act. Carl explained that people came to Huber's to be mocked, even humiliated; they enjoyed the attention. I would invite a member of the audience up onstage, sit him or her in a chair, put on my blindfold, and then razz the person with music. I asked my spirit questions, aloud, and answered with the piano. Popular tunes and dusty hymns did the trick. What brings this gent to New York? "A Hot Time in the Old Town Tonight." What lies in the young lady's future? "The Wedding March," of course, unless she was already married, in which case I tossed off a sour, jumbled rendition of "Home, Sweet Home." Where will this man find happiness? "In the Sweet Bye and Bye." I read a person's type at a glance, looking for wedding rings or the state of a man's cuffs or how expertly a shopgirl used rouge. If I were wrong, it only added to the fun. It was all very cheap and easy, and I took no pleasure in it, yet my dour expression added to the comedy.

And I performed regularly with Carl, our duets the finale of his act. He played the violin quite well, or rather, as well as a gifted amateur with fingers. With his instrument strapped to a stool, he gripped the bow in one foot and worked the frets with the other. His best pieces were slow, such as the Meditation from *Thaïs,* but he wanted to tackle more difficult work, the "Spring" and "Kreutzer" sonatas. We cheated, rearranging the impossible parts, and I hid his mistakes, playing loudly over his screechy arpeggios. But our audiences were mightily impressed, fooled into enjoying Beethoven by this spectacle of virtuoso feet.

I still disliked being an accompanist, even now, and bending my music to another man's tune. You would expect me to have no pride anymore, but a snakebite of vanity remained. Carl got all the applause, of course, and he made what I did look like child's play. Yet I was grateful to Carl and grew quite fond of him. For all his tough wisdom, he had his own tender illusions. He actually hoped that he might one day be treated as a serious musician, as if his music could move people so deeply they would forget its contorted, simian source.

Our household was settled by spring, more or less. We had an income and a dwelling, such as they were. The children started at the local public school. Alice walked them there each morning, a fierce bantam hen protecting her chicks. She made a home for them, and for me as well, cooking, washing, cleaning, sewing, alone, without a servant to help her. Our fine clothes joined the rude public displays hanging over the yards out back. I would return exhausted from Huber's each night, long after the children had gone to bed, and find a warm plate of food waiting for me in the oven, homely fare salvaged from bad cuts of meat and week-old vegetables. Alice bought carefully, and her cooking was not as bad as I had expected. She often joined me in the small, dark kitchen while I glumly ate and would talk to me, idly retelling the children's tales of school or complaining about a miserly grocer or even asking about my day at Huber's, which she refused to visit—it sounded much too vulgar and depressing. Or sometimes she said nothing at all but just sat with me, as if for company. I was surprised to think that Alice might be lonely. She was such a disciplined, intimidating sphinx, yet even sphinxes can be lonely. When I asked if she'd met any neighbors, however, she sharply tsked at me and said, "Don't be ridiculous. I have the children and this flat to look after. I don't need company. Besides, the women here are fools."

I waited for her to bring up Isaac. Now that we were settled and could think about the future, I thought she would want to look for him. I never believed her claim that she did not hope to find our fugitive. Yet she didn't mention Isaac, not once. I was afraid to bring him up, since I was to blame, and talk of him would only reopen that wound when there was nothing we could do about his absence.

Finally I found something. One night I sat down in the kitchen, ate a few bites, and casually announced, "Oh. I had an idea today. Look at this." I took out the slim newspaper I'd discovered that afternoon, *The Freeman,* a colored weekly based in New York. "It has national circulation," I said. "What if we place a notice here? Maybe *he* will see it and at least learn where we are."

She stared at me as if she didn't know whom I was talking about. "What makes you think I want to find him?"

"You must," I said. "Don't you?" I was confused by her calm look and implacable tone. "Why else haven't you told the children that he's gone for good? Don't they ask about their father?"

"Tristan does. Augusta doesn't." She lowered her eyes and grimaced, an annoyed, exasperated look. Her foot was tapping beneath the table. I expected her to lose her temper and bark at me for raising the subject. Instead she drew a deep breath and said, "You are right. This silence cannot be doing them any good." And she got up from the table.

"Where are you going?"

"I should not postpone this any longer. I must do it now."

She went straight to the bedroom where the two of you were fast asleep. She left the door open, and I heard her gently wake you. "Oh, my lambs. My poor, poor lambs. I just received terrible news. Your father . . . your father is no more. He is with the angels. I just received a telegram."

I remained at the kitchen table, stunned by her quickness, her instant need to be done with this. The mere mention of Isaac had hurt her into doing what she must have intended to do long ago but couldn't, it was dammed so deep in her heart.

"I heard nobody at the door," said Augusta.

"You were asleep. Because a telegram arrived and said your father was killed. In a train wreck in Montana."

"He was on his way back to us?" cried Tristan.

"No. He was still looking for a home for us. A nice home. But now we shall never see him again."

Tristan burst into tears. I heard no sounds from Augusta. But then Alice's voice began to choke with sorrow as she told you that God was good and your father was in heaven. She was crying herself. Yet it was so cruel what she did, her anger with Isaac making her cruel toward you, just as Isaac's anger with himself had made him cruel to all of us.

Alice came out and softly drew the door shut. Her face was streaked with tears. "There. It's done," she said. "I have killed my husband. Killed him for good."

I could hear Tristan still sobbing in the bedroom.

"If he returns?" I whispered. "How will you explain that?"

"He won't return. He washed his hands of us. Don't you under-stand that yet?" She drove the heels of her palms over her cheeks, wiping off the tears. "I must finish washing my hands of *him*," she said. She turned to the deal cabinet in the corner, opened a drawer, and took out a flat box. She knelt beside the parlor stove and emp-tied the box onto the carpet-patterned lino, a scatter of letters and papers.

"What is that, Alice? What are you doing?"

"I am finishing what I began." She unfolded a letter. I recognized Isaac's plump, round handwriting. She glanced over it, then thrust it into the stove.

More pieces followed—postcards, photographs, other letters. She did it methodically, piece by piece, inspecting each one, careful not to stuff the stove and fill the room with smoke.

I sat in a chair and numbly looked on. "Don't you want to save anything for the children? To remember their father?"

"No. Their lives will be easier once they forget him."

She stared into the canyon of coals, watching another scrap of Isaac curl and ignite. It gave her no pleasure, yet she could not look away, and I used the opportunity to scoot a few things from the pile with my foot: a couple of letters, a studio photograph from Amsterdam. She was destroying my life with Isaac as well as hers. I hid them under the coal scuttle.

The sobs in the bedroom had died away by the time Alice finished, and the stove was full of black-velvet roses. She slowly stood up and frowned at the empty box, confused by what she'd done. "Don't look at me like that, Fitz," she said softly, without even a glance at my face. "I have not gone mad. I have not become a monster. This was not the right thing to do tonight. But I did not know how else to handle it."

"I didn't think you were mad," I said. "I was only thinking that you must be in great pain."

"Yes. Of course. But it will pass. Someday. Good night."

She went to bed, and I took out the things I had saved from the fire. But you cannot really save the past, just as you cannot fully destroy it either. I promptly put them away, unable to bring myself to read the letters or look too long at the picture.

The next morning we all sat down to breakfast, and nobody mentioned last night. Tristan, in fact, sleepily played with his food as if he had forgotten it, like a bad dream. Then he looked up in alarm, remembering, and burst into tears.

"Stop it, just stop it!" cried Augusta, "I can't stand your boo-hoo-hooing!"

But Alice said to let him cry. "For as long as he wants, until he feels better."

She walked you both to school, and I didn't see you again until the next day, when you appeared to be back to your quietly content infant self. But a few days later I took you for a stroll down Hudson Street, to visit the new puppies at Schreiber's livery stable, and we passed an ice wagon driven by a colored man with a beard. You took a deep, excited breath—and burst into a fresh torrent of tears. I didn't know what to do except buy you a stick of barley candy.

After that, however, you wept no more for your father. Well, you were only six and perhaps already beginning to forget him. Augusta, however, remembered her papa all too clearly. She remained reserved and stoical, like her mother. Yet she seemed more guarded around Alice and less tolerant of Uncle Fitz, as if knowing that we had not told her the truth. Children have their own form of clairvoyance.

I went ahead with my scheme, however, for my own sake, needing to do something to learn what had become of *my* friend. Without telling Alice, I visited the offices of *The Freeman* and took out an ad. "Regarding Mr. Isaac Kemp, gentleman of color, formerly of Virginia, New York, and Europe. Will he or anyone knowing his whereabouts please contact F. W. August at 112 Bank Street, New York City. Responses will remain confidential." I paid for the ad to run three months, which should be long enough for one issue of the paper to come before Isaac. The transaction felt strangely religious, like praying to a god who might not exist. He existed, all right, but, as with any god or ghost, one did not know if he would respond in words or signs or silence.

I am still bedridden after two weeks. I don't get better, and these bitter memories are bad medicine. There are few things sadder than a sick blind man, the universe reduced to a bedful of humid flesh, aching joints, and caked, wheezing lungs. I miss the vast, articulate landscape of my keyboard.

Wouldn't it be a sorry joke if the Angel Azrael bundled me off before I finished our tale? What do they call those rambling new jokes with no punch line? Oh, yes. Shaggy-dog stories. Perhaps that is how this one will end, but as a Shaggy-God story.

55

MONTHS passed. I did my twenty daily shows at Huber's, ten alone and ten with Carl. And the children grew, more quickly than seemed possible, already outgrowing the pretty clothes of our salad days despite Alice's constant altering and mending. She altered my clothes, too, taking them in at the waist and neck. The past year had returned me to a leaner, hungrier shape.

Then summer arrived, and it was dreadful. Not only did the city become a steaming swamp of bad air and rotting garbage, the pavements puddled with horse sweat, but the theaters and dime museums closed shop for two months. While Carl took his wife on a vacation by the sea, we had to use our meager savings just to keep ourselves housed and fed. Unable to find interim employment, I was reduced to spending my days sitting on our back porch in shirtsleeves and no collar, like a common workman, reading newspapers or playing dominoes with the children.

"Why aren't you working?" grumbled Augusta one afternoon after I beat her at yet another game. She was not nasty about it but coolly righteous, sounding like her mother.

I kept my temper. "Why aren't *you* working?"

She arched her eyebrows as if it were the most ridiculous thing ever said. "I can't. I'm a little girl."

"That you are," I replied. "That you are." Nevertheless she'd hurt my feelings, making me feel unappreciated. "Well, I'll go back to work in September"—I hoped—"and you won't have lazy old Uncle Fitz whipping you at dominoes anymore."

When the theaters reopened, Carl was promptly hired by Tony Pastor's down the street. I panicked for a day or two, until he persuaded them to hire me as well. So I got up in the world and entered a vaudeville house, where the pay was better, the audiences less rowdy—people actually stayed seated during performances. I remained a comic novelty act, which was fine with me. The passion that makes art possible appeared to have left my soul for good. But I continued to learn new tricks. I had to keep up with the new songs, of course, and found I could always get a laugh if I took an old song, an unctuous church hymn or sappy parlor tune, and "ragged" it. I first heard ragtime from Lillie Langtry's accompanist during her two-week stint as a headliner at Tony Pastor's. The accompanist had heard it in St. Louis, where he reported that all the colored piano players were performing in this joky, stumbling manner. It spread quickly throughout the country, in secret, like a good dirty joke. There are similar syncopations in Schumann and others, but only for a few phrases. Now whole pieces were played with these extra one-two beats that simultaneously loosen a tune and support it on a second rhythm, like a jaunty dance by a man with a limp and a cane. Carl dismissed it as a trashy novelty, "cathouse music for coons," but my audiences enjoyed it, and I was happy to oblige them.

Carl had still not met Alice or the children. Alice refused to bring them to a vaudeville house, even when I assured her it was respectable, no liquor was served, and families often came to matinées. There were other reasons, of course. She did not want the children to know that we lived off fraud and nonsense, and she was reluctant to meet the other performers, especially my friend with no arms. But I also suspect she did not want them to meet *her*. Alice's proud, prickly solitude carried a whiff of shame, as if she feared the opinion of strangers. Her only social life was her regular attendance with the children at St. Luke's Church on Hudson Street. An Episcopal church, it was a bit Romish for Alice's liking but was nearby and attracted a good class of people, a fine example for her lambs. I stayed home, of course, enjoying a brief spell of quiet in our crowded rooms.

For a long time Carl teased me about my secret, clandestine life, until he decided I was telling the truth when I said the woman I lived with was not my bedmate. "You live, then, like two old maids? Ridiculous. If I had arms, I would use them to embrace a comely lass. Or lad, if that is my bent." He had his suspicions, but, like most show people, was not shocked by much.

Yet that "bent" had unbent in me. I felt no physical desire of any kind. When I wandered down to the docks that first summer for a breath of breeze, I would see the mobs of river rats out at the end of a pier, dozens of slum boys scrambling in and out of the oily water, sun-brown and naked as worms. The sight elicited nothing in me except sorrow and pity. I was too old for desire, I decided, though I was not yet forty. I must have missed it, however, or I would not have visited the Slide that winter.

I cannot remember how I heard of this infamous watering hole. I probably read a scathing description in a paper. The penny press indulged in lavish accounts of vice—prostitution, gambling, drugs, divorce—in the name of moral uplift, of course. The Slide was a reputed gathering place for "sexual criminals." It was on Bleecker Street, in our part of the city, just a few blocks away in the tangled maze of lanes, though it might have been on the other side of the moon. I stopped by there on my way home from work one night, out of grim curiosity. At first glance it looked like any saloon in New York, half empty at this hour, with only a handful of men and a couple of tarts. Then I realized that the tarts weren't women and not all the men were fully male. A quartet of beardless fellows sat at a table in back, smoking cigarettes, not cigars, and screaming like parrots at their own jokes. Most of the manly men were Italians.

I remained at the bar, where I was soon joined by a thin creature with rouged cheeks and violet eyelids. "Ain't seen you here before, mister," he said, snaking himself against the oak in a manner that would seem overly feminine in a female. His name was Alexander. He was clearly a prostitute, though he didn't volunteer the information, and I knew better than to ask. I couldn't understand why he painted himself like a woman and told him so. He said it made him feel pretty. I washed away his paint in my imagination, but the skinny lad underneath, no more than sixteen, awakened in me only a desire to feed him. So I bought the boy dinner. We sat in a corner, and I watched him eat—he was as hungry as a wolf—and I found myself wanting to touch him, a friendly hand on his shoulder or arm across his back. Suddenly there was a knot in my gut, a gagging in my throat, as my body remembered: My embrace was fatal. I was the one real criminal in that place. "Sorry, I didn't know it was so late," I told him. "Much too late. A pleasure meeting you, my boy. Good night." And I hurried out into the cold, dark street.

No, I could not forget Freddie. I did not remember the boy in words or images—I didn't dare—and I never dreamed about him either—I didn't dream at all—yet my body remembered in silence. My sleep remained silent, dreamless. I had not had a single dream since Constantinople. You might think slumber would be a lovely rest without visits by plodding horse spirits or wild visions of spectral hellfire. Yet it was a dry, dead thing, as if I only slept on the surface of sleep, like an invalid in a hospital.

I could not forget Isaac either. I waited for my ad in *The Freeman* to receive some kind of response. But there was nothing, not a letter from the man himself, not even a rumor passed on by a stranger. Instead, within a year the newspapers began to fill with stories about lynchings in the South.

The increase was real and not just in my eye. We think of Negro-lynching as a timeless Southern custom, but this was a whole new brutality, a golden age of the rope. No month passed without reports of a fresh atrocity. They became so common that the better papers treated them as minor misfortunes, like earthquakes in India, while the penny press continued to pour on the lurid details. Men were lynched all over the South, in Georgia, Alabama, North Carolina, and Texas, in villages and cities. It was no longer done in secret by night riders and Klansmen but often in broad daylight, with whole towns joining in. The victims were not just strung up but beaten, mutilated, even burned alive. And they were no longer killed for political acts but for rape. It was always rape. The South was obsessed with rape, claiming its freed slaves had regressed and turned bestial without the firm hand of white masters. Two or three assaults might be believable, but this epidemic of animal lust had to be a mass delusion.

I became obsessed with these stories, hunting them down, reading each and every one, looking for Isaac's name. I never believed that Isaac could be charged with rape. I didn't. But I could imagine him coming to the aid of an accused man, standing up for him, and protesting his innocence. The mob would promptly hang him alongside this friend or stranger. I had nothing to support such a story, only my knowledge of Isaac, and my memory of a picture he had shown me after dinner at Yali Ashe and how much it meant to him. He had returned home to atone for his sin of righteousness. He would be willing to die for his people.

That is, if he went back to the South. Maybe he went out West instead. I imagined him living like a hermit on a mountain. "I do not deserve the company of other people," he had told me, and so maybe he exiled himself in an isolated shack, alone with his conscience and God. Or maybe he was off in God's ocean, still working as a ship's carpenter, losing himself in shipboard anonymity and the wide blue vistas of watery eternity.

But I didn't know. He could be anywhere. Absence was such a vast kingdom, a faraway region as mysterious as death.

I did not think of Isaac steadily, mind you, but now and then, usually after a new lynch story. Which was probably why I read them so fervently, so that I might think about Isaac. When he invaded my thoughts, I would sometimes stay late at Tony Pastor's and play the piano to myself, hoping to get news of him. My spirits still knew only that ghost waltz, but they had always been more accurate about the dead than the living. Yet the waltz did not come so easily to me now. I had to hunt for it, deliberately dream it into my fingers. The dancing ghosts would soon show themselves in a little pocket mirror that I propped on the piano, Freddie with the others, yet they were beginning to fade, becoming as faint as breaths. But Isaac never appeared with the dancers, which confirmed that he was still among the living.

I did not mention any of this to Alice, of course, neither the lynchings nor my metaphysical groping. She had become less fierce since Isaac's fictional death. She kept her hard shell of propriety, but the pain and anger contained by that shell seemed to be subsiding. I could not risk bringing them back to life.

Another year passed. And a book appeared. It was more a pamphlet than book, a dime novel in fact.

Shadrach the Transparent Man visited me at Tony Pastor's one afternoon with a gift. His alabaster skin and milk-glass hair gave new meaning to the concept of "white man." He handed me a pamphlet. "I think this might amuse you," he said, a transparent look of mischief in his pink eyes. Shad was our friend, but he still envied me and Carl for having escaped Huber's.

The pamphlet bore an illustrated cover of garish red and pale yellow. A grinning Mephistopheles with a pointy beard banged a piano, and a swarm of tiny devils poured out and swirled around the title: *The Crimes of Doctor August: An American Tale of Musical Terror in the Orient.* By M. L. Cunningham.

"Where did you get this?" I demanded.

"At my newsagent's. Is it really you?"

"It's lies," I said. "I can tell you that before I read a single word."

I read it that afternoon between performances, and it *was* lies, but the lies were all mine. I was shocked that they had followed us across the ocean. It was the very tale I'd told Cunningham, repainted in purple prose and damning adjectives. "A dastardly warlock of the keyboard . . . fiendish sonatas . . . band of musical half-breeds." And he added a new twist of his own: I had released a demon in the house not from carelessness but malice, out of my burning resentment for the wealth and happiness of Lady Ashe.

I took the book to Carl in his dressing room, hoping for advice on how to smother this libel. He set the book on the floor, toed through a few pages, and began to smile. "Excellent, Owgoost. Most fine. Here is good graft." Which was what we called the merchandise we sold to audiences—souvenirs, sheet music, and how-to manuals. "And you did not have to write it yourself, but have it given to you on a silver plate."

"I can't sell this, Carl. I want to bury it."

"But vhy? It is silly story. You should make a buck off it. You purchase in bulk and sell at twenty-five cents. You might even grow a beard, so you look like the man on the cover."

He was so pleased with my good fortune, and so practical about it, that I began to see the dollar signs myself. "Whatever I decide," I told him, "I refuse to grow a beard and turn myself into that reptile."

I took the pamphlet home and showed it to Alice, expecting her to be appalled. Her righteous indignation would kill the temptation to profit from this. She made a sour face while she flipped the pages of cheap paper. "Does it name the children?"

"No. They're referred to as simply my 'dusky brood.' But you're called 'Mrs. Kemp, the mulatto concubine.' "

And she snorted, with a bitter smile balanced between a smirk and a frown. "I do not care what is said about me." She closed the pamphlet without reading further. "I want only to protect the children. So long as they aren't named, I say go ahead. Use it as you wish."

"But I want to forget what happened. I don't want to have it in front of me every day as a trashy tale."

"I can understand that. All too well." She gave me a sad, weary look. No longer clenched against her own furies, Alice could express uncertainty now and then, even sympathy. "Still," she said. "The children need new shoes. Another summer is near. Someone is making money off this. Why shouldn't we benefit, too?" She glanced at the pamphlet again, then looked me in the eye. "Do you really believe, Fitz, that you'll ever forget what happened?"

"No," I said. "Never."

"Then it will make no difference, will it?"

No. It wouldn't. I was surprised by her tenderhearted ruthlessness, but she was right.

So I went ahead and used the damn thing, telling myself that this trash was a fitting punishment for my crime, a hairshirt worn in remembrance of Freddie. But as soon as I began hawking it at each performance, the tale lost much of its sting. It became harmless frip, moneymaking graft, and my chief pain was the loss of pain, the numbing of memory.

The booklet sold quite well, and notoriety can be as good as fame when one wants a good breakfast. The publisher was in New York; I purchased bales of it without their ever suspecting that their best customer was the villain of the piece. It had been pirated from an English edition, so there was the consolation of knowing that Cunningham never saw a penny from my sales. He was an intermittent shadow in my life, a minor comet who appeared every decade or so, as indifferent to me as I was to him, yet the man left as deep a mark on my identity as any loved one.

I began each performance by announcing that I had learned my lesson from my terrible crime—"Which you can read about in this work of fine literature, available for a limited time at twenty-five cents"—and wanted only to entertain people, not frighten them to death. Which immediately piqued everyone's interest, although some were disappointed by my reform.

We shod your feet that winter and the next in old sins and purple lies.

56

Such a gray, dreary, stupid time. For me, at least. Your own memories must be different, Tristan. After all, this was your childhood, an age of wonders and dramas, good *and* bad. And we did all that we did for the sake of you and your sister.

The children were our cause, our church, mine as well as Alice's. You were my children, too, now, by default. You would still have a father if not for me. You might not even exist if I hadn't inadvertently stampeded him into marrying your mother. So you were my doing, and I accepted the responsibility. I did not play father—I didn't dare offer discipline and was never asked for advice—but I could make money. I ached to do well by you, perhaps out of a secret feeling of penance, an unexpressed hope that I might atone for one child with two.

No, that makes me sound too moral and deliberate, more like Isaac than my unprincipled, thoughtless self. Because the truth of the matter is, I could not imagine living without you and Augusta and your mother. I needed your company, though not the pleasure of it, to be frank. Life with your mother was never easy. But I no longer believed in pleasure. I needed Alice and her brood as an anchor. They were often a ball and chain, and sometimes a crown of thorns, but they were also an anchor.

We need to include an account of the children here, from my very limited perspective.

School never appeared to be a problem. Alice had taught her darlings well, so well that the teachers wanted to jump them ahead in their classes. Tristan started in third grade, but Augusta insisted on staying back in fourth, with girls and boys her age. She did not wish to stand out more than she already did.

From the beginning Augusta suffered a keener desire than her brother to fit in. She was overjoyed when she outgrew the last frilly dress and could wear the simple gingham smocks and starched white pinafores of her classmates. She needed other people, hungered for their company. She began to spend time after school at Greenwich Hall, the neighborhood settlement house, where the do-gooding middle-class ladies adored her and let Augusta help them with their packs of slum tots and orphans.

She continued to grow, becoming a long-legged colt with full lips, pale complexion, and wiry gypsy hair. Tristan grew, too, but his father's height did not kick in until later. He had his mother's turned-up nose and weak-eyed squint and wore glasses by the time he turned ten, steel-rimmed windowpanes that made him look old and wise despite his freckles, a constellation of dots over his sepia cheeks and nose. He was a bookish lad who would tuck himself away in a snug corner on the floor behind the sofa with volumes of Robert Louis Stevenson or Alexandre Dumas.

The children lived in one world while I lived in another. The twain were kept apart. Then one afternoon at Tony Pastor's, I finished my finale with Carl and followed him offstage. I had thirty minutes before my own act started again. And there, standing in the wings among the ropes and canvas flats, were two children in their school clothes.

"What's wrong?" I asked. "Your mother's had an accident?"

"No!" said Augusta, startled by the very idea. "Trissy wanted to hear you play. So I saved my pennies and brought him."

I was touched and delighted. I didn't know what to say. The little orchestra out front struck up the cue for Mademoiselle Aquitaine, who stood a few feet away with her plumed fan and feathered gown, glaring at us over her powdered shoulder.

"Come with me," I whispered. "We cannot talk here." I led them backstage through the beaverboard warren of dressing rooms to the alley out back. It was cooler there, and Carl already sat on a stool outside the door, massaging one foot with the other. He looked up in surprise when I appeared with two children.

"Carl, this is my niece and nephew. Children, my good friend Carl Unthan."

They stared at him, of course, but he was staring at them. "Such pretty children," he declared, which was what all well-meaning people said when they recognized your heritage.

Augusta gave him a sickly smile, but Tristan was wide-eyed, fascinated. You must have been eight or nine. When Carl stood up and bowed—his equivalent of a handshake—Tristan bowed right back at him, his own arms pressed to his sides in instinctive sympathy. Carl bade them good day and went back inside.

"You should have told me you were coming," I said. "You don't need to spend your pennies. I'll get you passes, and you can come anytime you want. You can bring your friends. But you must never tell your mother, you know."

"Mother," muttered Augusta with a roll of her eyes. "I don't know why she doesn't want us here. I didn't see anything so awful. Just a lot of silly people doing silly things."

"You caught my solo act?" I asked worriedly.

"Yes. You were quite rude to that man with the red nose."

"You were funny," said Tristan.

"It's a joke," I said. "All in jest." I wanted Augusta's approval and was sad when I didn't get it.

"At least you didn't play the piano with your feet," she conceded.

When she drifted over to the door to hear Aquitaine's song— "The Boy I Love Is Up in the Gallery," trilled like opera—I told Tristan, "That was very sweet of your sister to bring you here."

"Gusta was nice today," he said with a shrug. "Tomorrow she

might be mean again. But this is a jolly place. You have a very jolly job, Uncle Fitz."

I told him to visit anytime he wanted, but it was too far for Tristan to walk here alone, and Augusta did not come again.

She was such a complex, unpredictable child. She wanted to be like "other people"—civilized, well-off people—but she did not want to betray her family. She had much love to give, yet she preferred to give it to strangers. She loved her little brother, but he embarrassed her.

They were once so close. They shared the same bed for years, and Augusta doted on Tristan, scolding, comforting, commanding, like a second mother. Then a change took place. It started at school, I think. One day I encountered her on the street with a posse of pretty girls, conspiring on a stoop like pigeons. Augusta reluctantly introduced me, and they asked if I were Portuguese. "No, my uncle is from my mother's family," said Augusta, flushed and annoyed. She had been telling her friends she had a Portuguese father. The presence of a darker brother threatened to give away the truth. Was she cruel to you, Tristan?

Please. If I am to tell my story, I must also tell yours. A few words from you would not be remiss in this account.

You sound surprised I noticed. I noticed so little, but I did notice that. I was even aware of her acts of extreme kindness at home, as if to make up for betrayals at school.

A stepbrother? What a cunning little minx she was.

Really? How confusing that must have been for you.

You are including your words, too, I hope.

Why not? You think silence will protect you? You want to remain the invisible hand? Nobody reading this will guess how much you have reworked my sentences, cleaning up my old-fashioned thickets of prose. You make me sound positively modern at times.

Very well, then. I have no control over what you write. And when I am gone, you will do with my words what you please.

> Nigger, nigger, never die,
> Black as night, with shiny eye.

Hearing the rope-jumping girls chant that on Bank Street, the same little girls whom I'd met on the stoop, I wondered what you and Augusta made of the rhyme, if it sounded like a curse or a promise of immortality.

Was there one day when you said to yourself, "I will not live as white but as colored?"

Uncle Tom's Cabin? Oh, my. We were so tactful and protective that you had to read Harriet Beecher Stowe to solve the mystery?

The tragic mulatto. Novels and plays were full of them, as if no man's lot were sadder. Was your life a tragedy?

Good. I didn't think so. And if one must have tragedy, we want our own, not those that the world foists upon us.

But it was not an age for tragedy. It was a time of optimism and hope, for most Americans. New York boomed with new buildings, cloudscrapers climbed the skies, electric trolleys replaced the horsecars, and a dreadful new machine, the gramophone, began to appear in penny arcades. The present was too exciting for people to want to dwell on the past. Even Decoration Day, which began as a commemoration of the Civil War dead, was no longer a day of mourning but a celebration of the future.

Every year there was a parade up Broadway and Fifth Avenue. You could hear it all over the city, brass band on top of brass band, nothing but Sousa marches piling into one another. Theaters suspended performances for the afternoon, and I always joined the crowds, first on Union Square, then, when the vaudeville houses moved uptown and I worked on Twenty-third Street, at Madison Square. The contingents of veterans wearing faded campaign caps with their Sunday suits grew older and smaller from one year to the next. There were fewer men who, like me, had "seen the elephant." Instead the street filled with ladies wearing American flags over white robes and mobs of flag-waving children, also dressed in white. The whole country was turning white. It was the color of choice after the Chicago Exposition of 1893. Every house, every new building, even our battleships were painted in neoclassical white. Such a clean, pure look after decades of clutter, yet when I was in a mortuary mood, it made me feel that the entire country had become one big whited sepulcher.

I returned to the theater after watching the parade one year, feeling unusually old and moribund, to find Tristan waiting for me under the marquee. He was pacing back and forth, hands at his back, in a military manner completely at odds with his Buster Browns. He broke into a boyish grin when he saw me.

"Uncle Fitz? Did you see the parade? Wasn't it stupendous! It makes one proud to be an American."

"Yes? I suppose. To what do I owe this unexpected pleasure, my boy?" He visited so rarely, even after he grew big enough to explore the city alone.

"I wanted to talk to you, Uncle Fitz. Man to man. This is not something I can discuss with Mama. But I want to enlist. In the army. The Tenth Negro Cavalry."

I was startled you named the *Negro* Cavalry. It was my first indication that you had chosen a race, or it had chosen you. "The army, my boy?" I said with a nervous laugh. "You're too young to think about the army."

"I am fifteen."

I was startled again. I had not noticed you get so old. But then, I did not want to acknowledge that this boy in my care had reached a sensual age. I took on a distant, colder, manly tone.

"That's still too young. You've been reading too many adventure stories."

"I finish high school next year, Uncle. And I must decide what to do with my life."

"But the army, Trist? War is an ugly business. Do you want to kill Indians? You once wanted to be an Indian, remember?"

"I was a child. Now I am a man. I want to live a man's life. Riding, shooting, marching. In the company of other men."

"Think of your poor mother. What would she do without you?"

He frowned and turned away, looking like a child again. "I would miss her. But I can't be her little boy my whole life."

"Well, for another year at least. Finish high school and think about it again. But don't be fooled by the brass bands and banners. War is nothing but murder. Mud and murder. Your father and I saw it firsthand, and there was no glory."

I was not above using your father to make my point. I argued out of self-interest as well as for your sake and your mother's. I did not want to lose you. I was afraid of getting too close to you, but I did not want to lose you either.

The martial urge had passed by the time you were graduated. So you were spared the Spanish-American War, where so many soldiers, colored as well as white, died in Cuba of yellow fever. Instead we sent you to business college, a private college in the city, where you learned the shorthand and typewriting skills that an old man now mercilessly exploits.

You loved your mother very much, and she loved you. She loved both her children, of course, but you were easier company, quiet and self-contained. You kept all troublesome thoughts to yourself.

Augusta, on the other hand, troubled her. The changes of mood increased as she grew older. She was sullen one minute, sweet the next, with ten minutes of sulk to each minute of joy. She tried to keep it bottled up in good manners—nobody was more ladylike than Augusta in her teens—yet, unlike her brother, she was not afraid of talking back to her mother. There were arguments, first about clothes, then about the hours spent at Greenwich Hall—"You give more time to strangers than to your own family." The disagreements became so commonplace that Alice stopped reporting them to me. I was present, however, for the very worst one.

It was a Sunday, my day of rest, and raining. I was sitting by the parlor stove in my dressing gown, sipping a cup of tea, when Alice and Augusta came back from church. I heard them bickering on the stairs and bickering in the hall as they shook out and hung up their waterproofs.

"Absolutely not," repeated Alice as they came through the door. "You must tell him no."

"But why, Mother? Explain," demanded Augusta. She was a full head taller than Alice, and height gave her authority. Alice still wore the heavy brown brocades of ten years earlier, so she looked even older than she was, and less intimidating.

Alice frowned at me. "Not another word. We'll continue this when we're alone."

But we were rarely alone, which was how we managed to avoid discussing so many things. I do not know where Tristan was. Perhaps the first strains of argument on the walk home made him decide that this was a good day for a stroll, despite the rain.

"Mother, I am no longer a child," Augusta persisted. "I am eighteen. I require an explanation."

I offered to leave, but Augusta said, "No, I want Uncle Fitz to hear this. Let's find out what he thinks."

"Your uncle's opinion is of no matter here."

It didn't matter to Augusta either, but a new ear gave her a chance to start over again, which she did, mother and daughter standing before me like two lawyers arguing before the bench.

The situation was simple enough. Augusta regularly took tea at the home of one of the Greenwich Hall ladies, a Miss Schiff. Last week Miss Schiff's younger brother joined them. He was quite taken with Miss Kemp, visited Greenwich Hall a few days later, and invited Augusta to accompany him to the theater next week—without his sister.

"The proper response is obvious," said Alice. "You must thank him for his attention but tell him it's out of the question."

"But *why* is it out of the question?"

"I do not trust this young man's intentions."

"How can you say that? You've never met him."

Alice's gorge was up, but she kept her temper. "Just ask yourself, missy. What does he want from you? Since marriage is out of the question."

Augusta glared at her mother. "Why?" she demanded. "Because he's a Jew?"

All the ladies at Greenwich Hall were German Jews, but Alice had not yet considered that barrier. She did not want to say it, but Augusta was forcing her hand.

"No," she began. "It is because of what . . . *we* are."

There. It was said. But Augusta faced her mother as coolly as ever. "Don't you mean because of what I am?"

"Please, my love. Be reasonable."

Augusta drew herself up. "You will not *do* to me what you did to our father!"

Alice's face fell open. "What? What do you mean?"

"You will not make me feel inferior. You will not drive me out because of the color of my skin."

Alice swayed, then grabbed the back of a chair to support herself. She stared at me with wide, shocked eyes, as if I could explain how her daughter had arrived at this assumption.

"Augusta," I said, "we did not drive him out. We loved your father. Your mother loved him very much."

"Then why did he leave us? And don't tell me he was looking for work, because I've never believed that."

Alice remained too stunned to speak. She felt her way around the chair in her hands and sank into it.

"He left because of me," I said. "Because of things I said and did. He blamed himself for the death of Lady Ashe and her son. I tried to dissuade him, but he feared he wasn't good enough to be your father. It was a mad, spur-of-the-moment decision."

I was afraid she'd ask for details, but she had too many other questions to bother with strangers from her childhood.

"Is he dead?"

I looked at Alice. This was her decision. She faced me with blank, frightened eyes, not knowing what to tell her daughter.

"Yes," I finally said. "He is."

"In a train wreck in Montana?" Augusta sneered, daring me to repeat that preposterous fabrication.

"No," I said. "We lied about that. We did. And we regret it. But the truth was so awful."

I kept pausing, so that Alice could jump in and contradict me with the truth. But she only watched in stunned silence, letting me, the better prevaricator, take charge.

"He died in Norfolk, Virginia," I said. "When a mob was about to lynch an innocent colored man and your father came to his defense. They shot him down in cold blood."

Augusta gasped. Alice turned away.

"We learned about it only after we came home from Europe. He had written us, in care of your mother's cousin in Stamford. He was going to rejoin us. Then a friend in Norfolk, an old barber with whom Isaac had been staying, wrote to us with the terrible news." I drew on the stories I'd been telling myself but chose a kinder, quicker death. "We didn't know how to tell you. For the longest time. And when we finally did, we could not bring ourselves to tell you the full, awful truth."

Augusta burst into tears. She fell on her knees and buried her face in her mother's lap. "Oh, Mother. Forgive me. Please forgive me. All these years I have blamed you for Papa's leaving."

Alice sat quite still, finding no relief in my lie. Then, gently, timidly, she began to stroke her daughter's hair.

"I do not hate your father," she said. "I have never hated your father. Nor despised the part of him that's in your blood. Do not think that. Never think that."

"We were going to tell you the truth," I said. "One day. When you were old enough to bear it. Have you discussed this with Tristan?"

"Never. Because he's too young, and I want to protect him," she admitted. "No, these are things I have thought and suspected but shared with nobody."

"When I tell you to say no to this young man," said Alice, "it's because I want to protect *you*. Not because I don't think you're good enough for him. I couldn't bear for you to be hurt."

"I know that, Mother. I knew that even when I said those awful words to you. I should never have said them. Can you forgive me? Will you please forgive me?"

"Of course. Will you forgive me?"

"Yes. I will. And I will be a better daughter. I promise."

They remained in that tableau for a full minute, barely moving, a sculpture of sighs and tears. Then Augusta slowly rose to her feet. "I will not mention this to Tristan."

"We will tell him, too," said Alice. "One day."

"But later," said Augusta. "When he is older. Uncle Fitz," she said, "you will not hate me for the things I said?"

"No, my dear, I could never hate you."

She stroked her own hair, the coarse, telltale hair of her father. "I need to be alone with this news," she said. "I am going for a walk." And she kissed her mother on the top of her head, took up her waterproof and umbrella, and went out.

Alice remained seated, stunned, all the moral stuffing knocked out of her. She looked so sad and helpless. I leaned forward and took her hand in mine. She did not snatch it away.

"Oh, Fitz," she said. "I did not want the children to hate their father. But I never dreamed that they might hate me."

"She never hated you, Alice. Even when she blamed you, she didn't hate you."

"It has come home to roost. All the lies and errors. I feared they would. And we have only covered it with a new lie." She actually said "we."

"But it should make Augusta easier and more affectionate."

"Perhaps. But her life will be as complicated as ever. Only instead of blaming me, she will blame herself." She shook her head. "There is no lie that can protect her from the trouble in her future. Still, a dead father is a more admirable example than a live one who abandoned her." A new idea crimped her eyes. "But he could be dead by now," she said. "The lie may be true."

"He's not dead," I told her.

She jerked her hand away and stared. "He writes to you? You've heard from him?"

"No. I am in touch with some spirits. They're more like ghosts than spirits now. But according to them, he's still among the living."

She did not scoff or sneer. She peered deep into my eyes, a long, worried gaze. Then she closed her lids and said, "I should be glad of that. I should not want him dead. But it would take the bitterness from my heart if he were."

Whether she believed me or not was of no matter. She was lost in her defeat, so lost and frail that I could not understand why I had feared her all these years. There is no other name for what I had felt. I had experienced sympathy, too, and admiration and some gratitude, but the chief emotion had been fear. I recognized that only now, when the fear was suddenly gone.

The next night I stayed late at the theater and played my ghost waltz again, in order to confirm what I had told Alice. I did not bother with a mirror—the ghosts were too faded now, but I could still glimpse their shadows on my closed eyelids. Isaac was not among them. Yet the dancing shades looked tired, dull, their turns as mechanical as the gears of a clock. The dead had driven out my spirits, and now they, too, were dying on me. But I was ready to let them go. Yes, it was time I let them go.

*　　*　　*

Tristan heard the new story of his father's death soon enough, first from Augusta, then his mother. It did not grieve the boy, however, but filled him with pride and romance. He barely remembered his father, but the story told him he had a hero's blood in his veins. I suspect it helped give Tristan his secret ballast in the years to come, his quiet strength.

Augusta did not attend the theater with young Mr. Schiff. She did not mention young men again but threw herself more fervently into work at Greenwich Hall. She became a full-time volunteer there after she finished high school, without pay, as if she came from a well-to-do family. Alice tried to persuade her to go to a teacher's college and get a certificate, so she might get a salary, but Augusta insisted this should be done for love, not money, and she wanted to do good, like her father.

Alice had been right. Her daughter remained as contradictory and divided as ever, with more guilt in her unstable mix of guilt, ambition, and love. Her unpredictable states of mind continued until she left home in 1899. Augusta went off to the Philippines with the Thomasites, a band of teachers sent over "to educate the heathen." She went as an assistant to her devoted friend, Miss Schiff. Augusta wanted to follow in the footsteps of her father, she said, but I suspect that she also needed to get away from us, her mother and brother and me, people whom she loved but who made her life so terribly complicated.

We took her to the train station, the old Grand Central Terminal, where the missionary ladies and gents gathered with their suitcases, steamer trunks, and tennis rackets. There was a sad, tender farewell. Augusta was openly warm with her brother—you were remarkably tolerant of her changing moods—and mother and daughter forgave each other all over again, swearing eternal love, which was easy to do at a parting.

Alice went into mourning after Augusta's departure, a week of deep melancholy followed by an angry burst of dissatisfaction. "Look at this flat," she said. "Look at this squalor. No wonder she had to

leave us." And Alice threw herself into a mania of cleaning, washing, and scraping, replacing curtains, even repainting the walls—
quite badly, I might add. Her fit lasted a month, until she burned
off her demons and seemed fine again, her frayed ends singed and
tucked neatly back into her heart.

After all, we still had Tristan. And I had a new job. That was
the summer that I started work at Coney Island.

57

PARADISE blazes in the night sky: luminous palaces, spectral towers, a radiant city of light. Constellations turn slowly along the horizon, like stars come to earth in great wheels of chance. There's the bubble and buzz of human bees, a singing of calliopes, the shrieks of joy from the pleasure engines.

No, it's not a dream. It was always too noisy to be mistaken for dreams. And I remained dreamless, without even a nightmare to my name. But this was Dreamland, so fantastic that it did all your dreaming for you.

I am getting ahead of myself. My first experience of Coney Island was at Steeplechase Park, where I performed in the summer when the theaters shut down. Dreamland was not yet built, but Coney was already amazing.

It was not the tawdry resort of dance halls and sideshows that it became after the Great War but a fantasia of the future, a vision of things to come, joyful, democratic, electric. Most homes and all streets were still illuminated by the sputtering jaundice of gaslight, but Edison's invention ruled here, incandescent bottles of blinding white curls whose beams were as bright as day. The Electric Eden was most spectacular at night. It glowed like an aurora borealis from the sea.

Most New Yorkers came and went on excursion boats that docked at the steel pier. We who worked there arrived at the back door by train; the subway did not reach Coney until after the war. People came to bathe in the sea, of course, and the beaches were thick with men and women in wet black cloth, like colonies of seals. But after their swim they visited the utopias of bliss.

There were three parks strung along Surf Avenue. The oldest was Steeplechase, with its downhill race of mechanical horses, naughty Blowhole Theater, and famous leering face atop the Pavilion of Fun. I was there for several summers, playing in the pavilion, enjoying the extra income and the ocean breezes that blew through the open glass panels.

Up the avenue on the land side was Luna Park, newer and fancier, with twice as many lights, fantastical fairyland architecture, and herds of elephants who freely wandered the grounds like towering stray dogs. I never worked there yet enjoyed visiting, just to look at the buildings and elephants.

But the finest park of all, the masterpiece, appeared one year after Luna Park, rising opposite it on the ocean side of Surf Avenue, a luxurious vision of the future: Dreamland.

People were so in love with the future back then, trusting that the new century would be heaven. Even I began to fall in love with the future, believing that the arrival of the future would mean we had escaped the past.

I need to get out of bed. I want to think at the piano. I feel terribly restless today. It must be the spring thaw outside, an aroma of blossoms and mud. But I suffer a restlessness like health. Let's continue this at the piano in the parlor.

We should go back to a spring day in 1905, on Twenty-third Street, where I still played the vaudeville houses, often without Carl. Unthan the Armless was frequently on tour, and I never joined Carl on the road but would perform with him in Hoboken or Brooklyn. I finished my three-thirty and went to my dressing room, where the stage manager gave me a card: SAMUEL W. GUMPERTZ. He said the man was waiting for me outside the stage door.

A scarlet motorcar filled the alley, a mammoth Stanley Steamer. Automobiles were not yet commonplace, and I warily approached the chugging machine. A goggled chauffeur stood beside it, holding a door open.

"Step right in!" a voice called out. "Welcome to my office, Doc." I entered a red morocco-leather interior occupied by a fat man with a bald head and beard who resembled the late Boss Tweed. He had a cheaply bound book in his lap.

"Gumpertz is the name, Sam W. Came today 'cause I been reading about you." He held up the book: *The Man Who Broke the Bank at Monte Carlo and Other Tales of Americans Abroad.* By M. L. Cunningham. The dime novel had gone out of print years ago, yet the pernicious old yarn was back, reborn in cloth. "You *are* the notorious Doctor August, ain't you?"

Gumpertz was not a detective investigating an old crime, however, but worked for W. H. Reynolds, an entrepreneur building a new park in Coney. Reynolds was a mogul of amusement, a Rockefeller of joy. Gumpertz was his right hand, booking acts for their first summer.

"We'll pay you two hundred a week. But we want this man." He slapped the book. "Not the two-bit comedy act I just saw."

"You want me to terrify people?"

"Don't want you giving anyone apoplexy. Just amaze 'em. Read minds and leave 'em wowed. The old table-rapping guff, wrapped up in good music. We're a class act, you see. How you do it is none of my business. But if you can manage it, hell, we'll give you your own theater. All right, then. You got my card. Give me an answer in a day or two. Now, get out of here, Doc. Time is money. Good day." He waved me out of his office with a smile, the chauffeur climbed into the front seat, and the rubber-wheeled teakettle released a hiss and chugged away.

I discussed the offer with Alice that night. It was more money than we'd seen since Europe. And the chance to have my own theater? But I needed a partner, a "gideon" who could work the crowd and pick up the secrets needed by a mind reader. The gideon might also serve as a plant, a spectator who could faint or scream or cry out, "Yes, yes, that's the spirit of my dead sister!" or what have you.

"Do you think Tristan would be interested?"

"Absolutely not," said Alice. "We cannot expose him to that life. Besides, he has a very good job."

He had finished business school and was working at *The New York Age*, a colored newspaper uptown, the same weekly, in fact, that once called itself *The Freeman*. Tristan wanted to write but worked in their business department, which actually paid better.

"I'll have to find someone I can trust," I said. "I will ask around the theater. Maybe Carl will have some ideas."

Alice put on her deadest deadpan face. "What about me?"

"*You?*" I laughed—it was a good joke, but Alice didn't even smile. "You're serious?"

"Why not? Just look at me. Who would expect such a gloomy spinster to be part of a deception?"

I could not argue with that. "But the deceit, Alice? The dishonesty. You would not enjoy it." Nor be good at it either, I thought.

"I have spent my life deceiving people I love," she replied. "It should be a relief to deceive strangers. And I want to go back into the world. I am sick of my own company. Please, Fitz. Give me a chance. Maybe I'll be bad at it, but I want to try."

"Very well, then. Yes. We can try."

And so we went to Dreamland, Alice and I together.

Gumpertz and Reynolds were determined to outdo the competition, and they succeeded. Dreamland was a monumental affair of white façades around an artificial lagoon, a horseshoe of alabaster like the Chicago Exposition. Imposing by day, it was magical at dusk, when the sky faded and the lights came on, a million electric lights. Each cornice, corner, doorway, and window was outlined in bright white beads. Everything melted in halos. At the end of the lagoon, looming over the park like a motionless waterfall of light, stood Beacon Tower, a replica of the Campanile in Venice, but taller, electrified. A pair of searchlights at the summit stroked and lanced the starry heavens.

It was all plaster and lath, and all replicas: the Casino of Monte Carlo, the Doge's Palace—the front for a Venetian canal with singing gondoliers—a few of acres of Alps, and a squashed mosque said to be Santa Sofia. Pieces of my life cartooned in plaster of paris, they housed such shows as The Fall of Pompeii or The Galveston Flood. It had been years since the last war—"a splendid little war" with Spain did not count—and people adored catastrophes. A structure called Fighting the Flames featured a burning tenement put out twice a day by trained firemen. Watching the artificial blaze during my dinner break—I worked next door—I remembered all my old dreams of fire. But our new century had tamed fire, reduced it to spectacle. We had tamed hell, too, and one of the most popular attractions was Hell Gate. A giant winged figure of Satan peered over the roof of a funhouse where audiences filed past living tableaux of devils seizing boys who drank a single glass of beer or girls who admired themselves too long in a mirror. They dragged them down to a perdition of fluttering paper flames while the crowds laughed in godless glee.

So no, Dreamland was not as high-toned as it pretended. We had the Dreamland Chute, a high pier that jutted out over the ocean and sent little boats screaming down a slide to skip like stones over the lagoon. But we also had The Infant Incubators, a display of glass wombs that saved actual premature babies from death. There was a zoo with lions, tigers, zebras, and a giraffe; a wax museum full of infamous murderers; and Lilliputia, a toy village populated entirely by midgets.

All the wonders of the world, past, present, and future, were concentrated in sixty acres, and I was one of them.

I had my own theater, the Pavilion of Harmonia, a copy of the Paris Opéra, or so they claimed, tucked between Fighting the Flames and The Canals of Venice. The façade was three times as high as the tar-roofed interior, with six-foot-tall papier-mâché busts of Beethoven and John Philip Sousa flanking the door. It seated only two hundred, which was a good size for my act. Six shows daily. Ten cents admission. "Come hear the music of the spheres," cried our monkey-suited ballyhooer, Big Mahoney, whose brother, Little Mahoney, worked the lights and curtain. "Uncanny! Unearthly! Mysterious!" he shouted, and if that didn't get them, added, "The notorious Dr. August! His supernatural sonatas once terrified a family to death. Are you brave enough to listen?"

Men and women in summer whites and identical flat straw hats purchased tickets and poured into the foyer, working-class people out for a taste of aristocratic luxury, good middle-class folk come to escape the girdle of propriety. They were kept waiting in the foyer, where a solitary bespectacled lady in old-fashioned brown brocade always waited with them. A harmless-looking biddy, she went from one conversation to the next, asking the nosiest questions. The poor thing was lonely, people thought. When the doors finally opened and the crowd entered the theater, the lady slipped off to look for "facilities," never to return.

Alice made an unconvincing plant, which required acting abilities beyond her, but she turned out to be an excellent gideon. She played the part with surprising ruthlessness, or no, she was not ruthless, but remarkably tough, sly, even vindictive at times. "That haughty dowager in the front row needs to be brought down a peg or two," she would report when we stood at the peepholes in the curtain. Or "A spoiled boy of ten is making life miserable for his mother. You might put the fear of God in him." But she could be kind, too. "There's a mother with a sick child at home. She can't stop fretting about him. Tell her something to make her feel better."

The audience settled in and faced the closed curtain. The theater was warm and airless; we kept the sidings down to make people sleepy and suggestible. Then, without warning, the lights went out. There is nothing like plunging an audience into darkness to disorganize their wits. They gasped, murmured, and giggled worriedly. Then they heard music, this music. Remember, Tristan? My "Dreamland Waltz Variations"—"Meet Me Tonight in Dreamland," played softly, so softly that everyone became utterly still. The curtain whispered open on a dark stage like a softer darkness, and people saw only the faint shape of a grand piano that appeared to be playing itself. The keyboard was turned upstage, and I played bent down, hiding behind the piano. I slowly sat up, a silhouette rising from a coffin. And then, as I leaped into Saint-Saëns's *Danse Macabre*, a red lightbulb on the music stand was turned up, illuminating me from below, a demon playing a bed of burning coals.

Simple, so simple, yet audiences loved it. The opening always earned me a murmur of spooked appreciation, followed by applause when I got up and came forward.

"Ladies and gentlemen," I began, "my name is Dr. August. I bid you welcome. To my strange world of music and spirits."

What followed was more or less the same act I'd been doing since Huber's Palace Museum, but performed with solemnity, eerie lighting, and genuine revelations, courtesy of Alice. I called people up, sat them in a spotlight, put on my blindfold, and read their musical souls. The difference was chiefly in their expectations. When people come to laugh, it's easy to make them laugh. When they come to be scared, the same material can unnerve and disturb them. Each performance ended as it began, in red light, darkness, and silence. When the houselights came back on, I heard them outside the curtain, confused and light-headed, but pleasantly so, as if after a strong cigar.

I was pure mountebank now, never pretending to myself that my performances represented any kind of truth. Alice treated our work as a charade, a game, a job. The only satisfaction she would admit to was the opportunity to discover again and again that people were

not what they seemed. Yet she was secretly amused by her partic-
ipation. She would never confess it, but she was tickled to be part
of something so improper. She was not even distressed by the company we kept.

One afternoon our first summer, after the house emptied out and
we opened the curtain and stage door to air the place—the stage
door faced an alley and the back wall of the Canals of Venice—I
stood down front and loosened my tie, glad the next show wasn't
for another hour.

"August? Dr. August?"

I looked out and saw nobody in the haze of dust that floated
under the lights after each crowd departed. Then I looked down
and saw her, an ugly child with a tiara and a silk fan, like a porcelain doll in a cotton-boll wig.

"I am the Countess Magri," she said in an eerie grown-up soprano. It was one of the midgets from Lilliputia.

"How do you do," I replied and bowed, a bit ironically.

"You have a lovely touch at the keyboard. Pity you have to play
trash. Am I mistaken, or did I catch a few bars of Schumann?"

Nobody remembered Schumann now, and I was instantly all respect. I offered her my hand to help her up the steps, so that we
might discuss Schumann with less difference in altitude.

Alice came out. She blinked nervously as I introduced her to the
royal homuncula. I thought she would flee, but she gathered up her
courage and said, "We were going to have tea before our next show.
Would you care to join us?"

"I can't say that I'd mind a taste," she replied. I brought out a
footstool for her, Alice brought out the tea, and we had a nice little
tea party right there on the stage.

Magri was in her seventies and actually was a countess, by marriage to Count Magri, an Italian midget. They were the stars of
Lilliputia, though Lavinia—born Lavinia Warren Bump—once
knew greater fame. She had been discovered by Barnum when she
was twenty and married off with much publicity to his world-

renowned headliner, General Tom Thumb. The newlyweds visited
the White House and met President Lincoln. But it was not a good
match. Thumb was a souse and a boor, said Lavinia, while she loved
art, literature, and good music. She had her own piano at their
cottage in Lilliputia—only the Lilliputians lived at Dreamland—a
child's Bösendorfer with a reduced keyboard but a much richer
sound than my instrument. She invited me to come play "real music" for her, which I began to do regularly.

Alice and I ended many evenings as the guests of the count and
countess before going home, two freakish giants stooping under a
low ceiling among the child-size furniture. "Oh, the times we have
seen, August, the times we have seen," Lavinia would sigh after too
much Schumann and sherry, then launch into another tale of her
past. We amiably competed with one another over encounters with
the great, though Lavinia won hands down. As for Count Magri, he
was a stuffy little poppet who enjoyed basking in his wife's fame.
He didn't seem to mind when she still referred to herself as Mrs.
General Tom Thumb.

A new gentility was creeping in, and vaudeville grew uncomfortable with freaks, which was what brought Lavinia to Dreamland.
Carl, too, found life harder, and was reduced to performing in car-
nival sideshows. I brought him out for a few summers, happy to
repay him for his years of friendship by making him part of my
act.

So Alice finally met Carl, as well as Lavinia and other curious
folk. And she was perfectly at ease with them, much to her surprise
as well as mine. "I am sure they pity me," she confessed one evening
on our long train ride home. "But I pity them, and so it makes us
equals."

As Alice took a kind of comfort there, so I took mine in animals.
If I could not have spirits, I could at least have beasts. In addition
to admiring the elephants at Luna Park, I often visited the Dreamland zoo, gazing at the giraffe, tropical birds, and sleeping lion.
There are those wonderful lines by the Good Gray Poet:

I could turn and live with animals, they are so placid and self-
contained,
I stand and look at them long and long;
They do not sweat and whine about their condition.
They do not lie awake in the dark and weep for their sins....

That was what I wanted for myself, their dumb state of grace, their perfect peace. And there were days when I thought I had obtained it.

We were doing quite well now financially. We had one fewer mouth to feed and two incomes—Tristan became the business manager at the *Age*. He still lived at home, which pleased Alice but worried me; I wondered if the example of his parents' marriage had frightened him into bachelorhood. And we got out of Bank Street and moved to the country, or rather, the suburban reaches of Harlem. We bought a whole brownstone there, the very house where we sit today. The subway had opened up the rock-strewn wastes to the north, but the developers overbuilt and were desperate to sell off the row houses stranded in clusters on the wide, treeless avenues. The down payment was surprisingly low. The developers even allowed a few colored families in, good middle-class churchgoers who moved here from San Juan Hill, the Negro neighborhood.

As for Augusta, she spent three years in the Philippines. She wrote to her mother every month, then every two months. Then she wrote from San Francisco and said she would not be returning. She was staying in California to teach, and she had met a man, a successful businessman who seemed quite smitten with her. The next letter invited us to their wedding. She carefully worded her regret that San Francisco was probably too far for us to attend.

"He is white," said Alice. "He must be. Or she would bring him east. A gentleman of color would have no difficulty accepting us. But a white man might not understand."

"I'm sorry, Alice. It must be a grave blow to you."

"Don't be sorry," she said. "I am glad. I truly am," she insisted. "I'm happy for my daughter. She can live as white, and her life will be easier. It's sad to say, but it's true."

Augusta sent us a set of wedding photos, with a note from her husband thanking Mrs. Kemp for raising such a fine daughter. He said he was sorry that we could not come to the wedding but hoped we would get to California one day. The pictures showed Augusta, prettier than ever in a bridal veil, standing beside a wedding-cake groom with big teeth, big mustache, and skin as white as salt.

Alice knew her daughter so well. She understood and forgave her, and it seemed sincere, but I noticed she was harsher than usual to young women during our act that summer, bringing me more reports of ungrateful girls who showed greater love for clothes or parties than they did for their mothers.

58

AND yet, when all was said and done, we had made a good life for ourselves. A good enough life.

You think your life is over, that all that remains are a few more years and death. But here in the new century we achieved a workable happiness, a good enough life.

No wonder I still believe in life after death. I lived so many lives after death here on earth.

It took me time to recognize the change, however, to understand that our grim melancholy was over. The idea that we might even be happy didn't strike me until our picnic in Central Park, a farewell party for Unthan the Armless Wonder. Carl and his wife were going home to Germany.

There were a half dozen of us in a bosky woodland glade, camped on the green grass with tablecloths, hampers, and stools. From a distance we looked like any social club on a quiet Saturday. Only when people strolled closer did they notice our oddity: the count and countess like two pugs in fancy dress, Carl with his serpentlike torso, and Shadrach, untransparent in a suit but his head as pale as candle wax. Even the "normal" folk were odd: fat Frau Unthan, who did not speak a word of English after all her years in America; Alice, with her pince-nez "nippers" and long buttoned sleeves of the last century; and me, a desiccated elf whose oversize ears had reappeared as he lost his hair. We all looked remarkably old that day, especially in the presence of a tall young man in a celluloid collar and necktie. You were the finest specimen there, Tristan, handsome and easy, with a manly silence and infinite patience. You sat at your mother's feet like a courtly lover and passed her a plate of cold chicken.

"How luflee to be vith friends," Carl suddenly announced. "Life is good today. But I haf had a good life in America."

I was about to argue and remind Carl that he was going home because his vocation here had become humiliating. But then Alice—Alice, of all people—said, "Yes. Life can be wonderful. We'd be fools not to enjoy it."

If Alice could feel that, then it must be true. If she were happy, then happiness was real.

"You are a lucky woman," Lavinia piped up and nodded at Tristan. "To have such a wonderful, devoted son."

"Oh, yes," said Alice with a smile. "Only we must not say so in his presence. It embarrasses him."

All the old folks gazed on Tristan in admiration and envy. Tristan looked down, but even in embarrassment he was a good sport. He accepted us with a placid smile, amused by the gentle comedy of his mother, uncle, and the other freaks.

Tristan had more important things on his mind, a whole other life apart from us. Work at the *Age* involved him in literary and political talk down at Marshall's Hotel in San Juan Hill, the watering hole for what Dr. Du Bois called the Talented Tenth. Tristan admired W. E. B. Du Bois, editor and author, so much that he grew a chin beard and mustache like his hero's, although it reminded me of his father's beard—Isaac's beard on Alice's face. Tristan never chastised us for being innocently white or politically naïve. He was as private about his politics as he was about so much else, yet he did spill an occasional scornful remark about Booker T. Washington, "The Wizard of Tuskegee." Tristan believed that Du Bois's politics offered the best road into the future, while Washington preached only humility and submission. Tristan went to Niagara Falls, not for a honeymoon but for a political convention: Du Bois was organizing a new association to aid the Negro.

It was too complicated for me to follow, and Alice did not want her son involved in anything dangerous, but I was glad that Tristan had something to believe in.

So the new century looked good. We now know that it wouldn't begin until 1914 and that this was only the Indian summer of the old century. My own nineteenth century ended a few years before the Great War, yet the modern age was already making itself felt.

I saw my first aeroplane at Coney Island. It was 1909, and the newspapers were full of reports of these mechanical sprites. One afternoon we heard a buzz over the ocean, like a Moslem call to prayer. A hush came over the park, and we rushed outside to see why. People were staring at the sky, as if Jehovah Himself had appeared in the clouds. There it was, an aeroplane, like an elaborate box kite without strings.

That was the summer that Sigmund Freud visited Dreamland.

I actually met the man. I didn't know who he was at the time—few people did—but he visited New York and came out to Coney Island one afternoon with three other doctors: an American, a Hungarian, and a Swiss with a shaved head. The American brought the others up after my performance, a pack of professors as giddy as schoolboys on holiday. When I misheard the name of the man with the gray spade beard as "Dr. Fraud," I briefly thought they were vaudeville artists like myself. The spade beard and the shaved head did not appear to get along. The American did all the talking, laughing over the fact that "We scientists of fairy tale have come to Dreamland." The spade beard grumbled in German, pointed at my piano, mimed playing a keyboard, and said something about *"le vice solitaire."*

Meanwhile the "flickers" had arrived. There had been peep shows and kinetoscope parlors and brief screenings at variety houses, like moving magic-lantern shows. But now there were one- and two-reeler movies with *stories,* and theaters that showed nothing but flickers. The pictures themselves did not impress me, but I was intrigued by the musical accompaniment. It was usually a violinist and a pianist—full orchestras did not come until later—and they told the story better than the dumb show on the screen. It resembled my own spiritual improvisations, only everyone saw the images that produced the tunes. Well, I thought, if people grow bored with my mystery, I can always find a new career as a singer of shadows.

A heady time of science and technology, the future looked grand, glorious. The only portent of things to come was the electrocution of an elephant.

It happened at Coney Island, not at Dreamland but across the street at Luna Park. One of their elephants, an old pachyderm named Topsy, killed a man who fed her a lit cigarette. The management decided Topsy must be destroyed. They initially wanted to hang her in public and sell tickets, but after protests from the Society for the Prevention of Cruelty to Animals, they decided to give her a private, modern death instead. Thomas Edison's scientists had discovered a new use for electricity. What better place to test it than here in Electric Eden?

Alice could not understand why I wanted to witness this barbarism. I liked the elephants at Luna Park, their peace and grandeur, but couldn't distinguish one from another. I had no special feeling for Topsy. No, I went out of morbid curiosity.

It was a gray, foggy morning. The Edison laboratory brought dynamos over from New Jersey, and a motion-picture camera to record the deed. Fifty of us gathered in the empty field in overcoats and derbies. No women were present. We waited for half an hour. Then Topsy emerged from the mist, a dark, lumbering shadow led by a pack of handlers. Her keeper did not participate but stood at the far end of the field, watching in disgust. One handler fed her handfuls of caramels as they approached. She looked so large and serene, as tall as a church, as solid as a pyramid, one live eye gazing from a dry wall of wrinkled flesh.

She stood by patiently while the handlers fussed with chains and the Edison people attached their cords, one to her right foreleg, the other to her left rear leg. The gasoline motor for the dynamo was turned on. The handler fed her one last handful of caramels and stepped back. We all stepped back, afraid she might explode or burst into flames.

"Now!" someone said, and the switch was thrown.

Topsy did not make a sound. She only stiffened, as though startled by a new idea, as if she suddenly understood everything. Puffs of smoke poured from the cords at her hooves, like she was getting a hotfoot. She abruptly keeled to one side and hung there a moment, suspended by a chain around one extended leg. Then she folded to the earth, and the earth shuddered.

A long sigh came from the mountain of flesh, like a death rattle of the cosmos. And there was silence, a silence deeper than silence, as though the world had stopped turning. Wisps of smoke rose from her mouth, ears, and anus.

Nobody laughed, nobody spoke. We stood around the great corpse, stunned by shame, confused by sorrow. An eye remained open. Her mouth gaped wide, a wedge of pink in an ash-gray face.

And I suddenly knew: He is dead. Isaac is dead.

I cannot say how I knew, or why. It invaded me in a rush: Topsy's death was a sign. It had already happened, long ago. My Metaphysicals chose Topsy to tell me that Isaac was no more.

We approached her, wanting to touch yet fearful, afraid the corpse would spark like an electric battery. Then one man touched her, and there was a laying on of hands all around. The flesh was warm when I set my own hand on her mammoth sculptural brow. Isaac is no more, I thought. Isaac is dead. I stroked a huge ridge of bone beneath the unknotted furrow of hide.

It took only minutes for the men around me to overcome their shame and decide this was just a dumb beast, its death a lark, a hoot. They joked among themselves and plucked thick hairs from her chin and ears for souvenirs. I turned and walked away.

As I crossed the avenue to Dreamland, the universe felt emptied by a sudden absence, and not just the death of an elephant. I entered the Pavilion of Harmonia. There was nobody here yet, and I sat at my piano. I was full of questions and fears and did not know how to answer them except to try my ghost waltz again. Would I see Isaac among the dancers? Would he dance alone? Would he dance with Freddie?

But the waltz was gone. Oh, I could play it from memory, but there were no ghosts now, no drafty presences. Isaac had died and taken my ghosts with him.

It was over. It was finished. And I was both sorry and glad. I was free from Isaac and my ghosts. I was no longer a slave to either. Yet I felt a confusion similar to what Isaac must have felt when he said good-bye to his masters.

I was suddenly full of things I wanted to tell him: You arrogant sinner. You were so full of principles. I had no principles, but you had too many. You believed that things were black or white and could not see that most of life is lived in shades of gray. Your wife and children were your heart and soul. You punished yourself by rejecting them, but you punished them as well. You could not distinguish your soul from theirs? I hope God understands and forgives you, because I certainly don't.

And yet I did forgive him, now that he was dead, even as I recognized how angry I had been. All these years. A knotted, complicitous, guilt-ridden anger. He had abandoned his family, increased my sin, trapped me in a difficult life. I had imagined brutal deaths for him so that I might feel pity instead of anger. I understood those fantasies only now when he was gone. Death put anger in the past tense. I recognized the depth of my fury even as I let go of it and forgave him. The dead are so much easier to forgive than the living.

Alice arrived at ten sharp, unpinned her hat, and irritably asked, "Did you enjoy your execution?"

"No," I said. "It was sad. Very sad." I hesitated. I swallowed. "Sad and meaningless."

Because I could not tell her. She would think I was mad again, insane to mistake the death of an elephant for the death of her husband. She wanted him to be dead, or so she said. But if she believed me, I did not know what it might do to her. No, it seemed cruel and pointless to upset Alice when she had finally found peace, and so I kept the revelation to myself.

I waited for my Metaphysicals to return to my music now that my ghosts were gone, but they had nothing further to say after the death of Topsy.

59

SUDDENLY it was 1911. Such an odd-numbered year means nothing now, yet it was the year of the Triangle Shirtwaist Fire. We thought we were through with fires, but there was a terrible blaze that spring in a ninth-story sweatshop near Washington Square. It was also the year of "Alexander's Ragtime Band," which wasn't ragtime at all but became wildly popular, a monster hit. I was required to play it constantly.

Coney Island did not officially open until Memorial Day—Decoration Day had been renamed in an attempt to make it serious again—but it fell that year on a Tuesday, and Gumpertz did not want to miss the weekend trade. We opened on Saturday with much of Dreamland not yet in service.

Business was slow, though it picked up Sunday afternoon. Alice gathered her nuggets and joined me backstage at the curtain. She pointed out the usual girl-in-love, an elderly widow—I still did widows, I regret to say—and a man who had won big at the races. "The quartet of youths in the third row?" she said. "The one at the end made a recent conquest. His friends are teasing him. They say it's love, but he denies it."

"The colored youths?" I said. "That might not be wise." They were dressed like college students and could not have been more proper. There was no Jim Crow policy at Dreamland, but white workingmen sometimes got nasty if Negroes were brought to their attention.

"If he gets mocked, he has it coming to him," said Alice. "He and his friends are sniggering over your 'musical flimflam.' "

"I'll have to take the measure of the house first." I sat at the piano and told Little Mahoney to hit the lights.

The opening worked its magic, and the audience was a good one. They were happy for the girl in love, sorry for the widow, and amused by the gambler, who denied his good fortune until I launched into "Camptown Ladies." He let out a laugh and said, "Damn me, how did you know?"

"There are no secrets from the spirits," I told him. "And no secrets from a man who knows their music." I escorted him offstage, returned to my piano, and drew my blindfold down again. "Ah, another musical sphere is making itself heard," I said. "The key of G minor, the key of masculine love. Yes? A young man. He is here with friends. Youths of a collegiate mien." I threw my head back as if straining to understand, but actually for a nose peek. His friends were already chuckling. "Yes, you, sir. On the aisle. Four rows back. No, three. Do you dare to learn what's really in your heart?" I stopped playing, pulled my blindfold up, and stepped forward. "Please, sir. You have nothing to fear. We are all friends here."

His chums nudged and poked and cajoled until he gave in. He was a slim youth of twenty with a pretty face and milk-chocolate skin. His straight hair shone like wet coal. There were no sounds of disapproval when I sat him in the spotlight. The audience was willing to follow me anywhere.

"Your name, sir?"

"Robert Brown." He spoke with a high, boyish tenor.

"Close your eyes, Mr. Brown. Do not attempt to block your thoughts. We shall see what I can discover."

I glanced over at Alice, who stood in the wings, safely out of the light. The boy looked nothing like a lady-killer, but she gave me a nod to indicate yes, this was the fellow.

I sat down again, readjusted the blindfold, and resumed playing. "Ah, yes, love," I said while I performed "I Could Love a Million Girls" in the style of Mozart. "You don't want it to be love, Mr. Brown, but it is love."

"Your spirits are certainly wrong there."

"Oh, no, my spirits are never wrong."

Conquest meant sex, of course, but that was too unseemly for me to mention in public.

"Your spirits can't ever guess who it is," he declared.

Out in the audience his friends laughed knowingly.

"It's not a matter of guessing, Mr. Brown. It's a matter of how much they will tell me. So there *is* someone."

"I'll say no more." He was on his guard now, and I needed to be more subtle.

"You should tell this someone your true feelings, Mr. Brown. Or else it might end badly." And to illustrate, I let my hands ease into the dissonant longing of Wagner's dreary old *Liebestod.* A European audience would have understood, but here I had to explain my musical allusions. "What's this? Wagner? *Tristan and Isolde.* And we know how their love ended, don't we, Mr. Brown?"

Silence.

I repeated the Wagner while I considered other ploys. There was a sudden mutter from the audience. I threw my head back again and saw that the boy was on his feet, glaring at me.

I stopped playing and removed my blindfold. "Mr. Brown. Have I offended you? I didn't mean to insult your love of Wagner," I joked, hoping to defuse his temper.

"Don't do this to me!" His voice was high, hysterical. "It's not fair! Why are you humiliating me?"

I had accidentally struck a nerve. It happened now and then. The subject went into a panic, and there was nothing I could do except ease him off the stage.

Brown stepped toward me, fists clenched at his sides. "He told me about your musical bosh!" He meant to whisper but was angrily audible. "My friends and I thought you'd be a laugh. But he told you about me. Didn't he? That bastard! And now you're telling the whole damned world!" Brown wheeled around and leaped off the stage, then plunged up the aisle and out the door.

I was stunned by his pronoun, paralyzed, but only for a moment before my stage persona reappeared. "Yes, ladies and gentlemen. There are secrets of the heart that we prefer nobody knows, not even the spirits. But as the Great Book says, 'Let he who is without sin . . .' "

The young man's panic made a good finish for this show. I bent over the piano and played the Dreamland waltz again, which was Little Mahoney's cue to snap off all the lights except the red bulb over the keyboard. Then he dimmed that one and closed the curtain. I did not stop playing until the houselights gleamed along the hem of the curtain. And I sat motionless at the keyboard, letting it all spill over me: He? The bastard? Who could the boy possibly mean? But I already knew.

Little Mahoney opened the stage door and stepped outside for a smoke. Only then did Alice come in from the wings. Her face was white, her lips bloodless.

"That was Tristan," she muttered. "Our Tristan. Who they were chattering about outside. But they called him 'her'? And that boy talked about him like some—some girl he had seduced?"

"No, it can't mean that. It must mean something else." But it meant something like that or else the name "Tristan" would not have instantly unhinged the fellow.

"That beast!" she said. "That vile little beast. He corrupted my son! He led him into vice! And came here today with his friends to laugh at us?" She clutched the open piano and stared into its steel nerves. "Oh, my God. My child has fallen into the hands of vipers."

"We can't assume he corrupted Tristan. He's younger than Tristan. Tristan is old enough to look after himself. He might even be in love with Tristan."

"Love?" She turned her outraged eyes on me. "That isn't love.

It's sin, it's iniquity, it's——" She blinked in confusion. "You *knew* about this? You've known such things were going on?"

"No. I never suspected it. Not in a hundred years." But we both must have suspected something, or we would not have understood so quickly.

She suddenly stiffened, much as Topsy had when the first jolt hit her. "Oh, my God," she said again. "*You* made him this way."

"Alice. No. We don't even know if he *is* that way!"

Her eyes were wide with horror. "*You* introduced him to this vice. You seduced him. When he was a boy? Like that other boy?"

I was too stunned by the accusation even to respond to it.

"That must be it," she said. "You seduced my son. You introduced him to your sin. Of course." She spoke rapidly, dryly, instantly imagining the worst. "I have shared my roof with a monster. And exposed my child to him. So it is my fault, too."

"No, Alice! No!" I jumped to my feet. "I have never touched our boy. *Our* boy. I have known him since he was a baby. I loved him and protected him as if he were my own. Believe me, Alice. Can't you believe me?"

She looked me in the eye, cold and fierce. I don't know what she saw, but it confused her horror, softened it. She had seized the idea much too quickly, as if she never quite believed it.

"But your example!" she charged. "Your presence!"

"He knows nothing about my past! And I have been celibate! I have been good! I have been as cool and manly around him as an uncle could be."

"But it wasn't enough, was it?" she snarled. "Your past, your spirits, your dreams—*something* did this to him!" She squeezed her eyes shut, then covered them with a hand. "It's like a punishment from God. I lose my husband, then my daughter, and now my son?"

"You haven't lost him, Alice—whatever this means. He still loves you. But we don't know what it means. We need to speak to Tristan and hear his side of it."

She lowered her hand and looked at me in alarm. "I cannot

mention this to him. I cannot let him know that I know. It makes me ill just to think of speaking to him about such things."

There was a loud knock on the stage door, Little Mahoney letting us know he was back. "People gathering out front. Mrs. Kemp might want to get out there."

"Thank you, Mahoney."

He departed, but his words had thrust Alice back into public life. She struggled to recover from her anger and confusion.

"I cannot go out there," she said. "When I think of how thoughtlessly I have handled other people's secrets? Never guessing that I would find one that would poison *my* heart. What a fool I have been. What a proud, arrogant fool."

"It's not the end of the world, Alice. Whatever the truth."

"But it is! I thought I had one perfect love. One love I could be proud of. But to know that my son is not pure? It hurts. I do not know why it hurts so much, but it does. I don't know how to live with it. I am going home, Fitz. I need to be alone with this wound. Good night."

I did the remaining shows alone. I performed badly, needless to say, without Alice's help and with so much on my mind. I was sorry for Alice, and sorry for Tristan. Like father, like son, I thought, yet could not say that to his mother. I was worried for Alice, frightened for her. But beneath my sorrow was a guilty feeling of hope, a curious gladness: Tristan and I had something in common? If he were "like that," I could advise and counsel my nephew. My hope was not romantic. Absolutely not. But I did feel oddly hopeful, as if I were suddenly less alone in the world. Yet the idea of such a bond opened me up to even more sympathy and fear for Alice. Her peace was not so deep or strong as she pretended.

You can burn these pages later. I know how humiliating they must be. But this, too, is part of the story, Tristan, and I need to share it. It's easier for me to tell when I can hear the *scritch, scritch, scritch* of your pencil. And maybe the chore of writing better enables you to listen as well.

60

Mother and son were both asleep when I got home that night. The park was closed to the public the next day. I did not have to be there until the afternoon to supervise preparations for the grand opening, so I slept late. When I went downstairs, however, Tristan was still home, reading a book in the sitting room. I feared words had already been said.

"You're not going in to work today?"

He said that his office was closed today.

"Where's your mother?"

"She has a terrible headache, she says. She wouldn't even let me come into her room. She said she cannot join you today."

"And that's all she said?"

"Yes. Was there anything else?"

"Oh, no. Nothing at all."

But the subject needed to be confronted. I wanted to confront it yet could not bring myself to do it here, with Alice up in her bedroom. Habits of privacy endured even when spread over three floors. And I found myself looking differently at Tristan, nervously, uncomfortably. He appeared as mild and private as ever, but I now knew the source of his privacy.

"Would you care to come to Coney with me today?" I proposed.

"Beautiful day. There'll be nobody there. You might enjoy the fresh air. And it would be nice to spend some time together."

And he promptly understood that something was up. "What did you want to discuss, Uncle?"

I took a breath, I took the risk. "A friend of yours came to the Pavilion of Harmonia yesterday. Mr. Robert Brown."

He did not shudder or blanch. He studied me a moment, adjusted his specs, and said, "I'll get my hat and coat."

We walked down the street toward the subway, an old man struggling to keep up with a young man's brisk, preoccupied lope. Neither of us spoke for the first block. Finally I said, "I brought him up onstage to read his mind. If I had even suspected you knew him, I would not have done it. Your private life is none of my business, Tristan. But your mother was there, and she understood what his words meant."

"What did the little fool say?"

I described what had happened, more or less. I feared that Tristan would blame me and my nosy spirits, but he frowned and said, "Robert is such a fool. I should never have told him about my 'musical uncle.' He wanted to show you off to his fairy friends. Serves me right. Yes, it serves me right. For falling in love with such a pretty fool."

He said it flatly, fearlessly, looking straight ahead and waiting a moment before he stole a sidelong glance at me.

"Are you disgusted with me, Uncle?"

"No. I am sad. But only for your sake. A fine man like yourself would make a good husband and excellent father. You should not let your parents' marriage deter you." I had not entirely given up on that as a cause for Tristan's failure to marry.

"But I don't love women," he said. "I never have. I love men. There's a name for people like me."

"Oh, yes. Sodomite."

"No. A medical name. Invert."

It did not sound like much of an improvement. "Well, a rose by any other name," I murmured.

"Is that why Mama took to bed?"

"Yes. It broke her heart. She thinks she's lost you."

"This has nothing to do with her. Nothing at all."

"I tried to tell her that."

We descended into the subway and could no longer speak. On the long ride downtown, Tristan sat beside me, calm and self-contained, an occasional fretful thought twitching his bland face. We crossed under the East River to the Brooklyn terminal and boarded the train to Coney Island. The car was nearly empty, and I decided that now was a good time to give him my advice.

"What I propose, Tristan, is this. Tell your mother she misunderstood. You feel only friendship for this boy. A romantic friendship, clean and virtuous. The boy's flattered to have an older man showing him attention, but there is nothing shameful in your relations."

"You want me to lie?"

"Lies are the oil that keep the machine of the world running smoothly, my boy. Hypocrisy is a virtue when there are other people to consider." I was tempted to admit my own hypocrisy and confess how much we had in common, but it would only confuse the issue. Instead I said, "Your mother has not had an easy life."

"I know." He frowned. "I do not want to grieve her. But it's such claptrap, Uncle. This living for other people. Do I have to wait till she's dead before I can live for myself?"

"Nobody is asking you to give up your life. Only that you live it discreetly, privately."

"Which I already do. Day in and day out. At the newspaper, at Marshall's, with my political friends. It's as private as dreaming." He let out a mild snort. "Well, my dreams anyway. But home should be a place for truth. A lie of omission is one thing, but the thought of a deliberate lie sticks in my craw."

"So you refuse?"

"No. I am only saying that I must think it over."

We arrived at Coney Island, walked up Surf Avenue, and entered Dreamland. The entrance arch was supported on the wings of a twenty-foot seminude woman, *The Creation*. Tristan looked up as we passed through and sighed. "Mothers." He had a droll sense of humor, which he didn't get from either of his parents.

Just inside the midway, in front of the cuckoo-clock façade of Lilliputia, we ran into Lavinia. "Hello, August. And young Mr. Kemp," she chirped. "Taking over for your ma this season?"

Tristan explained that he was only visiting and his mother would be back tomorrow.

"This new generation," she declared. "No sense of tradition. No desire to follow in the footsteps of their elders." She bade us good day and returned to her cottage to help the count with their house-cleaning for tomorrow.

The park was full of workmen renewing white paint, patching roofs with hot tar, replacing the clear beads of a thousand lightbulbs. There was more work to do at the Pavilion of Harmonia than I had anticipated, and Tristan excused himself to walk around and think things over, promising to return by dinnertime.

I was instructing Little Mahoney on how to hang the new posters outside when Big Mahoney came back from the front office. "Place is turning into Darktown," he grumbled. "Coons yesterday and more coons today." I thought he meant Tristan and nearly lost my temper before he added, "Pack of darky preachers getting a tour. Booker T. Washington's people. Come to New York to meet with King Coon hisself. Even they want to see Coney Island."

We were still out front when a pride of elderly ministers paraded past. No, not a pride but a shuffle of preachers. They looked awe-struck by Babylon. They were all from the sticks, this was their first time in New York, and they had never seen anything like Dream-land. The Wizard of Tuskegee was not with them. For a laugh, Big

Mahoney launched into his ballyhoo—"Come hear the notorious Dr. August, musical magician!"—and the preachers amiably smiled, all except one. I thought I saw one righteous eye glaring from the pack of smiles. I looked again but couldn't find it in the parfait of white hair, dark faces, white collars, and black coats. I had imagined it, a righteous eye like Isaac's. Isaac was dead, but talk with Tristan had put him back in my thoughts, and the sight of any gentleman of color made me think of him again.

I had forgotten the righteous eye by the time Tristan returned. He had picked up a bag of red hots for dinner, and we ate them outdoors, sitting on our handkerchiefs on the wide stone steps that led down to the beach. A powdery blue dusk sifted over the ocean; a sliver of moon rose over the gentle surf.

Tristan had come to a decision. "I *will* lie to her," he said. "Out of consideration for her feelings, however, not from shame. I feel no shame."

"Nobody is asking you to feel shame. I am only requesting that you behave with discretion."

"Discretion?" He snorted and shook his head. "Oh, yes, discretion. Like the sorry Uncle Toms wandering the park today?"

"You saw them?"

"Godly bunch of watermelon-eaters. No wonder my race is stuck in the mud."

"Well, it's no shame to be colored," I said. "Nor is it illegal. But it is illegal to love men. You leave yourself open to blackmail."

"Is that what stopped you all these years, Uncle? Fear of blackmail?"

I looked at him. His expression was not chiding, however, but kind and open. So he knew. Of course. I did not want to lie but could not tell him the full truth either. "Oh, I loved a few men in my youth. But now I am old, and all I want is friendship. I miss it. Sometimes. But my life is less complicated without it."

"Love does make life complicated," Tristan admitted. "I enjoy it each time it starts but am relieved each time it passes. Until it starts over again, and I think, 'Maybe this one will endure.' Robert is not my first."

"Nor the last?"

"I hope not." He laughed, a hearty laugh like a full confession that Mr. Brown was more trouble than he was worth.

And that was all we said. We did not talk about Mr. Brown or Tristan's other loves, or mine either, but we had said enough. We watched the light fade in an affectionate, complicitous silence. Then Tristan stood up to go home. He said he would wait for the proper moment to bring up Mr. Brown with his mother.

"Do not put it off too long," I warned him. "We do not want to prolong her suffering." And he agreed.

I told him I would catch a later train. "I have business to finish here." He thanked me for my understanding, friendship, and "discretion," we shook hands, and he departed.

61

THE ocean blended with the twilit sky, the low waves curled along the sand, and I remained on the steps, lost in a reverie of remembrance. Like father, like son, I told myself again. But Tristan was not sin-wracked and God-haunted like his father. And Isaac had never loved men, only me, and only briefly. He'd loved Alice longer, but that, too, had passed. Whom did he love now that he was dead?

The park was still a bright, noisy hive as I walked back to the Pavilion of Harmonia, with banging hammers and a rich aroma of hot tar. Lights turned on and off on as circuits were tested, and portions of the midway went bright, then dark again, as if the park were thinking. I told the Mahoneys to go home. It was a long day tomorrow, and I would close up.

I sat at the piano and opened the keyboard. I wanted to try the ghost waltz again. I hoped to see Isaac. The sweet agitation in my chest and arms suggested that it might happen tonight.

I began the tune. The phrases gathered under the closed lid, wistful, tentative, sad, but then evaporated in the dusty glare of the stage. I played it again. Nothing. Nothing at all. It was just music, without a spook in sight, like a sentimental old song once performed for a friend who was now gone.

When I played it a third time, I rebelled against the sentimentality and began to rag it, as a joke, a laugh, using the happy crippled hop to thumb my nose at the dead.

"Augustus Fitzwilliam Boyd?"

I heard a voice in the piano, a mumble of syllables in the bass notes. A cold chill passed over my spine. I stopped and stared at the keys.

"Fitz? Look at me."

A deep voice. Like Isaac's voice. I looked up from the keyboard. His ghost floated beside the piano. Or no, not *his* ghost but the ghost of an old man who could have been his father. His hair was gray moss, his beard a white frost around his mouth and scored cheeks. He wore a black patch over his right eye and a clerical collar around his throat. He held a cane in one hand and rested the other on the piano, a large, sepia hand with yellowish fingernails. He looked awfully corporeal.

I stood. The specter did not lose its focus.

"It's you," I said. "You?" I touched his chest with the flat of my palm. There was bone in the black shirt. "You're real? You're alive?"

"You sound disappointed."

"No. Not disappointed but— Surprised. Very surprised."

I was too stunned to feel joy. My knees were all nerves and water. I slowly lowered myself to the piano stool again.

We were on a bright, bare stage, like a scene from a play watched by two hundred empty chairs. But in a melodrama our reunion would be a joyful thing, and joy would carry us through the shocking strangeness. I felt only uncertainty, disbelief, and fear. Isaac, too, seemed afraid.

"When I saw you today," he said, "I couldn't believe it was you. But then that fellow started howling 'Dr. August,' and I knew it was you. Still up to your old tricks."

"So you *were* there. I thought of you when I saw those men today. But I did not see you."

"Well, I saw you."

"You've become a man of the cloth," I said.

"Yes. I received the call. Terrible sinner that I am, God came to me and asked me to serve Him. And I had to obey."

"You saw God?"

"No, I felt Him. In my heart. I was born again."

"Again? You were born again?" I worried the phrase around in my head. "Damn it, Isaac. You've been born again and again. You've had more lives than a cat."

"Yes," he admitted. "But I do not forget my old lives. I want to, but I can't."

This was so unreal, so unearthly that I began to tap a single key to assure myself I was awake.

"And Alice?" he said. "Is she well? Is she still alive?"

"Oh, yes. Quite alive."

"You see her?"

"I live with her. We work together. I helped her raise your children." I struck the note harder but refused to look at him.

Because I was angry that he was still alive. Inexplicably angry. I had forgiven him when he was dead. Could I forgive him when he was living?

"Augusta and Tristan?" he said. "Did they grow up as white or colored?"

"That's the first thing you ask about them?"

"Yes. Because all this time, Fitz, whenever the wrongness of what I did became too painful, I tried to tell myself that it was better for them. That without me there to prove otherwise, they might grow up white."

"Is white really so much easier?"

"Yes." His single eye watched me. "May I sit? Did you *want* to talk to me?"

"Of course. Aren't we talking now?"

He limped over to the mind-reader chair, a few feet away, dragged it toward the piano, and sat down.

I resisted knowing, but I had to know. "What happened to your eye?"

"I lost it," he said. "A long time ago. Soon after my return to America. I was beaten. In a town in Georgia. I won't dwell on it. It was too long ago to matter."

My finger tapped the key more quickly. I abruptly removed my hand. "You faced a mob?" I said. "You tried to stop a lynching?"

His eye opened wide. "How did you know?"

"I made it up. It was the lie we told the children. Only we said you were killed. That their father died a hero's death." I was stunned by the clairvoyance of the lie. But lies come from the imagination, and the imagination often hits upon the truth.

"No, I did not die. And I was not a hero," he said. "My children think I am dead?"

"Yes," I told him, without a trace of guilt.

He thought a moment. "Good," he said. "Yes. Good. I'm glad they think I'm dead. It's better that way."

I looked at his blind black patch and his naked, heavy-lidded eye. The eye was pure sorrow. I thought he was mourning his own demise.

"I was a fool, Fitz. A sin-proud, righteous fool," he began. "I understood that once my ship left Constantinople and started across the ocean. And I wanted to return, but the thought of my children living with a murderer still hurt too much."

He needed to tell his story, and I needed to hear it. I folded my arms and listened.

"My ship came to America," he continued, "and made its way down the coast, until we docked in Savannah, and I saw a land of negritude, thousands of men and women as black as I. I disembarked, thinking I could lose myself in their blackness. I wanted to be nobody, and there's nobody smaller than a colored man in Georgia.

"I wanted to eat spiritual dirt, but did not know I would eat so much. I knew that the lot of my people was bad, but knew it in my head, not my flesh. It was as bad as slavery—no, worse, since a slave had the protection of being owned. My race was now defenseless. I was witness to a thousand humiliations: grown men unable to shield their children from insult, children seeing their parents dishonored and abused. So much turned upon manners, not simply that you accept a life of insult but that you accept it with a smile. A frown suggested anger, and anger suggested brains. My own people were afraid of me, fearful that my speech and manner drew too much attention.

"I took work upcountry, away from the sea, with a white carpenter who had two sons—all of whom treated me as trash. I wanted to be treated as trash. 'What business you got speaking like a white man?' they sneered, until I learned to speak like Uncle Remus. I couldn't glance at a scrap of newspaper in their presence without one of them snarling, 'You think you can learn to read? Don't you even think on it. Reading only ruins a nigger.' I spent a year with these bitter, pitiless men."

"So you ate your dirt," I said. "You never considered returning to us after you got your fill?"

"Every morning, Fitz. Every night. But it was too late. I did not know where you were. I did not know how to find you. And I feared that if I left to hunt for you, it would only be so I could escape the punishment I deserved. But the longer I stayed, the larger my guilt grew. I was paralyzed in a wilderness of Georgia. Without a will of my own, without God. My guilt rose like a mountain between me and God."

"But the lynching," I said. "You stopped a lynching?"

"I didn't stop it. I failed there, too." He screwed his face around his nose, disgusted by the stink of failure. "We were building a store in a dusty little town, an ice-cream parlor, even though everyone was dirt poor in that wretched place. All except one farmer, a young black fellow who had switched from cotton to wheat. I spoke to him only once, and he was as proud as I had ever been. 'You do good work, Uncle. You can work for me any day.' He treated me like a child, a nobody without land. He had gotten up in the world and had no sympathy for those held down by their race. I can't say I liked the man. His name was Johnson. I never knew his first name.

"The boss and his sons and I were working one market day, when this farmer came into town, *in a horse and buggy*. He had just bought the rig and looked so pleased with himself. He ignored the resentful stares from the crackers standing around their mules and broke-down wagons. He went into the general store and— I don't know what happened, but there was a commotion, an argument. The farmer ran out into the street pursued by a red-faced clerk with an ax handle. When he took a mallet from his buggy to defend himself, everyone rushed over, including the boss's sons, not to watch a fair fight but to thrash an uppity nigger. I was so humbled, so broken in spirit, that I only stood by my boss on the sidewalk, wishing I were blind. Then somebody took out a rope and said they should make him an example for any nigger who took food from white folks' mouths. And I could remain silent no longer. I jumped into the street and cried, 'No! Think of the blood on your hands! How will you face your families with blood on your hands!' And the man looked at me, with amazement, gratitude, and disbelief. But suddenly I was in the dust, covered in white flashes that I slowly understood were boots and clubs. I expected to die. I was glad to die.

"But I didn't die. I awoke in the shack of an old man, a colored gravedigger who had watched from an alley until it was over, then came out to see if I were alive. My boss had left me for dead, but this stranger took me in. He was feebleminded, but full of Jesus, mad with hymns and prayers. He told me how the farmer had been tied to the back of his own buggy and dragged by the neck until dead, all the way out to his farm, where they presented the corpse to his wife and children. His family fled the county that night, abandoning the farm they had worked so hard to own. 'He be joyful in heaven,' the gravedigger told me. 'No white folk in heaven.' He was quite mad. But he fetched a doctor and nursed me himself, changing my bandages, washing my wounds. My eye was gone, my leg broken in so many places that it could not heal straight. I was laid up for months. The gravedigger prayed over me, and I prayed with him, but my own prayers were hollow words. I remained in a wilderness, without grace, without God.

"Then one morning I was kneeling on his dirt floor, giving thanks with the old man for our mush, when I repeated for the hundredth time that Christ had died for my sins. And I suddenly understood: I did not need to punish myself; Christ had already suffered for me. And a door opened in my heart. God wanted me to serve Him. He could use a man of my sins. Everything became clear. I had been blind with pride but could see with one eye. God needed me in His church. His need rode over my sins. Belief in His need and belief in His Son arrived in a hot paroxysm of tears. I embraced and kissed the old man.

"And when I was well, I left him. I went north to Nashville, to the colored seminary there, walking all the way. I studied there, learning how to preach and serve, paying my way with carpentry. And I became a minister in the African Methodist Episcopal church. And was sent to Cincinnati to tend a poor parish in that city of wolves. Where I am to this day. Protecting my flock as best I can."

I found it hard to look at Isaac while he spoke. It was impossible to remain angry with a man who had suffered so much, even as I resented his ability to armor himself in God and suffering. "So pain washes away pain," I said. "Blood washes away blood."

"I didn't tell this story to buy forgiveness, Fitz. It does not undo the grave wrong I did my wife and children. I did that to punish myself. But I know I punished them."

And me, I thought. And me.

"You never saw our notice in a Negro newspaper?" I said. "Asking after your whereabouts?"

"No." He was amazed to hear of it. "When was this?"

"Fifteen—no, twenty years ago. In *The Freeman.*"

"No," he said. "I saw so few papers." A startled crease appeared between his eyebrows. "Alice wanted to find me?"

"Not Alice," I said. "Me. I needed to know where you were. I never mentioned the notice to Alice."

"Ah," he sighed. "Of course. Alice could never forgive me." As if it meant nothing coming from me.

"But you never attempted to contact us?" I said. "Even after you found God?"

"No. Because it was too late. And I had forfeited my rights. I considered it, weighed it, but my shame remained too great. Do not think, Fitz, that knowing God washed away my shame. Shame keeps me close to God. But I continue to suffer. Not physically, but morally."

"Of course. But your suffering did not make us suffer less."

He crossed his legs, the good leg over the bad, and tapped his thigh with his hand. "I fear I did not suffer enough," he said. "I meant to spend the remainder of my life as a selfless man of God, a shepherd living for his flock. But the flesh is weak, Fitz. Being a minister exposed me to temptations. I regret to say it, but . . . I married again."

I set my right hand on the keyboard to steady myself and produced a jangle of notes. "To a woman?"

"Of course. Who else does one take for a wife?"

The very idea that he might love another man stung me, but Isaac couldn't even consider such a thing.

My hand began to play, tunelessly picking at keys, needing to protect myself with music. "You have children?"

"Yes. Three. Two daughters and a son. I became happy again. I am sad to say. I built happiness on top of sorrow."

Just as we had. Isaac, too, had made a new life in the ruins. Nevertheless I remained stung, furious. I had been working to forgive him, but to be told that he had married again—?

"Your new wife is colored?"

"Yes."

His people, Alice once said. His people. And we were not his people. "So you are finished with white people?" I charged. "You have put your old life behind you?"

"No. You are here," he said, placing his hand over his heart. "You will always be here. I know my children are grown, but talking to you makes me long to see them again."

"You can't. They think you're dead."

"Yes. I understand that. But I want to see Alice, too. I am afraid to see her, but I feel I should face her and tell her how sorry I am for all that I did. Sorry and ashamed."

"She won't want to see you."

"Are you certain?"

I wasn't, but I feared what his return might do to her. Already wounded over Tristan, this resurrection would destroy her peace for good. But stronger than my fears for Alice was the fact I did not want Isaac to see her. He did not deserve to see her.

"Yes," I said. "I am certain." My right hand found a tune, a sad pattern of notes that it idly tapped out like a telegram.

"Very well. It's for the best. Because I dare not face her."

"But you can face me? That was easy?" I was amazed at how angry it made me to understand that.

"No. It was difficult, Fitz. To come back here tonight and see you. I was afraid what I might learn. About Alice and the children. If they were alive or dead, healthy or ill, happy or in poverty. I prayed long and hard this afternoon, and God put the steel in my heart that enabled me to come."

I played with both hands now, irritably groping the keys.

"So you feared me only as a messenger? You did not fear *my* anger, *my* pain?"

"I feared it. I feared you as we fear anyone whom we have wronged. I caused the death of someone you loved. It was a sinful love, but I know that I hurt you. Out of righteousness made blind by jealousy. And yes, I was jealous, and it led me into evil."

What did jealousy matter when he could admit it so easily? Why did he even mention Freddie? I said nothing, only continued to play.

"God forgave the child and took him to heaven, Fitz. And He has forgiven you. In gratitude for all the good you have done my wife and children."

Such pious nonsense, such God-is-good blather. My fingers struck the keys harder to stop myself from listening. But it was no longer me playing. It was spirits! My spirits were in my hands! The return of Isaac, and my anger with Isaac, had brought my Metaphysicals back from oblivion.

"Stop that!" said Isaac. "I can't talk over your music."

"I can't stop," I said, grinning at my hands, then at him, an awestruck, scornful grin. "It's not *my* music. It's my spirits. They don't seem to believe in your loving God."

I heard my horse and piano galloping in the keyboard. They no longer trudged mournfully but charged through the keys, with Eusebius running alongside. *Eusebius* was back! Who had not appeared to me since Freddie's death! He kept the horse going at a clip, slapping its flank, pitching pebbles at its head, a naked, angry boy with tears streaming down his face.

Their music was a furious song in no single key, a fierce chromatic anger. I did not bang the piano but jabbed and knitted white and black notes in a clattering dissonance, a syncopated rage. What was Eusebius angry about? That Isaac was alive? That he once replaced me with Alice, only to replace her with another? Or that he had suffered so much. We brought such pain upon ourselves, but pain washed out pain and nothing remained. Nothing.

"Stop it!" cried Isaac. "Stop your damn noise!"

I heard Schumann in the cacophony, and my ghost waltz, and the frantic bounce of "Pop Goes the Weasel." The angry music swelled inside the cabinet. When I pressed the pedal and released the dampers, it roared forth in a fiery blaze.

"No!" cried Isaac, and jumped up. "Can't you hear me? Are you deaf? I told you to stop!" He grabbed my shoulder and pushed me from the keyboard. He pushed so hard that I fell over and hit the floor on my back.

The wind was knocked out of me; the music was cut off. Yet I could still feel it, a bass chord trembling in the earth. I heard sounds outside, shouts and bells, a chorus of bells.

Isaac stood over me, apologetically offering his hand to help me to my feet. He suddenly glanced up.

"You hear it, too?" I said. "That's my music out there. Released into the world." I scrambled to my feet, stumbled across the floor to the stage door, and flung it open.

It was like opening a door in a fairy tale: Over the alley's usual pattern of light and shadow was a wash of blood-colored moonlight, a fluttering tint as if I were literally "seeing red." I stepped into the eerie light, looked down the alley, and saw a bright specter across the lagoon, a trembling flower of flames.

How beautiful, I thought, a perfect apparition. My Metaphysicals had made up for their long absence by offering me the most extraordinary vision.

62

BUT it was not a vision. Dreamland was on fire.

You can read accounts of it in old newspapers, how Dreamland burned that night, a conflagration so great that people in Manhattan went up on their roofs to see the copper-colored sky over Brooklyn, an unearthly glow like the Second Coming.

But it began as one burning building, which is what I now saw from the alley, like a flaming paper lantern reflected in the lagoon's black water. The sight drew me down the alley to the midway. That was Hell Gate over there, a hundred yards away, and I slowly understood that it was not a mirage or even Hell Gate's red-crepe streamers but real flames that roared through the façade and licked the wings of Satan.

I was amazed. I had never dreamed my spirits had so much power, that they could create fire as well as music.

Bells were clanging all over the park, and workmen ran toward the blaze. A clattering silhouette plunged in front of me, a blur of horses followed by the spinning wheels and smoking boiler of a fire engine. Another engine followed, and another, the men of Fighting the Flames rushing out to fight the real thing. On the roof of The Fall of Pompeii next door to Hell Gate, eyes began to open, a sprinkle of sparkling eyes.

Isaac appeared at my side and gazed across the lagoon with a curiously detached look, as if this were any fire.

"That's my music," I told him. "My spirits did that. Eusebius and the others." I was breathless, excited.

Isaac stared at me. "Don't be a fool. It's not spirits. It's an accident. The hand of man."

A loud crash caused us both to turn, and we saw Hell Gate collapse and Satan tumble down. Flakes of burning burlap flew up into the night like fiery angels. The firemen swung their streams of water to The Fall of Pompeii, whose roof was already ablaze. The fire brigade of Lilliputia joined them, its toy engine and tiny firemen standing like shadow puppets against the inferno.

And then all the electric lights of Dreamland went out. There was only the fire, bright gyres blown clean of smoke. A steady breeze combed the flames and lifted fresh flocks of red angels high into the air. Beacon Tower stood above it all, wreathed in firelight, swirled in racing shadows.

"Like the wrath of God," Isaac murmured. "The fires of God."

"Not at all," I said. "It's the wrath of Eusebius."

We did not move but stood there, side by side, hypnotized by the spectacle across the water. Isaac was wrong. This was my fire, my doing. I had unleashed my spirits and their rage. I was horrified by what I'd done. But mixed with my horror was the strangest elation, an ecstatic feeling of power. I was exhilarated, appalled, electrified, and stunned, all at once. I seemed to have felt nothing since Freddie died and Isaac fled, but emotion now poured into me, twenty-five years of anger, joy, love, and hate. It left me breathless and staring as the flames leaped from Pompeii to the Casino of Monte Carlo, then to the domed roof housing *The Creation* at the end of the lagoon.

Who could have guessed that paradise would burn so easily? But it was a false paradise, a fraudulent happiness, a dishonest peace. The world was a cruel, violent place. I was thrilled to see the pretty lie of Dreamland go up in flames.

A new handful of fiery debris blew over the back corner of the midway, darting, flapping, shrieking. They were parrots and cockatoos, beating their wings in a frantic attempt to escape their blazing feathers, only to drop lifeless into the water or strike the ground in a spatter of sparks.

The fire had reached the zoo! There was the roar of a lion, a scream of monkeys. My caged beasts were no longer placid. And I realized with a shock: There are live things here, animals and people. I begged my spirits not to harm any more. Please. They do not deserve to suffer for my anger with Isaac and my spirits' rage with the world.

"Lavinia!" I said. "Oh, my God. Lavinia is here! Is she awake?" I started up the midway, toward Lilliputia and the fire.

"Where are you going?" cried Isaac, hopping after me on his cane. "We have to get out of here!"

I kept going. "You once said we'd burn in hell!" I called over my shoulder. "Well, here we are!" And I laughed like a giddy, tickled child. "This way," I said. "This way," and he followed me, thinking I was leading him to safety.

Midgets spilled from the gates of Lilliputia, in pajamas and dressing gowns, some of them carrying suitcases. They did not look panicked, only exasperated, as if all too familiar with calamity. Isaac blinked in alarm at the little figures swarming around his waist.

"Where's Lavinia?" I cried. "Is she out? Does she know we're on fire?"

"Of course I know," a voice loudly squeaked. She staggered through the gate with the count, the pair lugging a huge crystal chandelier. "A gift from Lola Montes. I can't let it burn up."

"Here," I said and grabbed it, a jangling mass of glass and firelight. I was going to carry it for her, but it was too heavy. "We'll throw it in the lagoon," I said. "You can come back for it later." I carried it toward the water. "Just go! Get out!"

"I'm going. Thank you, August. Much obliged." She and the

count ran after their fellows toward the beach. The ocean was the only way out now; the front entrance was a cataract of flame.

I had wanted to perform one good act, save an animal or midget, something to make amends for my music. But all I saved was an ugly tangle of glass and wire. I lifted it over the balustrade and flung it into the lagoon. I began to laugh again. Life was too ridiculous, the world too absurd.

"What the hell are you doing?" cried Isaac. "Do you want to die here? We have to get out." His eye bulged like the eye of a terrified horse in a burning barn. I did not know he was so afraid. I was too exhilarated to feel fear myself.

We started back down the midway, and there was nobody on our side of the lagoon. The midgets had vanished; the firemen were all across the water.

There was a squealing at our backs, like crying babies, and shadows suddenly flooded across the pavement, a mob of monkeys. A blacker shadow shot after them, like a cat but larger. A panther! Isaac and I jumped back. We pressed ourselves to the railing of the lagoon and froze as a tiger hurried past, followed by a lion with a singed mane and insulted, indignant frown. The zookeeper was freeing his animals. The beasts swung their heads left and right but did not look at us, only at the dark sea ahead. The giraffe galloped by on her wobbling stilts, the keeper himself running alongside, clapping his hands to keep the creature going. The man paid us no more heed than his beasts of prey had.

The wind turned, and I felt a furnace blast of heat. I looked up and saw flames overhead. We stood far enough back from the Canals of Venice to see its burning roof. Carried on the wind over the tarpaper rooftops, the fire had leaped ahead of us.

"Hurry!" cried Isaac. "Before we're cut off."

He headed toward the sea, and I followed, still feeling only exhilarated, exalted, drunk with excitement.

I heard a squeak of wheels behind me, a rush of tires. I looked back just as a bicycle flew past us, a high, old-fashioned cycle with

an enormous front wheel. It raced after the fleeing animals, furi-
ously pedaled by a small nude figure. At least he looked nude—
everything was red and pink in the fluttering glare—but then I saw
a boy's tapered back, a bare rump squashed against the leather seat.

Eusebius? I thought. *Freddie?*

But Freddie was dead, and Eusebius only a spirit. This must be
a young acrobat, I told myself, rudely awakened from his bed.

I walked more quickly, watching the cyclist sail ahead of us, a
sparkle of firelight on the spinning spokes of the huge wheel
pumped by his skinny legs.

Isaac didn't mention the cyclist, said nothing at all, only drove
himself along with his cane.

The cyclist came to the Pavilion of Harmonia, slowed his glide
to a wobble, looked back at us—he was too far away for me to see
his face—then swung under the portico roof.

As we approached the pavilion, however, I saw nobody. The portico was empty, the front door open. There were only the giant
papier-mâché heads of Sousa and Beethoven, the German's stern
features twitching and grimacing in the fitful light.

And then, just audible in the crackle of flame, I heard music.
Not piano music, and nothing like my keyboard cacophony, but
circus music, orchestral tremolos of theatrical fire, followed by a
quick, delicate two-four scamper of flutes. It sounded like a whole
orchestra was inside the Pavilion of Harmonia, and they played
Offenbach, the galop from *Voyage to the Moon*, Freddie's favorite
piece.

So the cyclist *was* Freddie! Freddie had returned to earth! His
very presence turned the musical blaze back into music again.

I experienced the strangest joy. Not grief or fear or guilt, but joy.
I slowed my steps as I understood. My spirits had set this fire for
me, then sent Freddie to signal that it was time for me to die. And
a little child shall lead thee.

Here it is, I thought. My fate. My death. Of course. Fire was my apotheosis. I always knew there would be fire. All my dreams had been of fire. My world would end in fire.

I would sit at my piano. Yes, a piano would be the perfect place for me to die. I would burn so beautifully, like a photograph in a stove.

"Just go!" I told Isaac. "Keep going. I am right behind you." I did not want him to die with me. No, he had died once already. This time was my turn.

He did not look back, did not even hear me, but continued down the midway.

I remained under the portico, peering through the open door, wondering if I would see Freddie before I died. I saw nothing, no boy, no orchestra, only a dribble of fire from the ceiling.

The music suddenly leaped into its fierce, triumphant polka, now a roaring cancan scored for brass, cymbals, and bass drum. Such a gaudy, vulgar melody, but exhilarant, ecstatic. You would think I'd die to Schumann or Brahms or even Wagner—or my lovely ghost waltz. But no, I was going to die to Offenbach.

The roar of music produced a fiery roar on the roof, and a shower of sparks fell around me, a beautiful spray of light. It stung like a cloud of bees. I laughed as I slapped at my hair and eyebrows and turned to blink cinders from my eyes. When I looked up again, the bust of Beethoven was blazing. Sousa remained cold and dead, but the German titan burned gloriously.

Something seized my arm. "Damn you, Fitz! No!" Isaac gripped my arm, his fingers digging to the bone. His teeth were bared, his eye fierce. "You will not add self-murder to your sins!"

I was too drunk with excitement to be surprised by his return or that he understood what I intended. "Let go!" I cried. "I have to go inside! Freddie's in there!"

He stared at me in horror. "Freddie is dead!" he cried.

"I know that!" I snapped. "Do you think I'm an idiot!" I tried to jerk my arm away, but he would not let go.

"Come away from here!" he shouted, threw aside his cane, and hauled me out from the portico with both hands. The old man had more strength left than I ever imagined.

"Isaac, no!" I cried. "He's come back for me. He's telling me it's time for me to die!"

Isaac did not answer, refused to argue, but pushed and pulled me toward the sea.

I tried to struggle out of his grip, but Isaac was too strong. I looked back at the burning portico, heartbroken. He had torn me from the boy once; he was tearing me from him again.

He dragged me down the midway, and I stopped fighting. It was all fire now, even Fighting the Flames, the lagoon a circle of fire, a ring of red and gold flames. And over it all, like a music of fire, was the joyful beat and bounce of Offenbach's *Voyage to the Moon.*

Isaac pulled me down the wide stairs to the beach. The tide was in; the beach was empty. The midgets and animals had escaped, but the towering piers of the Dreamland Chute were now ablaze, the creosoted timbers a spiderweb of flame. It cut off our escape on that side, while the pyre of the bathing pagoda cut us off on the other. There was nowhere to go but the sea. Isaac dragged us into the water. Waves broke around my ankles, and icy water filled my shoes, but we kept going. Until we were waist deep in ocean and Isaac collapsed, clutching the front of my shirt and pulling me down with him.

"Damn you, Fitz. Why do you want to die? Have we not suffered enough already? We have punished ourselves enough!"

"It wasn't for punishment." What a ridiculous notion. I did not want death for pain, but for— Elation? Joy? Love? Except where was the love in dying?

The coldness of the water was bringing me to my senses, and the sting of salt in my face. There was no music now. The music vanished, and there was only the crack and rumble of the fire. I sat in the heavy, rolling swells, Isaac still holding my shirt.

"Can you learn nothing from my example?" he pleaded. "Pain and death purge nothing. Live with your sin and go on with your life. God will take us when He is finished with us."

"It's my fire," I insisted. "My spirits started it. They wanted me to die in it. And I saw Freddie! On a bicycle!"

"There was nobody on a bicycle. You're talking gibberish, man! Lunatic gibberish!"

Not even the cyclist had been real? It was all a mad hallucination, a counterfeit vision? No, the fire was real. My spirits were immaterial, and they didn't start the fire but had used it like a dream to speak to me. "No, no, my spirits were telling me it was time to die."

"Damn you and your damned spirits!" he cried.

"Well, damn you and your damned God!" I tried to pull away, but he still gripped me by my shirt. And the tug of his hand made me understand: Isaac had saved my life. He probably would have saved any man's life. Yet Isaac saved mine, and it suddenly made my life worth saving. He loved me. He had always loved me. He did not want me to die. And my intoxication of death vanished.

There was a great roar from the shore, and a blaze of light illuminated the Old Testament face before me. Beacon Tower had burst into flame, a solid torch, a pillar of fire like the pillar that led the Israelites through the desert. As bright as the sun, it threw our shadows over the green waters behind us and lit up the beach down front. A lion paced back and forth there, a frantic silhouette of mane and muscles trapped against the ocean. The salt burned my eyes. My vision kept clouding over, and I could blink away the clouds, but they returned as soon as I looked back at the burning tower.

We could not go ashore while the lion remained. We might have waded around the burning pagoda, but we were too exhausted. So we stayed in the cold sea, rocking in the sluggish surge, waiting for the fire to burn itself out and the lion to go away.

A loud crack like a cannon shot was followed by a noise like applause, and the pillar of fire collapsed. The crash of plaster sent a final flight of angels spinning into the sky and over the ocean, their red-and-gold embers flaring and blinking until they died away among the stars.

63

I cannot say how long we stayed in the water, how much time
passed before the fire died, the lion departed, and we crawled ashore.
Or maybe we didn't crawl ashore, maybe only the tide went out.
But the next thing I remember is that Isaac and I lay on a shelf of
damp sand, side by side in sopping clothes and pulpy shoes, while
daylight the color of smoke crept in from the ocean.

There was the cold stink of a dead fire, the whole world reeking
like a smokehouse. I looked over at Isaac. He lay on his back and
breathed through his mouth. His eyepatch was off and hung around
his neck. The empty socket was a pale, puckered scar. The living
eye glanced at me, but he said nothing.

I remained blank and befuddled, waking from one dream into
another. Only the exhaustion in my limbs and crusts of pain on my
face seemed real.

I slowly sat up and turned around to look at the park, which
should tell me if I were awake or dreaming. A broad flight of stone
stairs climbed up from the beach into ... nothing, nothing but gray
sky. The great white façades, Beacon Tower, and the rest were gone.
I could hear voices and commotion just over the rise, but all I saw
were a few thin columns of smoke and the jagged steel frame of
the Dreamland Chute, a cage of twisted bars towering over the
water.

Then I saw my piano coming down the beach. Not the earthly Steinway from the Pavilion of Harmonia but my metaphysical piano, my musical familiar. She passed under the open cage, alone, on foot. Where had our horse gone?

She saw me. She recognized me. She stepped more quickly and lowered her hood. It wasn't a hood but a scarf. And it wasn't my piano. I hadn't dreamed about my piano in years, but I knew that my piano would never wear spectacles.

It was Alice, her face pinched in fear, her skirt spattered with ashes. She must have seen the strange light in the sky, heard what it was, and hurried out to Coney Island to look for me. She broke into a trot over the damp sand, overjoyed to find me seated stupefied on the beach.

Then she saw the figure beside me. Her steps slowed. She stopped.

Isaac had his head rolled to one side. He was watching her, his eye round with fear and awe, as enormous as when he had looked upon the fire.

She stared at him, a filthy, tattered stranger cast up by the ocean. Her eyes narrowed. She drew the scarf tightly around her shoulders.

I couldn't speak. Nobody spoke. Another wave growled along the sand. Trails of smoke passed silently overhead.

"Fitz?" cried Alice. "Dear God! You're hurt!" She forgot Isaac and went straight to me, bending down to my face. "Your head, your hair? You're burned."

My skull stung when I touched it. My scalp was naked, and I felt only cushions of blister where my eyebrows should be. It was hours before I saw a mirror, when my head was already swathed in white bandages; I cannot guess how ghastly I looked, roasted in a fire, washed in the sea.

"But alive," I said hoarsely. "Alive." I nodded at Isaac, wanting her to look at him again and acknowledge that this stranger actually was— But I didn't know how she might respond, what she could say. She frowned at me.

"Alice," Isaac whispered. "Alice."

He gathered himself off the sand. He went up on his knees and bowed his head.

She rose to her feet again, stepped back from me, stiffened her spine, and gazed down at Isaac.

"Forgive me," he said. "Forgive me. For what I did to you and our children."

She clutched one hand in the other, and I thought she would strike him. She kept her eyes wide, but the lashes trembled. Then she blinked, and a tear slipped down her cheek.

"Isaac," she said. "Husband." She set the hand on his shoulder, so gently, as if he were ashes and might crumble. "I have wanted you dead," she murmured. "All these years. But you are alive. And I am glad. I cannot believe how glad I am."

He took her hand and kissed it.

Tears spilled down her face, and my heart broke for her, seeing her joy at the return of a man who I knew couldn't stay. But she could not look at him. She abruptly turned to me and said, "When I saw fire in the sky last night, and people told me what it was, I was afraid for you, Fitz. Frightened. But you survived." She slowly turned back at Isaac. "We all survived."

She took her hand out of his hand and lightly touched the scar of his missing eye. "I forgive you. I do." She spoke in tones of astonishment. "I seem to have forgiven you years ago."

Isaac took her hand again and held it to his cheek. "I cannot come back," he said. "I know you wouldn't have me. But I have another life now. A new life."

"No, I can never take you back," she replied, without a moment of hesitation. "My love for you died years ago. In anger, hatred, and confusion. But I am glad you are not dead. And such gladness must mean that I forgive you."

I had feared that her strength was hard and brittle, like old iron. I should have known better. Alice was steel. She bent with the pain, which she felt keenly, yet she did not break.

* * *

I did not know how weak I was until I tried to stand. Alice and Isaac had to support me on either side. Even without his cane Isaac was stronger than I. He adjusted his patch back over his eye before he took me under the arm.

We climbed the steps to the midway. And it opened in front of us: acres of devastation, a desert of ashes. Here and there a gaunt frame of charcoal stood over the rubble, a lopsided remnant of wall, but the rest had been wiped away. A few small fires continued to smoke, exhausted workmen standing by as if they were burning trash. The remains of Beacon Tower filled the lagoon, slabs of charred plaster and snarls of chicken wire, with a crystal chandelier buried somewhere in the wreckage. The Steeplechase roller coaster next door stood fully exposed, like the skeleton of a mountain, singed yet undamaged. But Dreamland was gone. We trod over a landscape of hard plaster curds, feathery ashes, and the burnt black leaves of cloth and paper.

The daylight was too bright, and I could look up only for quick peeks. Alice held me on my right, Isaac on my left. You might say that they walked arm in arm over the rubble, using me as an oven mitt.

"It was unforgivable," said Isaac. "What I did to you and the children. I took one sin of pride and compounded it with a worse sin."

"I told you that back then," I said. "Don't you remember me telling you that?"

"Leave off, Fitz," said Alice. "We will not rake over old wrongs today. It is too late in the day to dwell on them."

Each pause in conversation was filled with a dry crunch of plaster under our feet.

"Our children?" said Isaac. "How are they?"

"Wonderful. Augusta is married and lives in San Francisco. But Tristan is still with us. He is everything a mother could want from a son. He has grown into an excellent young man."

I thought her praise only self-protective vanity, a refusal to admit that her life was not entirely perfect—she delivered it with a defiant thrust of chin—but a startled look came over her, a puzzled look of temptation.

"Yes," she repeated, "he is everything a mother could want." It began in nervous pride but settled into place over the next weeks, the decision to give no mind to your love life. She never asked about it either but tenderly averted her eyes. There's nothing like fire and resurrection to reorder one's grievances.

"Is Tristan here?" I asked, suddenly realizing that he could encounter his dead father. But Alice reported that he hadn't come home last night. "Oh, yes. Now I remember," I said. "He told me he had a late political meeting." With Mr. Brown, I presume.

How curious that for all my anger with Isaac, I never considered telling him that his son, like me, loved men. But that anger was merely personal, and the rage of my spirits had been directed at something larger than Isaac: life on earth? my life? Even now I cannot say why my spirits possessed me with a desire for death that night, why they sent Freddie as a sign. Only that the time seemed right, the moment auspicious: Isaac had returned, the park had caught fire, and I could pass from this realm to the next in a passionate blaze of anger, pity, sorrow, and love.

We passed a scrap of poster burnt clean of color. COME HEAR THE NOTORIOUS was all it said, and I looked up to see what remained of the Pavilion of Harmonia. There was an outline of rubble, a sketch of wires on the ground, a collapsed stage of burnt boards where a grand piano hung at an angle, gaping like an open coffin. The lid had slid off, and the veneer was cracked and scaly like alligator hide, but only the hottest fire can consume a hardwood piano.

"I should tell you," said Isaac, "it hurts me to confess this, Alice, but— I am remarried. To a lady of color."

Her little laced-up boots crunched over the cinders.

"Do you love her?" she finally said.

"Yes. As much as I loved you. No more, and no less."

"Good. It is not good for man to be alone. Especially you, Isaac. Alone you would grow only grim and morbid. I trust that she's a kinder, more loving wife than I was."

"But you were a fine wife. None could ask for better."

"And you were a fine husband. Until the day that you stopped being a husband and saw yourself as only a sinner. I forgive what you did. But I cannot forget it."

"No. We can never forget."

We saw tents along Surf Avenue up ahead, canvas shelters offering coffee and first aid, and began to pass people coming in, gawking men and boys from the neighborhood, even a few ladies, tourists visiting a disaster. Out in the street firemen from all over Brooklyn were still stowing their equipment and watering their weary horses, but Sam Gumpertz was already selling tickets to yet another catastrophe, this time his own.

Nobody died in the Dreamland fire, which is hard to believe for anyone who witnessed it. But the park went so quickly, like a paper house. It was so insubstantial that nobody was trapped in its buildings. Some animals perished, and eventually my eyesight, and a few illusions about the excellence of the new century. But no human beings.

Alice and Isaac took me to the hospital. They spent the day together in a hospital waiting room before they said good-bye. Forever. It was Alice's decision that they not see each other again. Isaac had a new life, a new family. He could not see us without betraying them, she said. "And you're a hero to our children," she added. "I do not know what they would think of you alive. Or of me for lying to them."

Her forgiveness was terribly complicated. Later she would give me a full account of the deep pain that had accompanied her joy at seeing Isaac. She had seized the joy, knowing it would be brief and sorrow would come later. Her forgiveness was genuine, but it removed the hatred that once armored her injured heart. There was no protection for her afterward except distance and silence.

But I prefer that earlier, simpler scene: Three old souls stumble over a desert of ashes, clinging to one another and speaking in sighs, the relief of discovering that they are all still on earth enabling them to make a start at forgiving one another, and themselves.

64

I was glad to be back at church today. Not even the windiest sermon can spoil the beauty of a soft, fragrant morning in May. And I loved hearing the congregation open their throats in song again, roaring hymns of praise shaped by a blind white pagan at the organ in the upstairs choir. Music is music wherever you play it—Monte Carlo, Coney Island, or a house of God.

Even though there is no God. At least not the Supreme Know-It-All that people evoke with that word. There are only spirits, millions of spirits, ambiguous, unpredictable, as slippery as quicksilver, yet more flexible than an all-or-nothing Almighty. It was nice of Christ to die for our sins, but one takes small comfort in a God so fond of torture that only the brutal death of His Son can persuade Him to torture us a little less.

I still believe in my Metaphysicals, even though I have done so badly by them. One needs to believe in something. I found others who believed in them after the Great War, when Alice brought me women from the neighborhood wanting news of deceased sons or husbands. There is nothing like a war to revive a belief in spirits, and nobody more convincing than a blind seer. I wanted to help these women, give them solace, and I did, earning every nickel they paid me. On the other hand, I do not mind misleading the people who play the numbers and still come to me for tips.

Luckily the congregation of St. Philip's doesn't know of these sidelines, or they might charge me with witchcraft. Yet they can be remarkably forgiving. Take this morning, for example, when they welcomed into the fold an unwed mother with a baby, James Arthur Jones, one year old. Old habits die hard, and I had one of my premonitions while I produced organ murmurs for the baptism: This child would achieve fame but under a different name.

St. Philip's was Alice's doing, of course. Blindness came slowly, beginning as a pretty white mist, then a white fog with shadows that slowly crowded in from the corners. Cataracts, the doctors said, like calluses produced by the blinding light of the fire. Alice became my eyes, first in theaters, then in church. St. Philip's was her church. She joined a Negro church, she said, because she liked the congregation's mix of fervor and propriety, and because she hoped it might attract Tristan. When she learned that they required a new organist, she promptly enlisted me, since I needed the work and she went there every Sunday anyway. As a blind man, I could never play the flickers, a pity since I would have been so good at it. Instead I play St. Philip's, their own King Oedipus at the keyboard, a bald little man in smoked glasses working the elaborate stops and pedals of a glorious pipe organ with a three-decker keyboard.

And now you are saddled with the duty of taking me to church each Sunday, Tristan, exposing yourself to more religion than is comfortable for your science-addled rationality.

There is no God, only spirits. And maybe fate. Which is not an invisible hand but more like an improvisation, a score that does not fully reveal itself until the piece is over. We were bound together by fate, Isaac, Alice, and I. We should have died on the same day but are dying as we were born, one by one.

I cannot believe that it has been five whole years since Alice, dear Alice, passed over. It seems like only yesterday when you took me to the hospital and I sat beside your mother's bed to say good-bye. I held her hand, a few ounces of sparrow bone sheathed in catfish skin. In all our years together we touched each other so rarely—even when she was my guide, I held only her sleeve or hard, sharp elbow—and we almost never held hands.

She spoke in the softest whispers. Her lungs were failing, worn out by double pneumonia, and she produced barely enough breath for words. She talked first of practical matters, telling me that she was leaving her share of the house to Tristan, asking me to look after him—though a blind man can hardly look after himself—then requesting me to assure Augusta that her mother went to the grave with no bad feelings about her, who had remained a perfectly good daughter by mail if not in the flesh.

"And promise me this, Fitz. One last promise. When I am gone, you will not try to call me back to earth with your piano."

I was startled. Alice had never believed in my ghosts, but she wanted to hedge her bets. "I promise," I said. "Besides, I know you'd never come."

"No, I wouldn't—I think. I believe I am going to a finer place. A more peaceful place." She drew a longer, more difficult breath into her lungs. "But we did not do too badly here, did we?"

"No," I said. "We did surprisingly well."

"And we were friends," she said. "You and I."

"Good friends," I agreed. "For all our differences."

"But we had one thing in common. One very important thing." She gave my hand a weak squeeze.

"Yes," I said, squeezing back and wondering in a panic if she actually knew how similar our loves of Isaac had been. But I could not risk cross-examining her. The love of his body as well as his soul should be of small matter to someone saying good-bye to her own body, but it would be cruel to send Alice off into eternity with a headful of thoughts about sodomy. "Did you want me to write to him?"

"Not necessary. I sent a letter yesterday. Dictated to a nurse. Who was startled to learn that an old lady had a secret lover." The nurse's response seemed to amuse her very much, she who had spent so much of her life unamused.

She passed away early the next morning. She died a modern death, in a hospital rather than at home. And we gave her a modern funeral, with a motor hearse and no horses.

But a few nights later I dreamed of my horse and piano. Only with the death of Alice did they return to my dreams, as if understanding that I needed company. As my eyesight faded, my dreams had resumed, but always of places, never people: empty rooms, deserted streets, vast landscapes. That night, however, I dreamed of an emerald-green forest, and there in a cool glade stood my horse and piano. I approached them, more closely than they'd ever let me come before. I was naked, yet my body was not an old man's sack of bones but smooth and taut, a youth's body with a flat belly and beautiful bottom. I was Eusebius? A most curious development. I had nothing in common with a larky, selfish, cheerfully heartless boy—only Eusebius did not seem so heartless now; I moved with a tentative, almost tender gait. Then the piano turned toward Eusebius—toward me—lowered its hood, and I saw Alice. Of course. I knew it would be Alice. She gazed down at me and nodded, as if to thank me for the loan of the horse.

So was the horse Isaac or music or something else entirely? I cannot say. That's the problem with symbols. They keep shifting their meaning on you.

But you see, Freddie was not Eusebius, and Eusebius was not Freddie. They were two entirely different beings.

I never saw Freddie again after the Dreamland fire, in any form. He no longer needed me, or, rather, I no longer needed him. No, that's not true. I do need him, or I wouldn't have brought him back for this story, in all his hunger, wrongheadedness, and sorrow, a victim of victims. I want to believe that the boy is at peace on the other side, calmly bicycling through the ether, riding the beautiful machine that he never mastered on earth.

*   *   *

And now only I remain. For Isaac, too, is gone.

Let us enter into the record the packet of letters that started us on this long voyage of words several months ago:

January 7, 1925

Dear Dr. August,

I regret to inform you that the Reverend Isaac Kemp of Cincinnati, my father, passed away this Tuesday last. He requested that I write to you with the sad news and send you the enclosed envelope.

I regret to say that I do not know who you are. Our father never mentioned you until this last request. I know that he had a troubled past, which he would not discuss even with our mother. But he lived a good life, a moral, loving life here in Cincinnati. He was a pillar of the community, respected for his clear judgment and kind heart. And no daughter could ask for a wiser, more affectionate parent.

I trust this letter finds you and yours in good health.

Yours truly,

Miss Augusta Kemp

Remarkable, isn't it? You were as stunned as I when you read out that name. He used it a second time? Out of love for your sister? Or do I dare say it, for me? Either way, there are now two Augusta Kemps in the world, one white, one colored.

There is his sealed letter. Very well. Let us enter his words into the account:

Dear Fitz,

When you read this, I will be no more. I have written a final statement for my son and daughter. You are permitted to look it over and decide if the time is right for them to learn the truth about their father.

I never fully thanked you for all that you did for Alice and the children. You were a better friend to me than I ever was to you. But I sincerely believe that you will get your reward in heaven.

With deepest love and admiration,

Isaac

He thought he was being so cagey, so discreet, not knowing that you would have to read this letter aloud to me.

Even in death he remains an egotist. Whatever I did, I did not do it for him. But let us continue to the center, the letter inside the letter inside the letter:

Dearest Son and Daughter,

I hope that I do not alarm you with these words from beyond the grave. Whether I am in the bosom of Abraham or another place, I cannot say. You believe that I perished long ago, soon after I left you, but the truth is that I did not die yet. Your mother, may she rest in peace, and your uncle told you an untruth. Be not angry at them. They did it out of love and a desire to protect you.

I ran away. There is no other name for my act. I did it not from lack of love, but blind love, misplaced love. A crime of pride made me feel unworthy of your love, and there seemed nothing I could do to justify myself again in my own eyes. I did not understand that only God's eyes matter, and He is more forgiving than we.

I grew up without a mother or father to teach by example the laws of love. I was born a slave and spent much of my life trying various ways of being free. I made many grievous errors along the path, a path strewn with sins, but no sin I regret more than my abandonment of you and your mother.

But God gave me a second chance. He told me to surrender my sinful self to the church. I was born again and made a new family, a new wife and children. They know nothing of my previous life but benefited from all I learned there, making me a gentler, wiser, more patient man. This does not atone for what I did to you, but know that you did not suffer in vain.

I hope you find it in your hearts to forgive me and pray for me. Pray for your mother. And pray for your uncle. He is a man riddled by unbelief and idiosyncrasy but has a good heart and may get to Heaven yet, just as Jesus allowed the eunuch of Ethiopia to be baptized and enter the Kingdom.

Your loving father

What do you make of that? Cant or wisdom? Five months ago I thought he was still hiding in God. One does not enjoy being compared to a eunuch, even though I've known some nice eunuchs in my time. And you can't take much pleasure, Tristan, in hearing that you were a rehearsal for a better, more moral life.

Today, however, his words sound wiser to me, his God more appealing. I envy Isaac's ability to push all the madness of life—the misfortune, violence, error, and pain—up into heaven, where it can be called God and given purpose. We are each of us full of sins, regrets, contradictions, and despair. Would that we could all dissolve them in a fire called God, a fierce music that purges the soul without destroying the body. Such a pretty phrase, "born again."

I do not believe in reincarnation. No, you get only one chance on earth, and then it's back into the immortal ether. So while we are here we should make the best of second, third, or fourth chances. Your father had the right idea. You should be born again, over and over, until you get it right.

I will not return as flesh after I am gone. But maybe as a dream or, better yet, music. You will turn on the radio one night—the radio is full of spirits—and there will be something different about a broadcast from the Savoy Ballroom, a spooky music full of amusement and longing. And it will be me. Strangers will hear it, too, but only you will understand.

If I still had eyes, I'd ask for a mirror, so that I might try the ghost waltz one last time and see if I can see Isaac. Dancing with your mother, perhaps?

But that's it. The end. Tomorrow we can start reading this

through from the beginning, decide if we want to sell it, and see what must be cut. And discover what it all means, if anything.

But let's end today with a final piece of music.

Yes, you're right, Tristan. It's not spirits. No, this is me. Just me.

Don't you recognize it? It's "Träumerei" again. With a new tempo and jazzy syncopation, turned into a sprightly, defiantly cheerful tune. Mad old Schumann must be spinning in his grave.

I bring the first theme back for a final appearance. It's the oldest trick in the book. The snake bites its tail, the circle is closed, the story ends at its beginning, but the meaning has changed.

You must be born again. And again. And again. And again.

AUTHOR'S NOTE

A lifelong love affair with American literature stands behind this novel—I leave it to the reader to identify the echoes and variations, conscious or unconscious—but the story itself was first triggered by a curious collision of nonfiction: *Patriotic Gore* by Edmund Wilson, *Gaiety Transfigured* by David Bergman, and an excellent film documentary, *Coney Island*, by Ric Burns and Richard Snow.

Other works of history provided useful information as I wrote: *Roll, Jordan, Roll* by Eugene Genovese, *Highbrow, Lowbrow* by Lawrence Levine, *Men, Women and Pianos* by Arthur Loesser, *Constantinople* by Philip Mansel, *Trouble in Mind* by Leon F. Litwack, *The Betrayal of the Negro: From Rutherford B. Hayes to Woodrow Wilson* by Rayford Logan, *Gay New York* by George Chauncey, and *Learned Pigs and Fireproof Women* by Ricky Jay.

Augustus Fitzwilliam Boyd is entirely fictional but was inspired by several real improvisational pianists, in particular Jesse Shepard (1848–1927), alias Francis Grierson. (If you want some idea of how Fitz's music might sound, I suggest visits to the piano repertoire in a loose continuum of Beethoven, Schumann, and Debussy, with a dash of Scott Joplin thrown in at the end.)

Cedric Tolley generously shared with me what he learned from his years as a pianist-of-all-trades; I would not have attempted this book without him. Paul Russell, Mary Gentile, Mary Jacobsen, Ed Sikov, Damien Jack, and Victor Bumbalo offered invaluable encouragement and criticism. Roz Parr passed along several important books, and Patrick Merla gave the manuscript a tough yet helpful reading. David Fratkin, Schuyler Bishop, and Bryan Byers were excellent companions in Turkey. Edward Hibbert, Neil Olson, and Peter Steinberg are more than agents; they are trusted friends. My editors, Colin Dickerman and Meaghan Dowling, have been rocks of wisdom and sanity. And Draper Shreeve once again provided more than words can say.

ABOUT THE AUTHOR

Christopher Bram is the author of six novels, including *Gossip, Hold Tight, Surprising Myself,* and *Father of Frankenstein,* which was made into the movie *Gods and Monsters.* He lives in New York City.